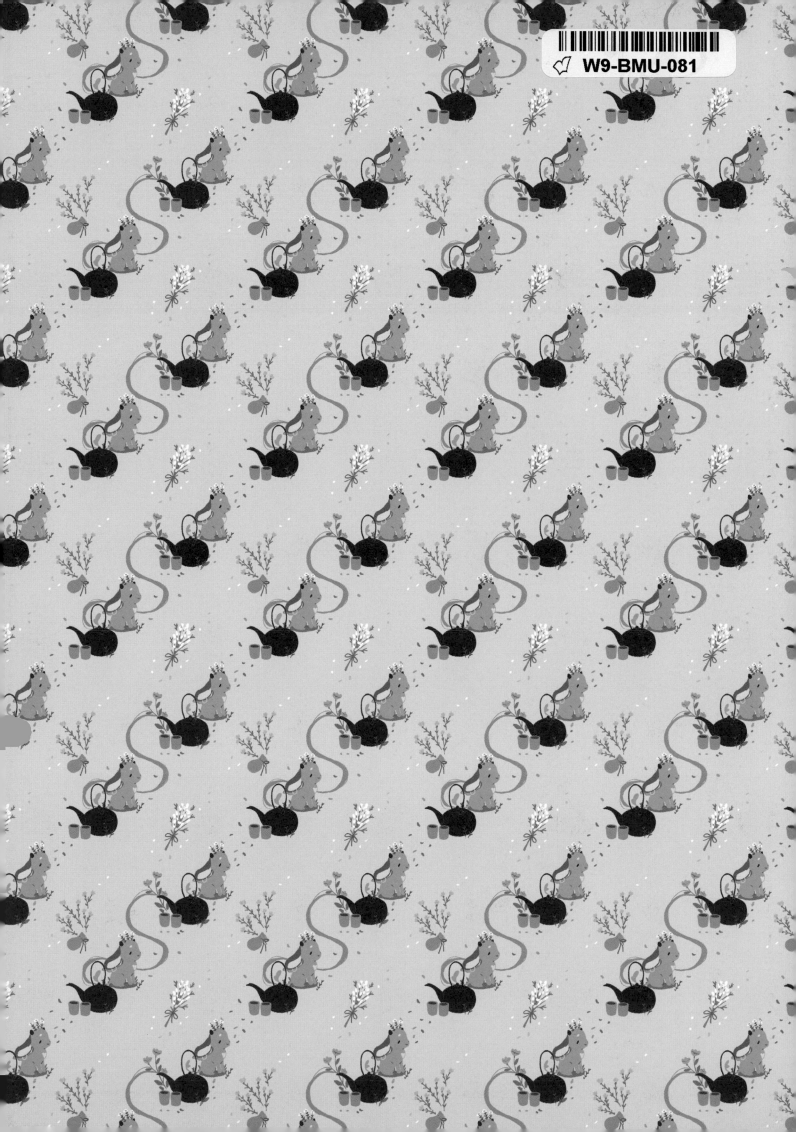

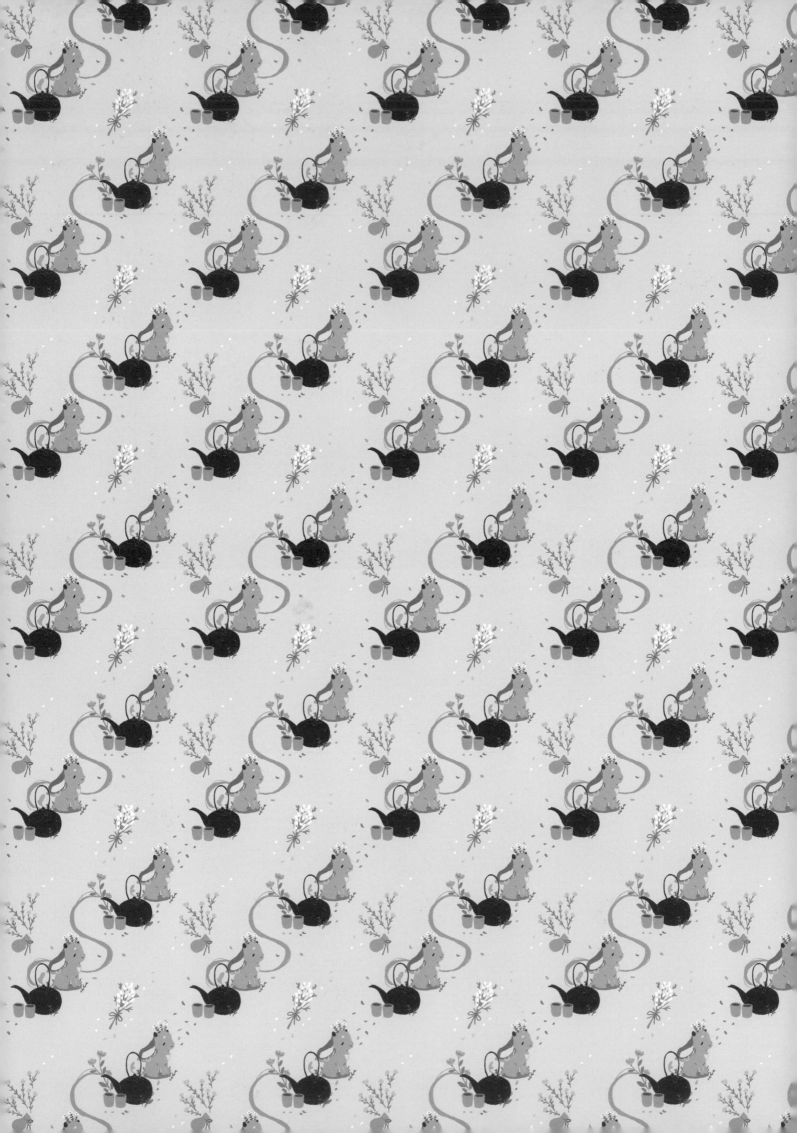

The Tea Dragon Tapestry

FOR

Frank, Jane
& Michael

The Tea Dragon Tapestry

WRITTEN & ILLUSTRATED BY

Kay O'Neill

LETTERED BY
Crank!

EDITED BY
Ari Yarwood

DESIGNED BY
Kate Z. Stone

ONI PRESS

AN ONI PRESS PUBLICATION

PUBLISHED BY ONI-LION FORGE PUBLISHING GROUP, LLC

James Lucas Jones, *president & publisher*
Sarah Gaydos, *editor in chief*
Charlie Chu, *e.v.p. of creative & business development*
Brad Rooks, *director of operations*
Amber O'Neill, *special projects manager*
Margot Wood, *director of marketing & sales*
Devin Funches, *sales & marketing manager*
Katie Sainz, *marketing manager*
Tara Lehmann, *publicist*
Troy Look, *director of design & production*
Kate Z. Stone, *senior graphic designer*
Sonja Synak, *graphic designer*
Hilary Thompson, *graphic designer*
Sarah Rockwell, *graphic designer*
Angie Knowles, *digital prepress lead*
Vincent Kukua, *digital prepress technician*
Jasmine Amiri, *senior editor*
Shawna Gore, *senior editor*
Amanda Meadows, *senior editor*
Robert Meyers, *senior editor, licensing*
Desiree Rodriguez, *editor*
Grace Scheipeter, *editor*
Zack Soto, *editor*
Chris Cerasi, *editorial coordinator*
Steve Ellis, *vice president of games*
Ben Eisner, *game developer*
Michelle Nguyen, *executive assistant*
Jung Lee, *logistics coordinator*

Joe Nozemack, *publisher emeritus*

onipress.com | lionforge.com
@onipress | @lionforge

ktoneill.com
@strangelykatie

First Edition: June 2021

ISBN 978-1-62010-774-4
eISBN 978-1-62010-795-9

Library of Congress Control Number: 2020934137

Printed in China.

1 2 3 4 5 6 7 8 9 10

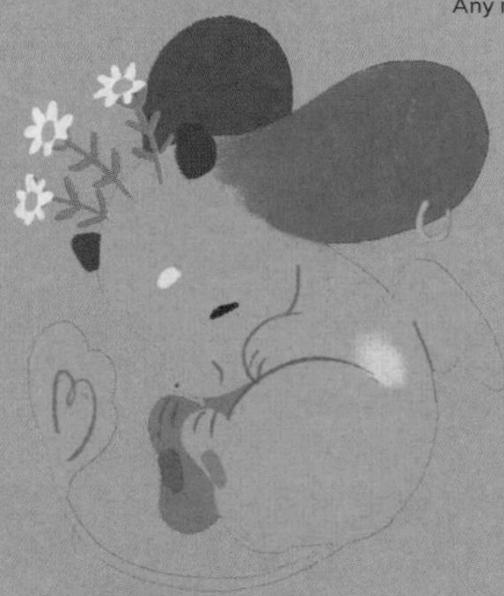

Chapter One

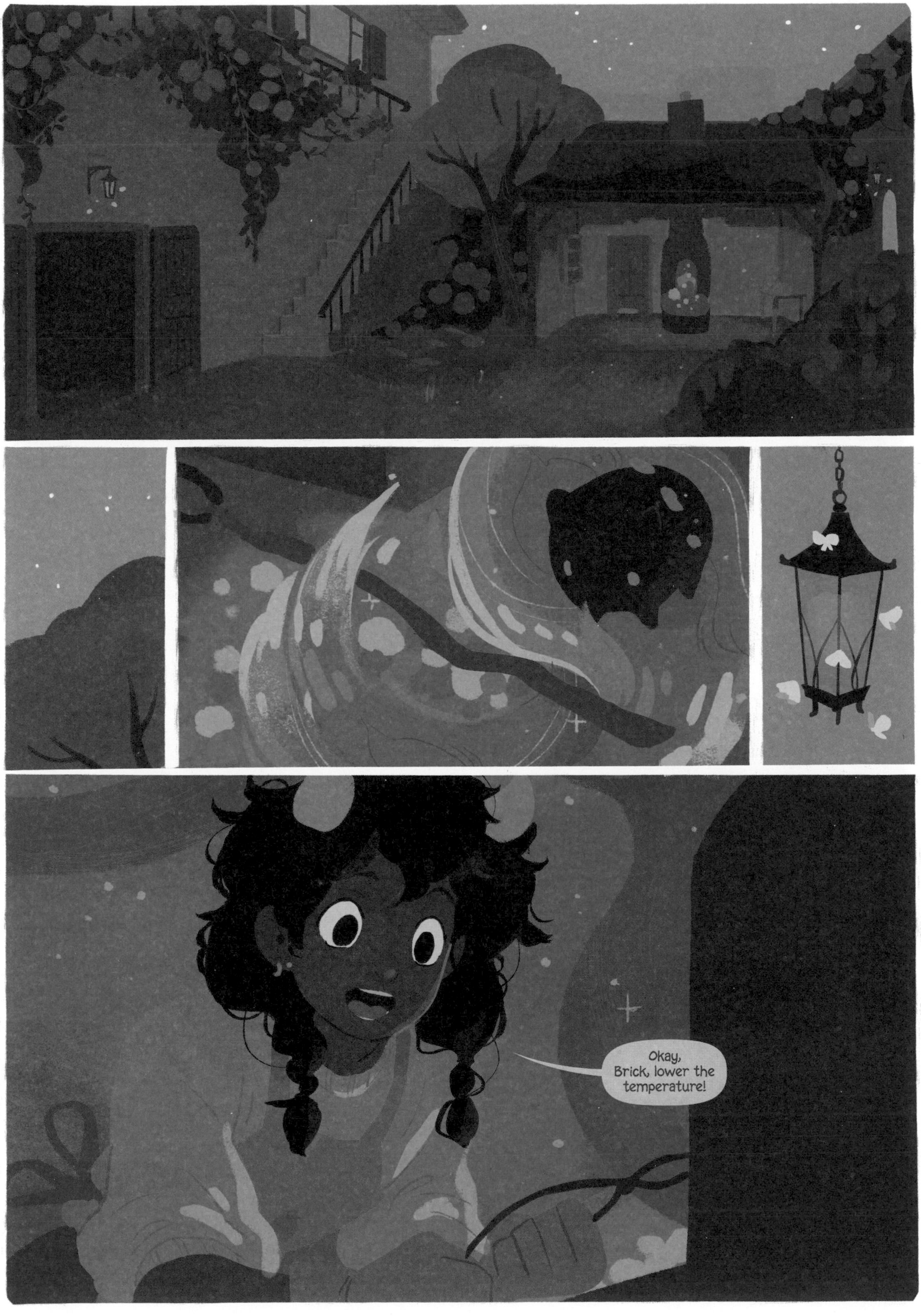
Okay,
Brick, lower the
temperature!

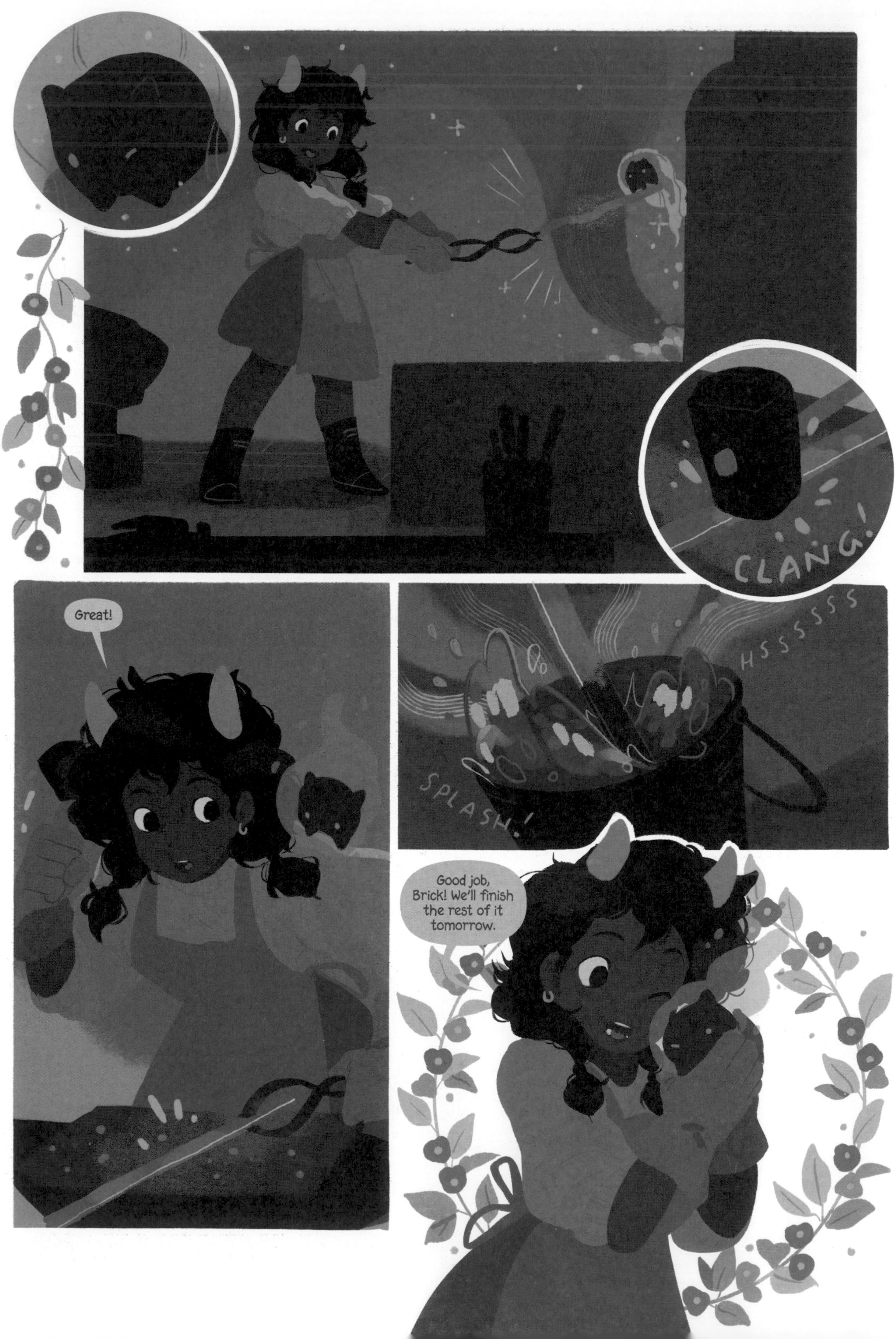
CLANG!
Great!
SPLASH!
HSSSSSS
Good job, Brick! We'll finish the rest of it tomorrow.

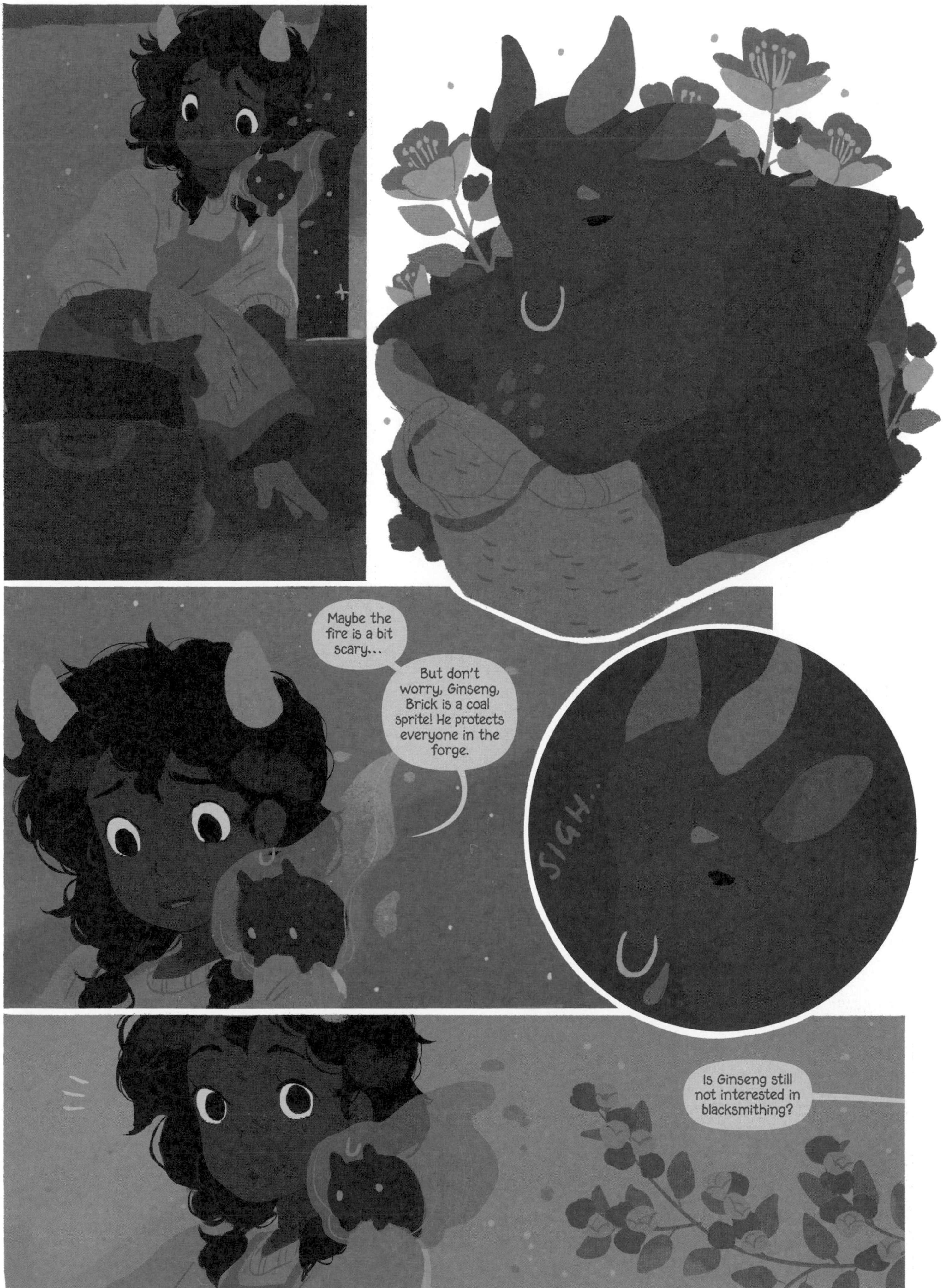
Maybe the fire is a bit scary...
But don't worry, Ginseng, Brick is a coal sprite! He protects everyone in the forge.
SIGH...
Is Ginseng still not interested in blacksmithing?

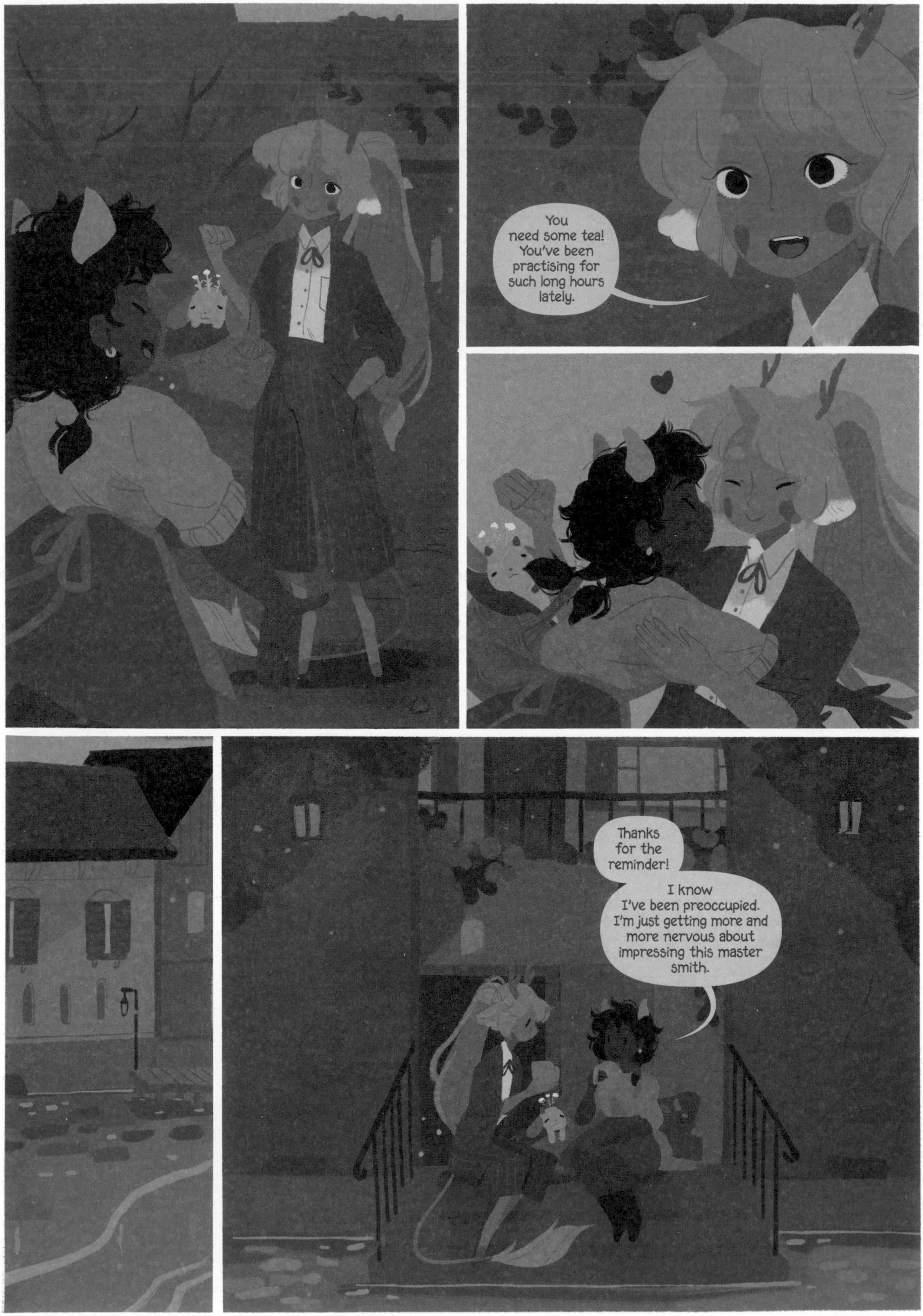
You need some tea! You've been practising for such long hours lately.
Thanks for the reminder!
I know I've been preoccupied. I'm just getting more and more nervous about impressing this master smith.

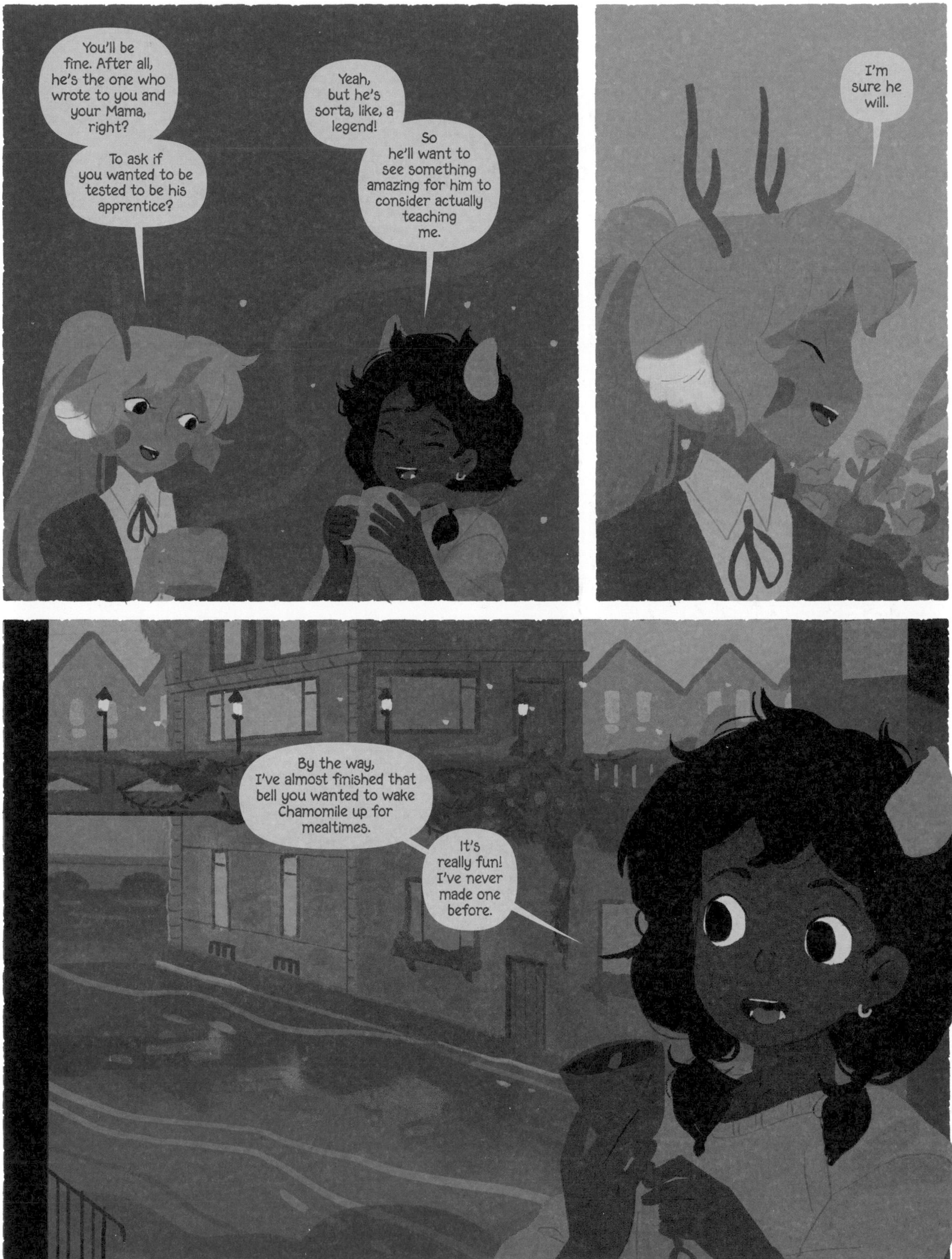
You'll be fine. After all, he's the one who wrote to you and your Mama, right?
To ask if you wanted to be tested to be his apprentice?
Yeah, but he's sorta, like, a legend!
So he'll want to see something amazing for him to consider actually teaching me.
I'm sure he will.
By the way, I've almost finished that bell you wanted to wake Chamomile up for mealtimes.
It's really fun! I've never made one before.

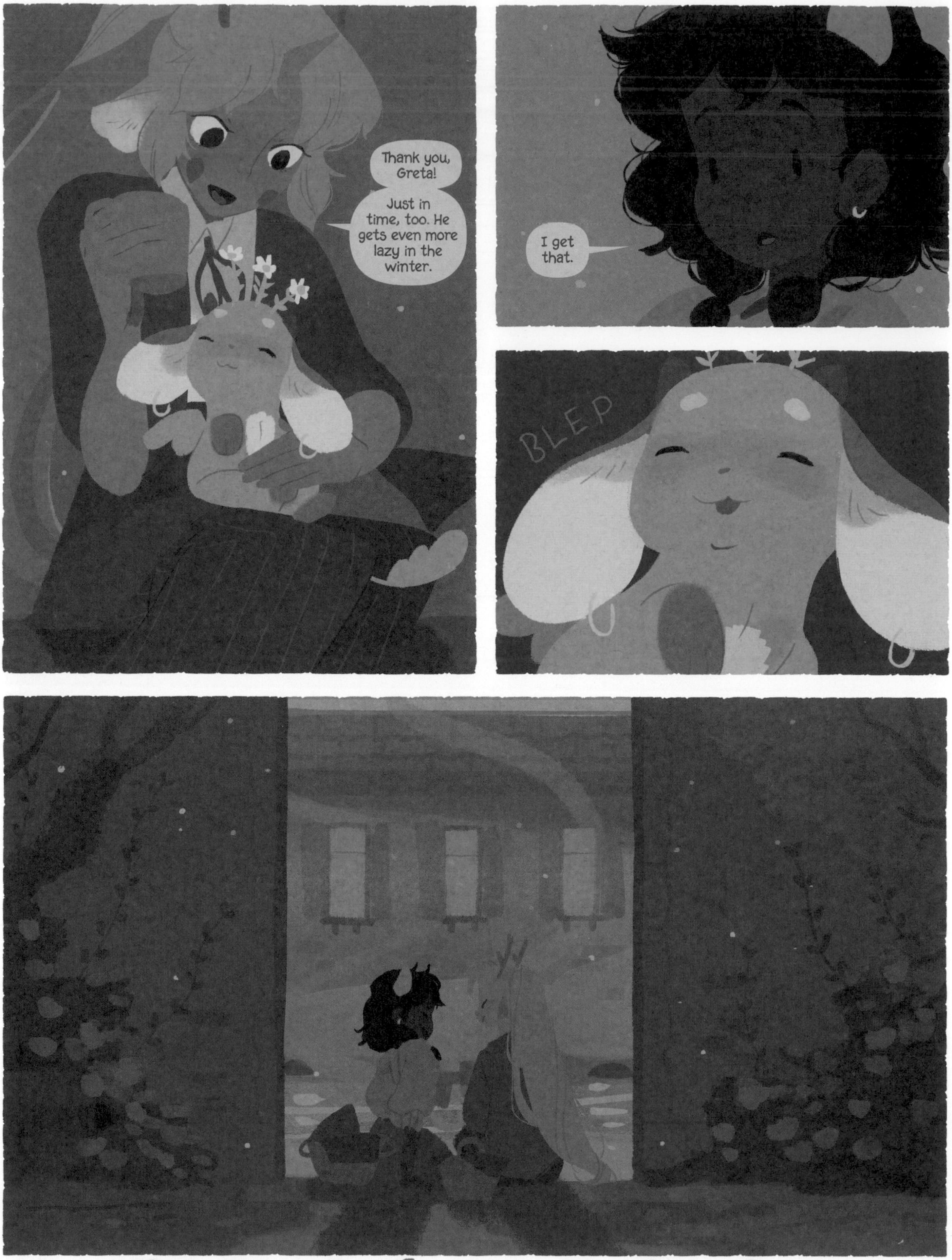
Thank you, Greta!
Just in time, too. He gets even more lazy in the winter.
I get that.
BLEP

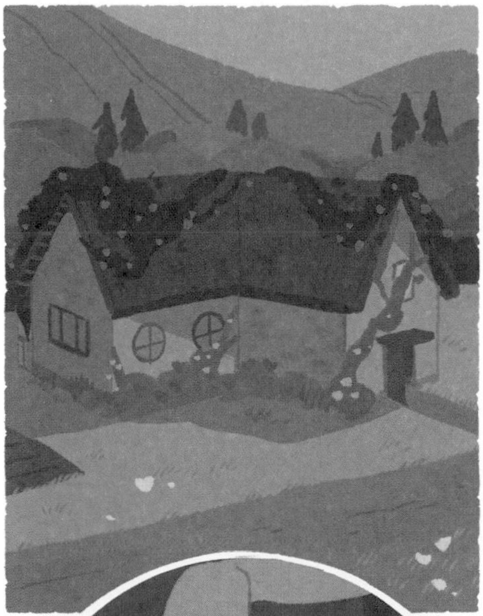

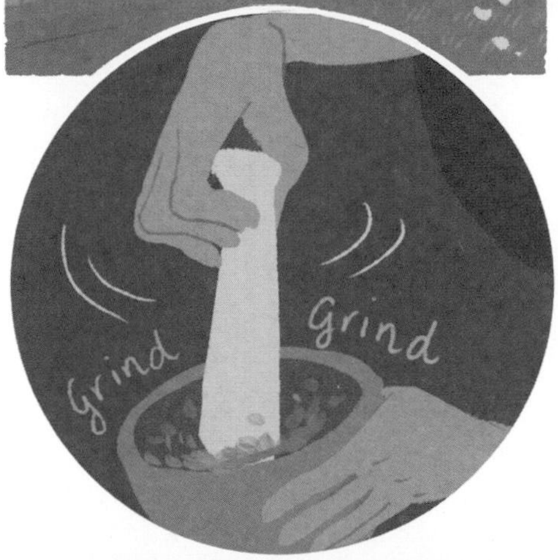
Grind
Grind

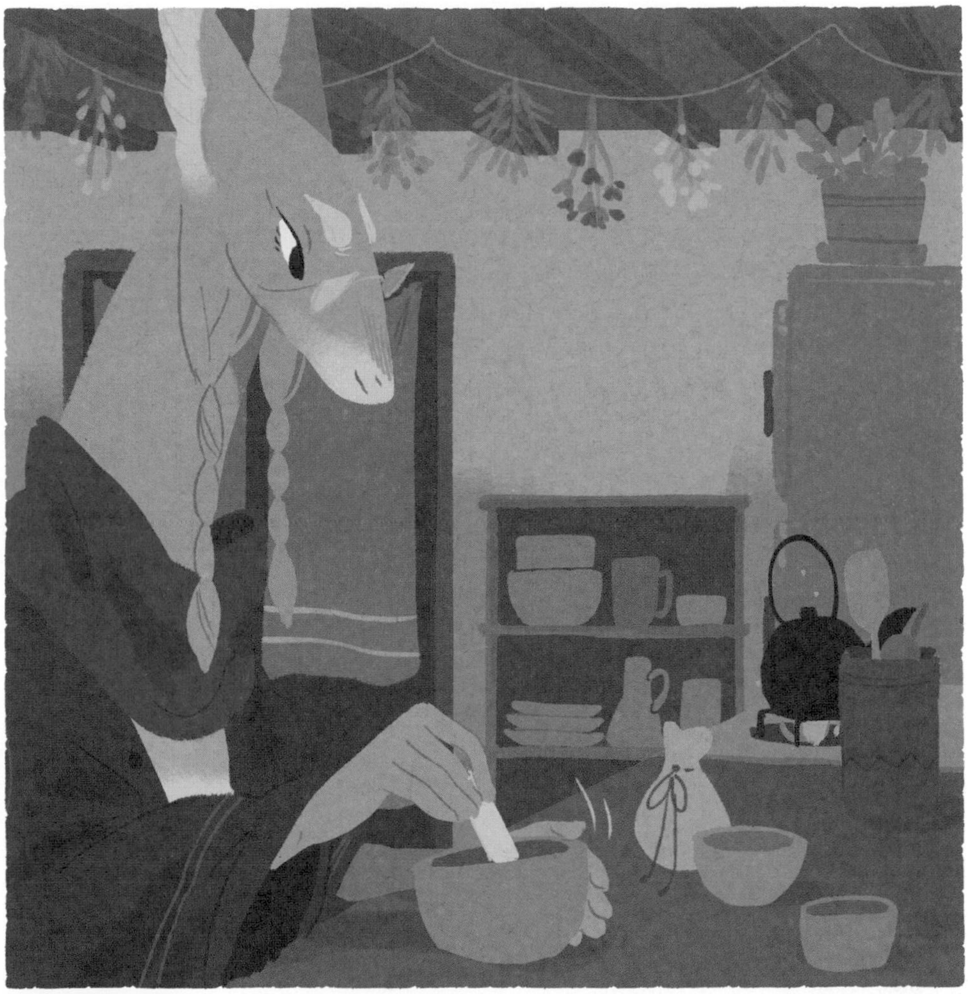

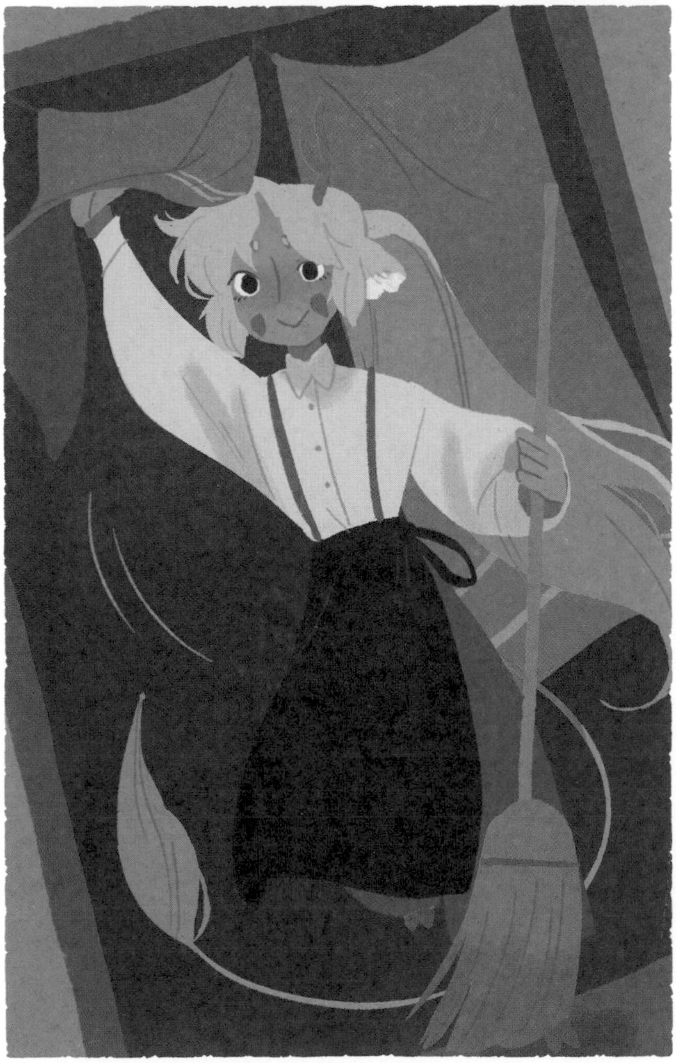

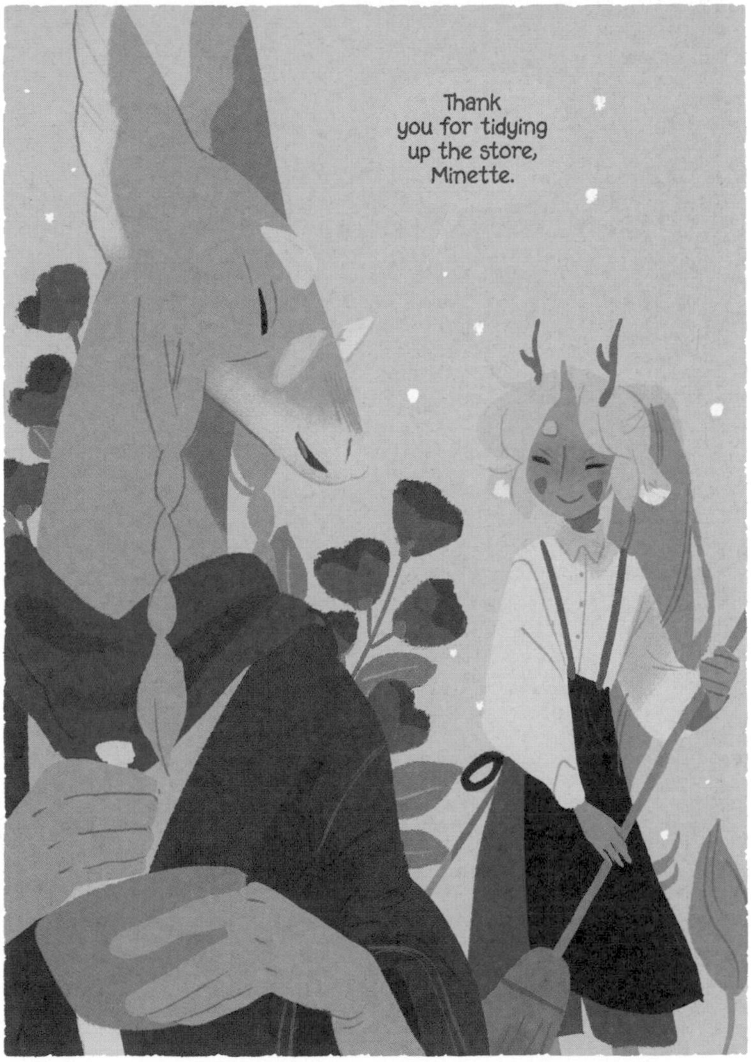
Thank you for tidying up the store, Minette.

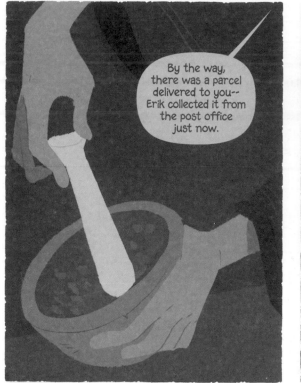

By the way, there was a parcel delivered to you-- Erik collected it from the post office just now.

From my family?

In a sense. It's on the table.

It's from the monastery!

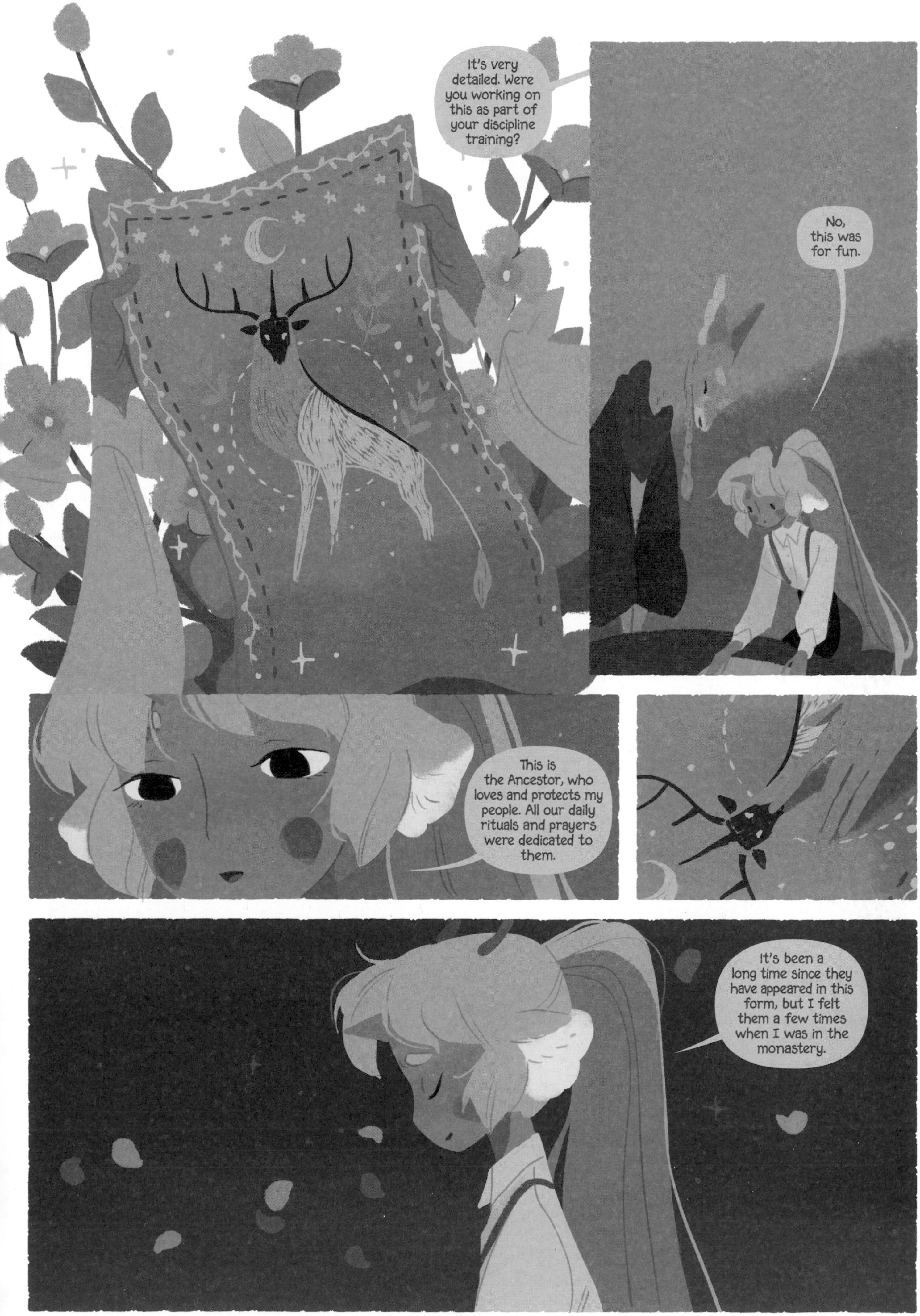
It's very detailed. Were you working on this as part of your discipline training?
No, this was for fun.
This is the Ancestor, who loves and protects my people. All our daily rituals and prayers were dedicated to them.
It's been a long time since they have appeared in this form, but I felt them a few times when I was in the monastery.

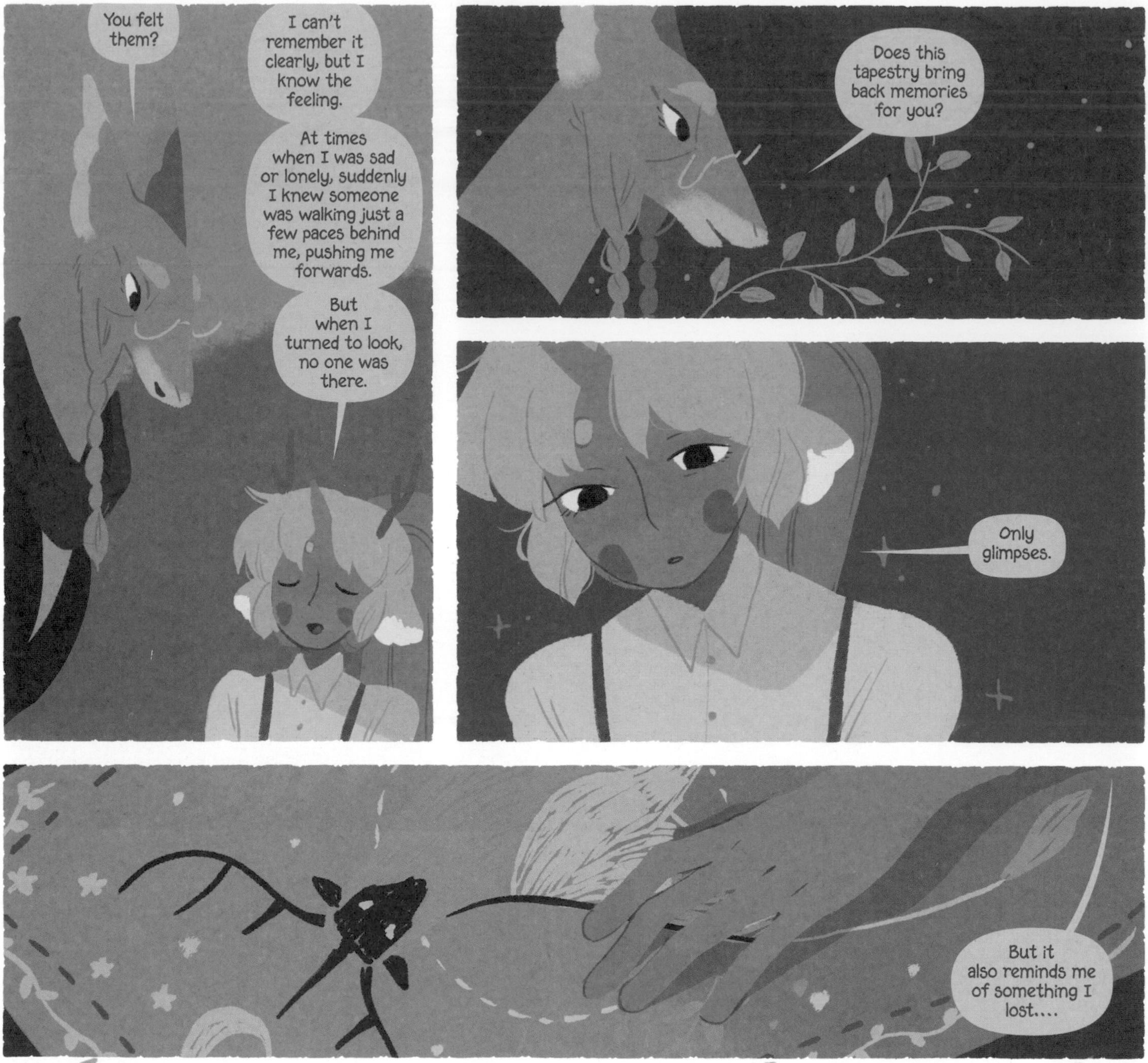
You felt them?
I can't remember it clearly, but I know the feeling.
At times when I was sad or lonely, suddenly I knew someone was walking just a few paces behind me, pushing me forwards.
But when I turned to look, no one was there.
Does this tapestry bring back memories for you?
Only glimpses.
But it also reminds me of something I lost....

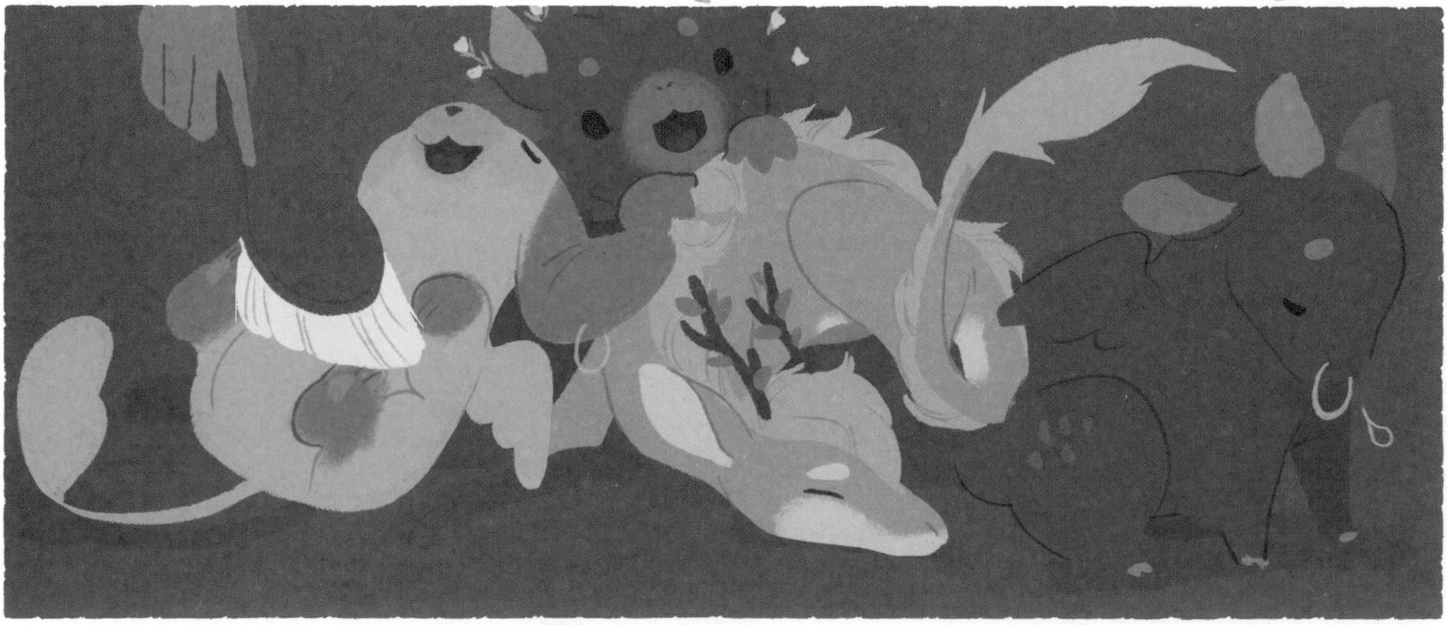

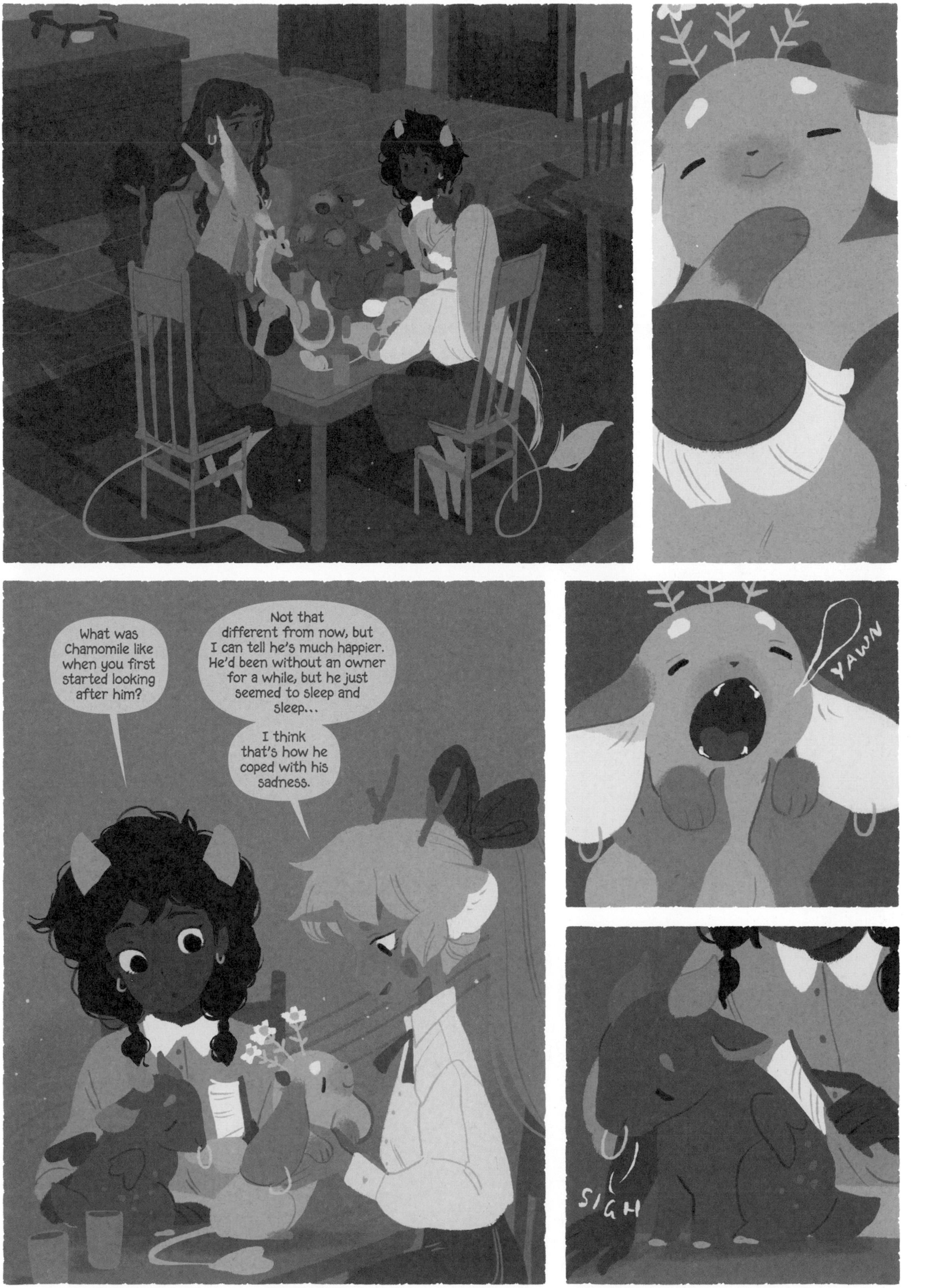
What was Chamomile like when you first started looking after him?
Not that different from now, but I can tell he's much happier. He'd been without an owner for a while, but he just seemed to sleep and sleep...
I think that's how he coped with his sadness.
YAWN
SIGH

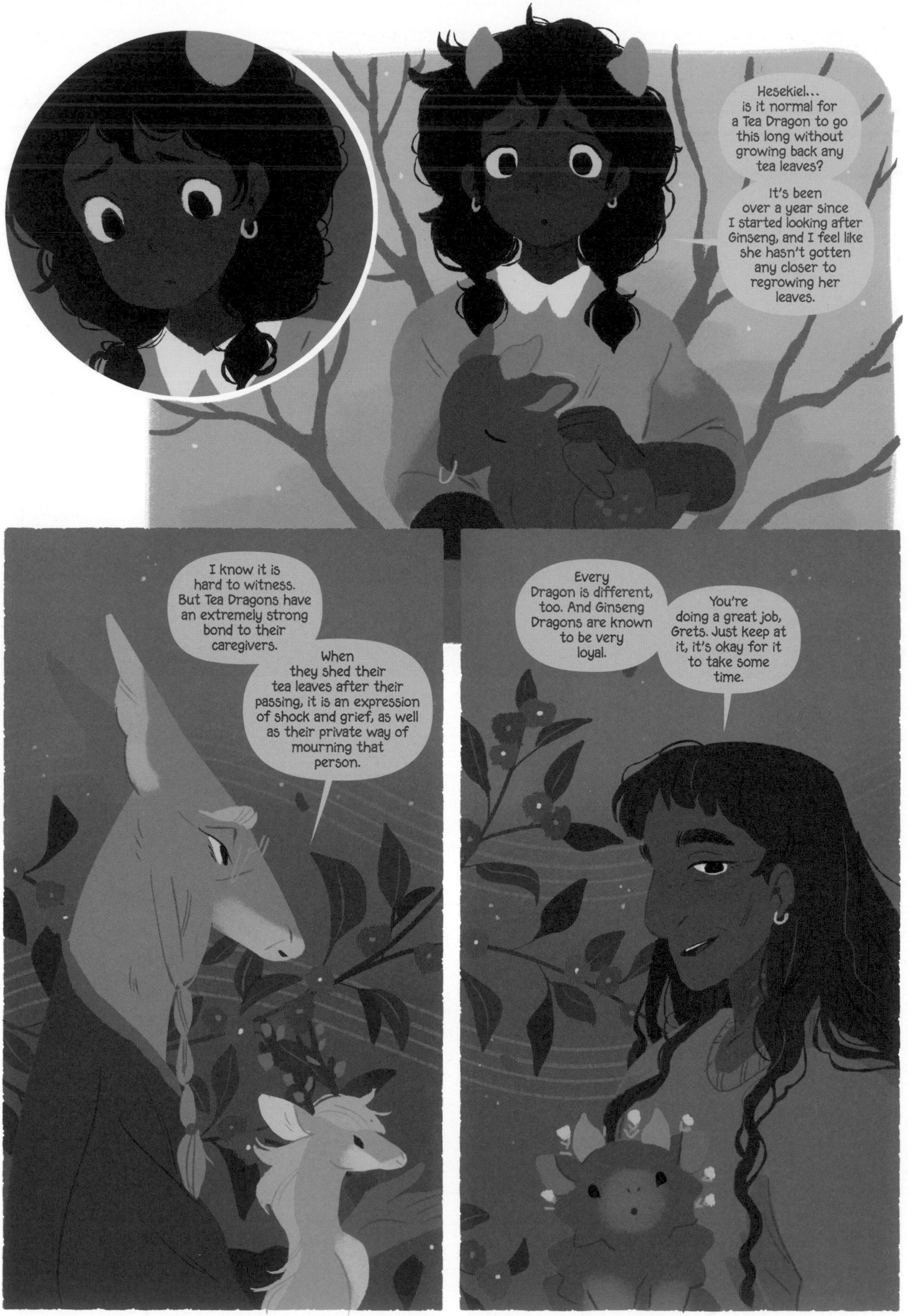
Hesekiel... is it normal for a Tea Dragon to go this long without growing back any tea leaves?
It's been over a year since I started looking after Ginseng, and I feel like she hasn't gotten any closer to regrowing her leaves.
I know it is hard to witness. But Tea Dragons have an extremely strong bond to their caregivers.
When they shed their tea leaves after their passing, it is an expression of shock and grief, as well as their private way of mourning that person.
Every Dragon is different, too. And Ginseng Dragons are known to be very loyal.
You're doing a great job, Grets. Just keep at it, it's okay for it to take some time.

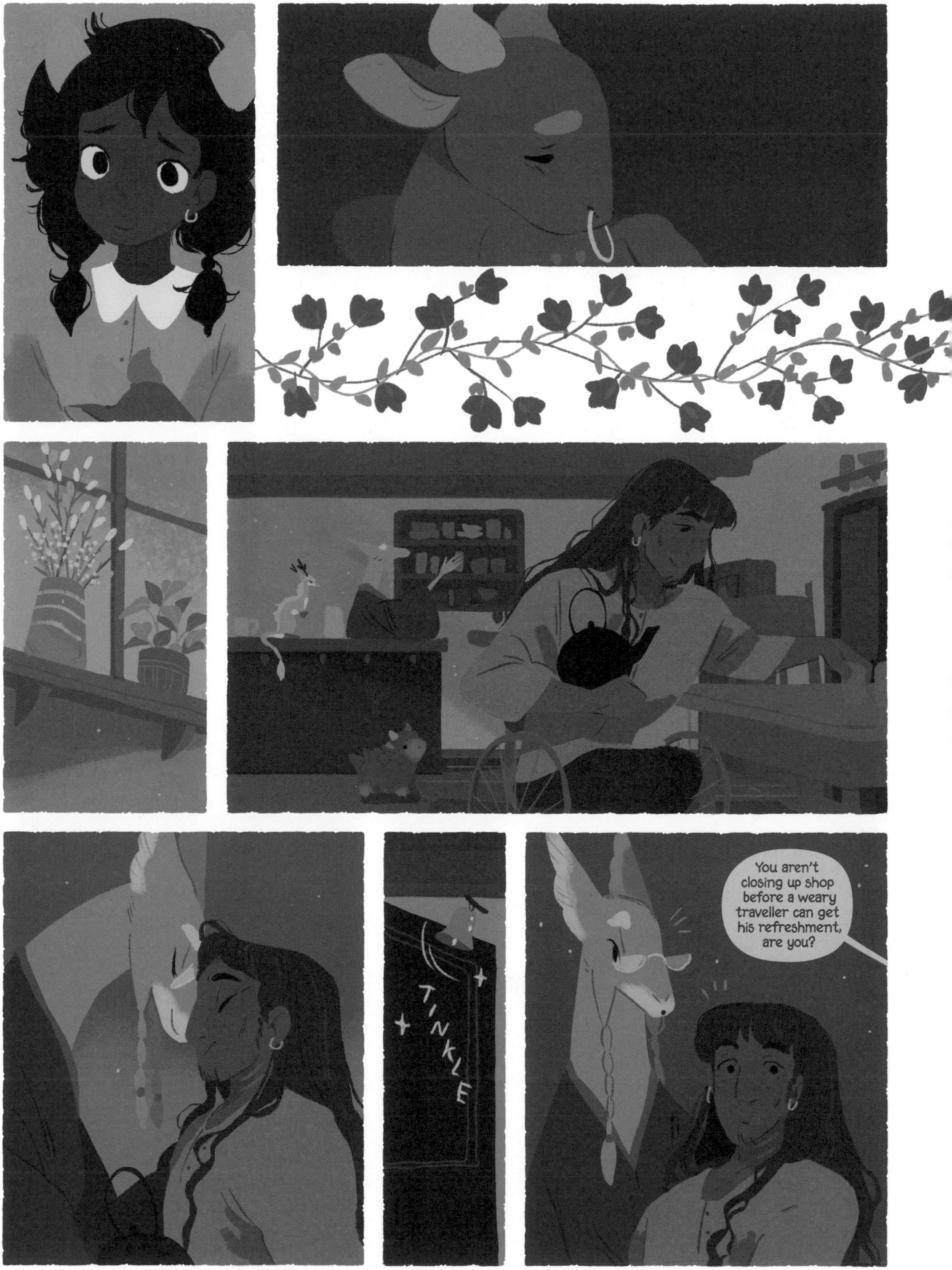
TINKLE
You aren't closing up shop before a weary traveller can get his refreshment, are you?

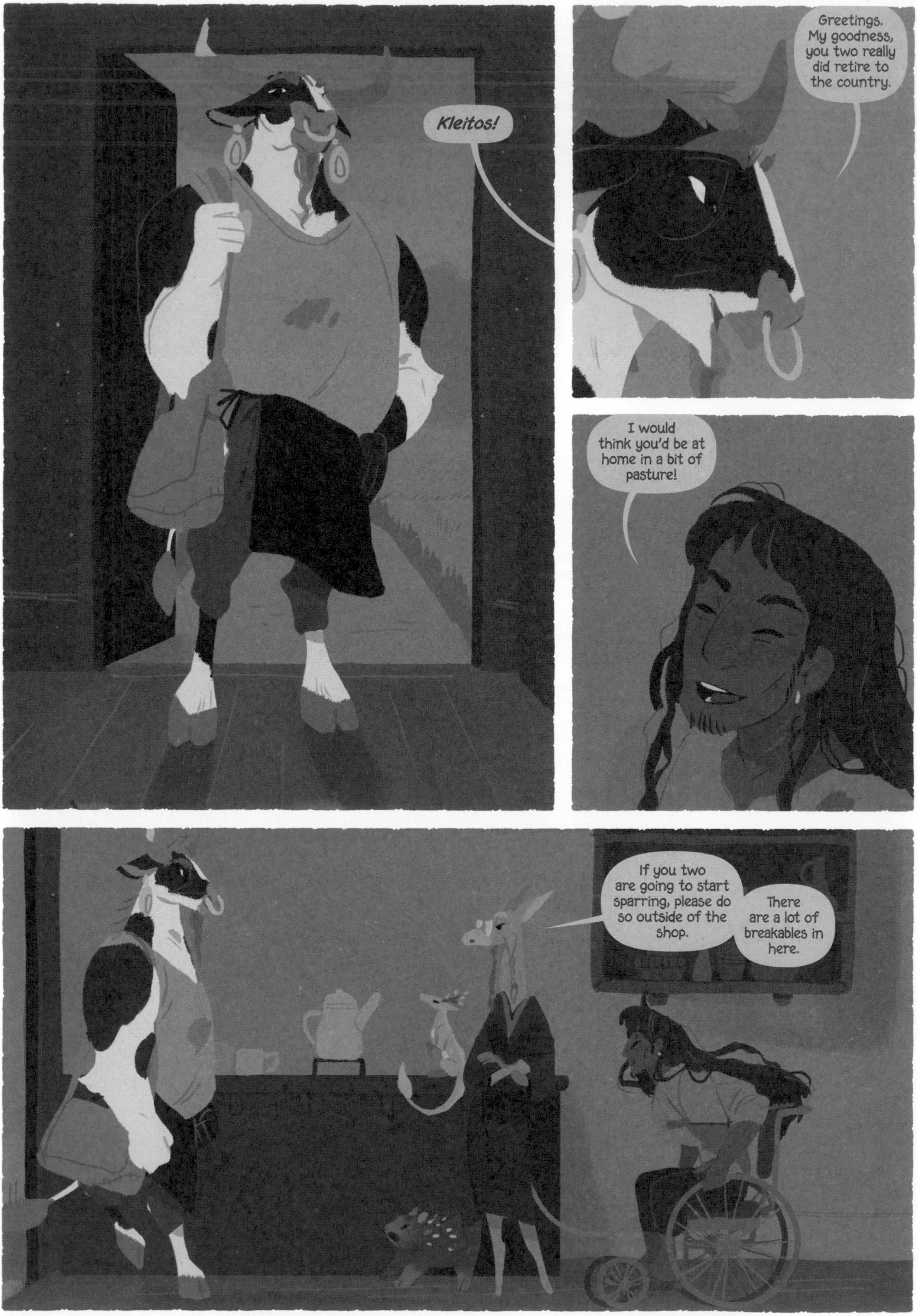
Kleitos!
Greetings. My goodness, you two really did retire to the country.
I would think you'd be at home in a bit of pasture!
If you two are going to start sparring, please do so outside of the shop.
There are a lot of breakables in here.

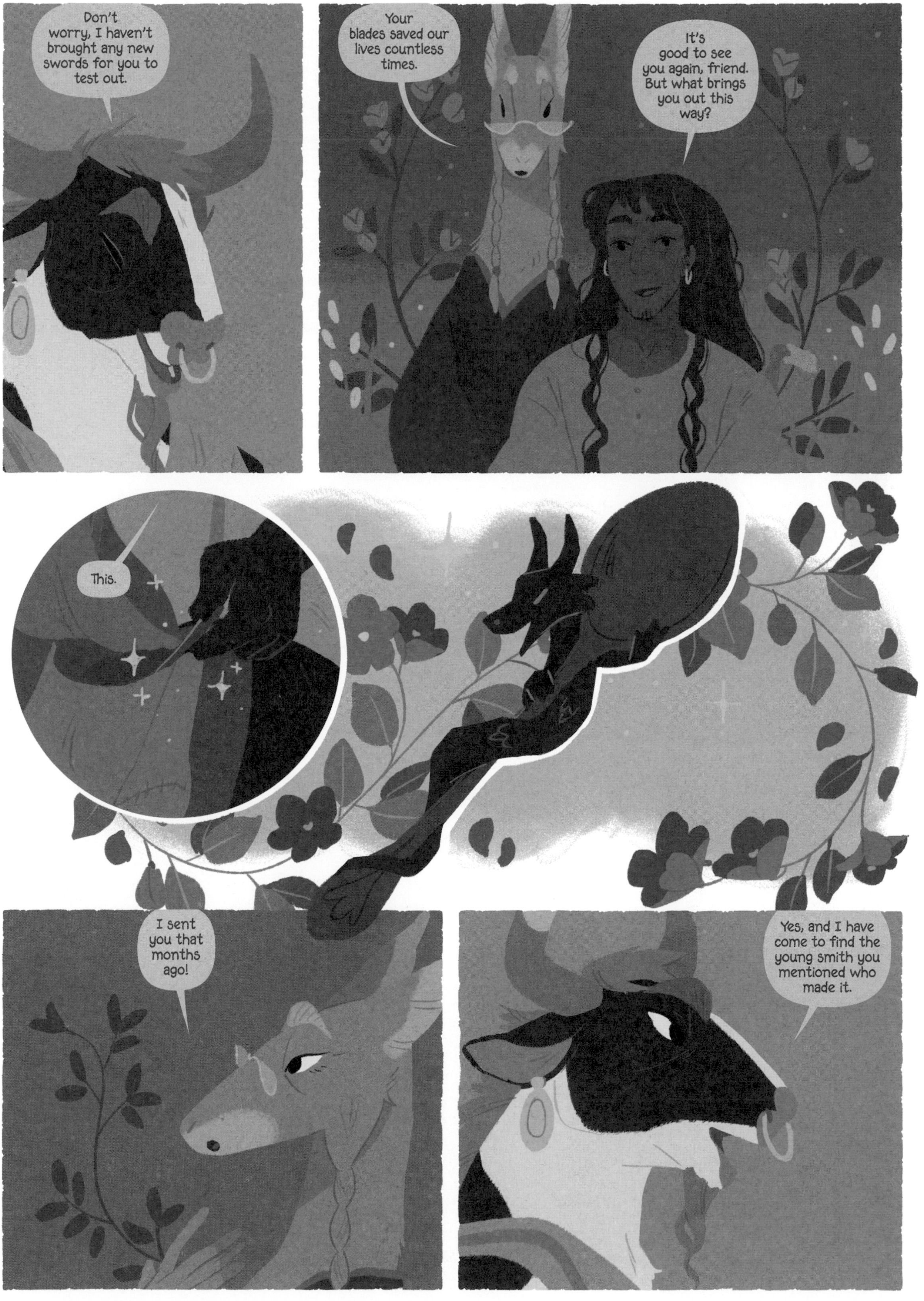
Don't worry, I haven't brought any new swords for you to test out.
Your blades saved our lives countless times.
It's good to see you again, friend. But what brings you out this way?
This.
I sent you that months ago!
Yes, and I have come to find the young smith you mentioned who made it.

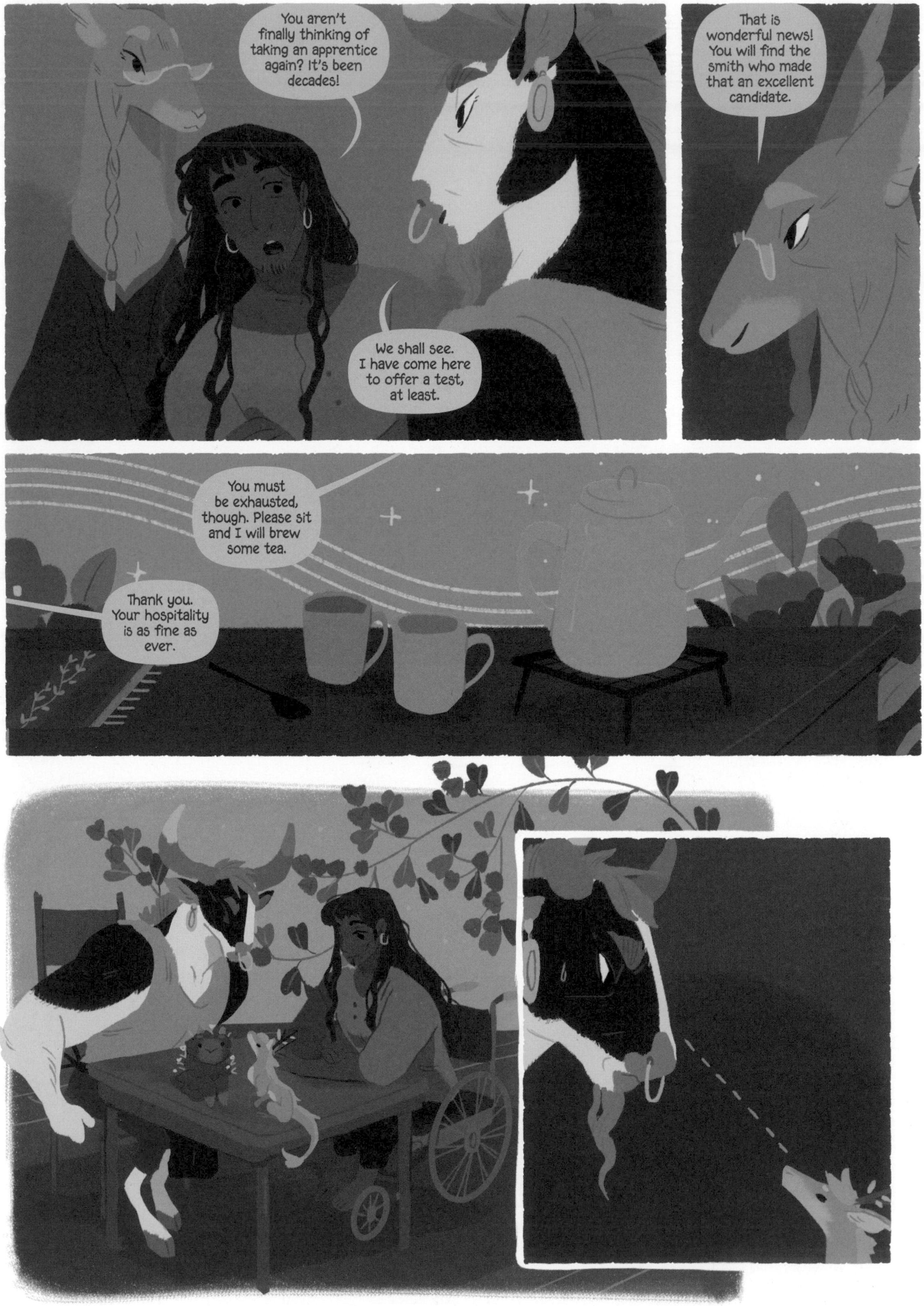
You aren't finally thinking of taking an apprentice again? It's been decades!
We shall see. I have come here to offer a test, at least.
That is wonderful news! You will find the smith who made that an excellent candidate.
You must be exhausted, though. Please sit and I will brew some tea.
Thank you. Your hospitality is as fine as ever.

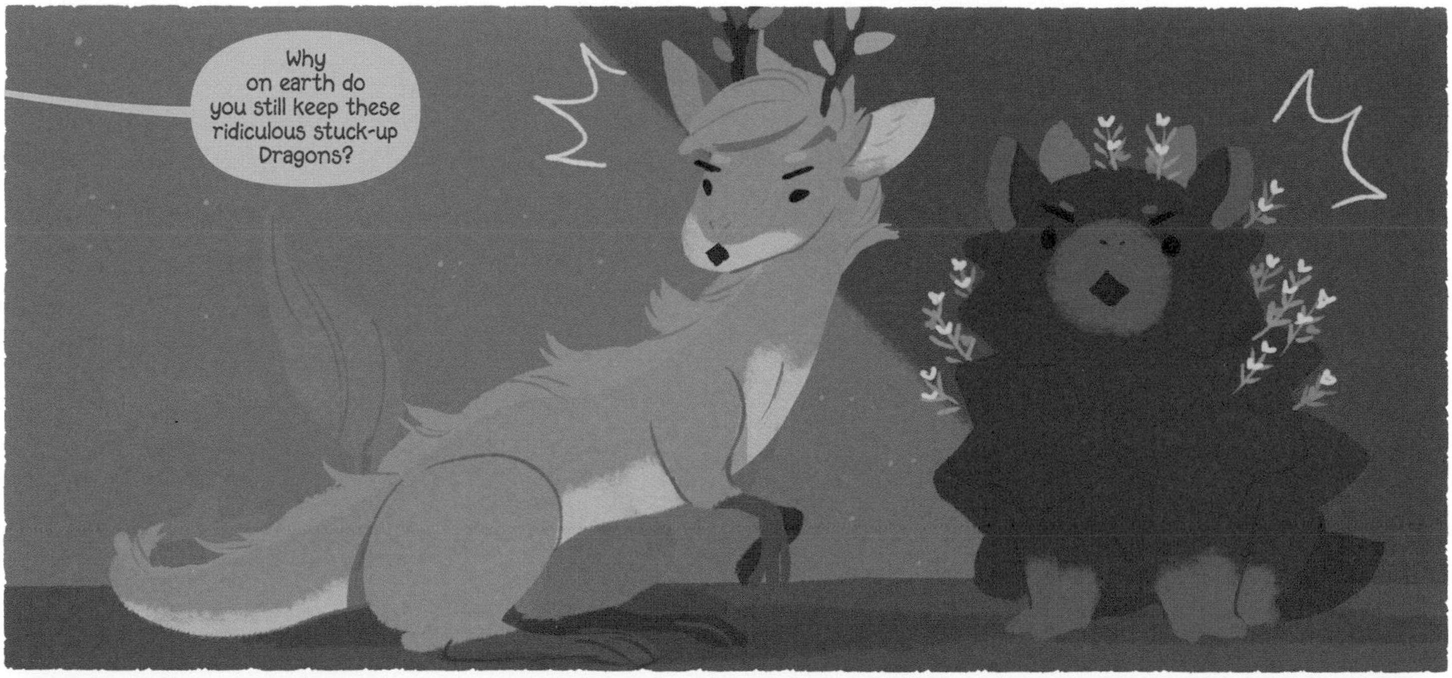
Why on earth do you still keep these ridiculous stuck-up Dragons?

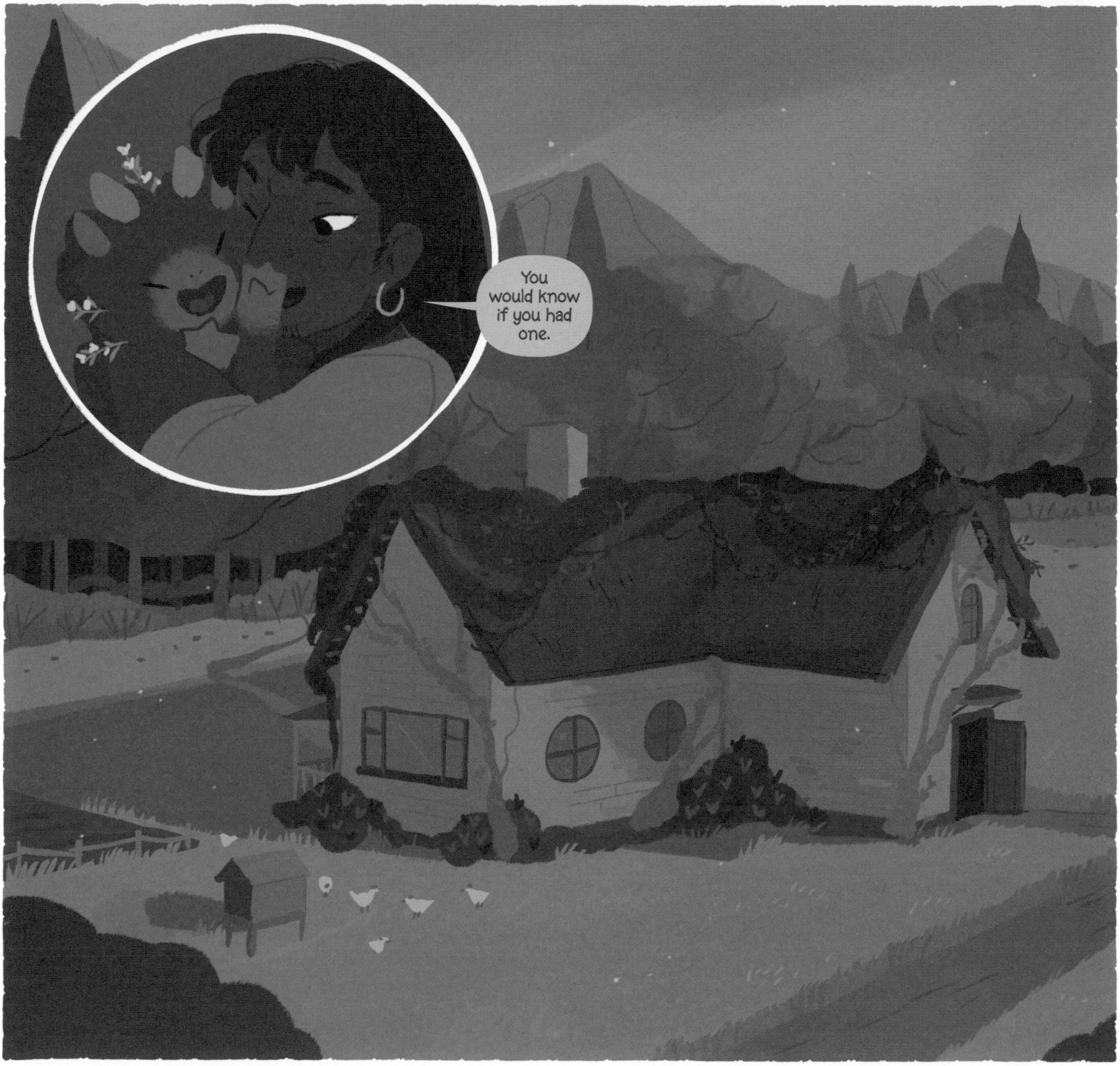
You would know if you had one.

Chapter Two

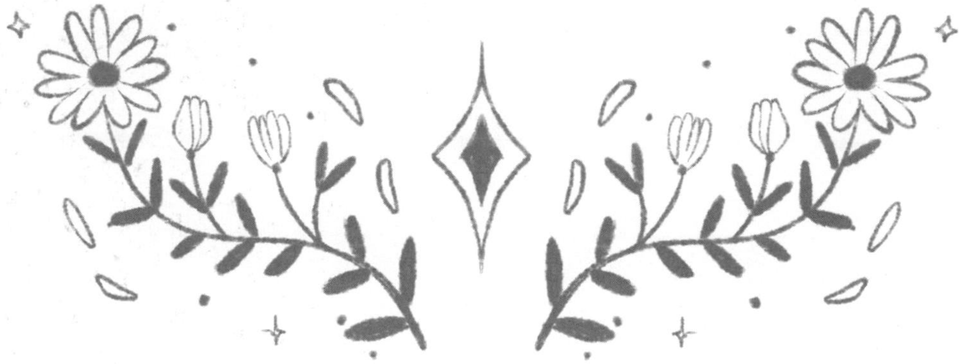

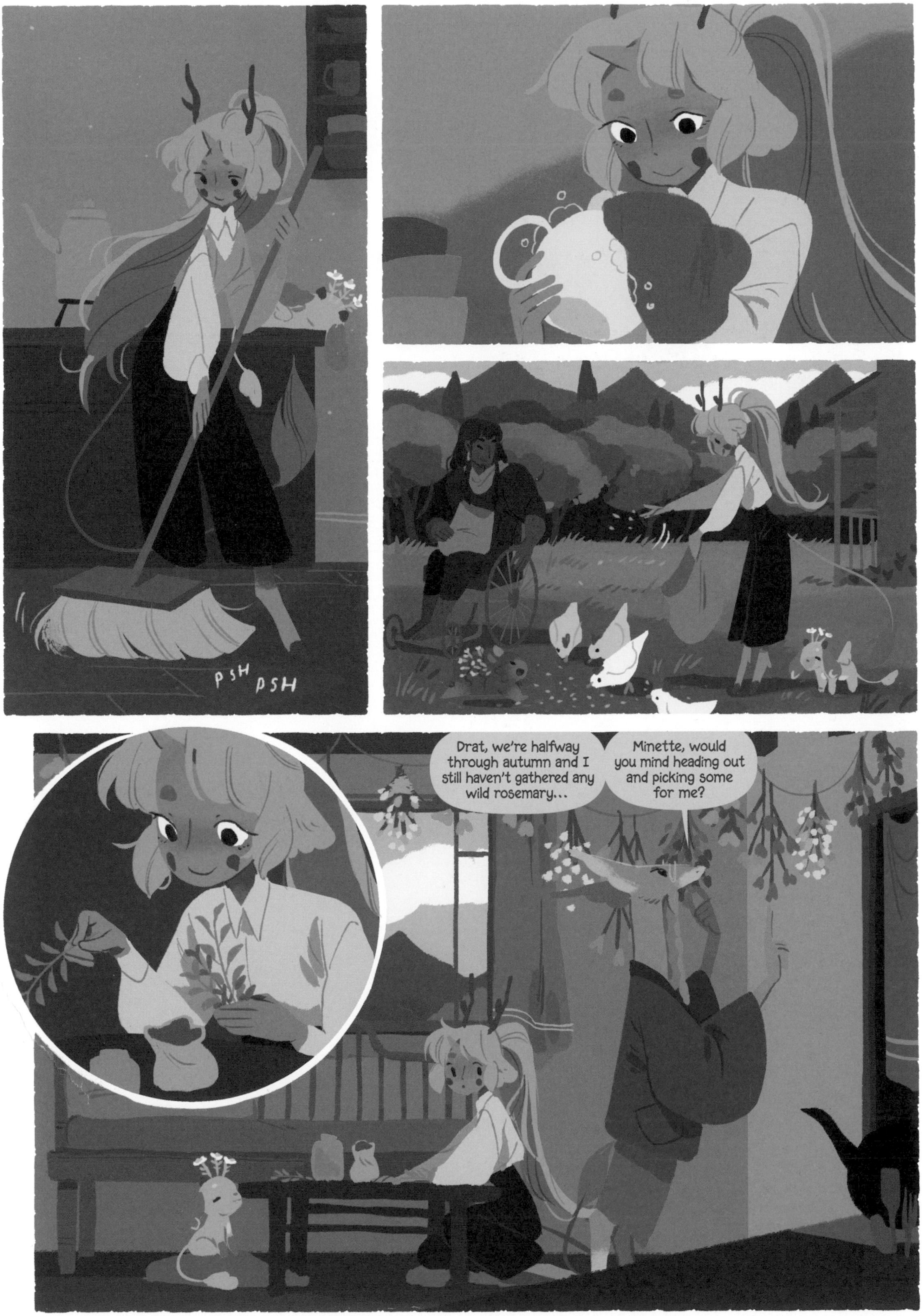
PSH PSH
Drat, we're halfway through autumn and I still haven't gathered any wild rosemary...
Minette, would you mind heading out and picking some for me?

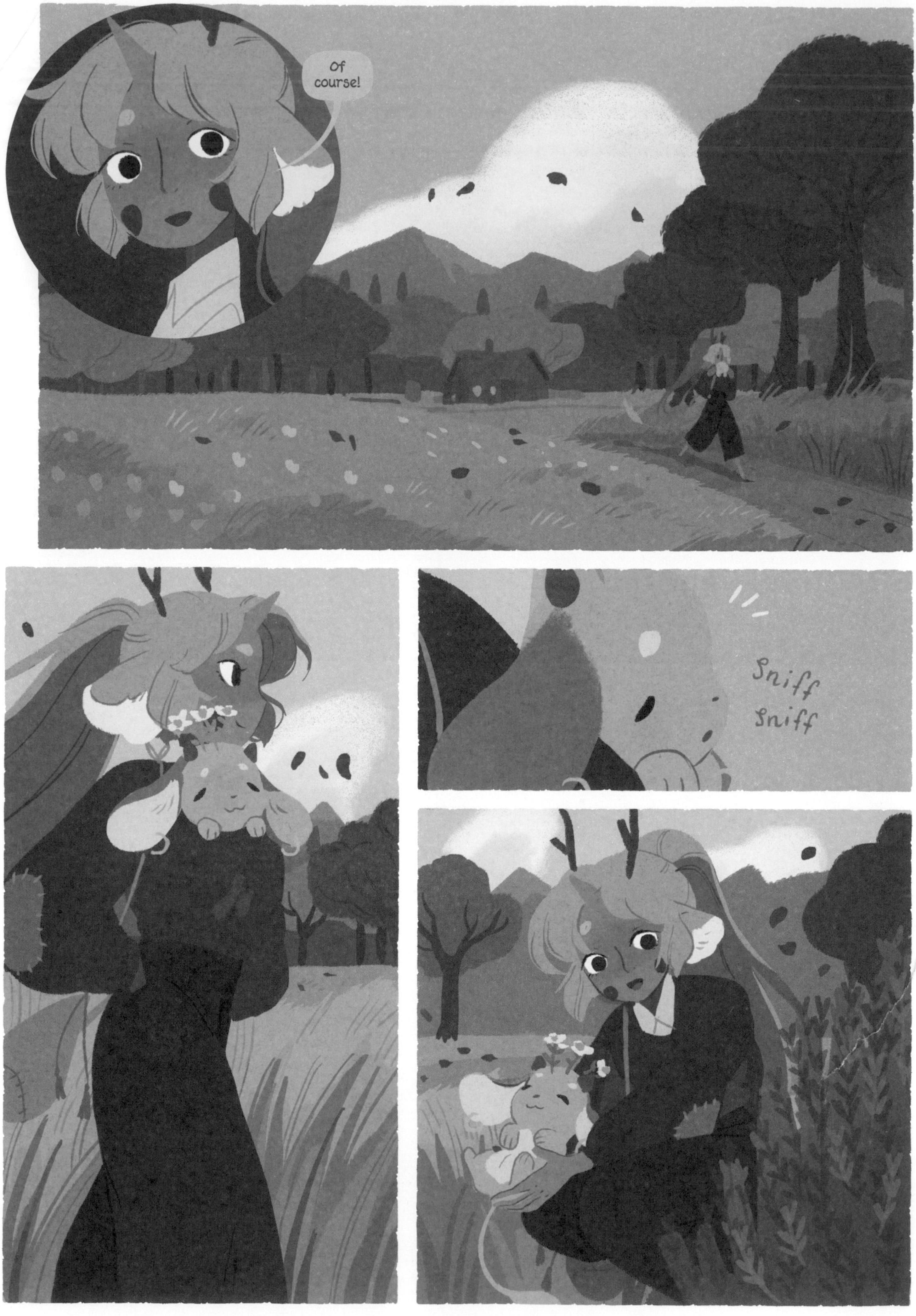
Of course!
Sniff
Sniff

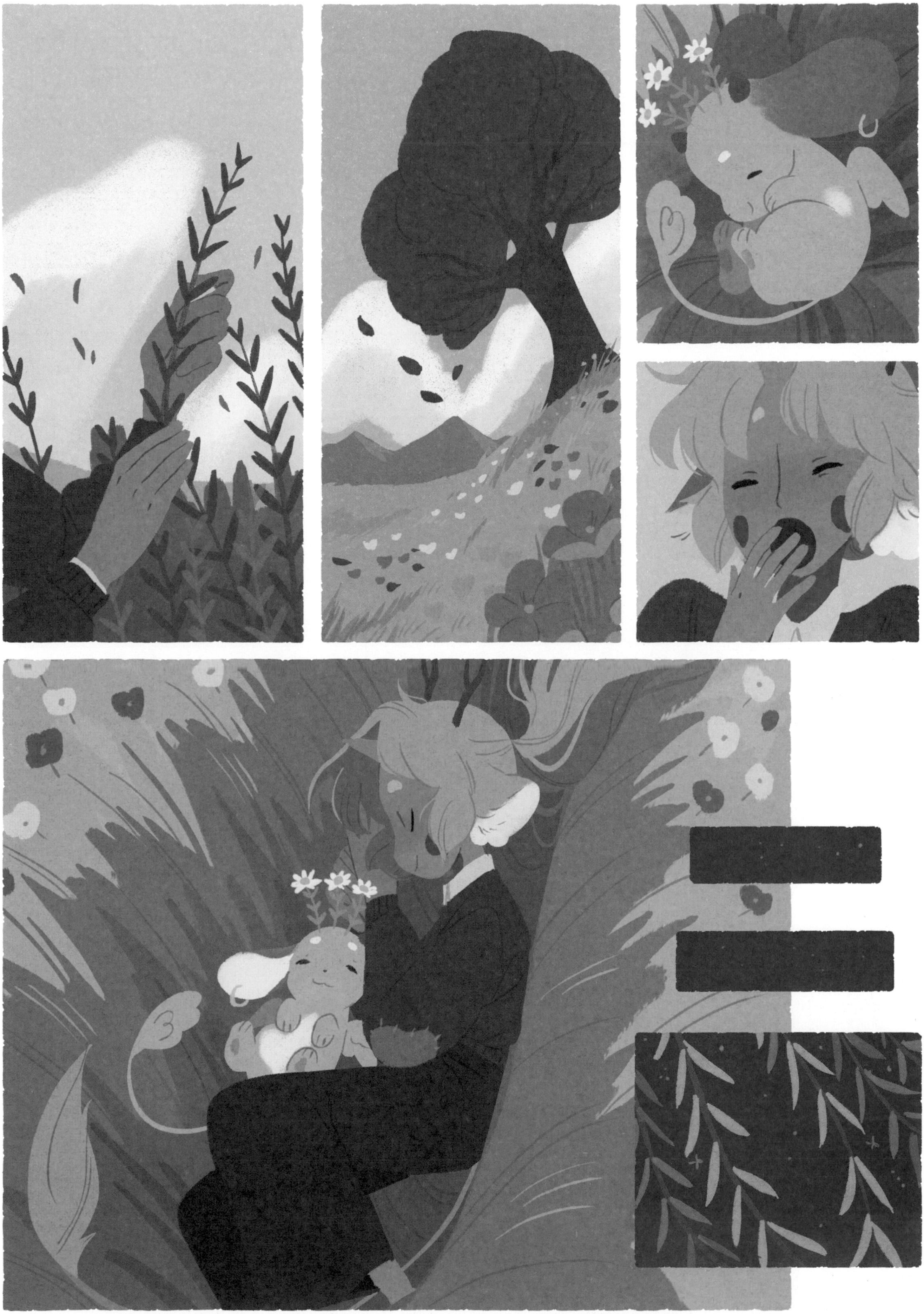

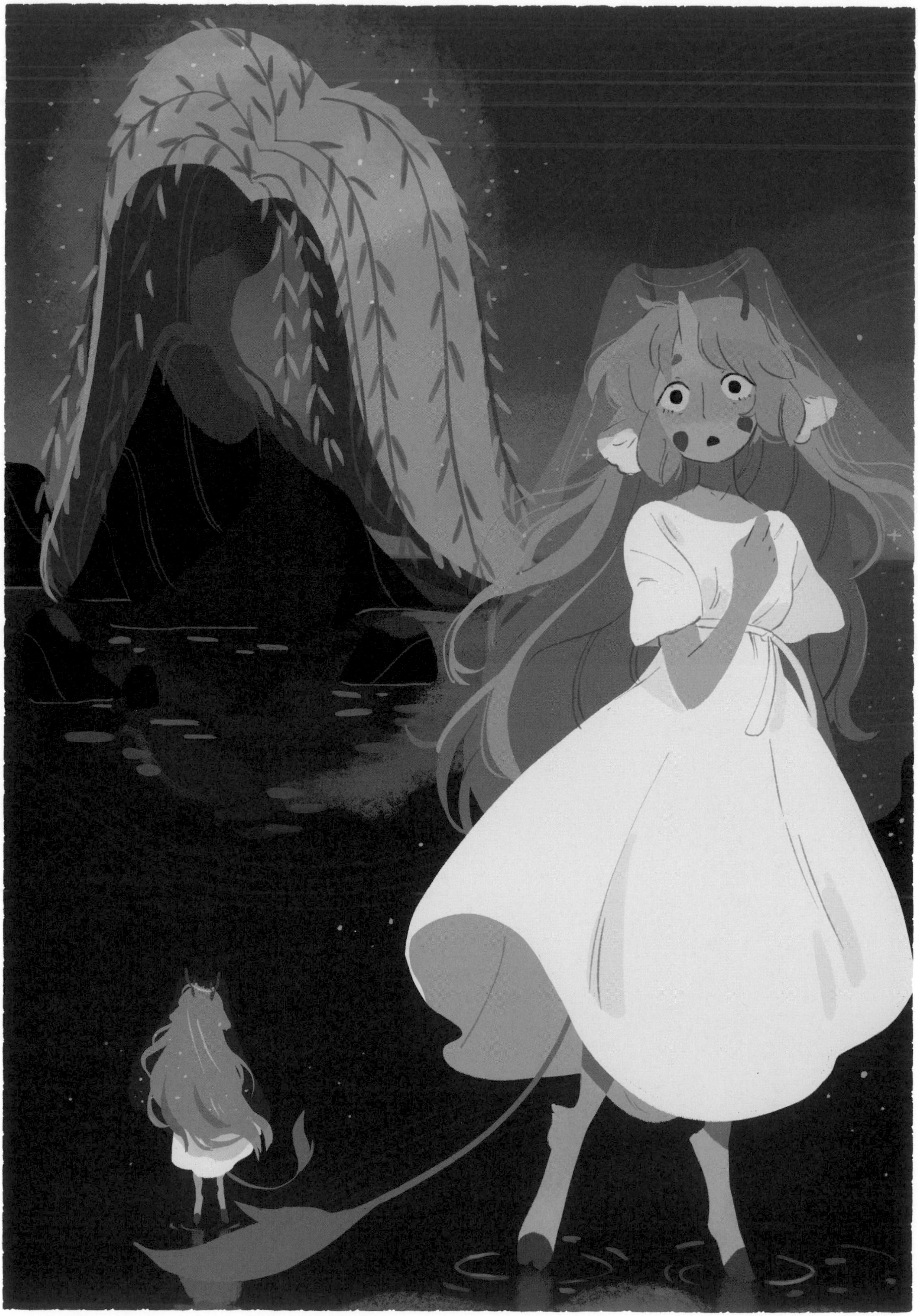

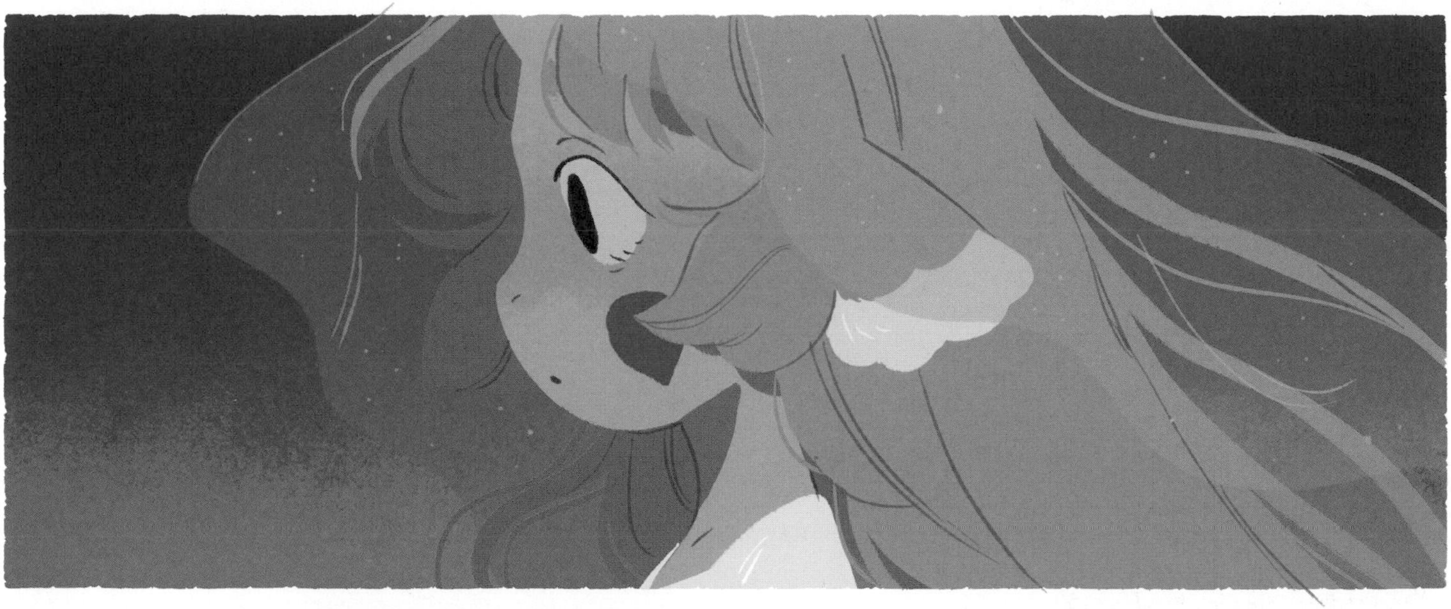
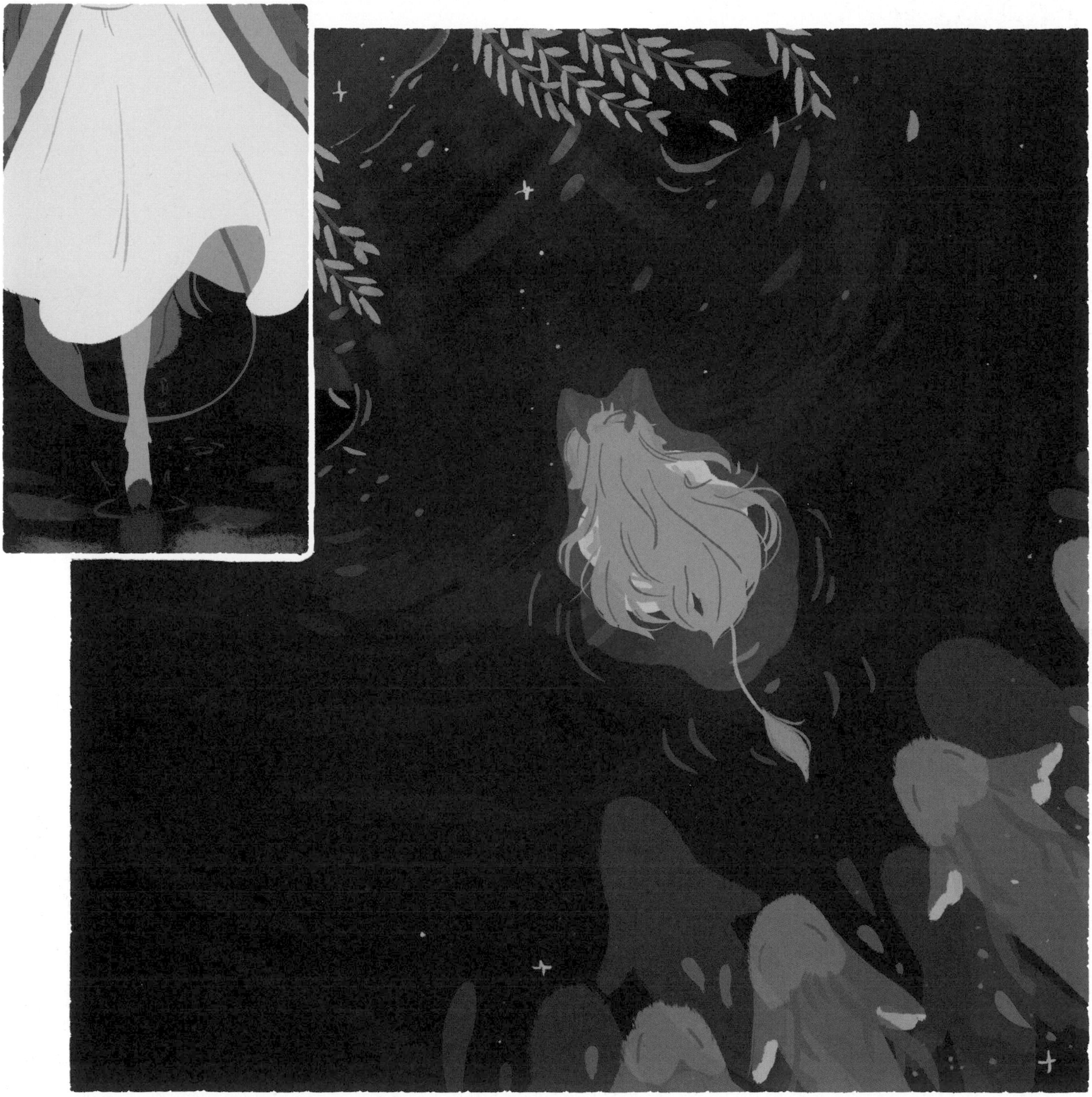

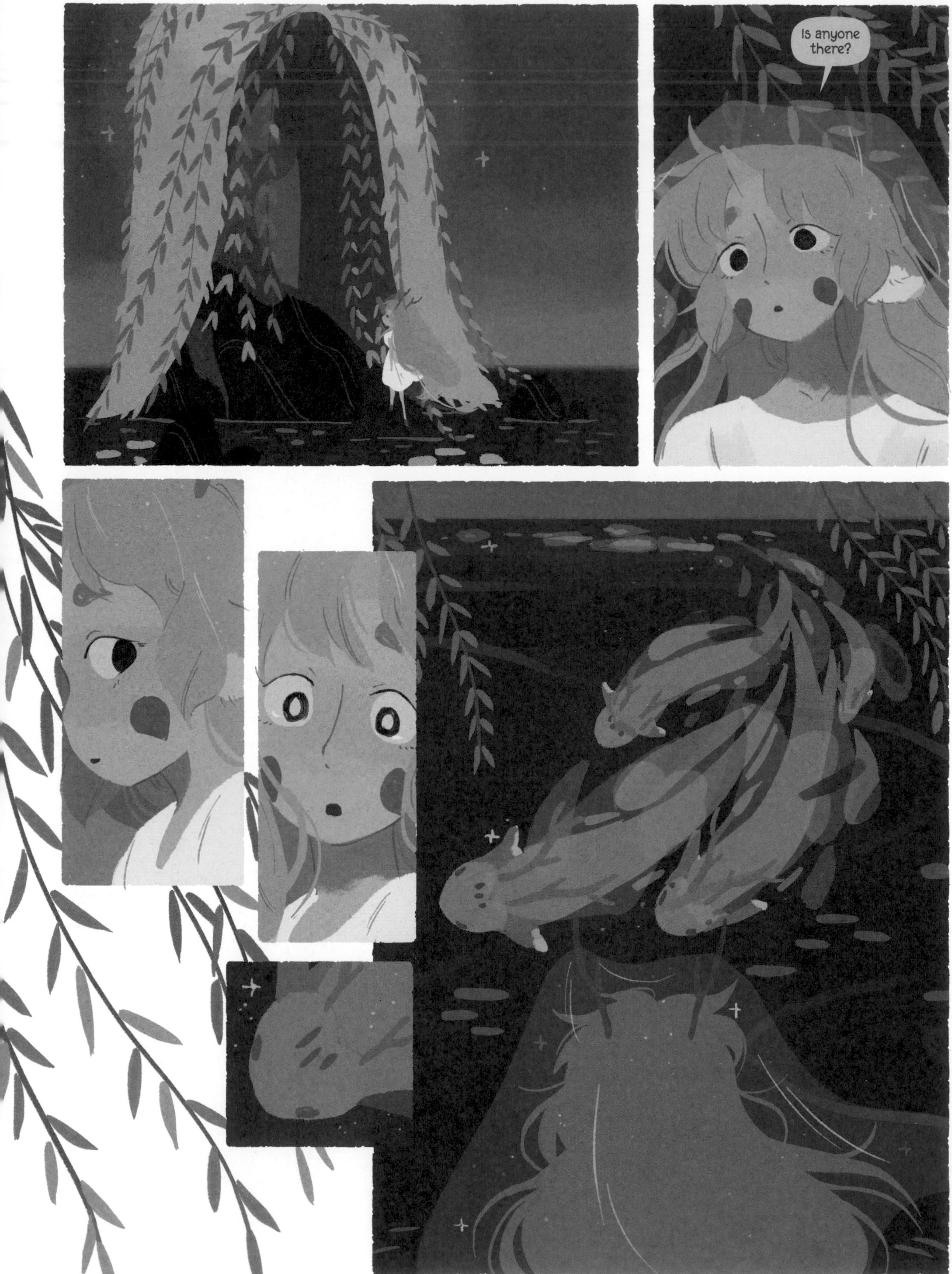
Is anyone there?

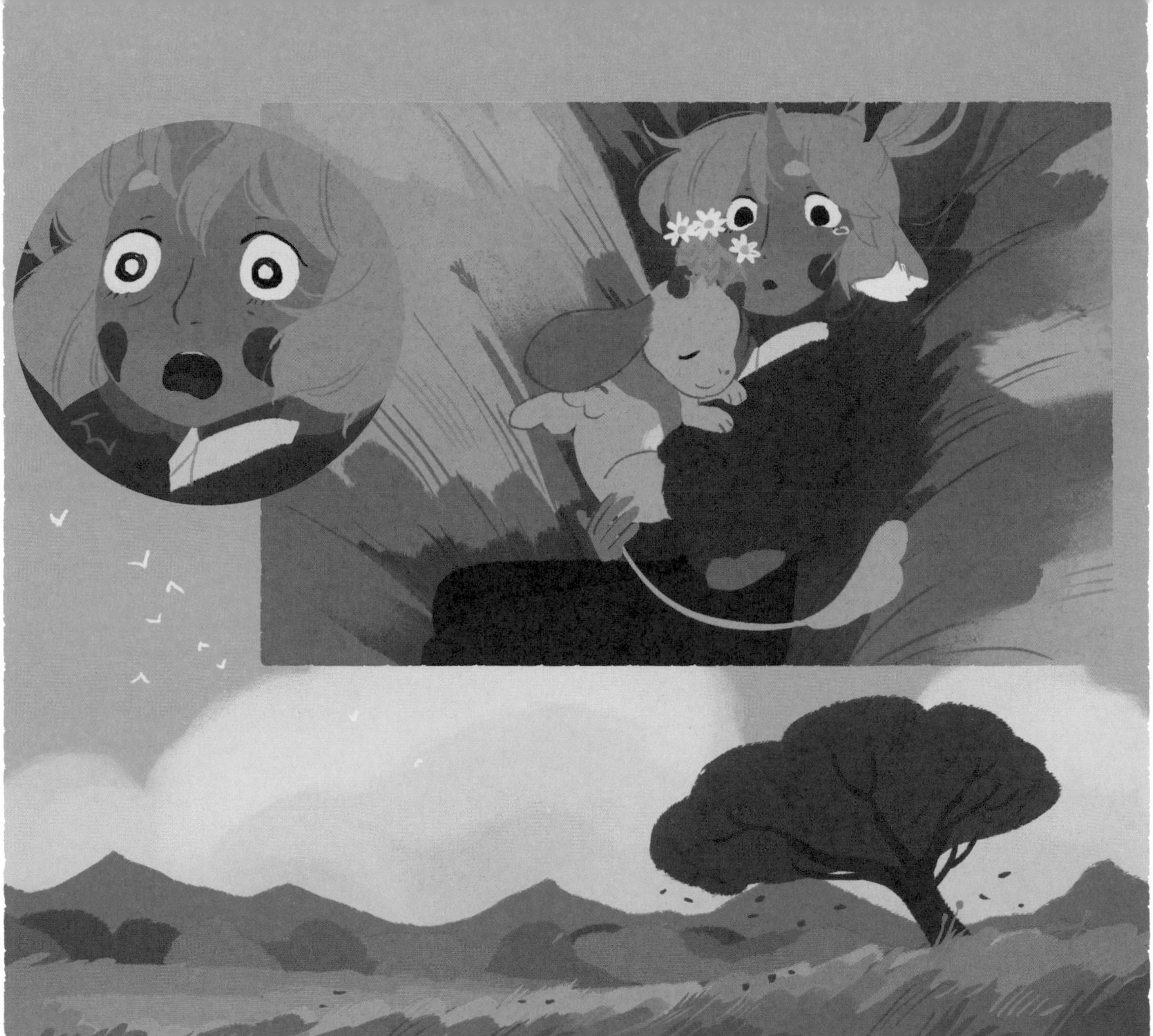

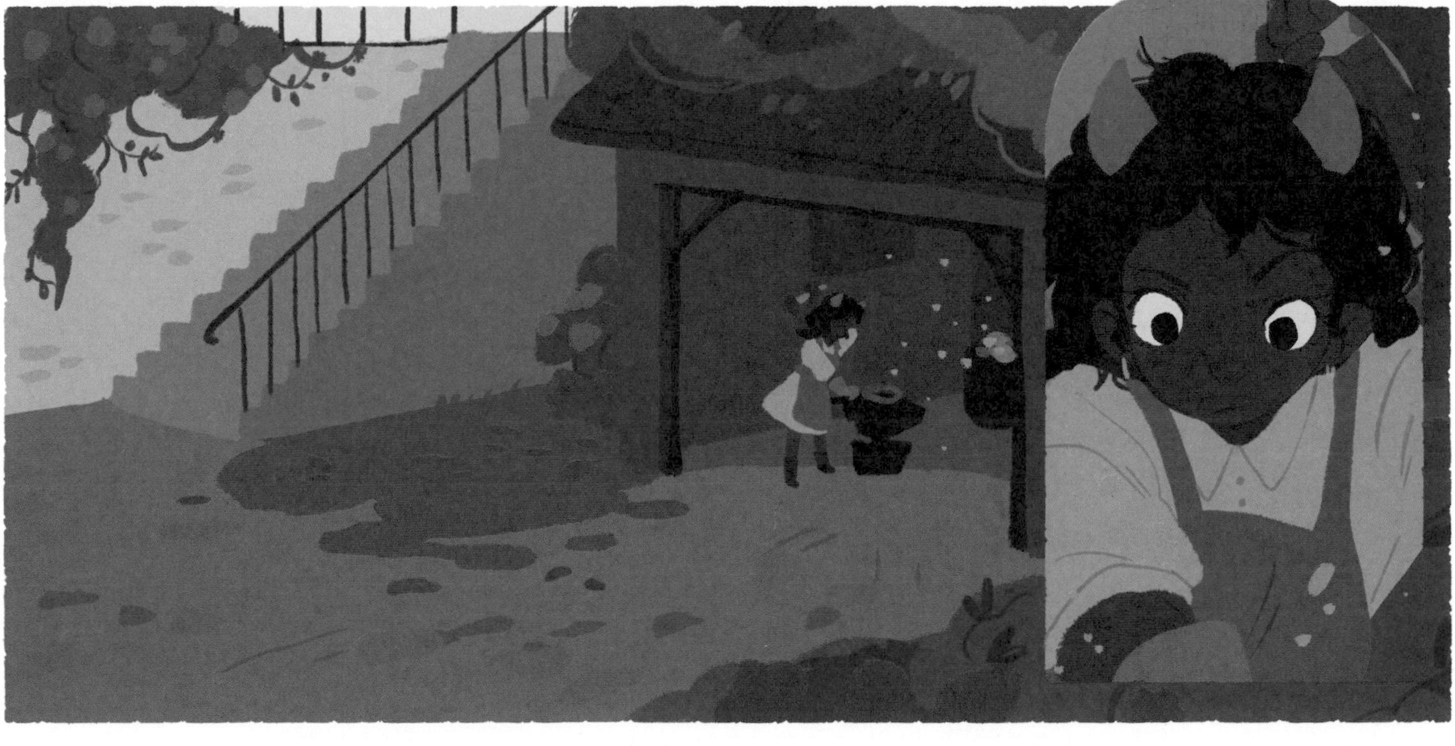

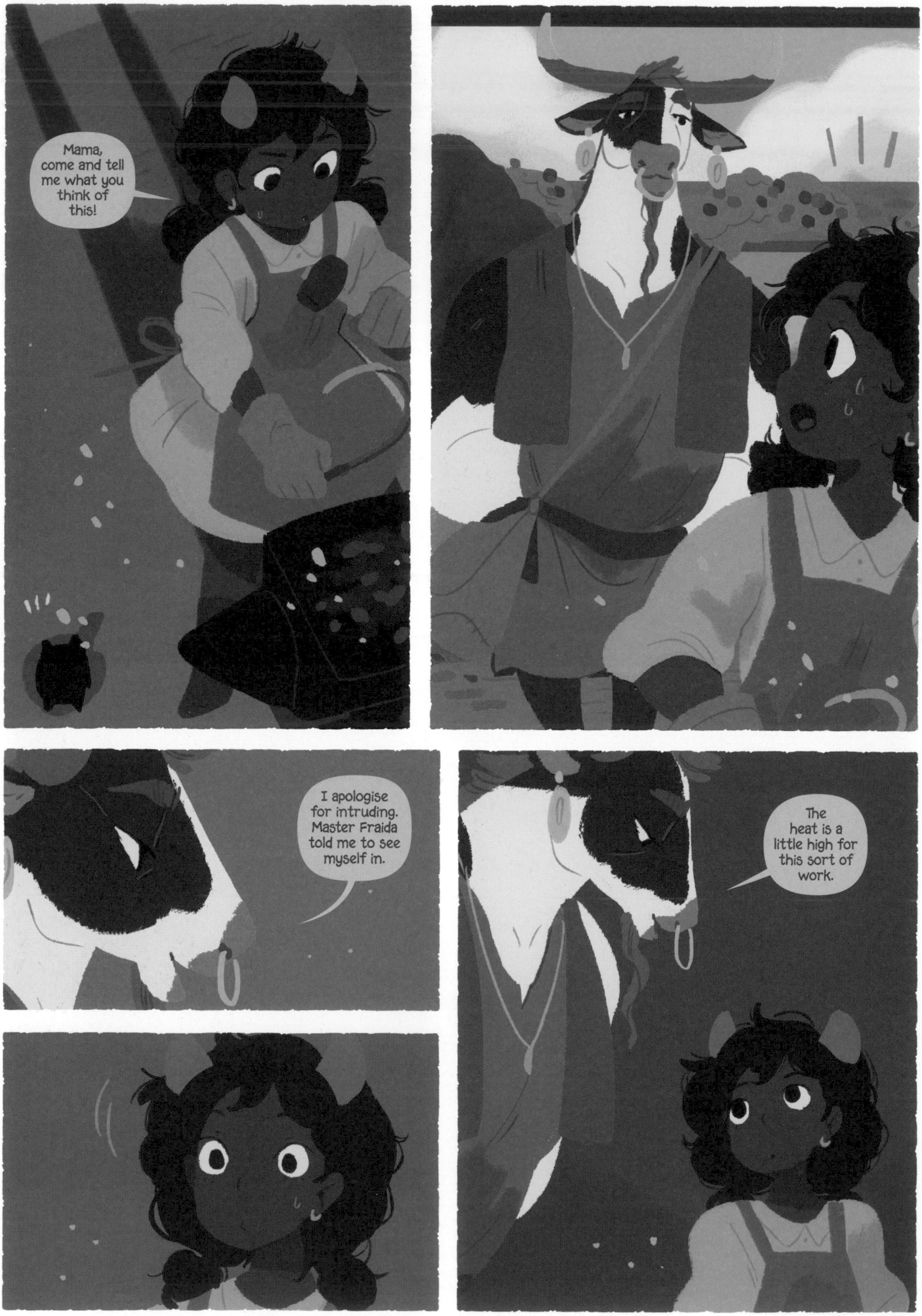
Mama, come and tell me what you think of this!
I apologise for intruding. Master Fraida told me to see myself in.
The heat is a little high for this sort of work.

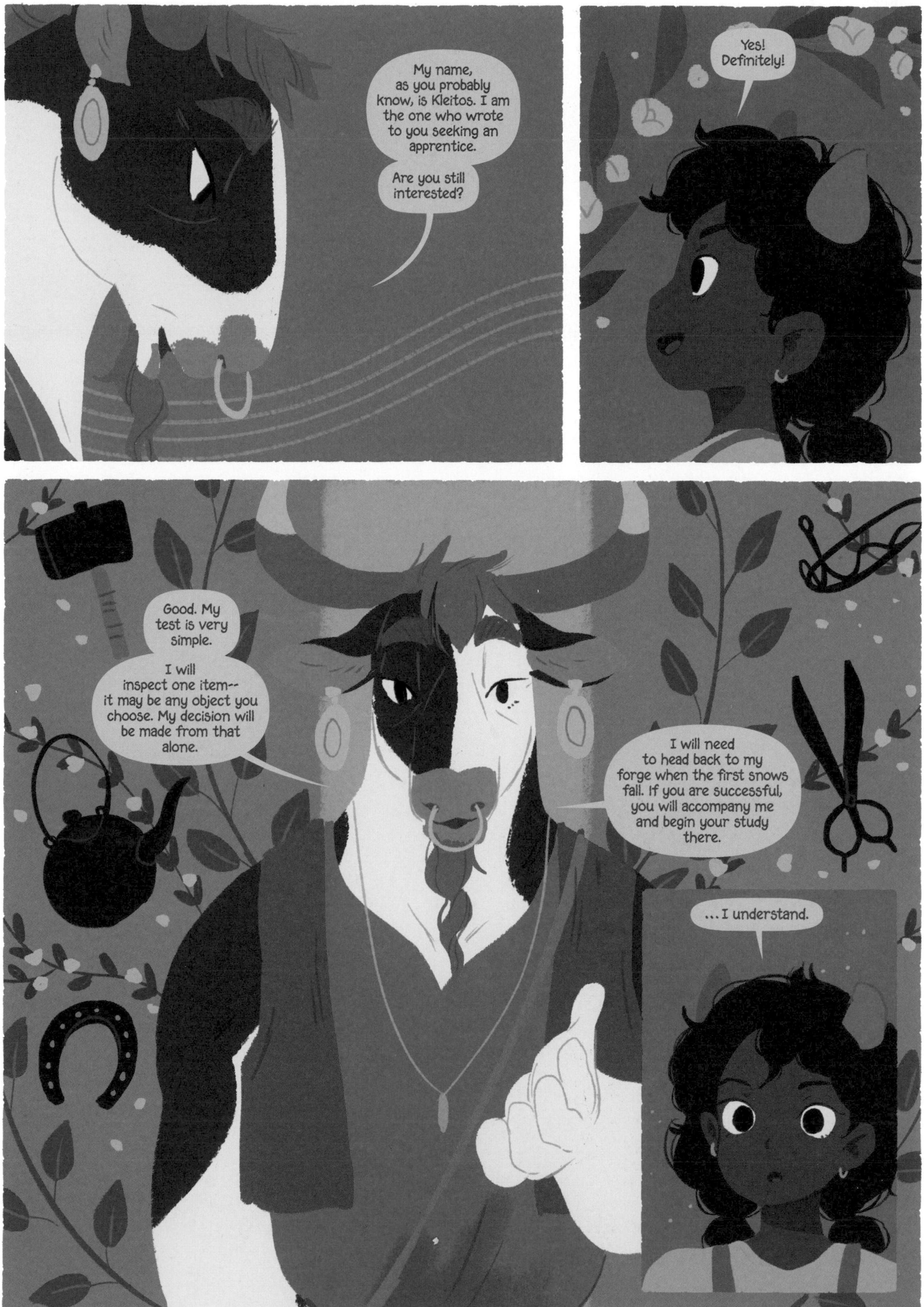
My name, as you probably know, is Kleitos. I am the one who wrote to you seeking an apprentice.
Are you still interested?
Yes! Definitely!
Good. My test is very simple.
I will inspect one item-- it may be any object you choose. My decision will be made from that alone.
I will need to head back to my forge when the first snows fall. If you are successful, you will accompany me and begin your study there.
...I understand.

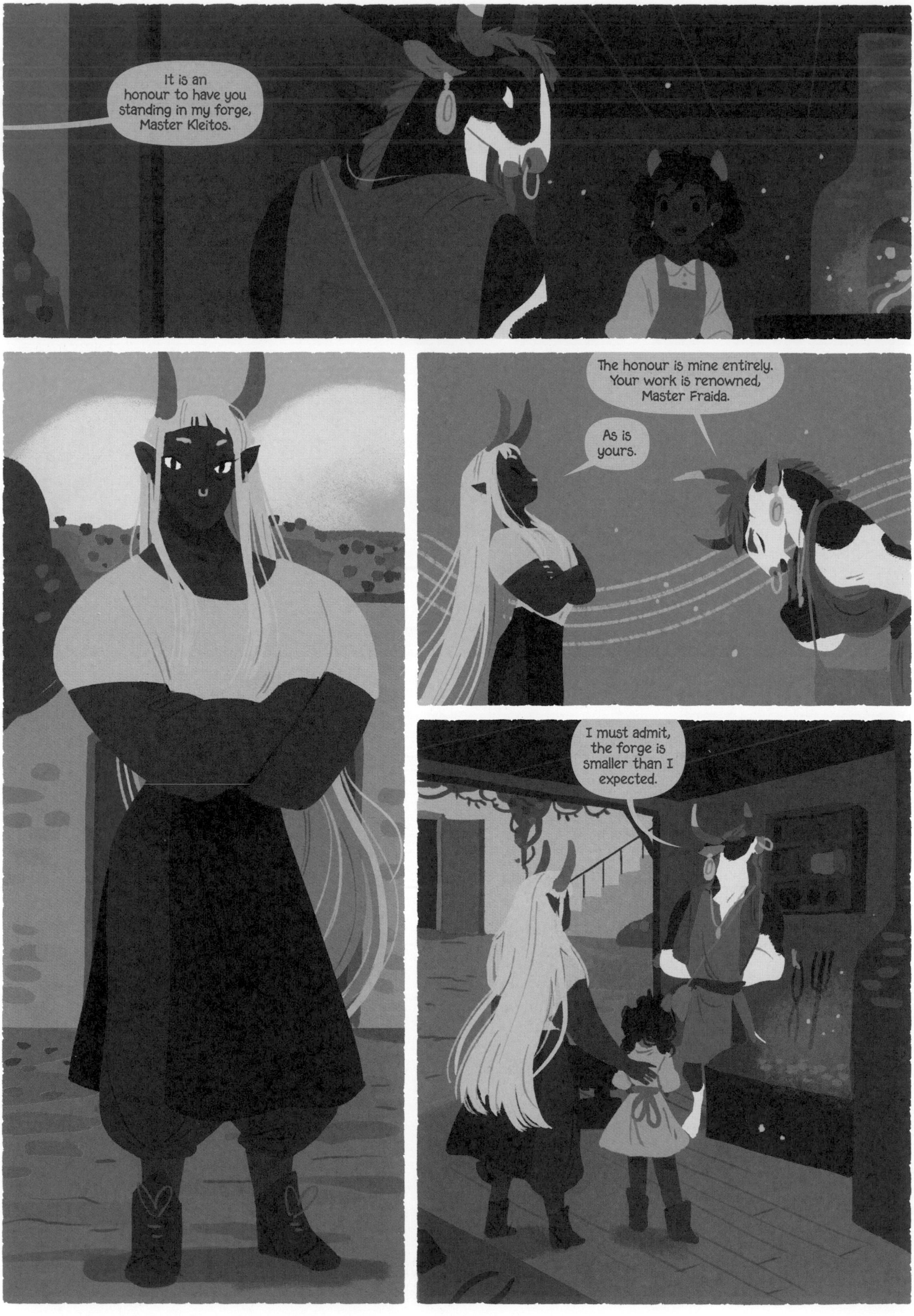
It is an honour to have you standing in my forge, Master Kleitos.
The honour is mine entirely. Your work is renowned, Master Fraida.
As is yours.
I must admit, the forge is smaller than I expected.

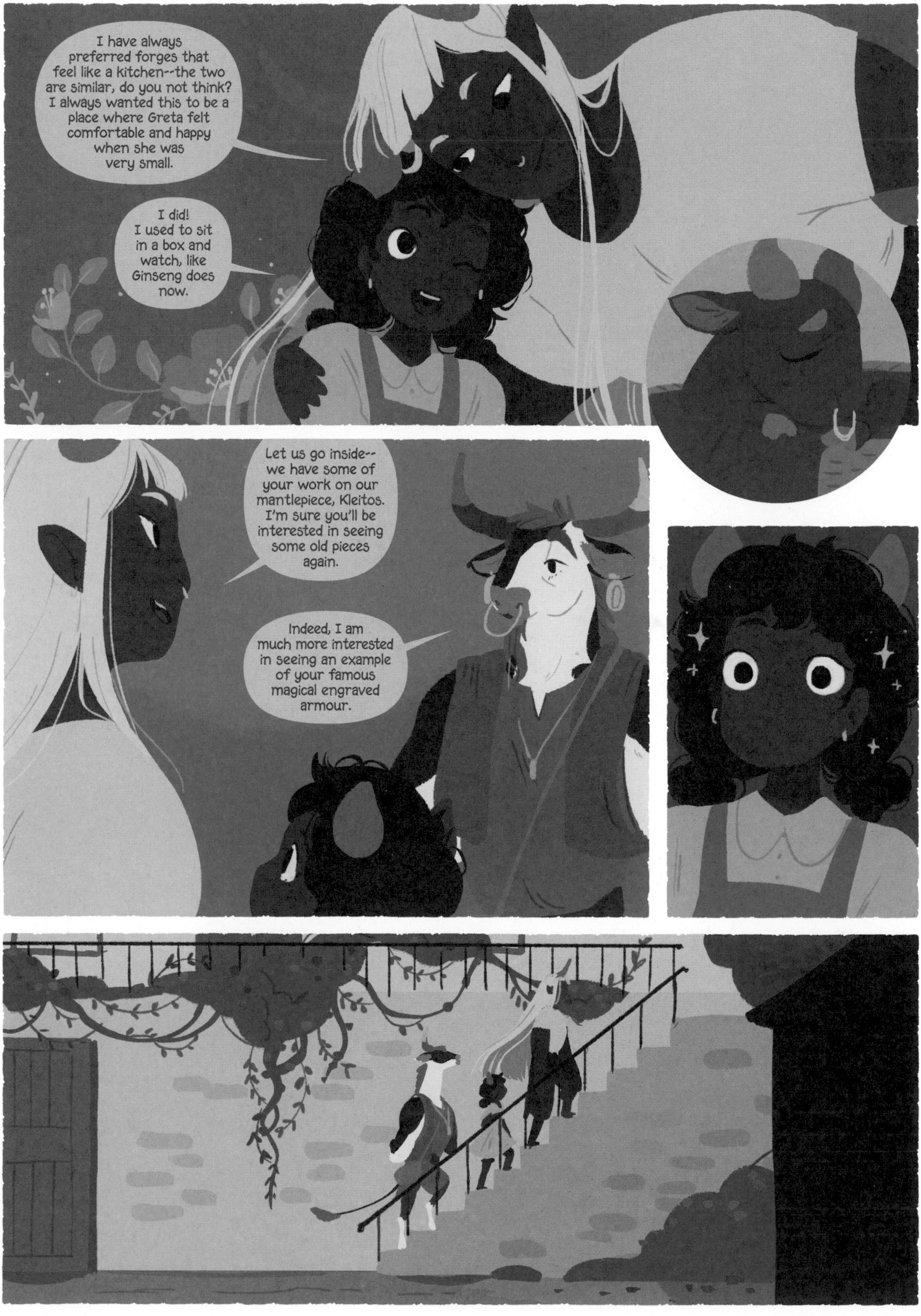
I have always preferred forges that feel like a kitchen--the two are similar, do you not think? I always wanted this to be a place where Greta felt comfortable and happy when she was very small.
I did! I used to sit in a box and watch, like Ginseng does now.
Let us go inside-- we have some of your work on our mantlepiece, Kleitos. I'm sure you'll be interested in seeing some old pieces again.
Indeed, I am much more interested in seeing an example of your famous magical engraved armour.

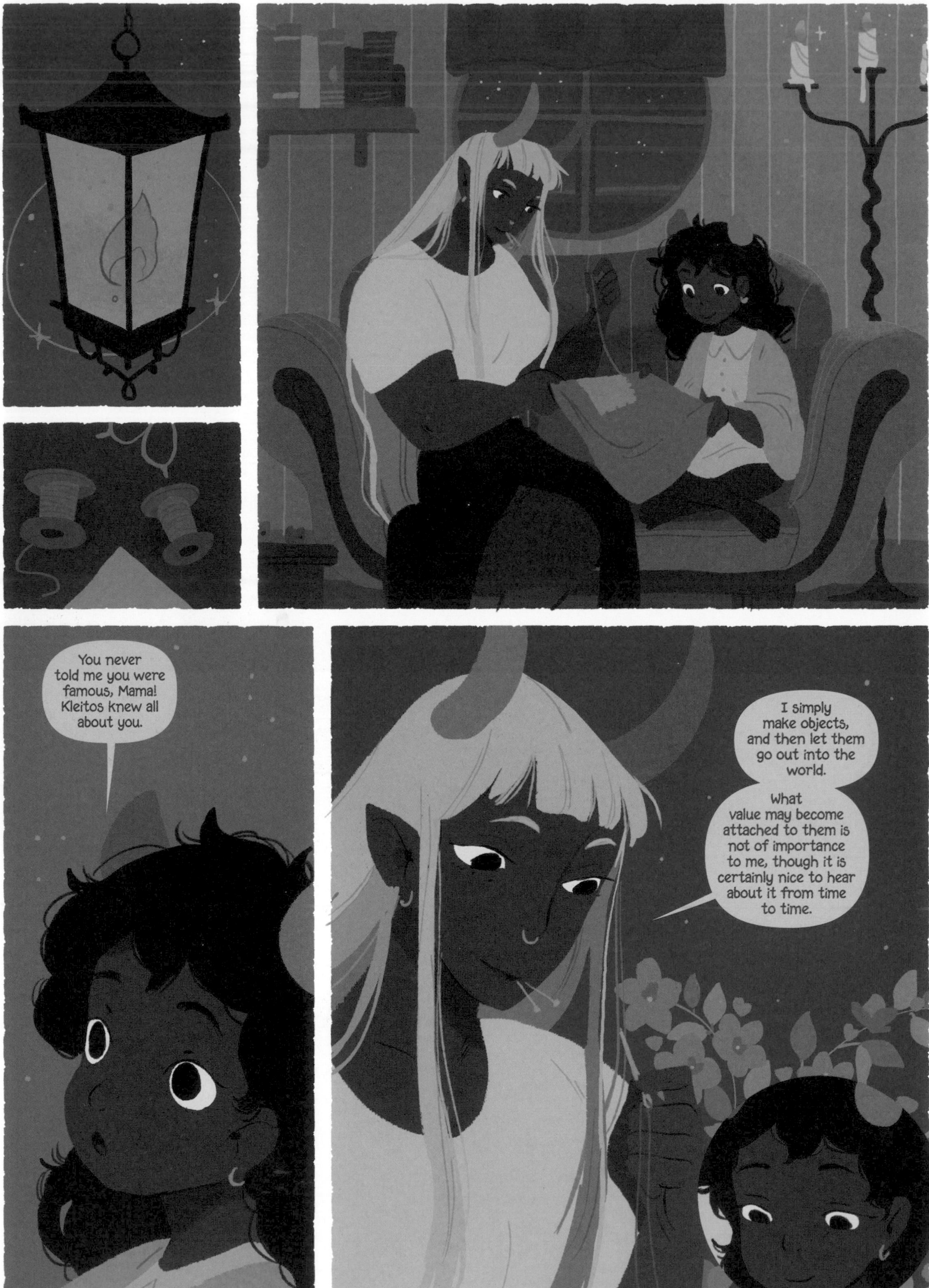
You never told me you were famous, Mama! Kleitos knew all about you.
I simply make objects, and then let them go out into the world.
What value may become attached to them is not of importance to me, though it is certainly nice to hear about it from time to time.

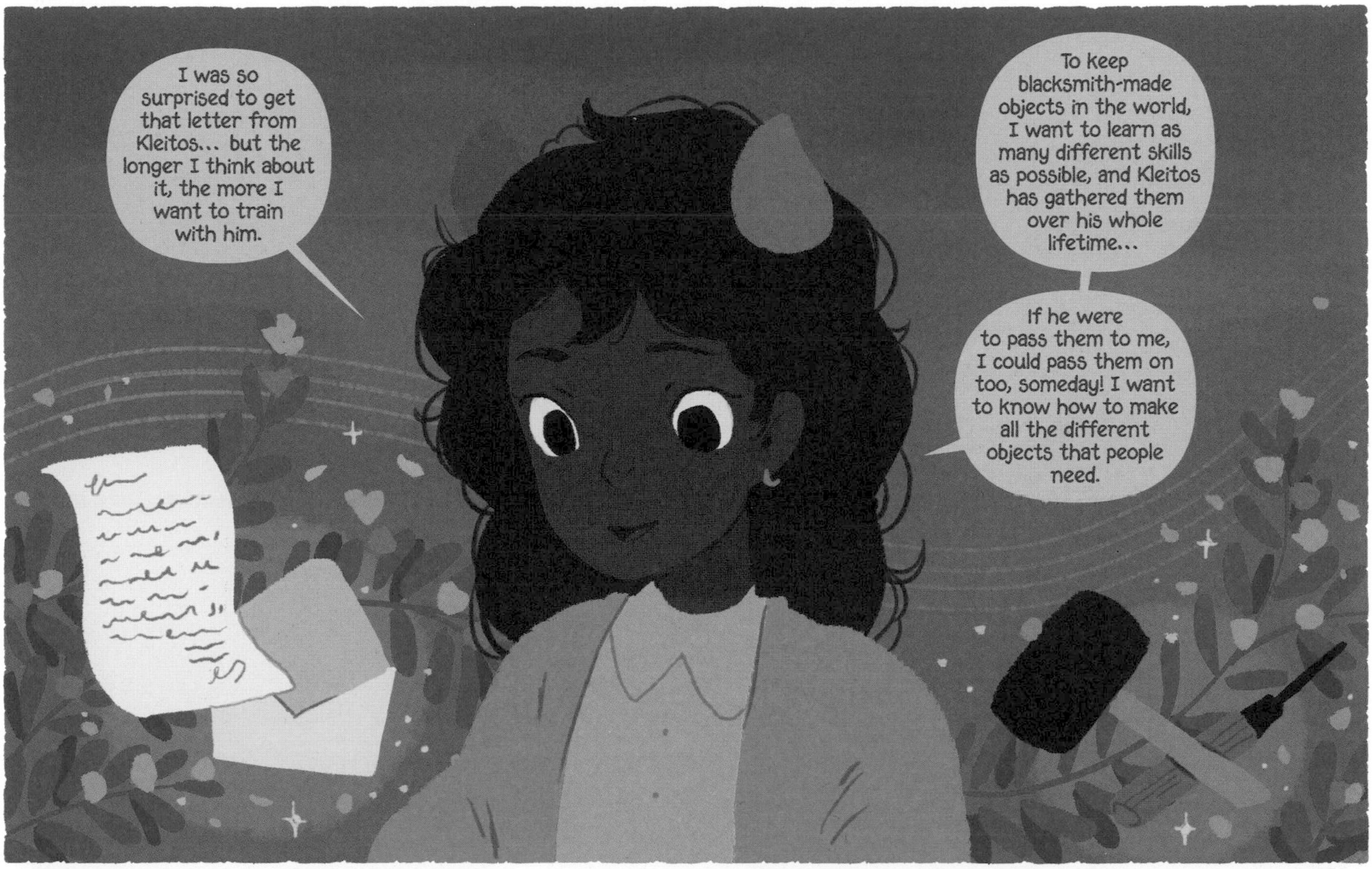
I was so surprised to get that letter from Kleitos... but the longer I think about it, the more I want to train with him.
To keep blacksmith-made objects in the world, I want to learn as many different skills as possible, and Kleitos has gathered them over his whole lifetime...
If he were to pass them to me, I could pass them on too, someday! I want to know how to make all the different objects that people need.

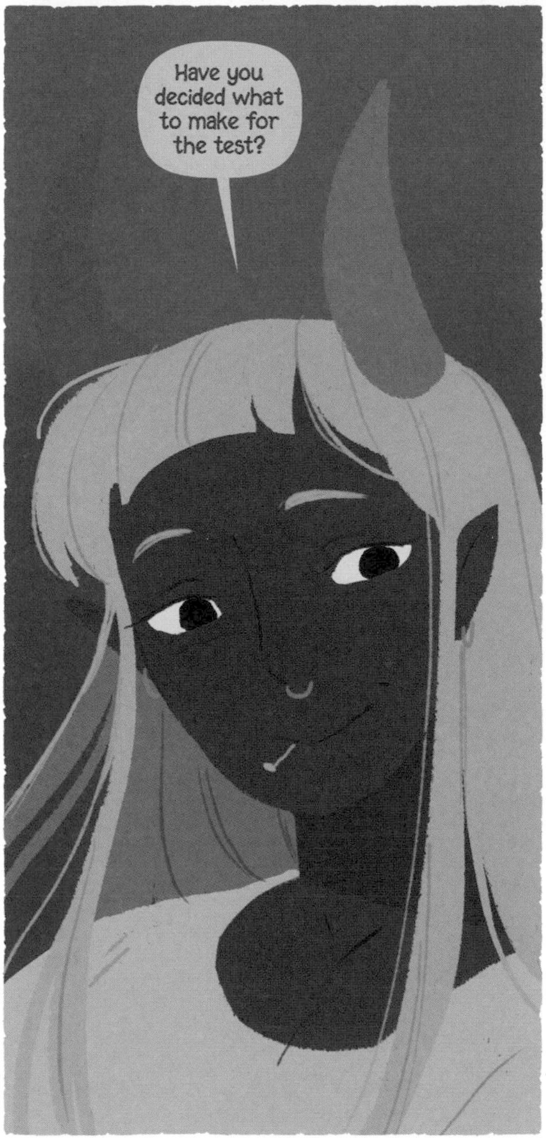
Have you decided what to make for the test?

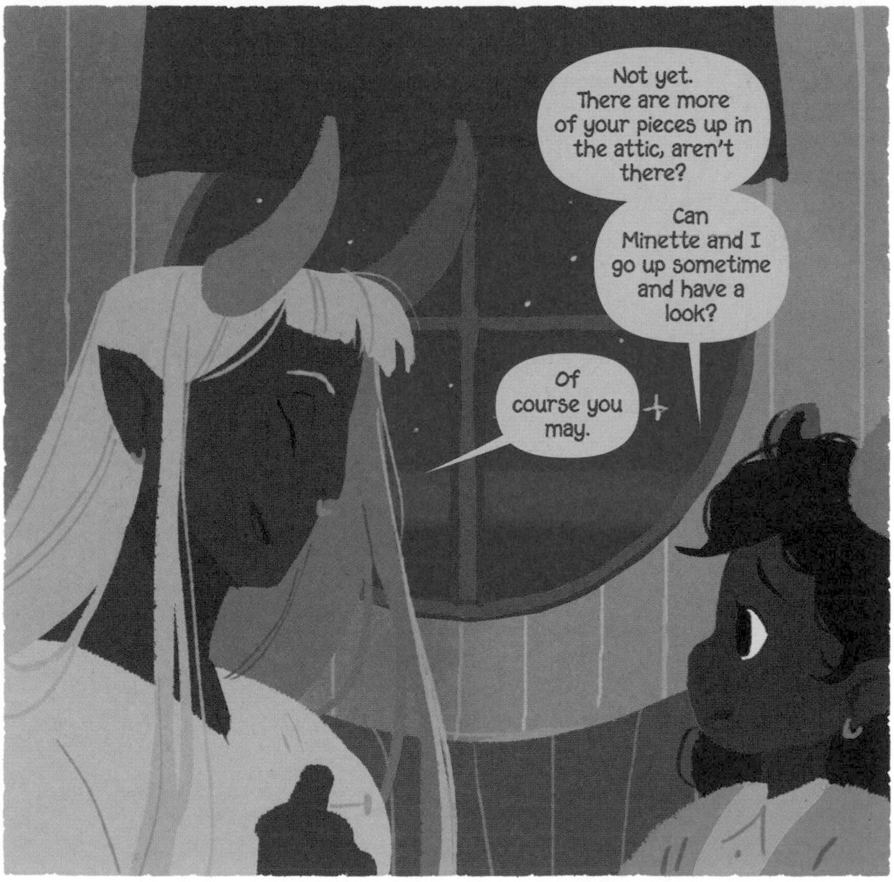
Not yet. There are more of your pieces up in the attic, aren't there?
Can Minette and I go up sometime and have a look?
Of course you may.

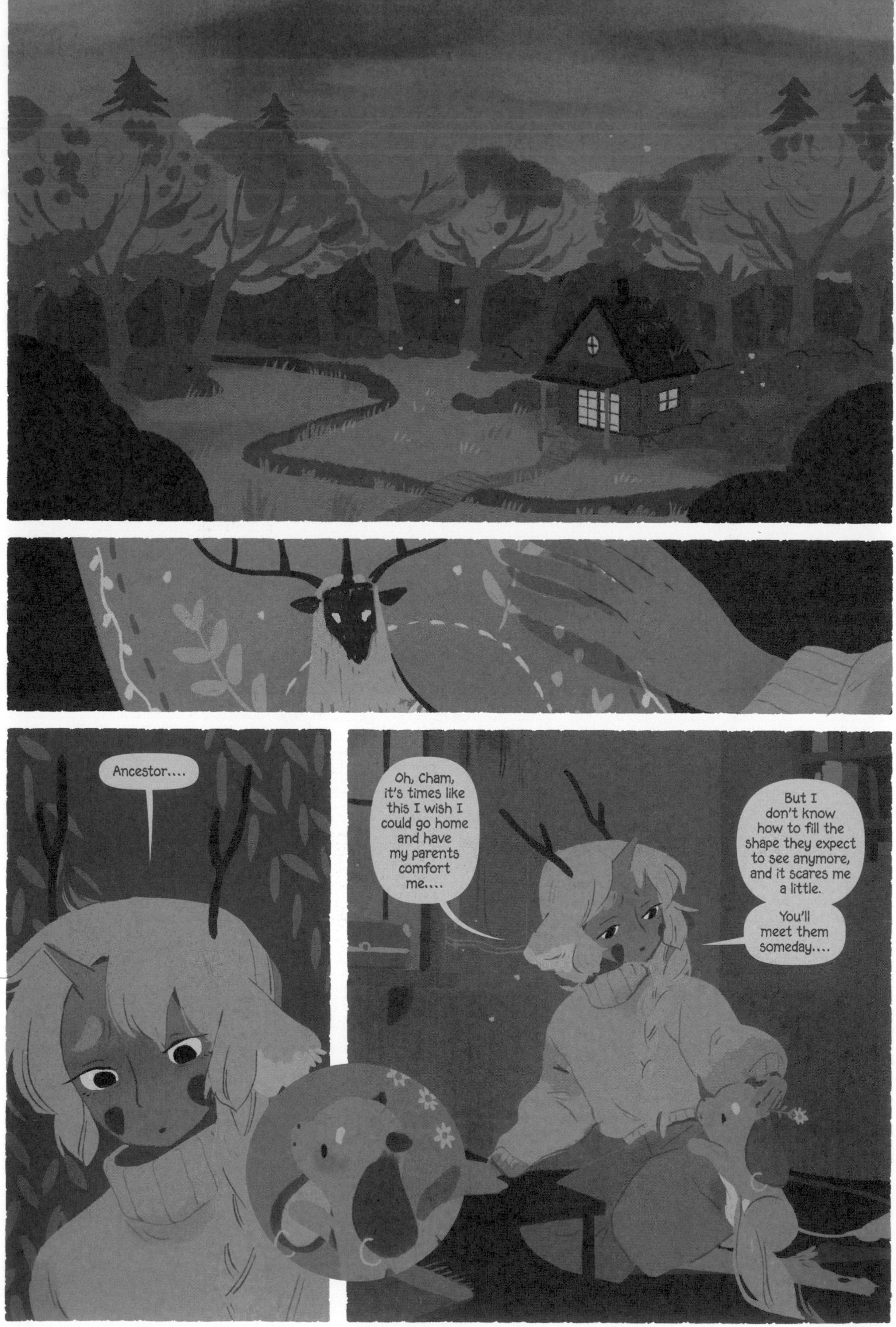
Ancestor....
Oh, Cham, it's times like this I wish I could go home and have my parents comfort me....
But I don't know how to fill the shape they expect to see anymore, and it scares me a little.
You'll meet them someday....

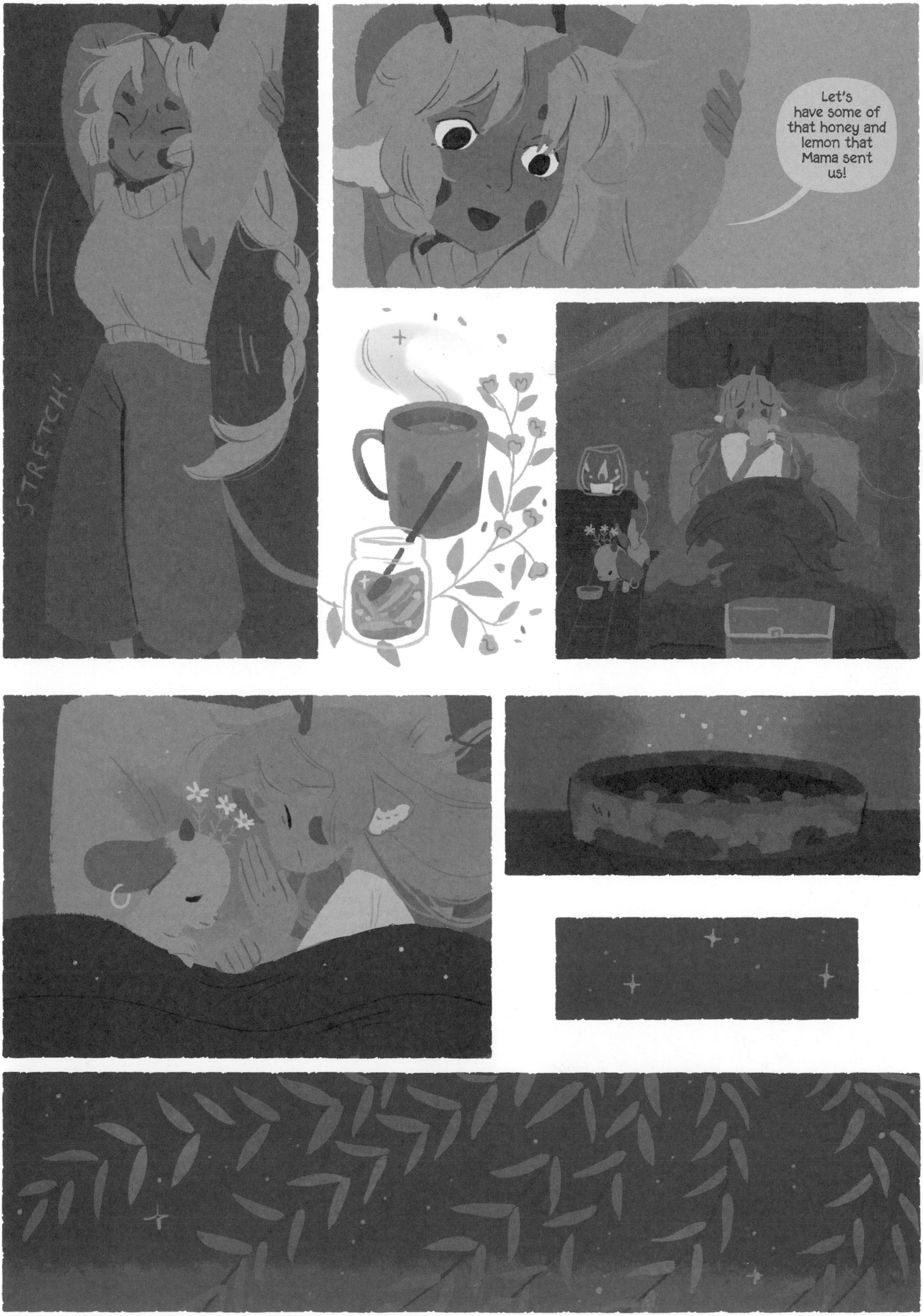
STRETCH!
Let's have some of that honey and lemon that Mama sent us!

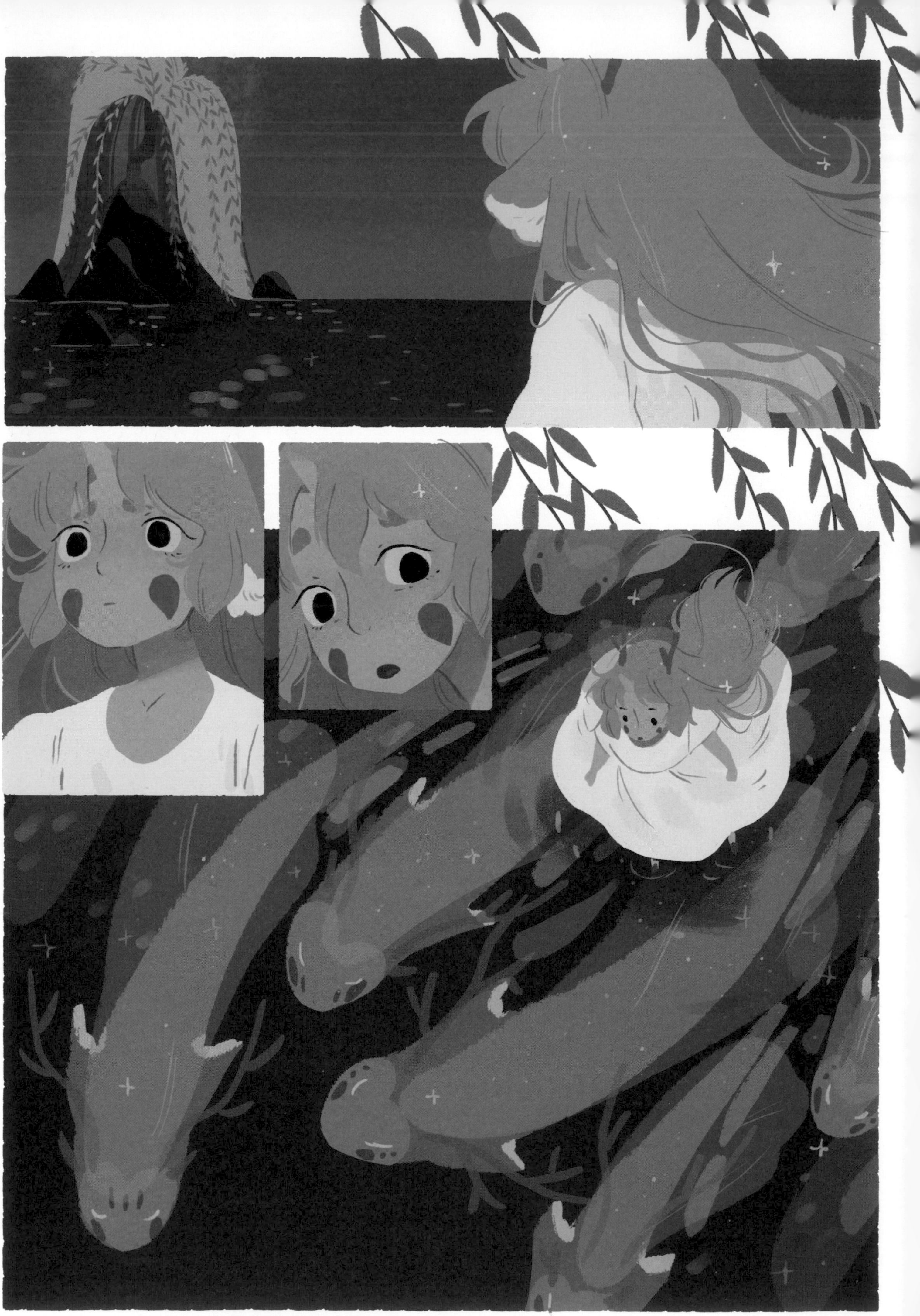

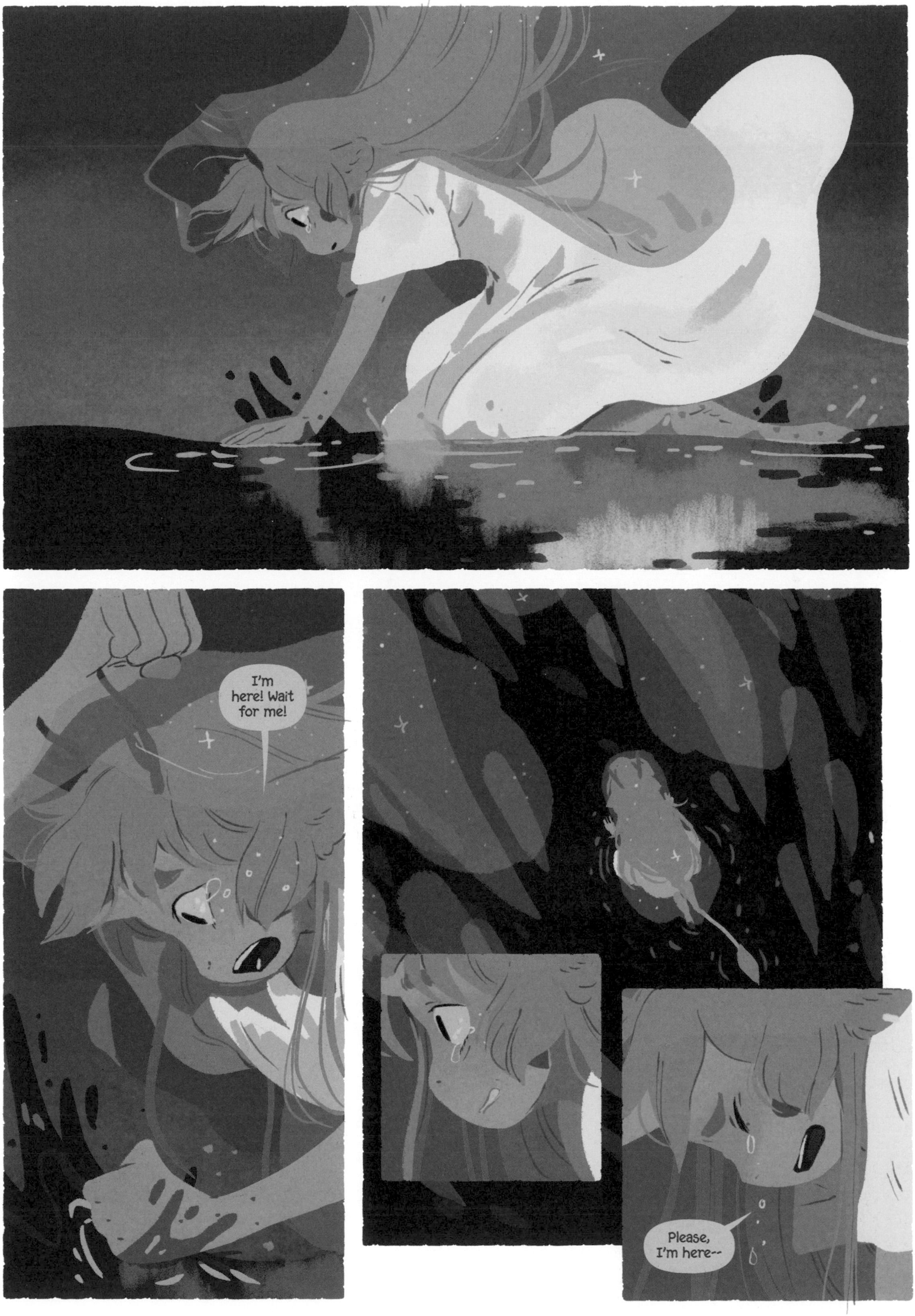
I'm here! Wait for me!
Please, I'm here--

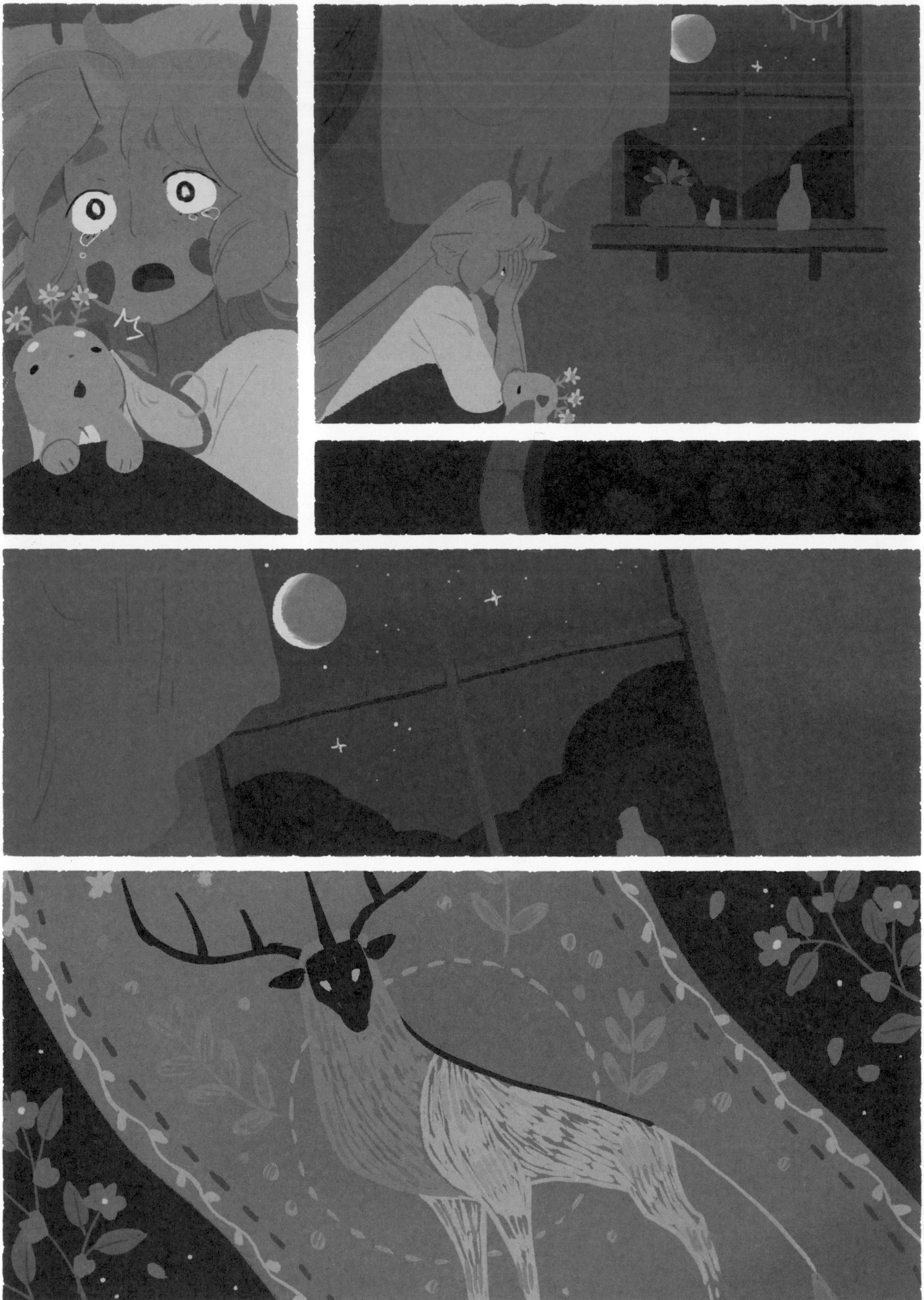

Chapter Three

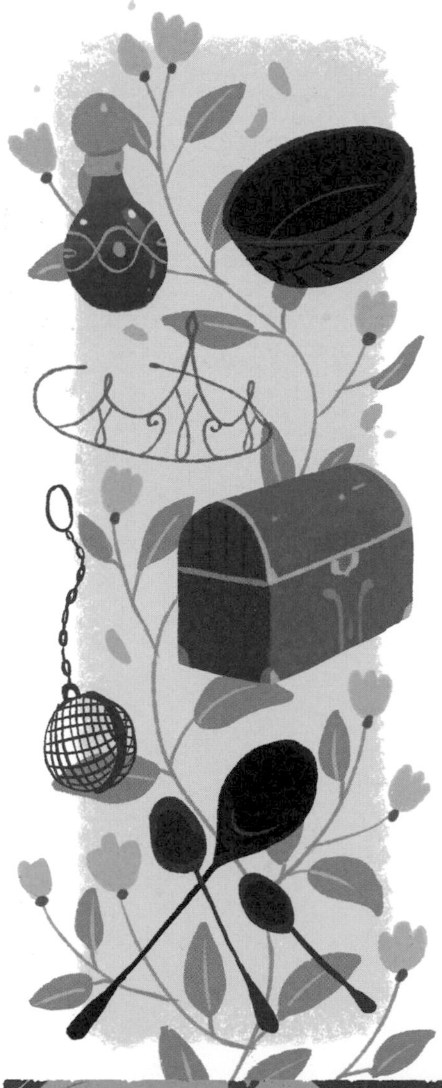

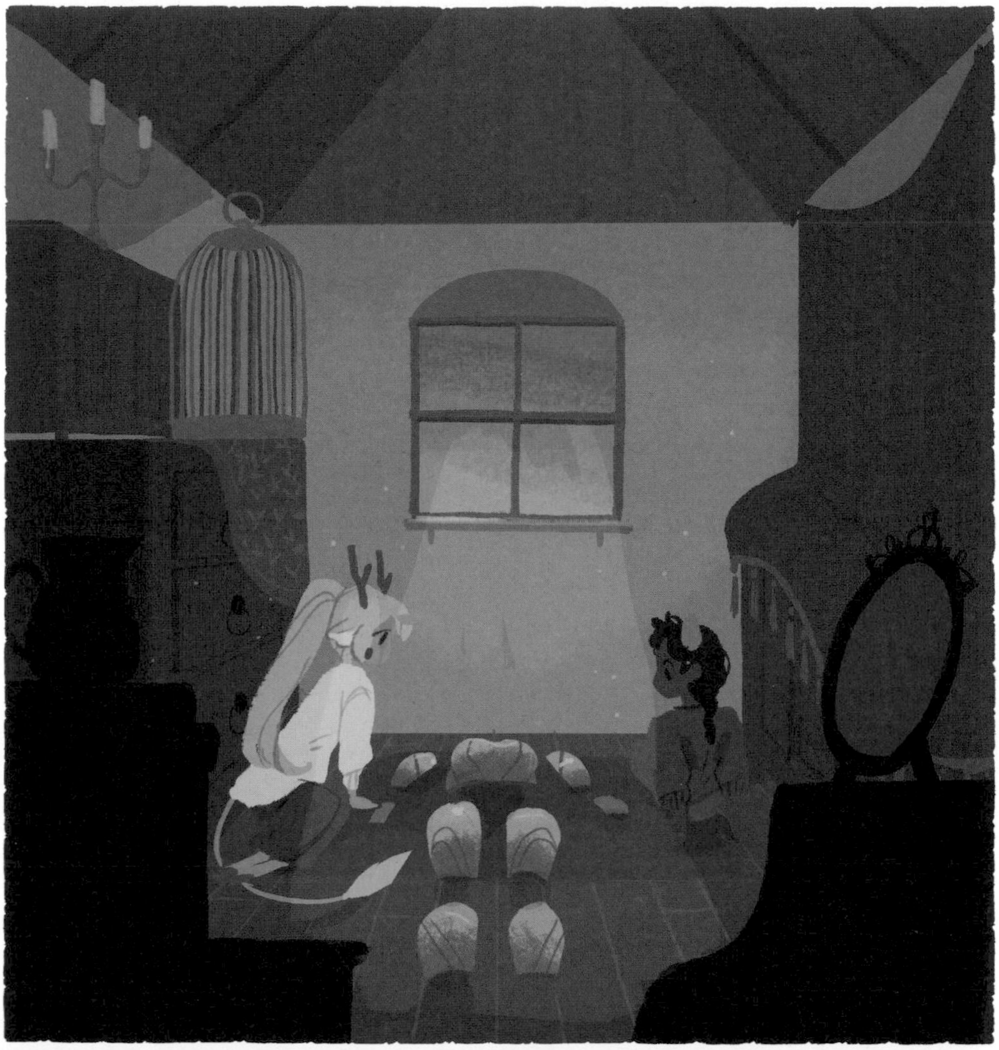

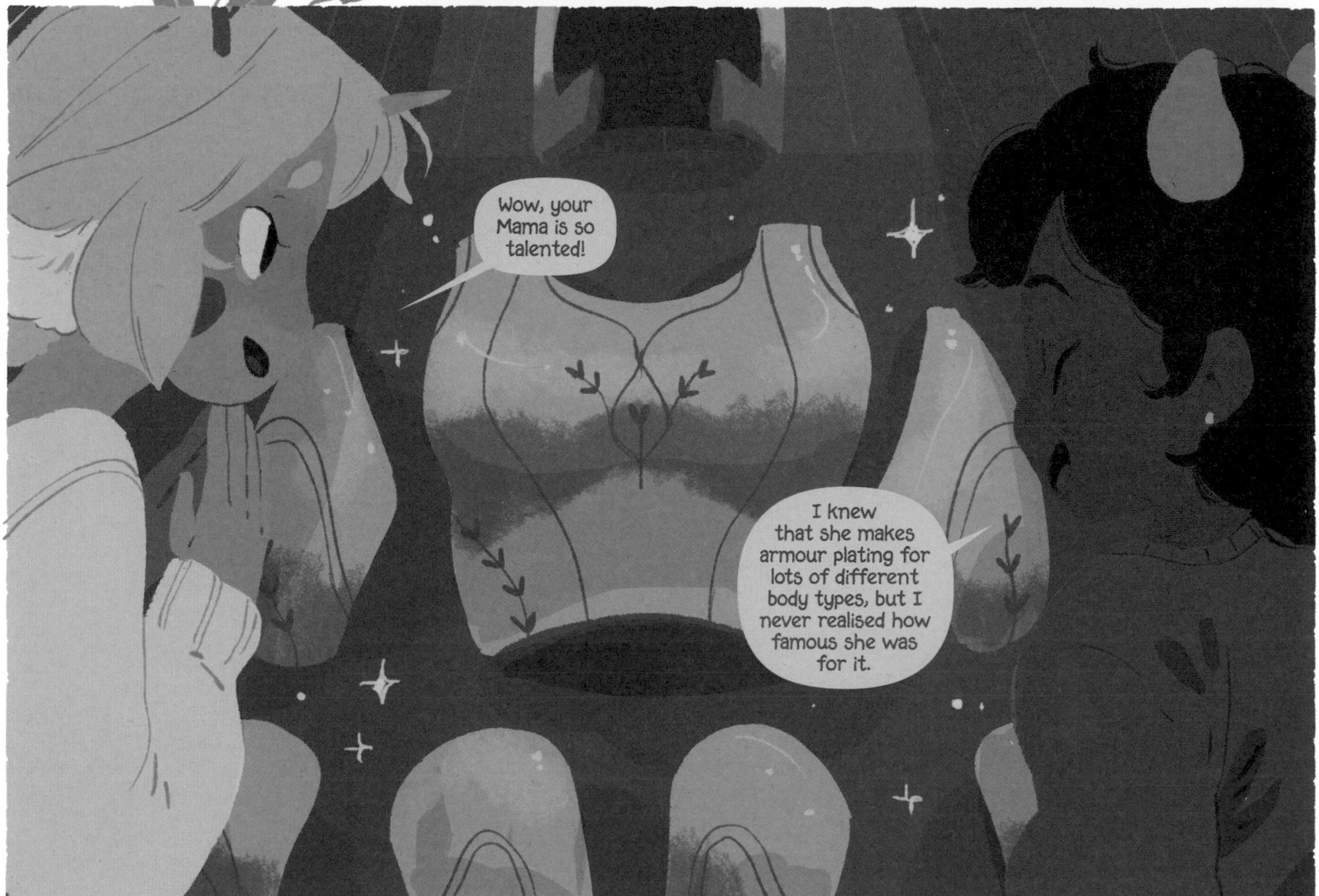
Wow, your Mama is so talented!
I knew that she makes armour plating for lots of different body types, but I never realised how famous she was for it.

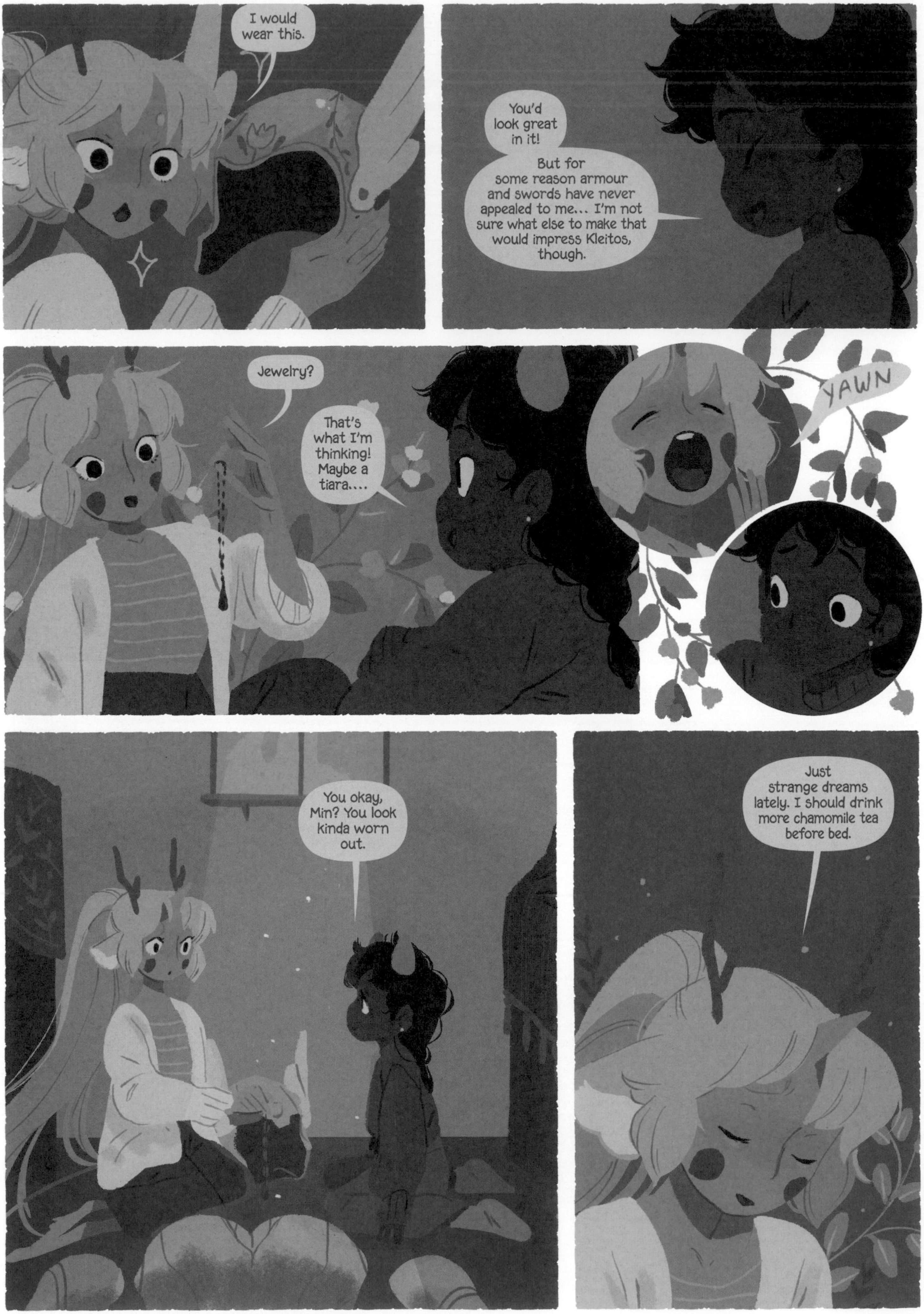
I would wear this.
You'd look great in it!
But for some reason armour and swords have never appealed to me... I'm not sure what else to make that would impress Kleitos, though.
Jewelry?
That's what I'm thinking! Maybe a tiara....
YAWN
You okay, Min? You look kinda worn out.
Just strange dreams lately. I should drink more chamomile tea before bed.

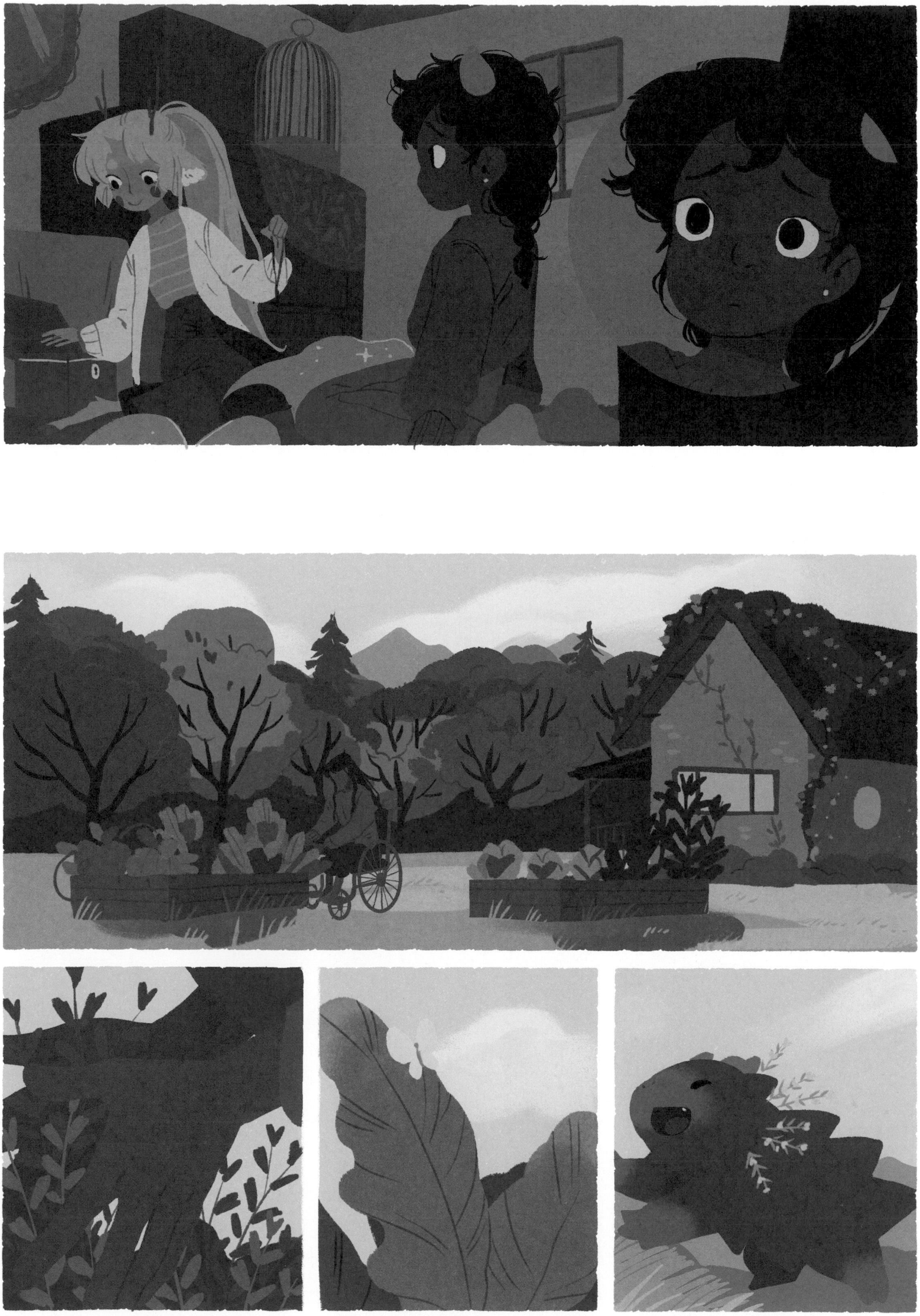

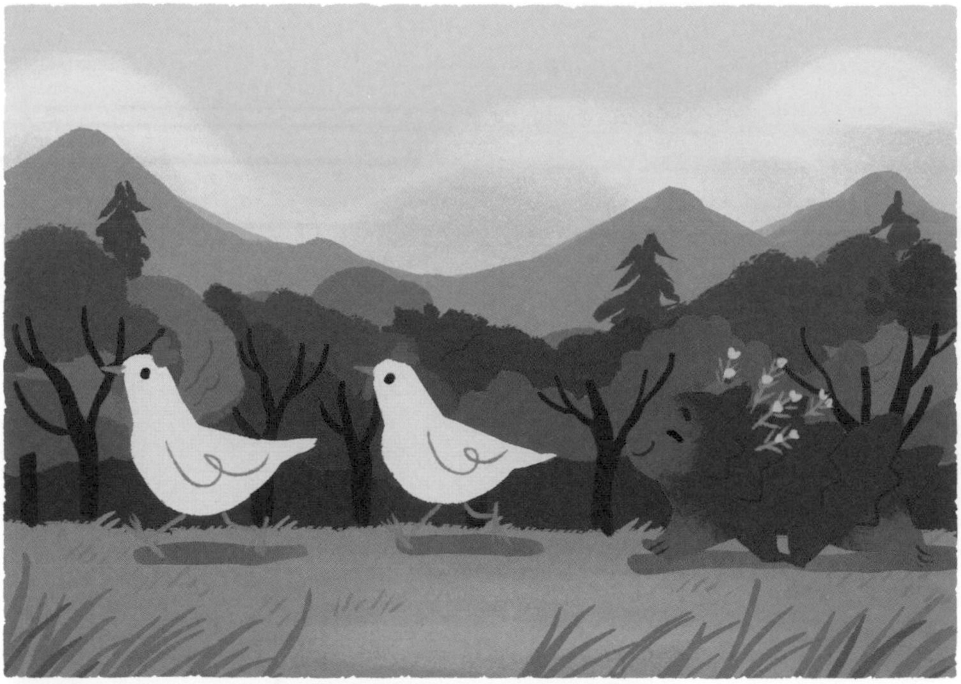

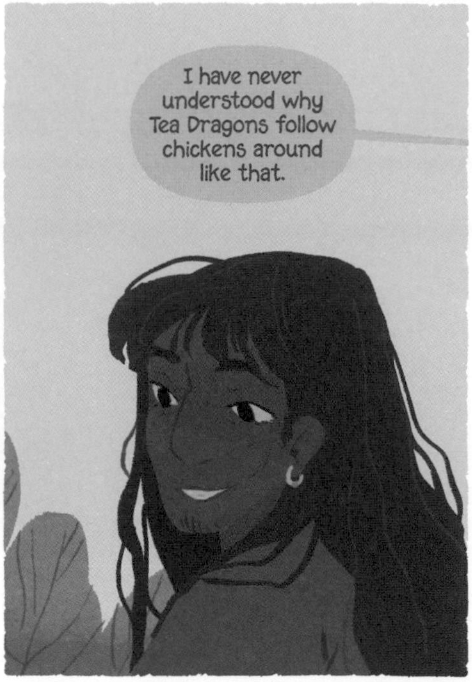
I have never understood why Tea Dragons follow chickens around like that.

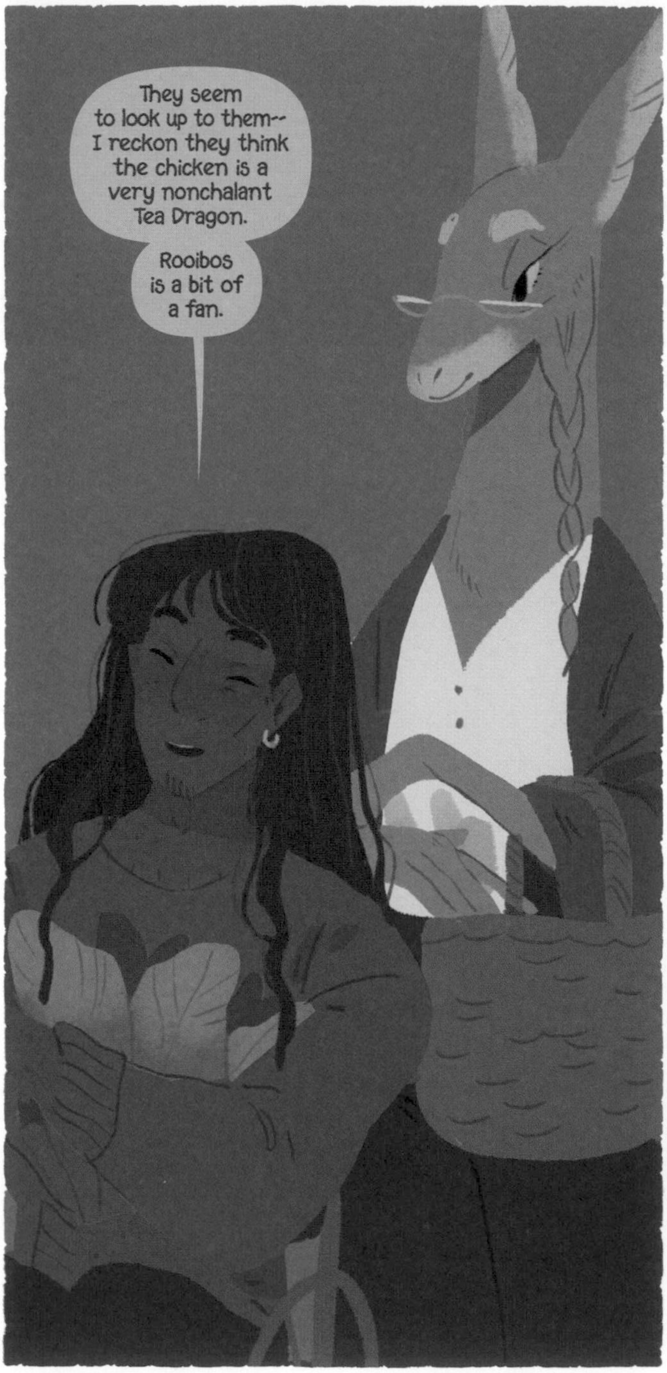
They seem to look up to them-- I reckon they think the chicken is a very nonchalant Tea Dragon.
Rooibos is a bit of a fan.

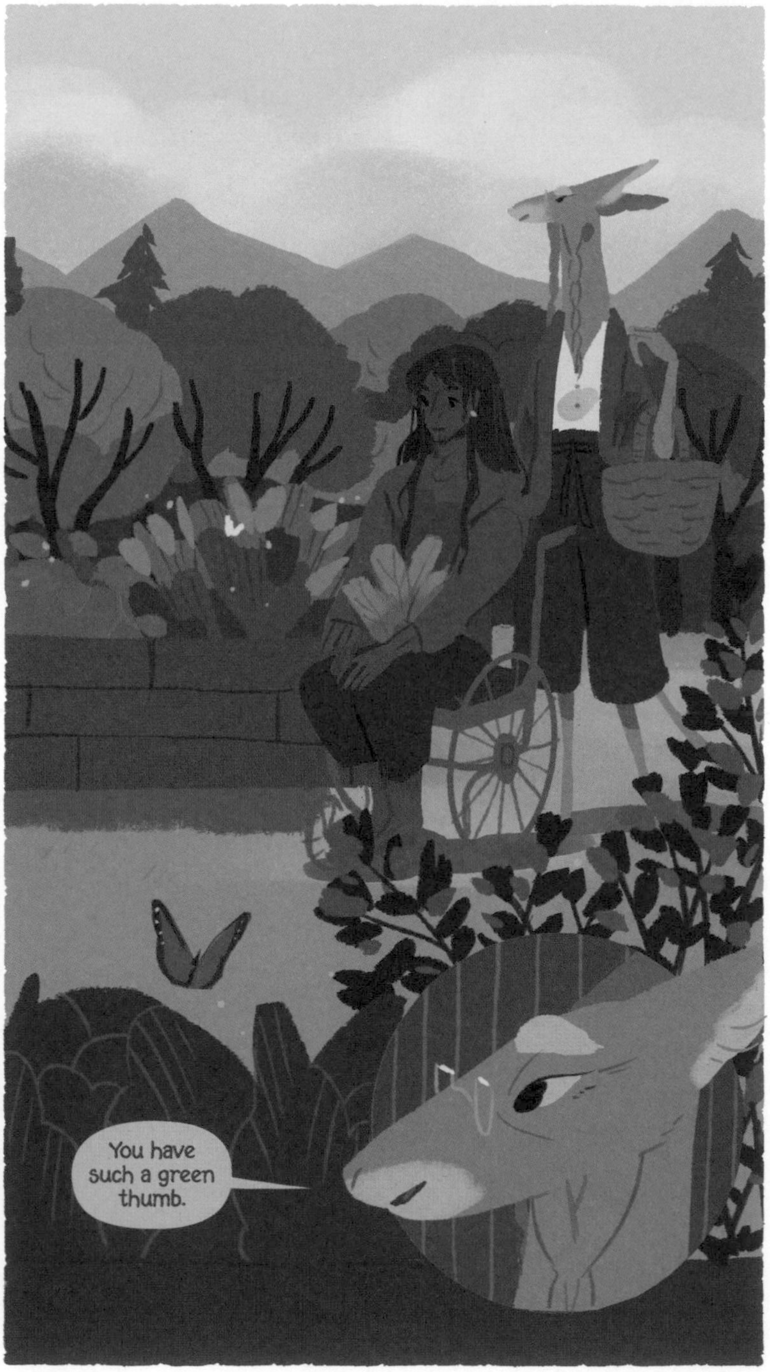
You have such a green thumb.

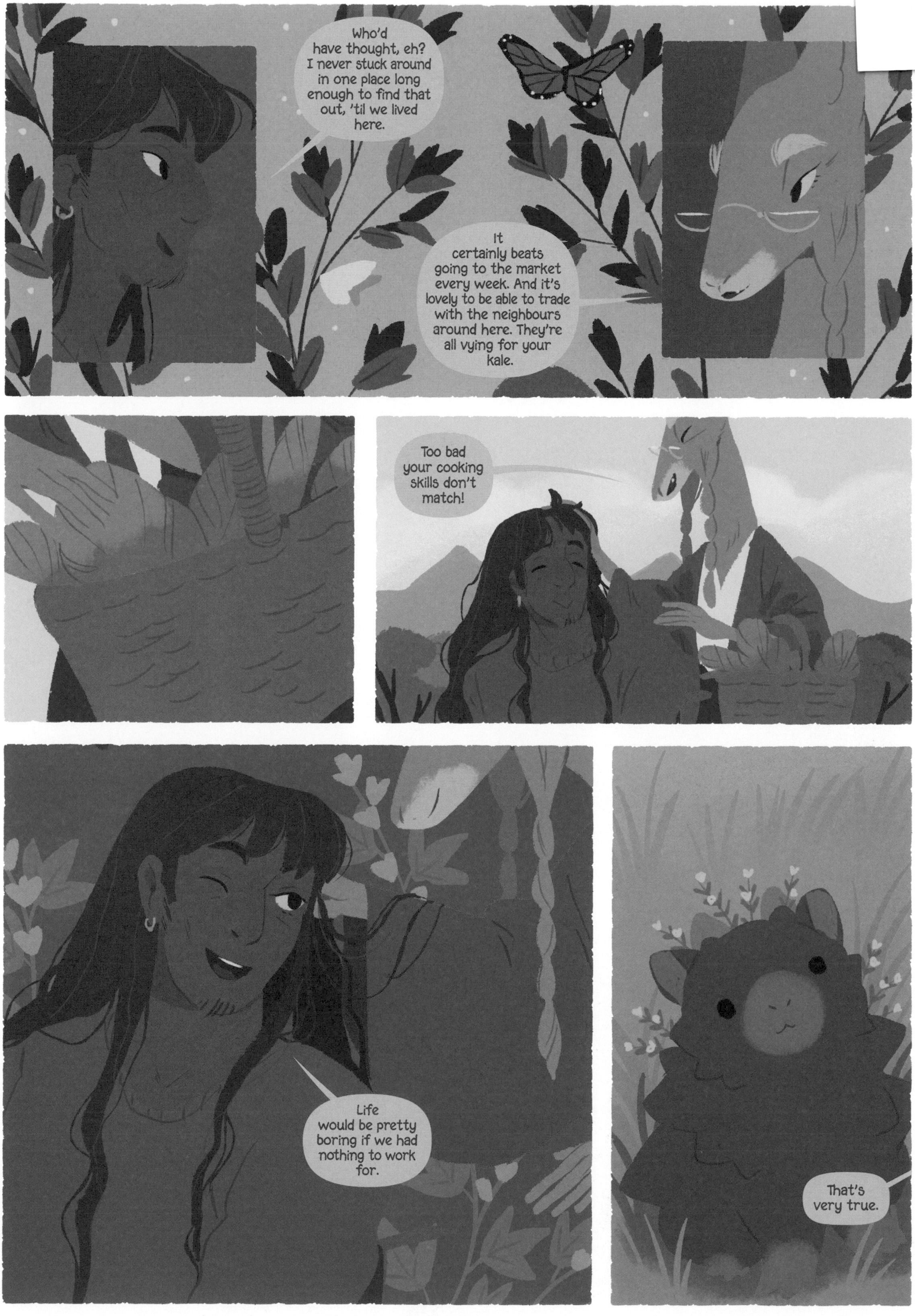
Who'd have thought, eh? I never stuck around in one place long enough to find that out, 'til we lived here.
It certainly beats going to the market every week. And it's lovely to be able to trade with the neighbours around here. They're all vying for your kale.
Too bad your cooking skills don't match!
Life would be pretty boring if we had nothing to work for.
That's very true.

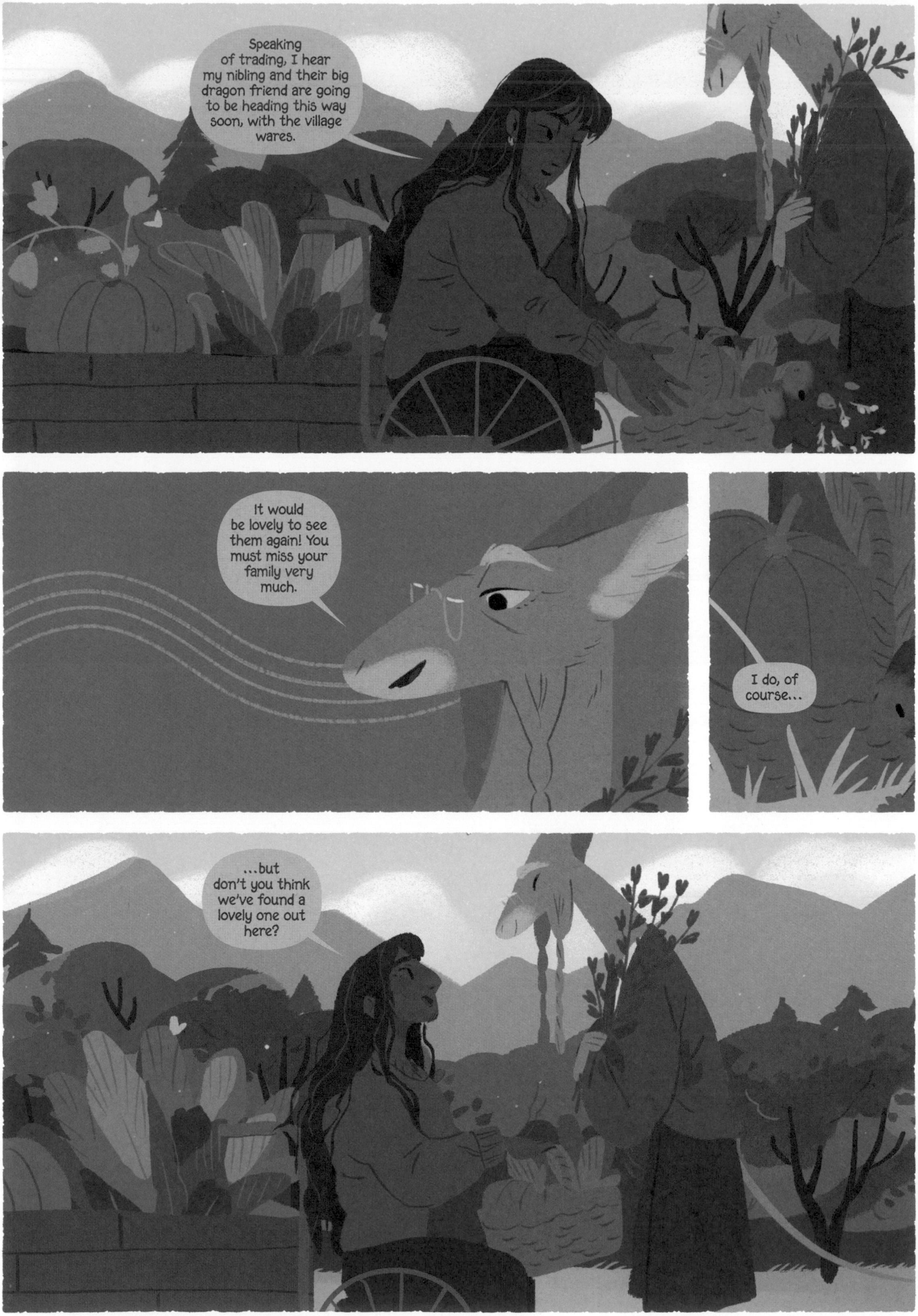
Speaking of trading, I hear my nibling and their big dragon friend are going to be heading this way soon, with the village wares.
It would be lovely to see them again! You must miss your family very much.
I do, of course...
...but don't you think we've found a lovely one out here?

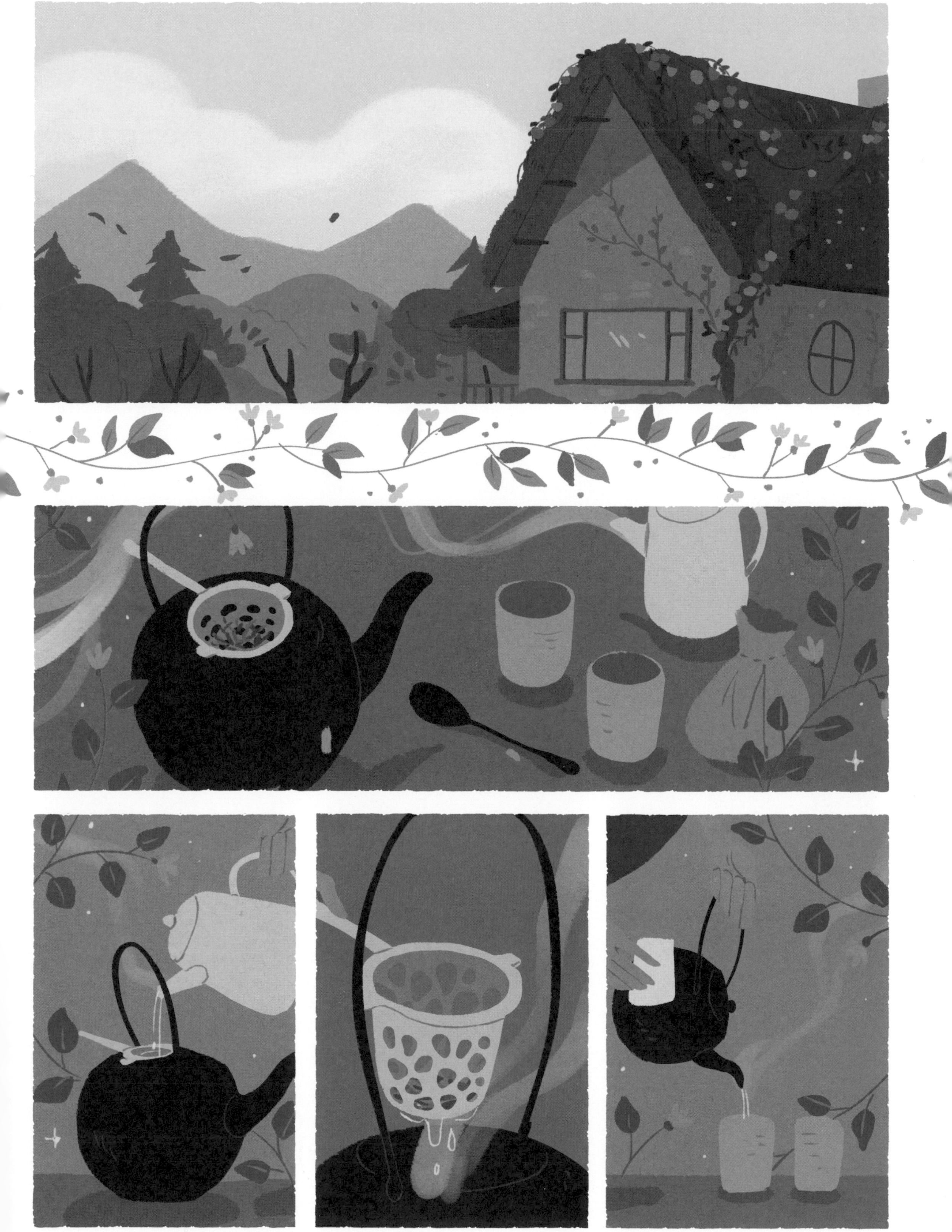

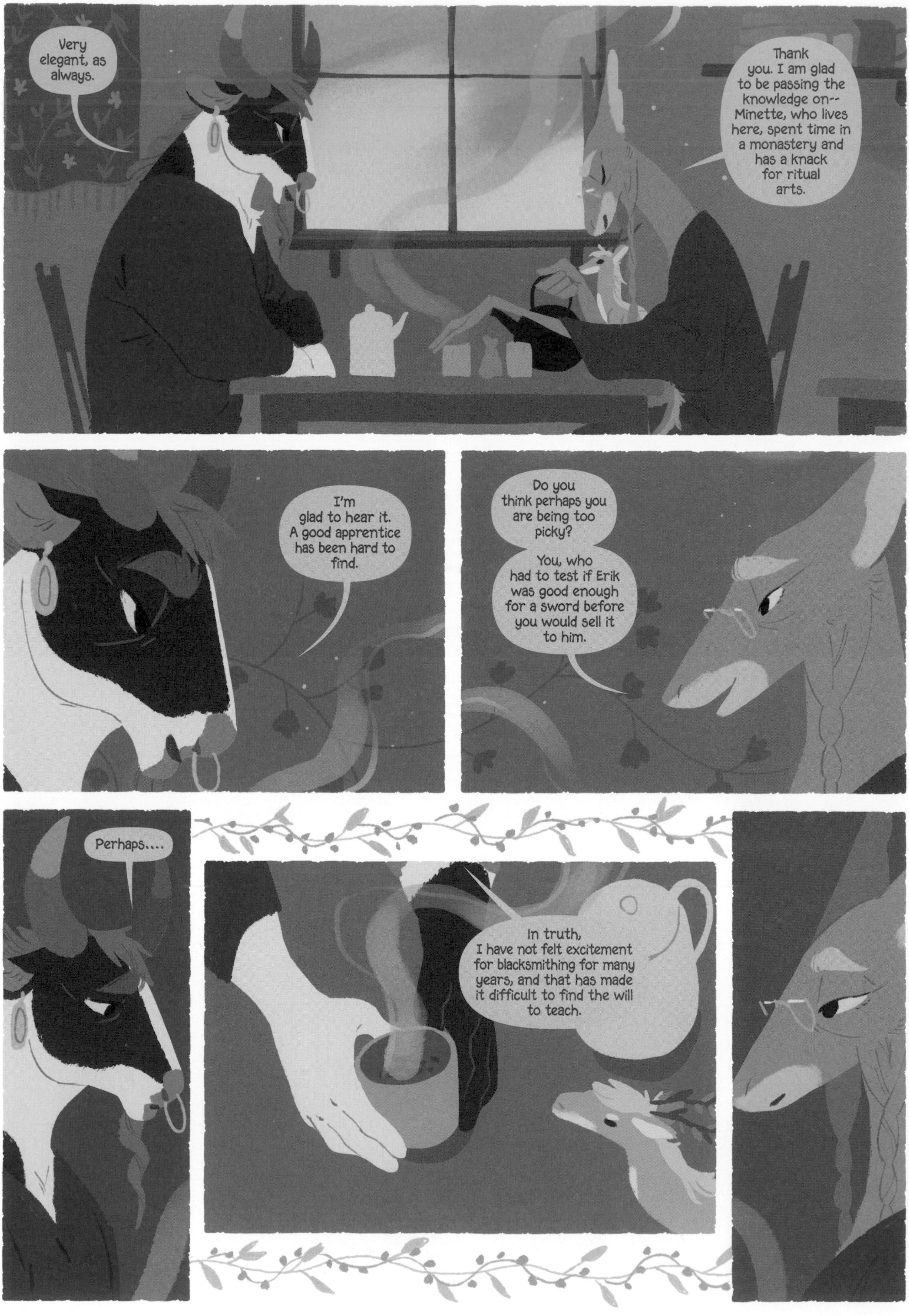
Very elegant, as always.
Thank you. I am glad to be passing the knowledge on-- Minette, who lives here, spent time in a monastery and has a knack for ritual arts.
I'm glad to hear it. A good apprentice has been hard to find.
Do you think perhaps you are being too picky?
You, who had to test if Erik was good enough for a sword before you would sell it to him.
Perhaps....
In truth, I have not felt excitement for blacksmithing for many years, and that has made it difficult to find the will to teach.

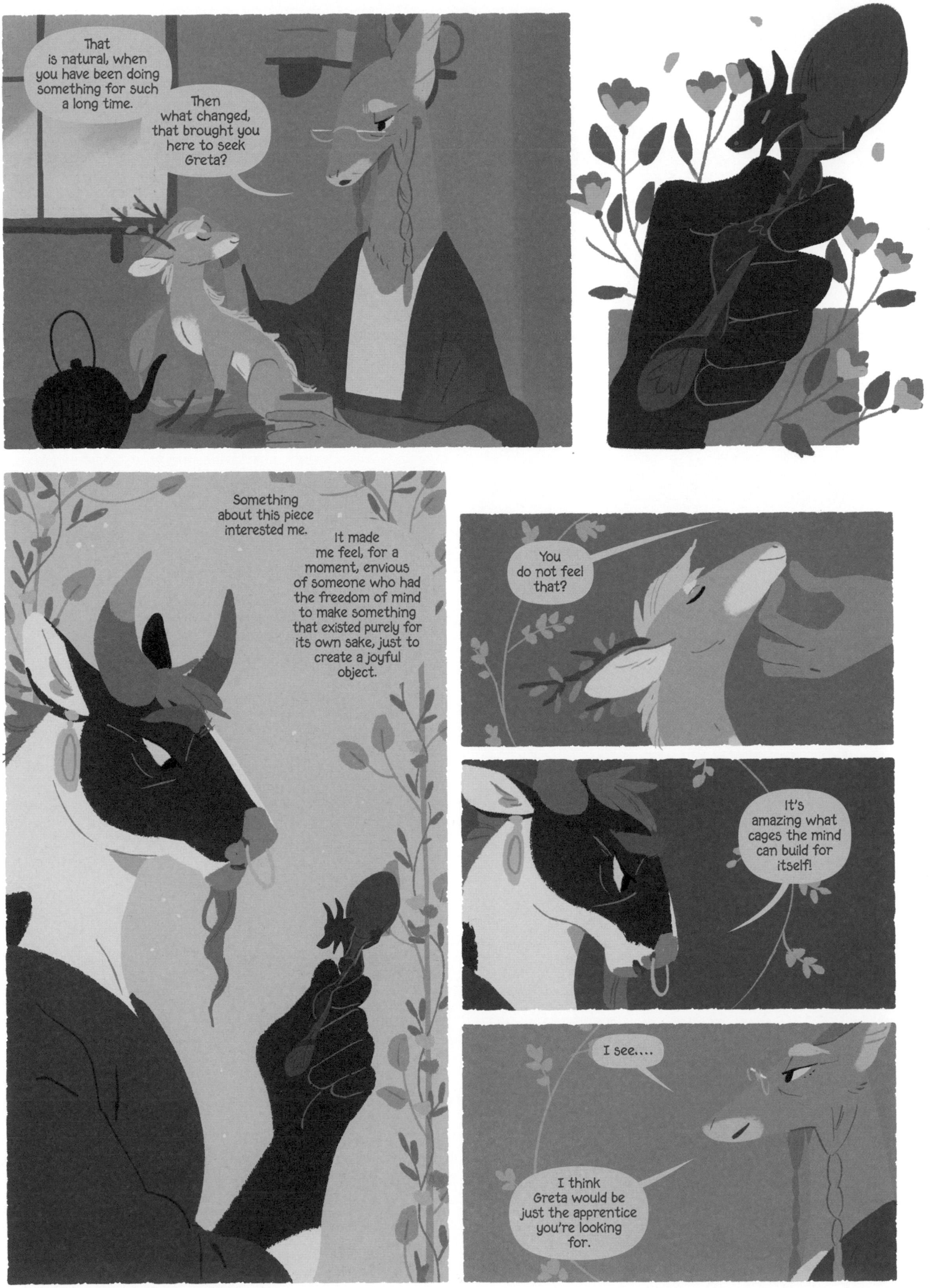
That is natural, when you have been doing something for such a long time.
Then what changed, that brought you here to seek Greta?
Something about this piece interested me.
It made me feel, for a moment, envious of someone who had the freedom of mind to make something that existed purely for its own sake, just to create a joyful object.
You do not feel that?
It's amazing what cages the mind can build for itself!
I see....
I think Greta would be just the apprentice you're looking for.

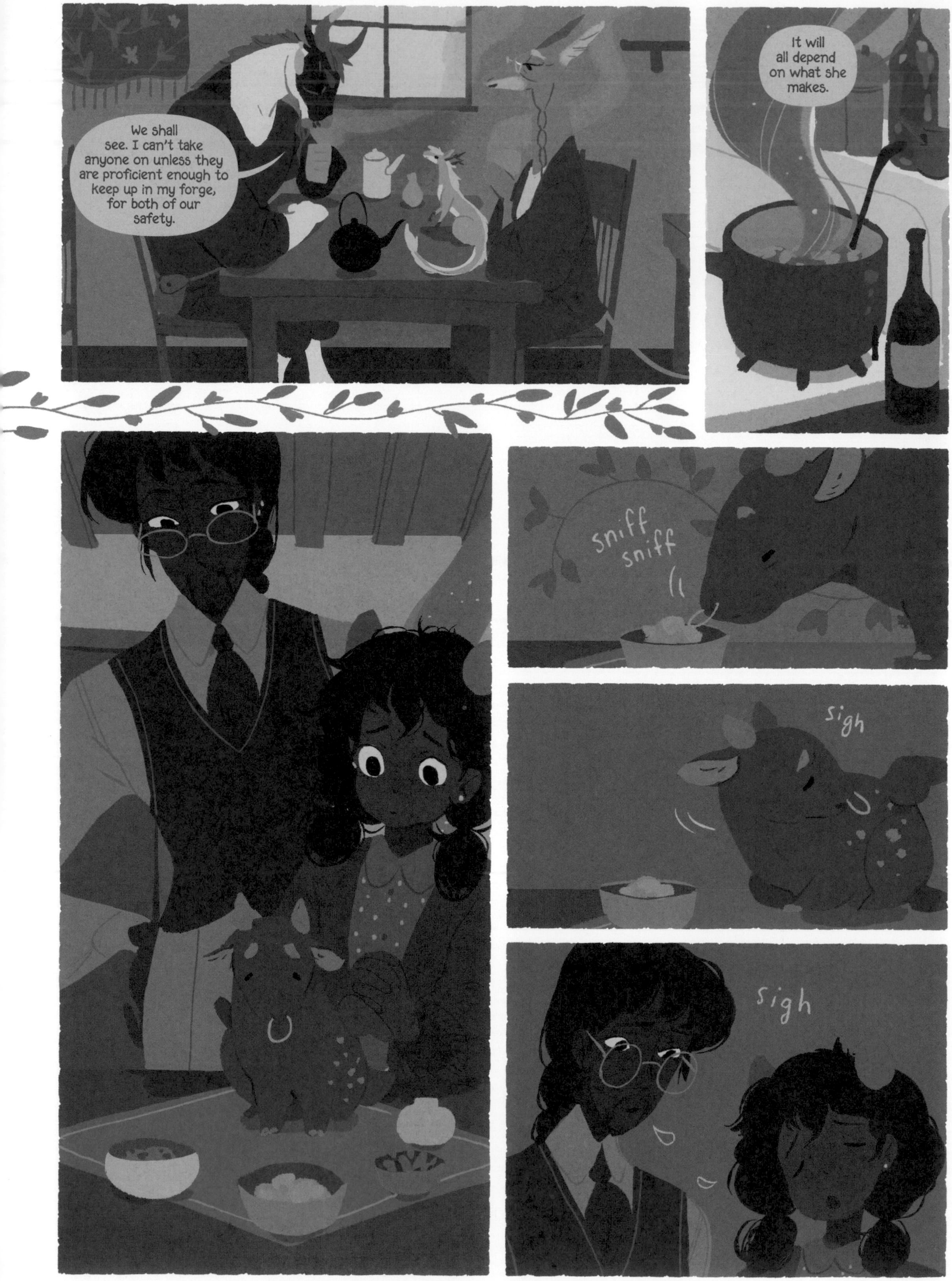

We shall see. I can't take anyone on unless they are proficient enough to keep up in my forge, for both of our safety.
It will all depend on what she makes.
sniff sniff
sigh
sigh

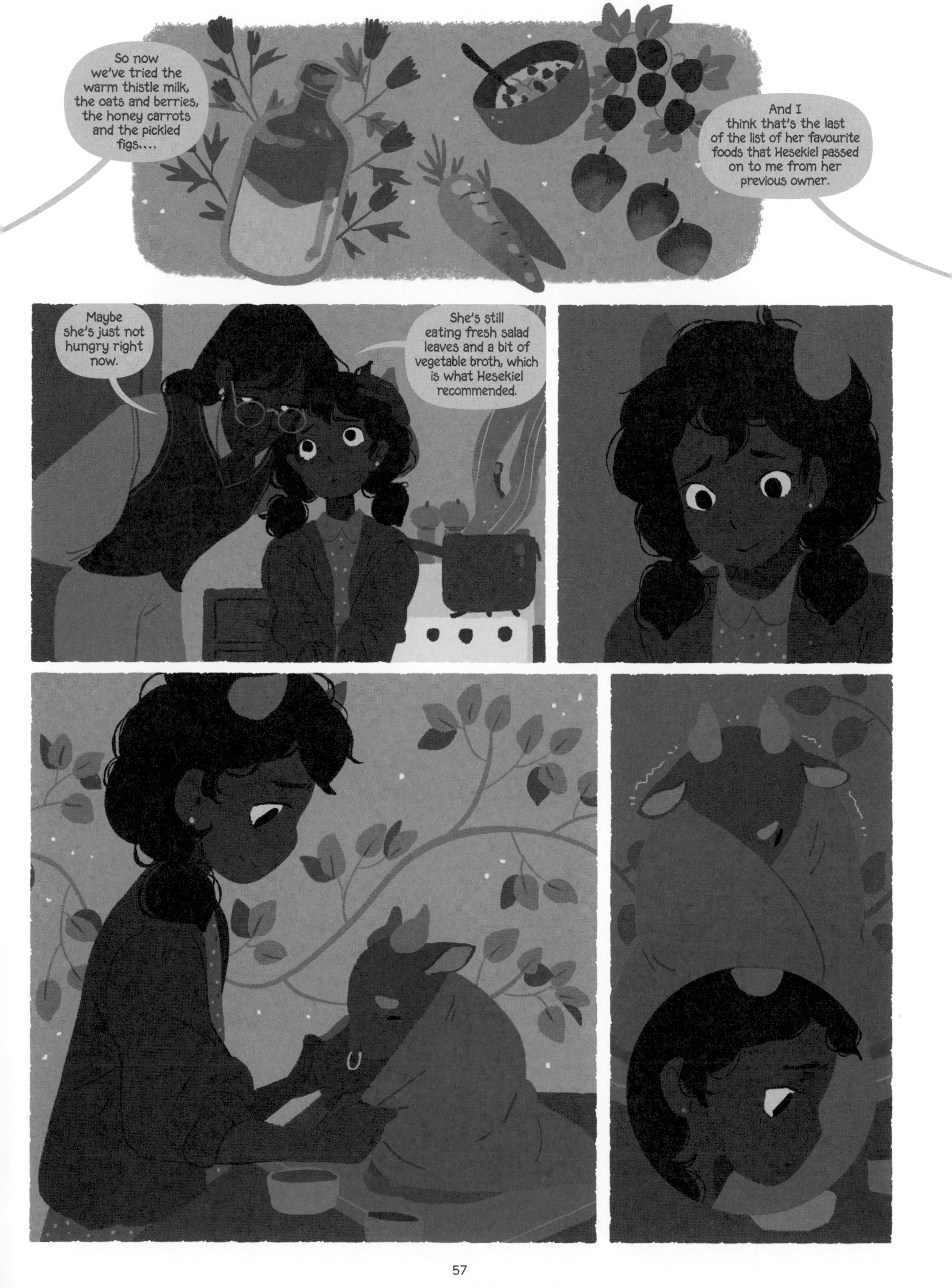
So now we've tried the warm thistle milk, the oats and berries, the honey carrots and the pickled figs....
And I think that's the last of the list of her favourite foods that Hesekiel passed on to me from her previous owner.
Maybe she's just not hungry right now.
She's still eating fresh salad leaves and a bit of vegetable broth, which is what Hesekiel recommended.

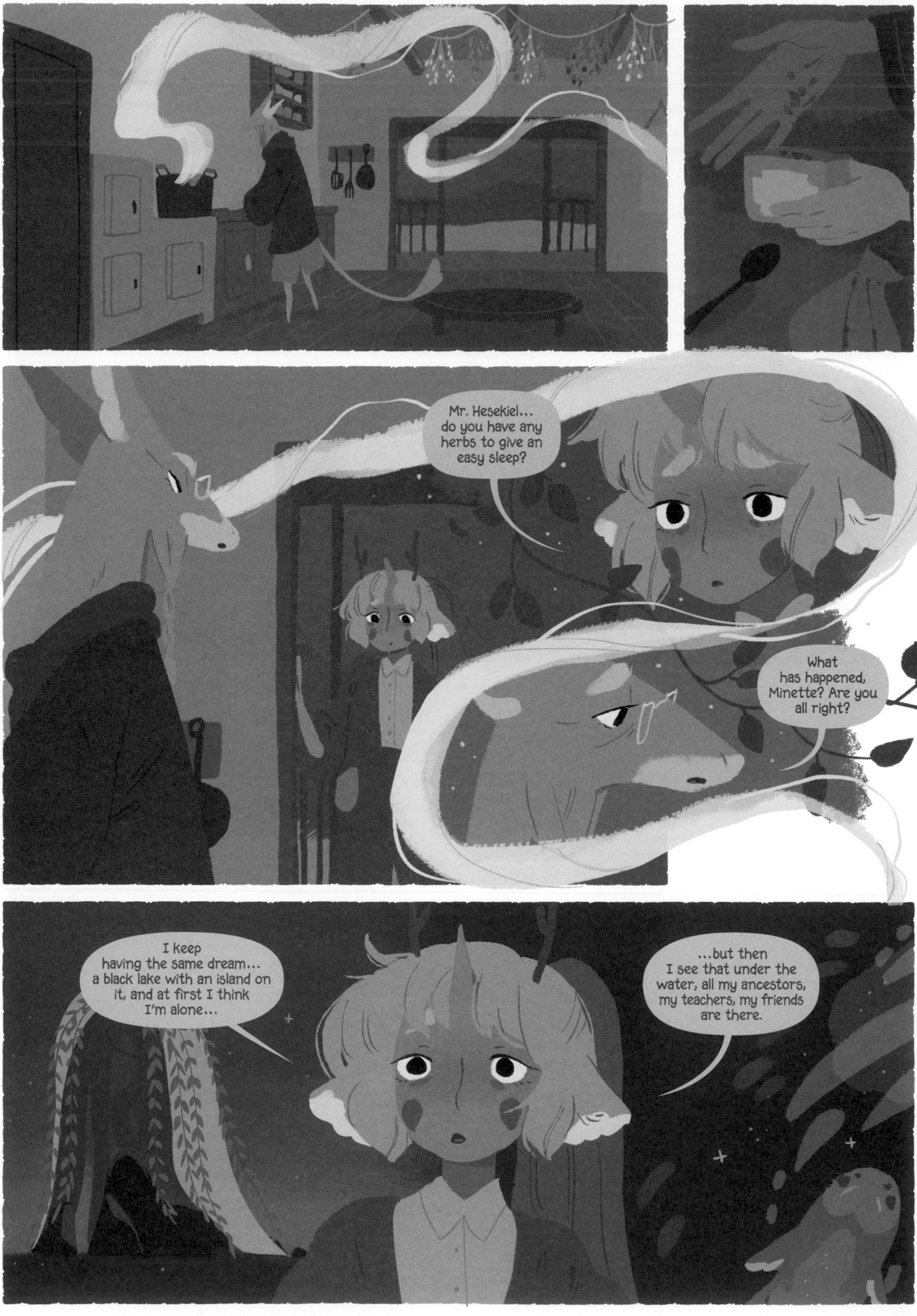
Mr. Hesekiel... do you have any herbs to give an easy sleep?
What has happened, Minette? Are you all right?
I keep having the same dream... a black lake with an island on it, and at first I think I'm alone...
...but then I see that under the water, all my ancestors, my teachers, my friends are there.

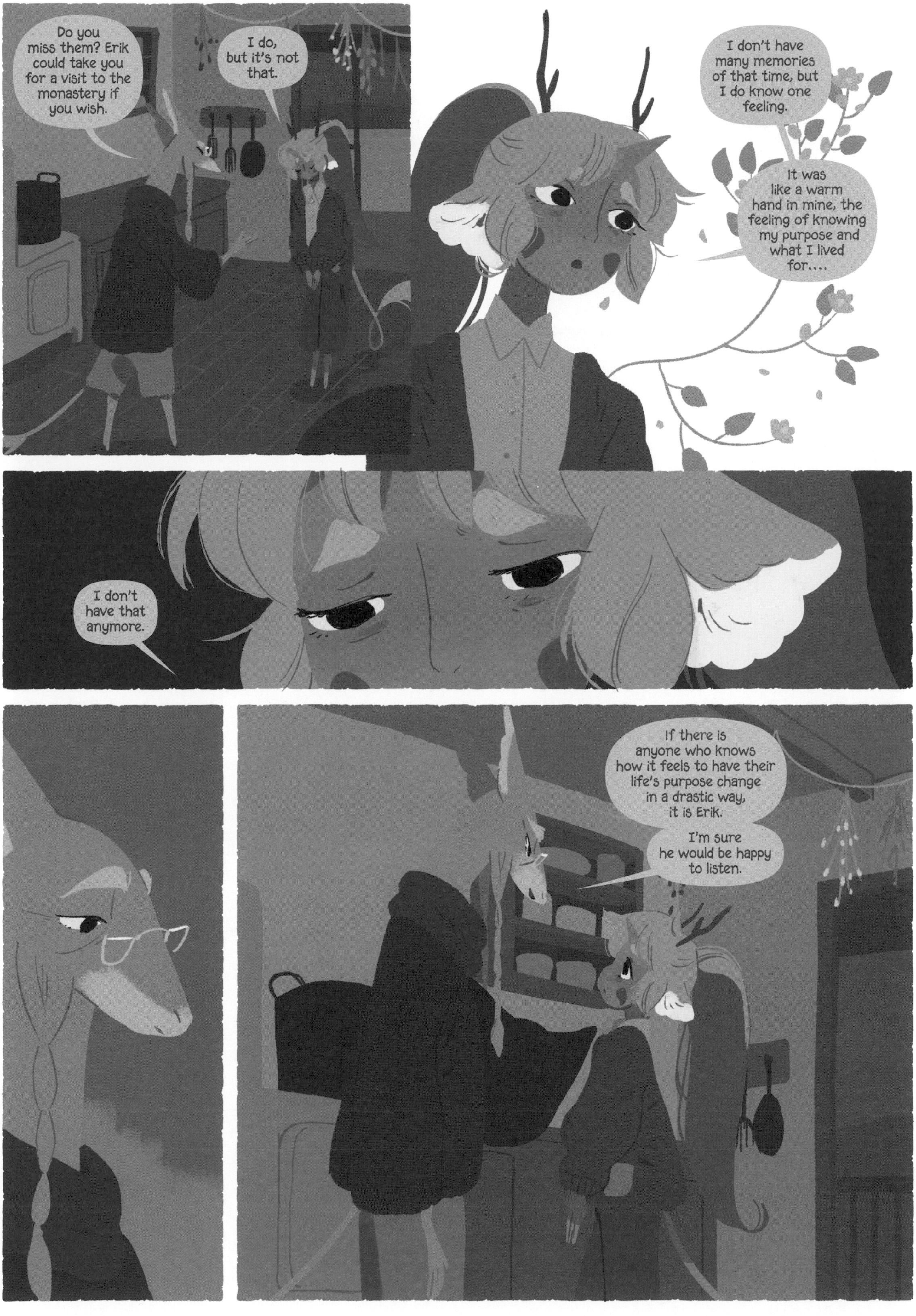
Do you miss them? Erik could take you for a visit to the monastery if you wish.
I do, but it's not that.
I don't have many memories of that time, but I do know one feeling.
It was like a warm hand in mine, the feeling of knowing my purpose and what I lived for....
I don't have that anymore.
If there is anyone who knows how it feels to have their life's purpose change in a drastic way, it is Erik.
I'm sure he would be happy to listen.

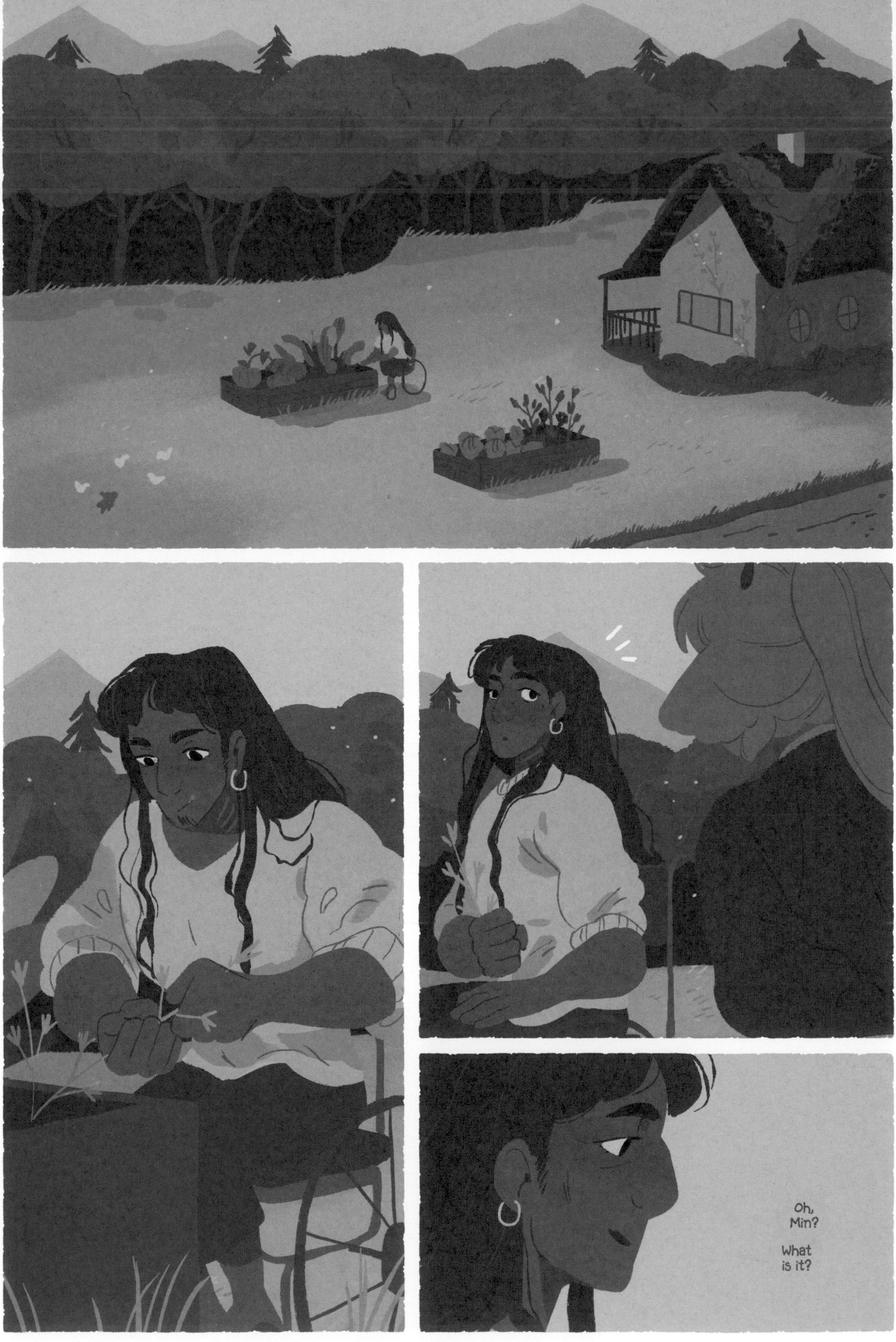
Oh, Min?
What is it?

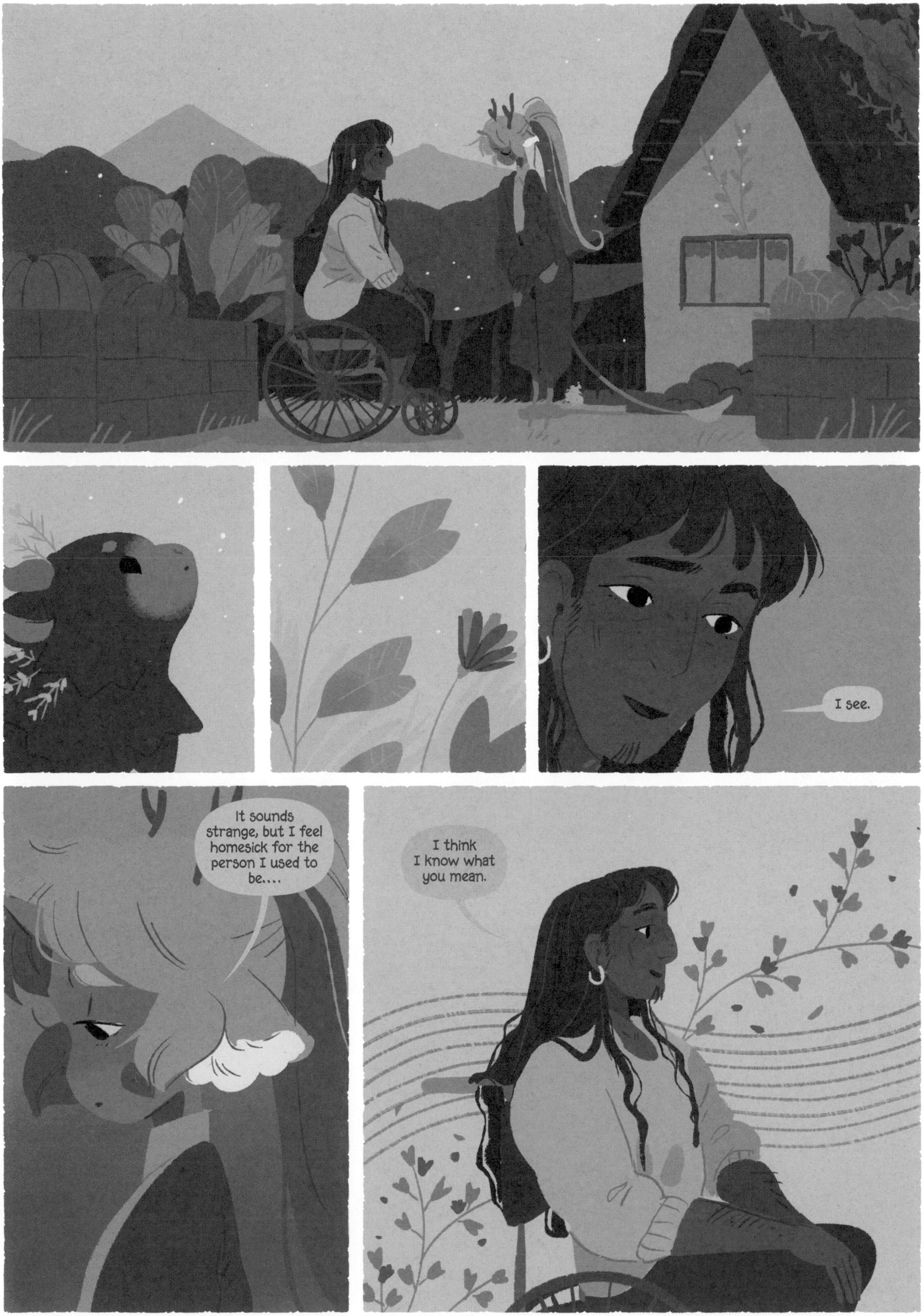
I see.
It sounds strange, but I feel homesick for the person I used to be....
I think I know what you mean.

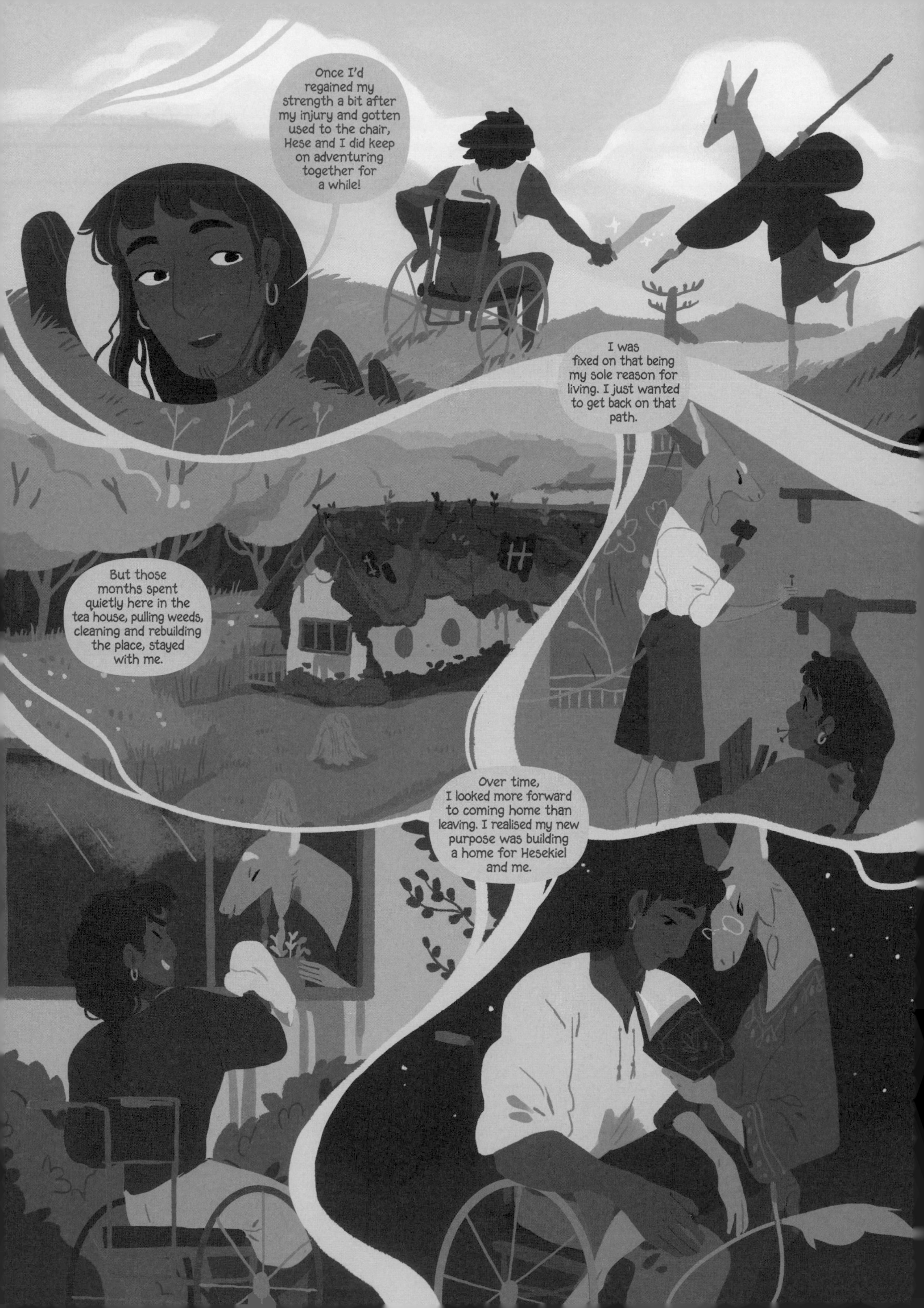
Once I'd regained my strength a bit after my injury and gotten used to the chair, Hese and I did keep on adventuring together for a while!
I was fixed on that being my sole reason for living. I just wanted to get back on that path.
But those months spent quietly here in the tea house, pulling weeds, cleaning and rebuilding the place, stayed with me.
Over time, I looked more forward to coming home than leaving. I realised my new purpose was building a home for Hesekiel and me.

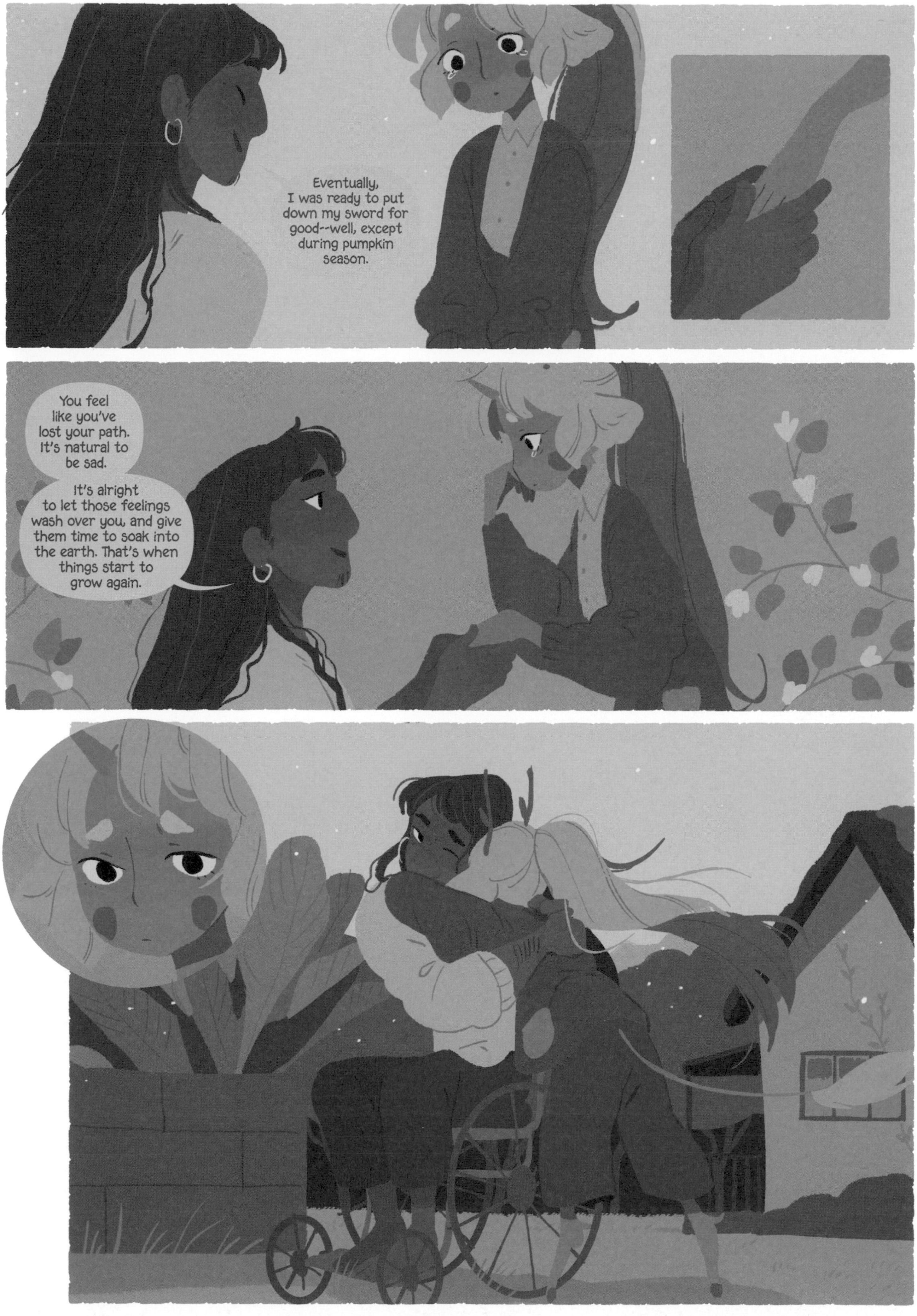
Eventually, I was ready to put down my sword for good--well, except during pumpkin season.
You feel like you've lost your path. It's natural to be sad.
It's alright to let those feelings wash over you, and give them time to soak into the earth. That's when things start to grow again.

Chapter Four

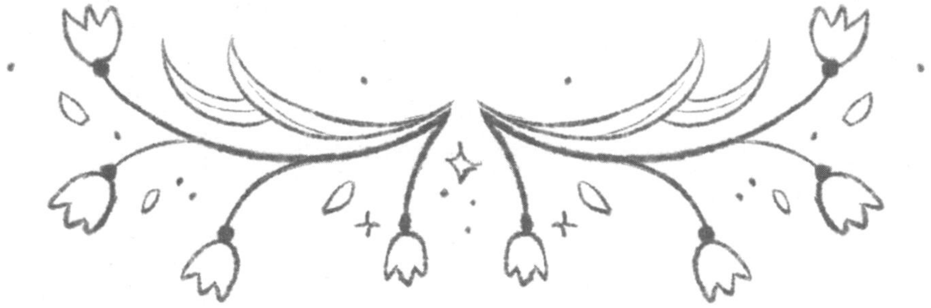

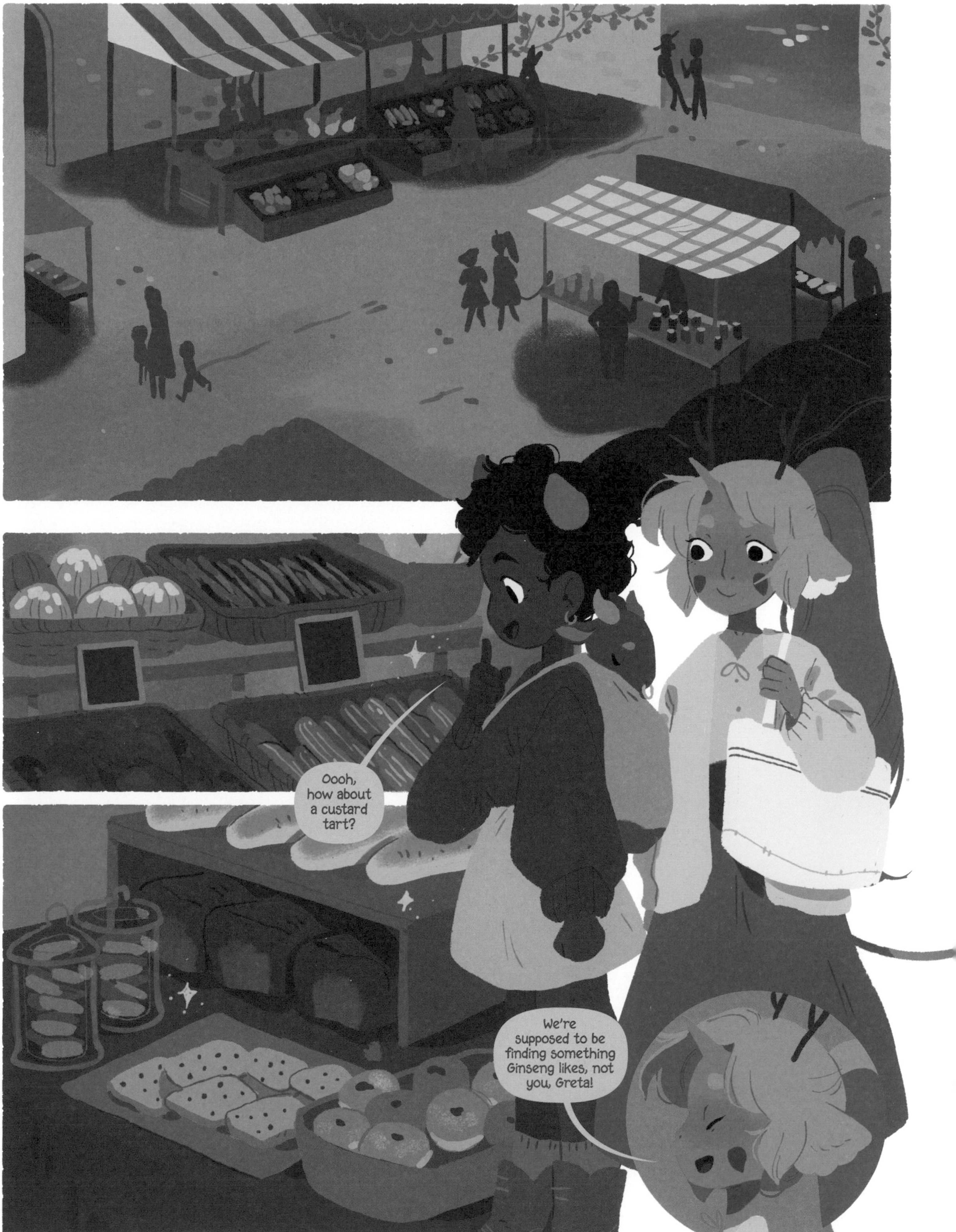
Oooh, how about a custard tart?
We're supposed to be finding something Ginseng likes, not you, Greta!

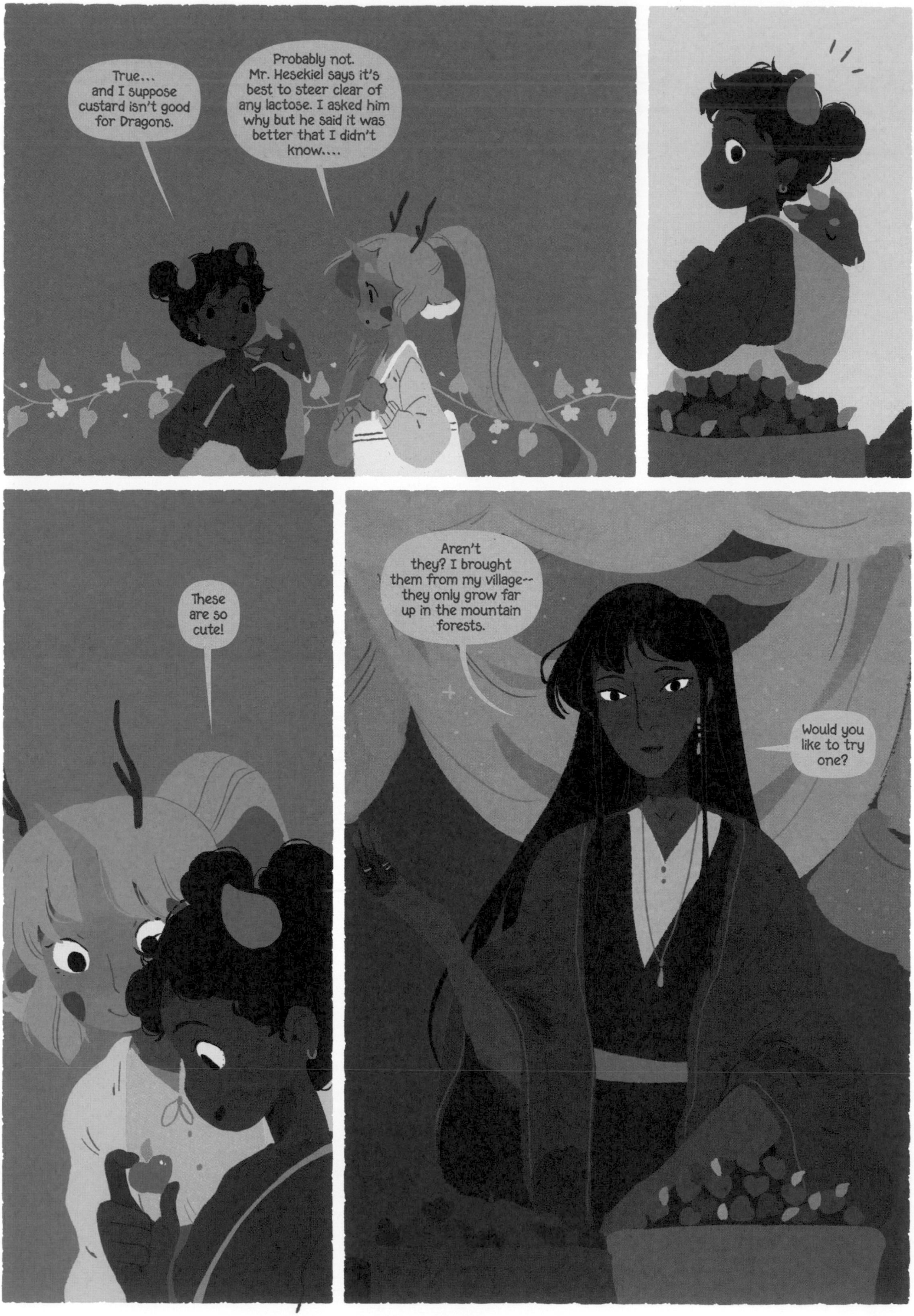
True... and I suppose custard isn't good for Dragons.
Probably not. Mr. Hesekiel says it's best to steer clear of any lactose. I asked him why but he said it was better that I didn't know....
These are so cute!
Aren't they? I brought them from my village--they only grow far up in the mountain forests.
Would you like to try one?

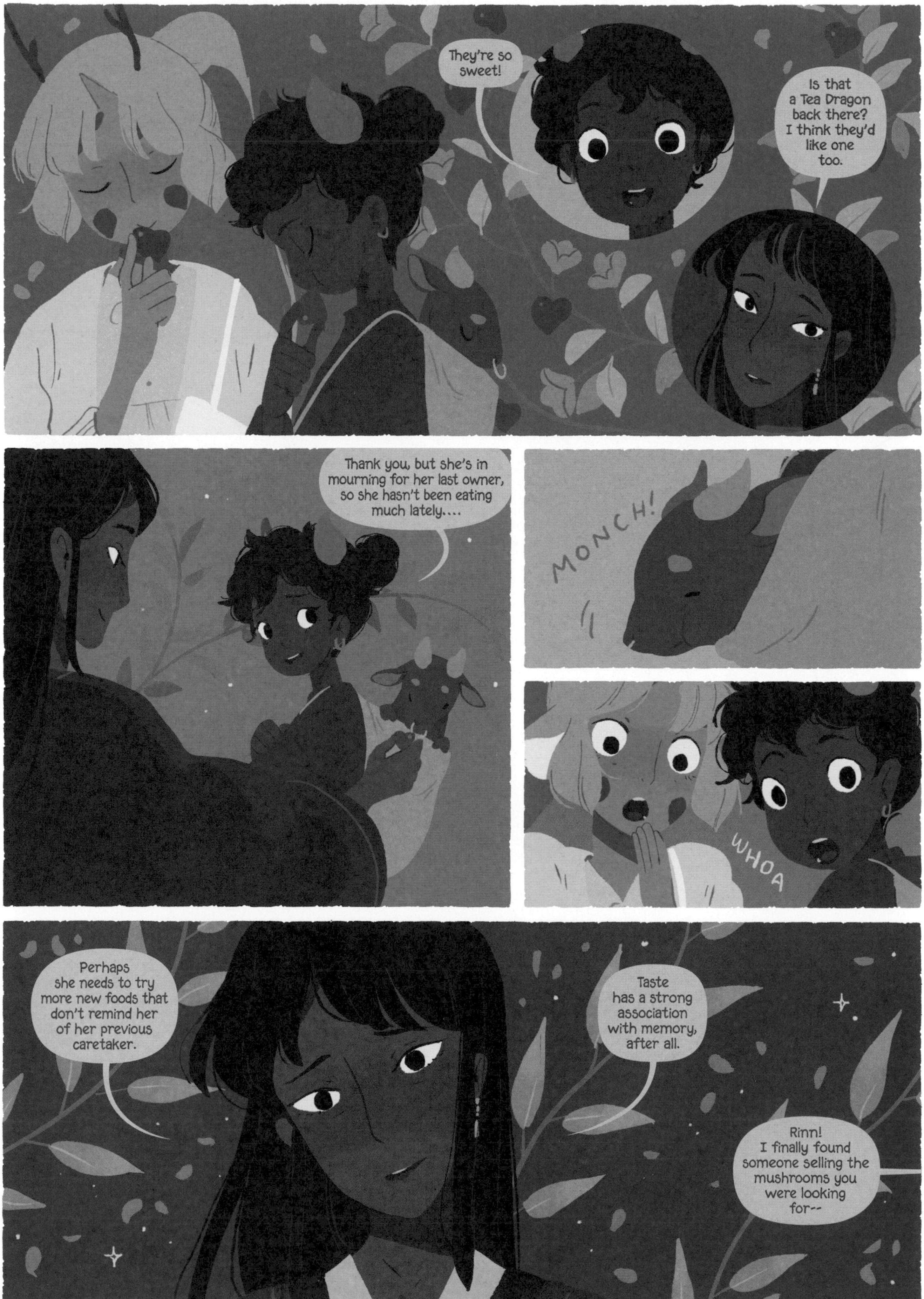
They're so sweet!
Is that a Tea Dragon back there? I think they'd like one too.
Thank you, but she's in mourning for her last owner, so she hasn't been eating much lately....
MONCH!
WHOA
Perhaps she needs to try more new foods that don't remind her of her previous caretaker.
Taste has a strong association with memory, after all.
Rinn! I finally found someone selling the mushrooms you were looking for--

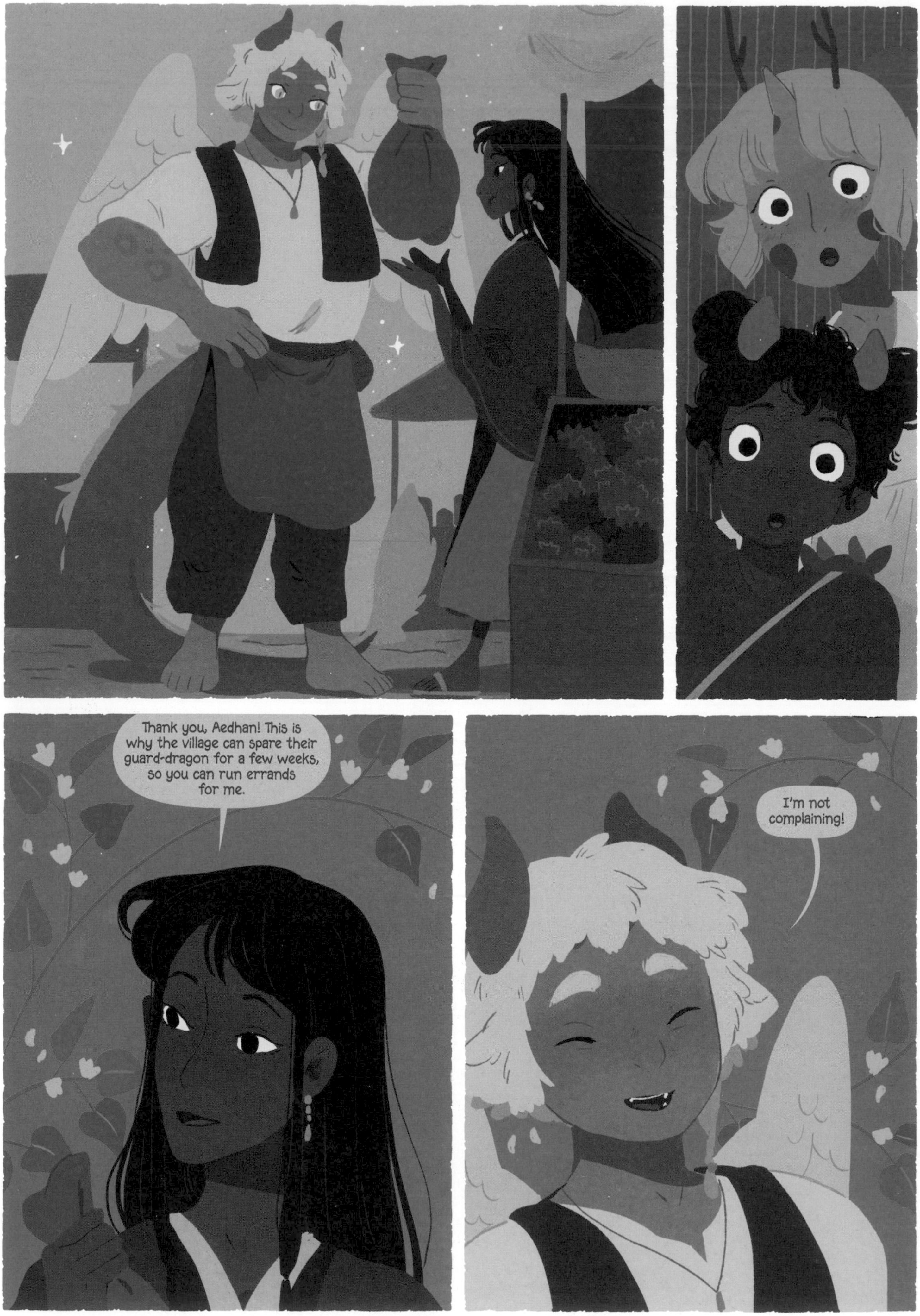
Thank you, Aedhan! This is why the village can spare their guard-dragon for a few weeks, so you can run errands for me.
I'm not complaining!

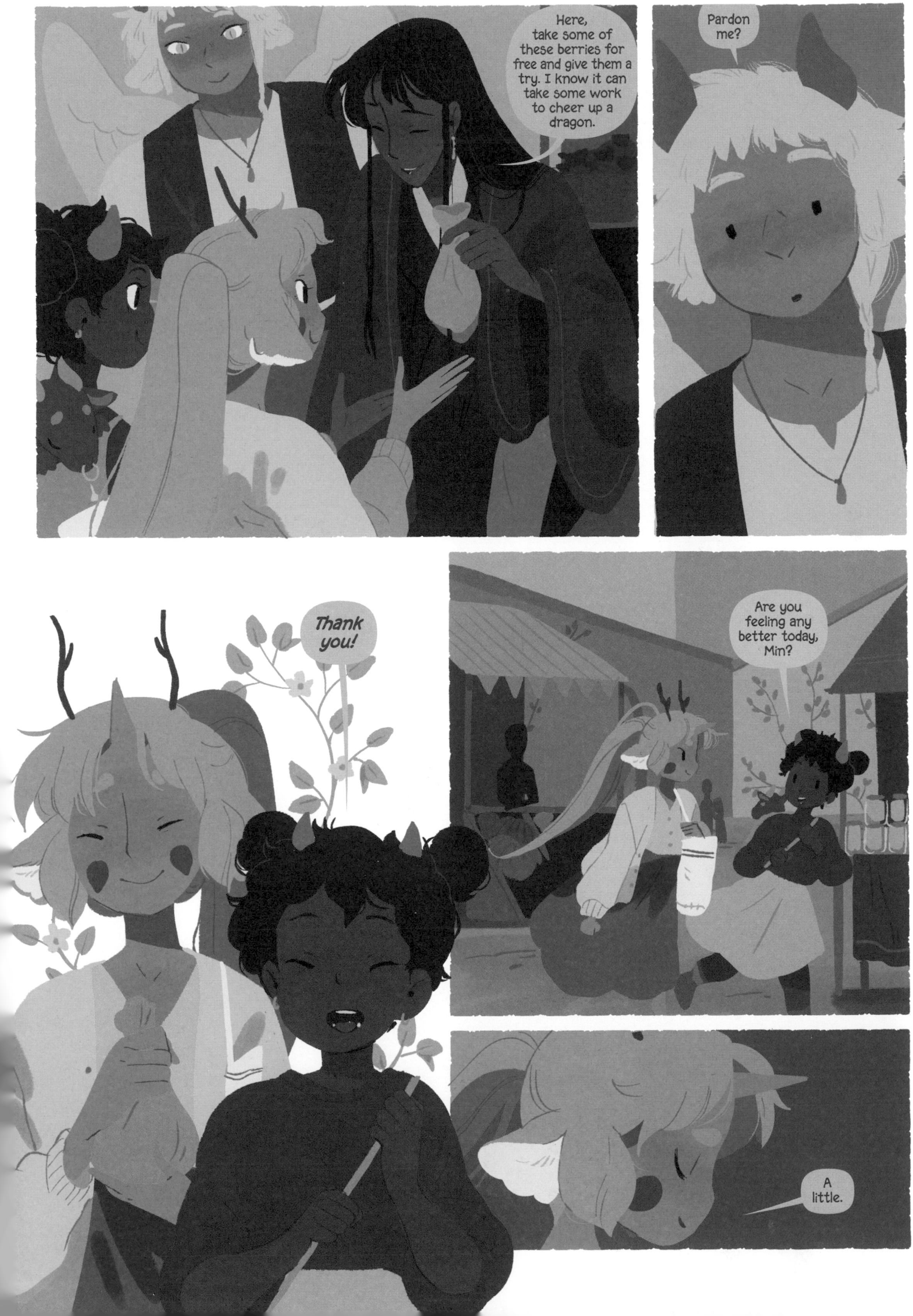
Here, take some of these berries for free and give them a try. I know it can take some work to cheer up a dragon.
Pardon me?
Thank you!
Are you feeling any better today, Min?
A little.

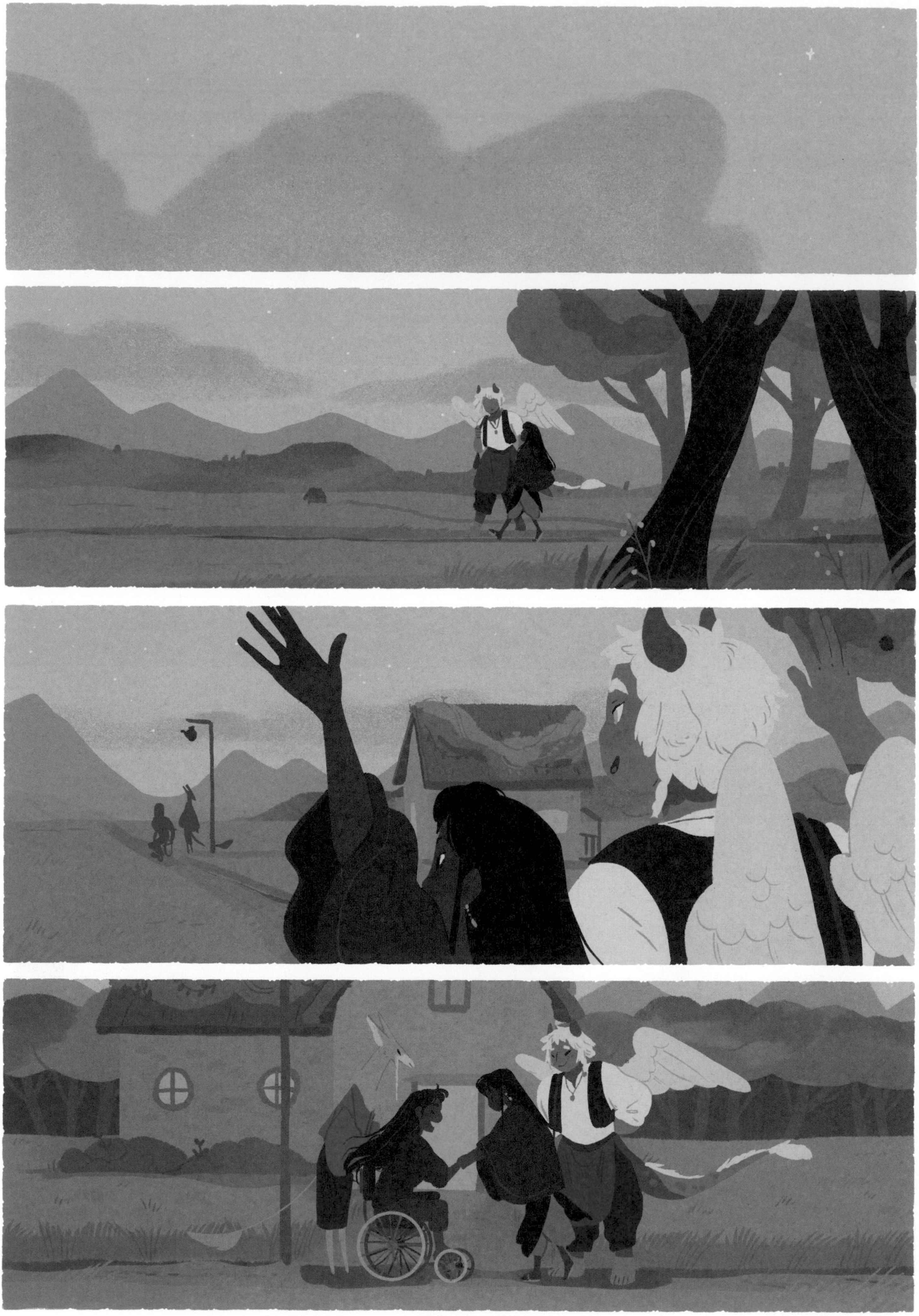

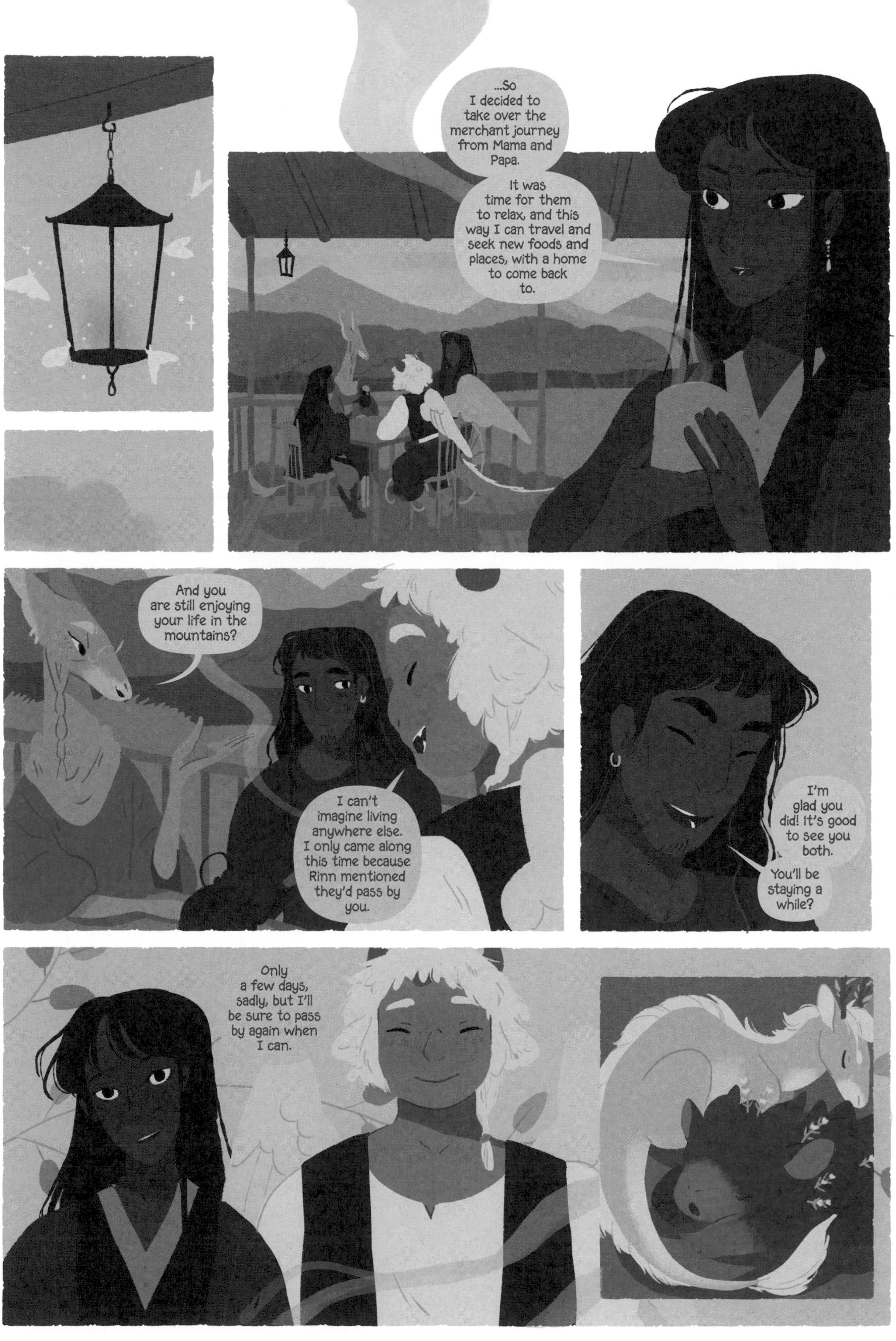
...So I decided to take over the merchant journey from Mama and Papa.
It was time for them to relax, and this way I can travel and seek new foods and places, with a home to come back to.
And you are still enjoying your life in the mountains?
I can't imagine living anywhere else. I only came along this time because Rinn mentioned they'd pass by you.
I'm glad you did! It's good to see you both.
You'll be staying a while?
Only a few days, sadly, but I'll be sure to pass by again when I can.

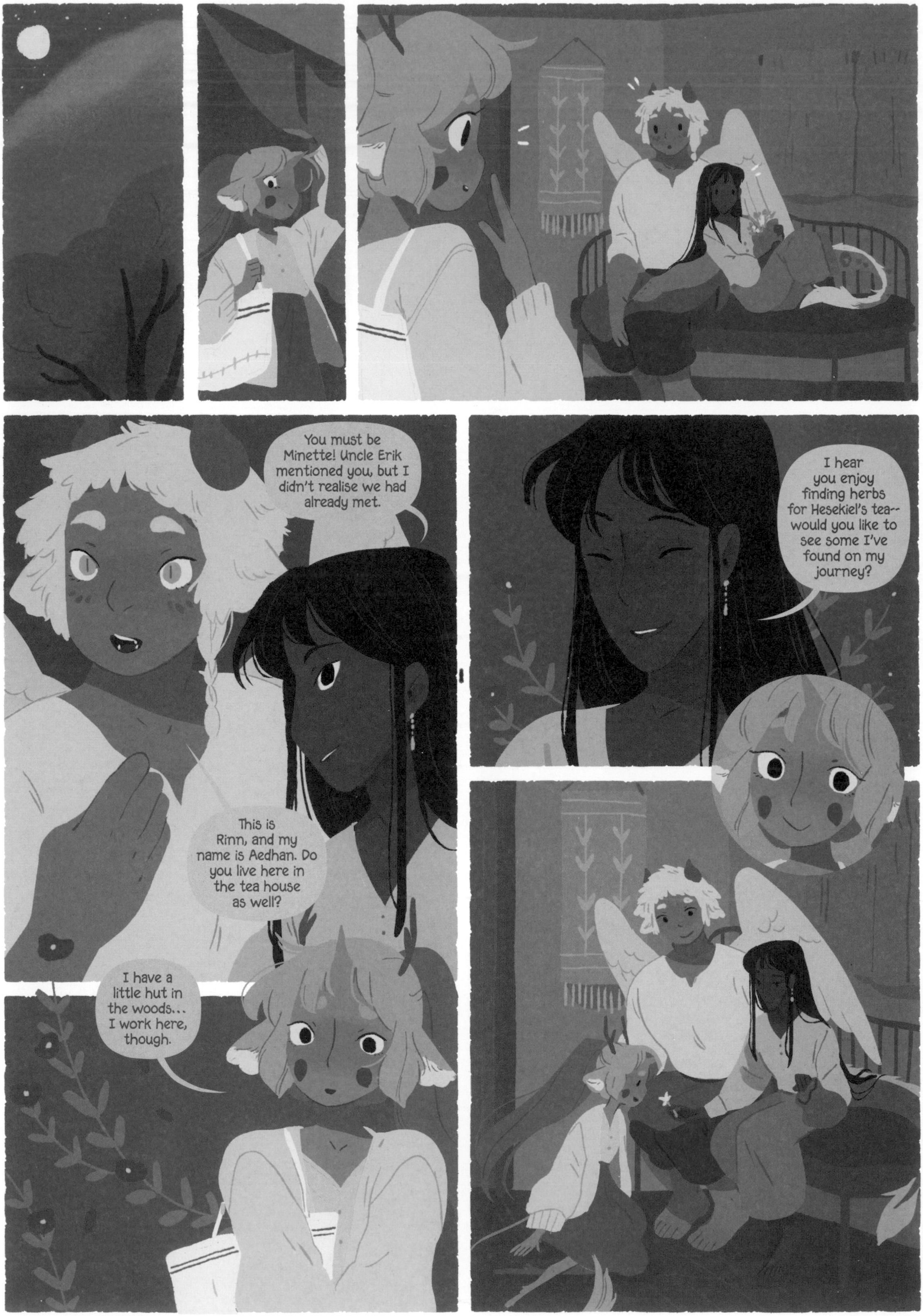
You must be Minette! Uncle Erik mentioned you, but I didn't realise we had already met.
This is Rinn, and my name is Aedhan. Do you live here in the tea house as well?
I have a little hut in the woods... I work here, though.
I hear you enjoy finding herbs for Hesekiel's tea-- would you like to see some I've found on my journey?

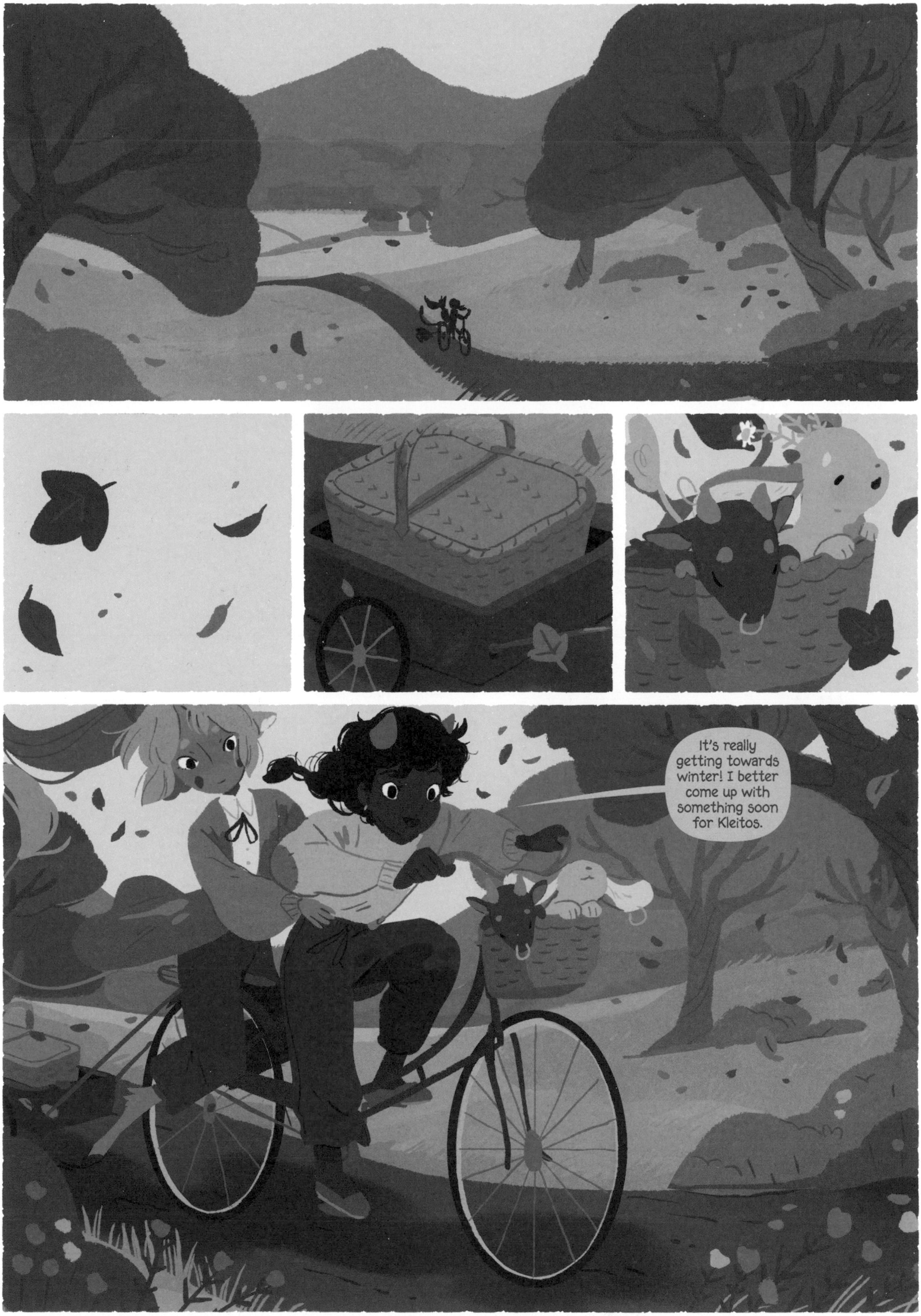
It's really getting towards winter! I better come up with something soon for Kleitos.

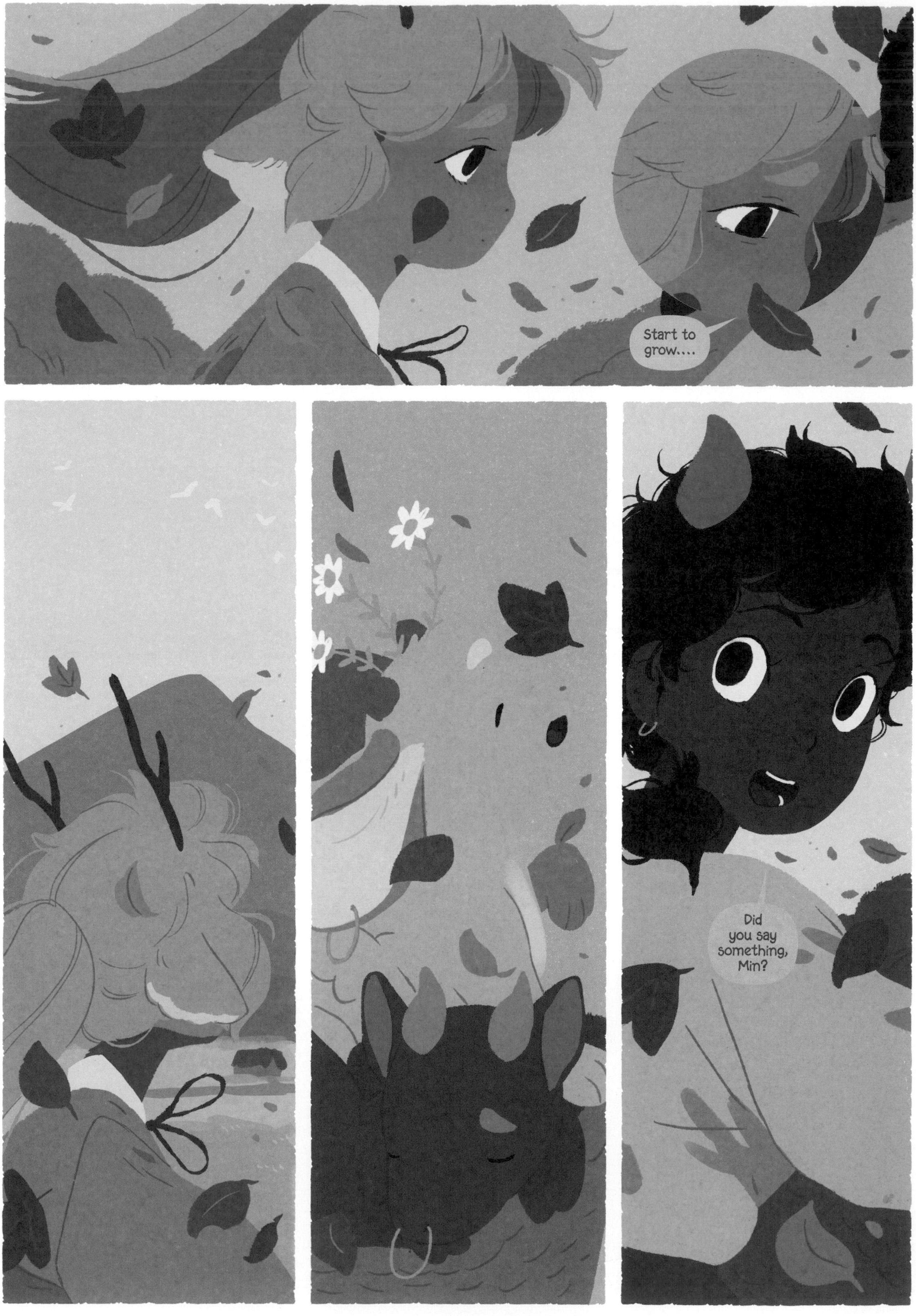
Start to grow....
Did you say something, Min?

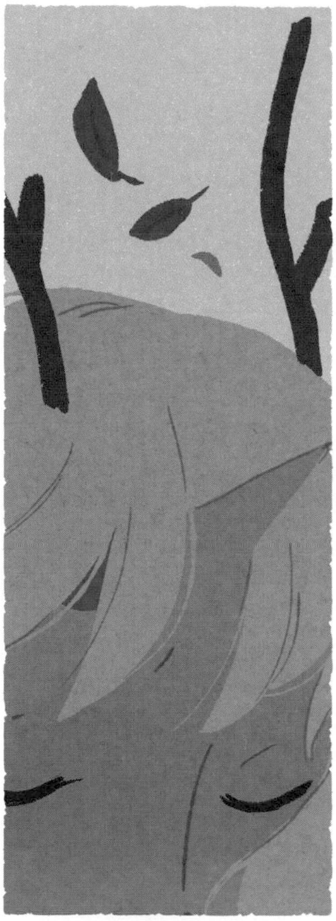

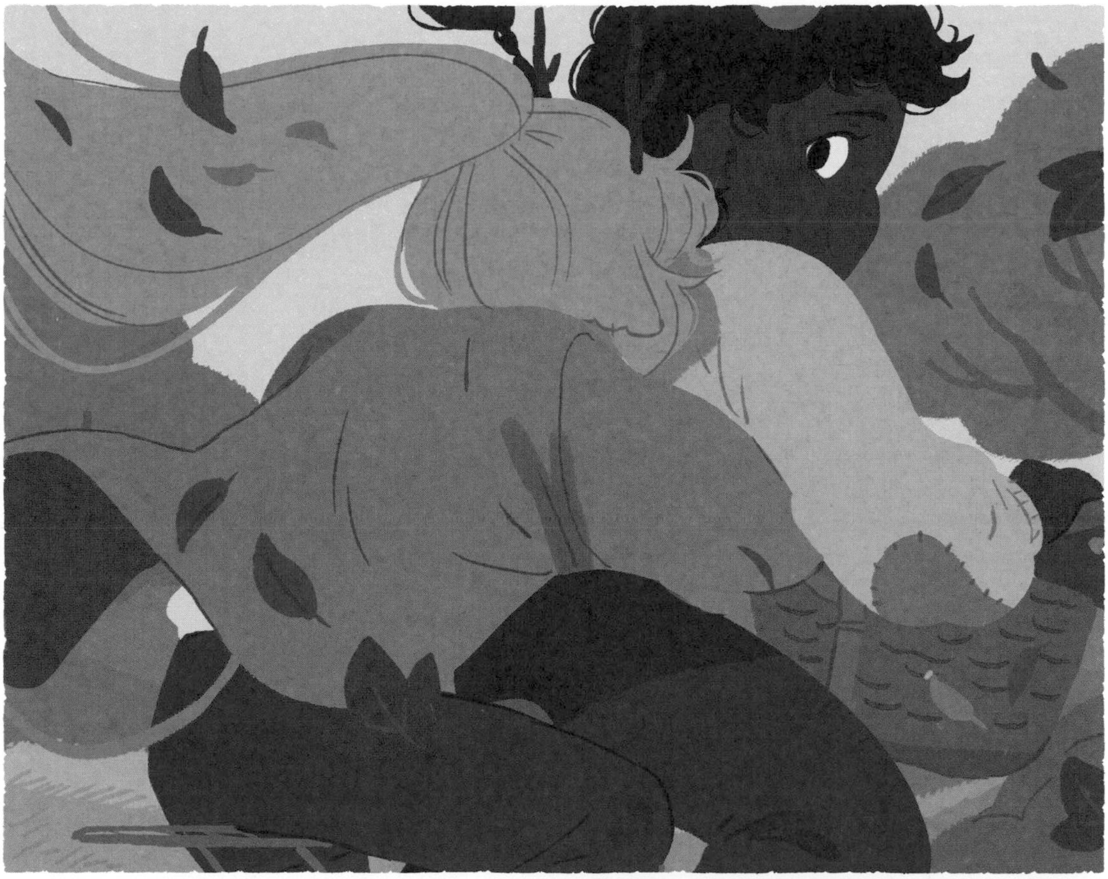

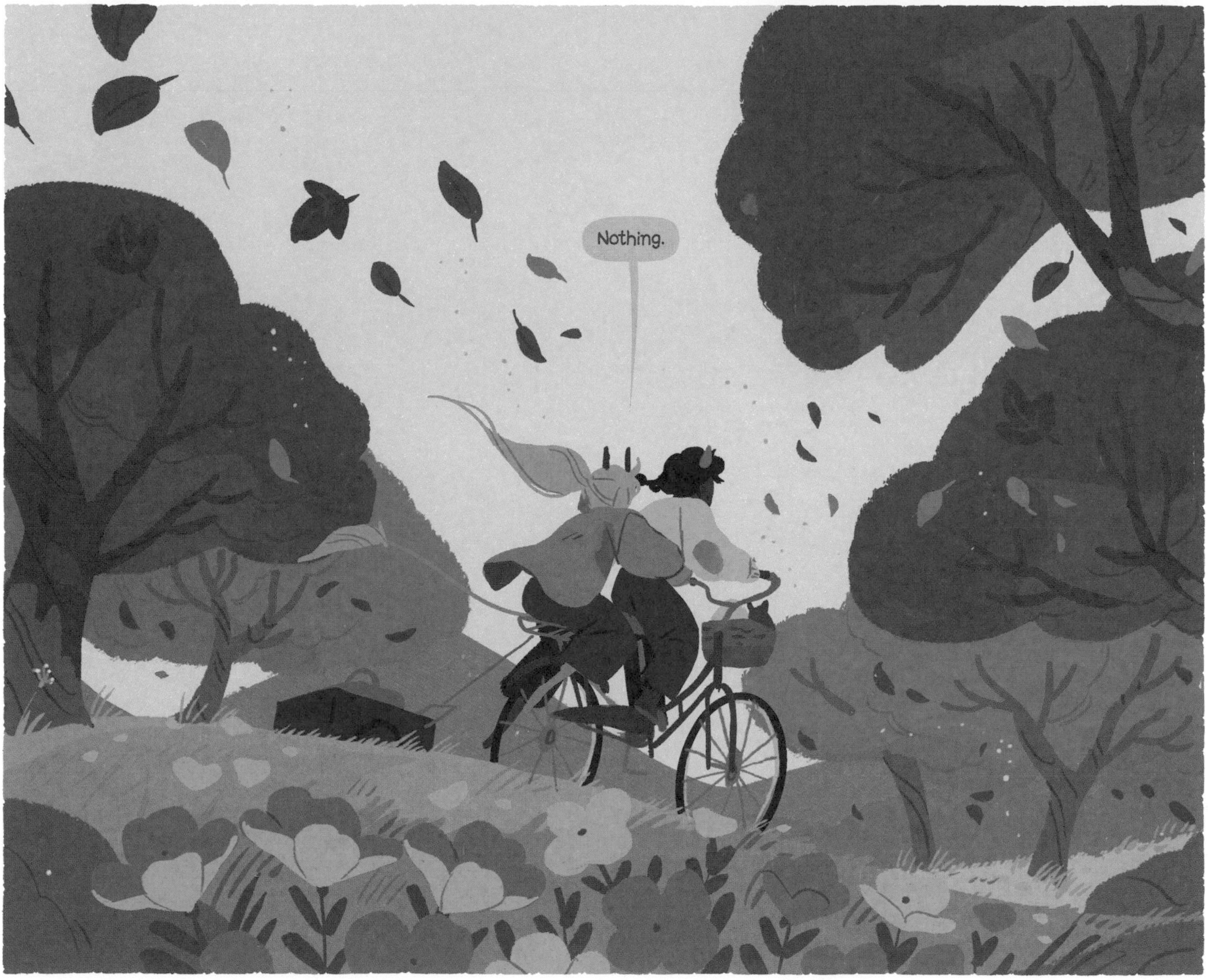
Nothing.

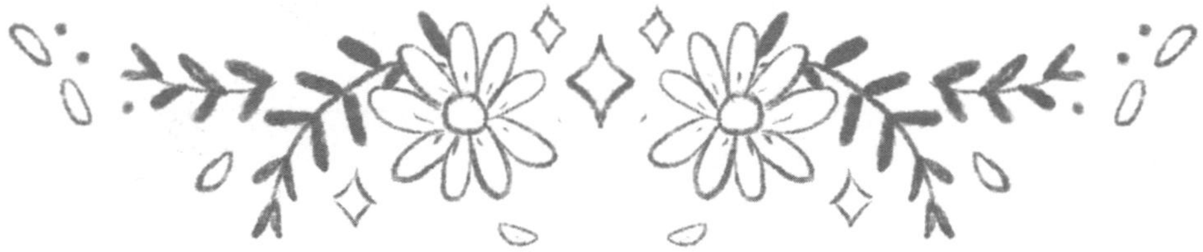

Chapter Five

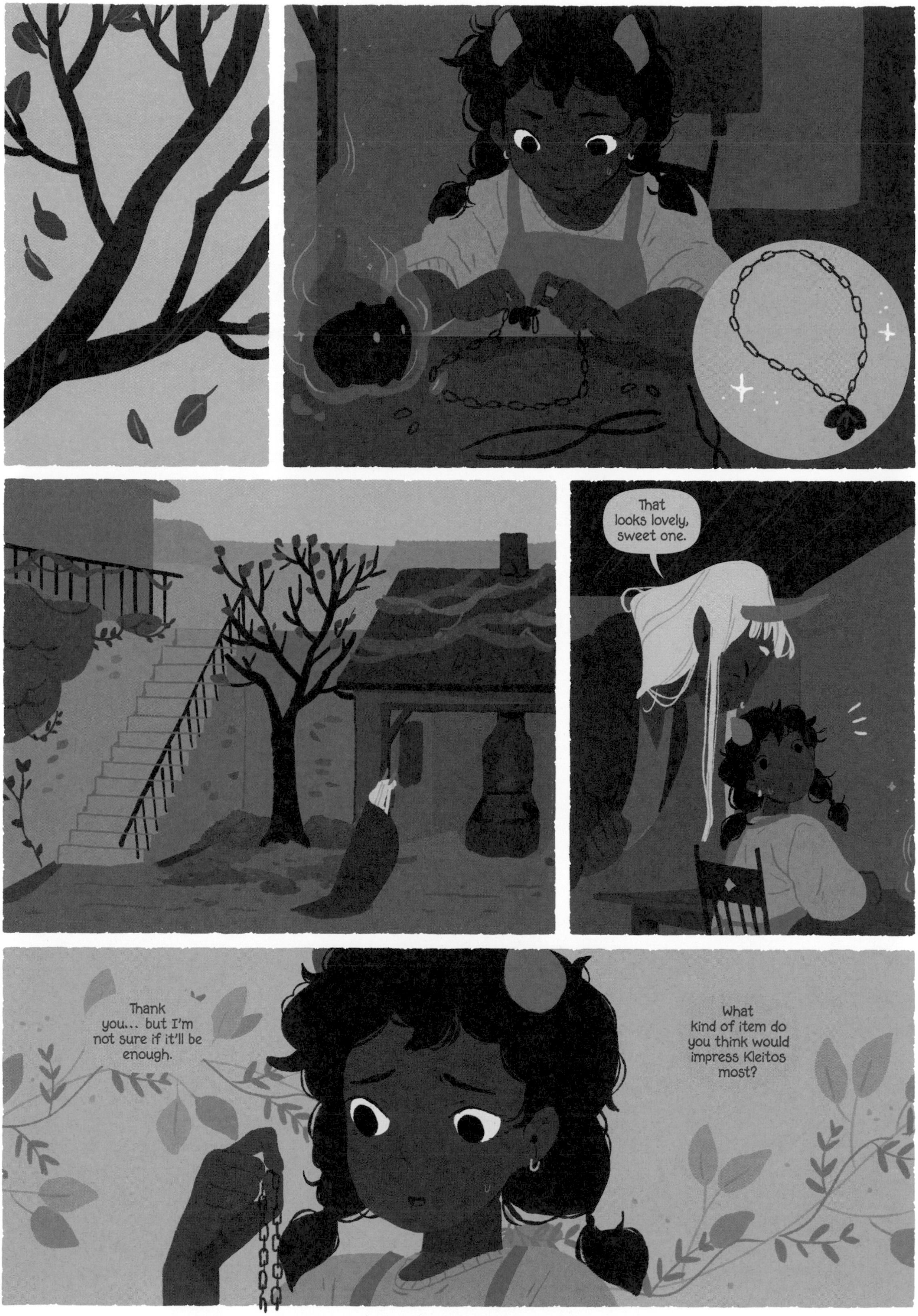
That looks lovely, sweet one.
Thank you... but I'm not sure if it'll be enough.
What kind of item do you think would impress Kleitos most?

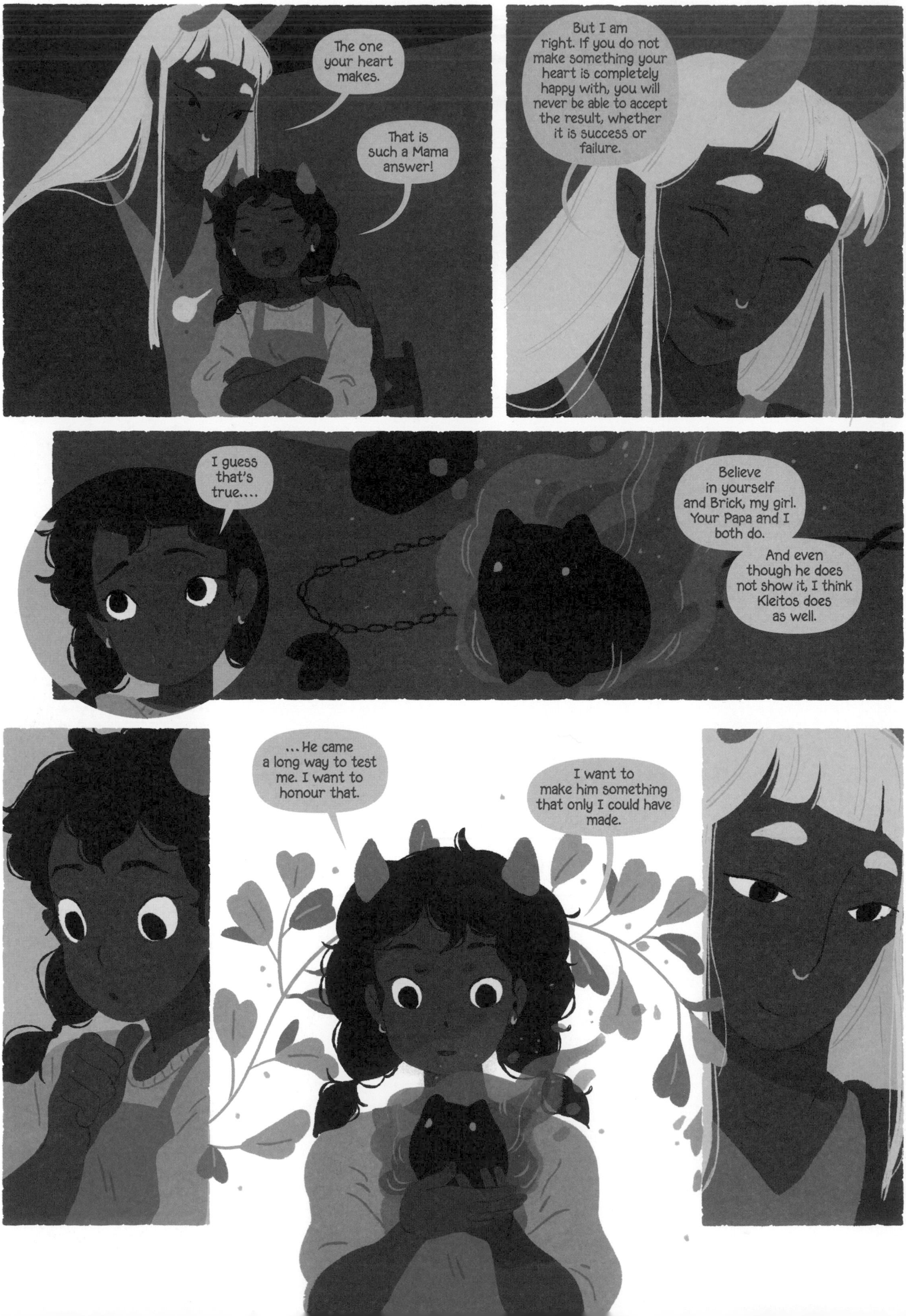
The one your heart makes.
That is such a Mama answer!
But I am right. If you do not make something your heart is completely happy with, you will never be able to accept the result, whether it is success or failure.
I guess that's true....
Believe in yourself and Brick, my girl. Your Papa and I both do.
And even though he does not show it, I think Kleitos does as well.
...He came a long way to test me. I want to honour that.
I want to make him something that only I could have made.

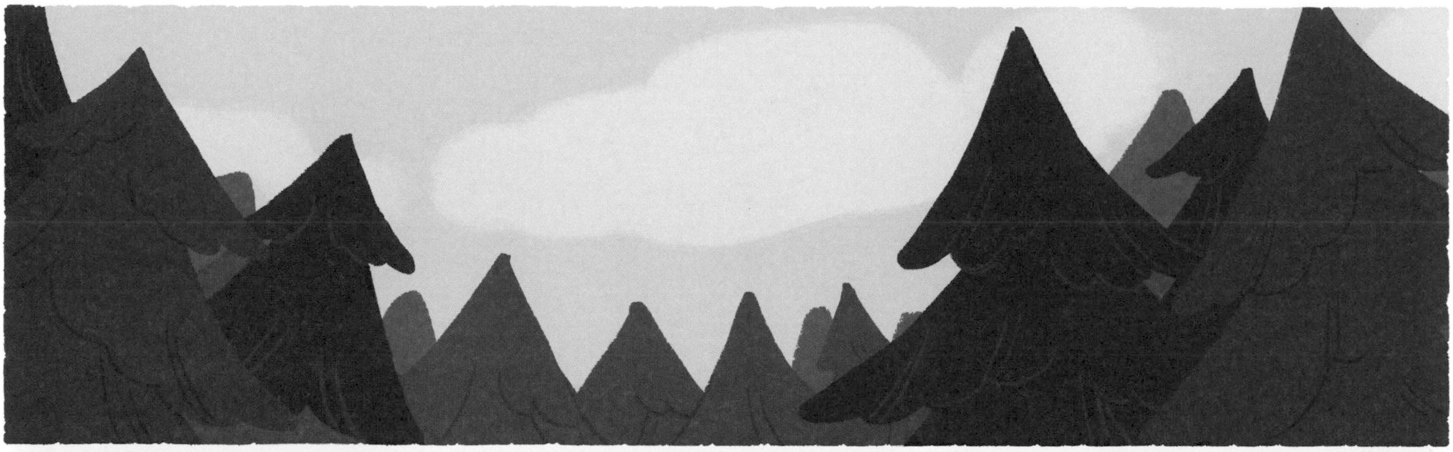

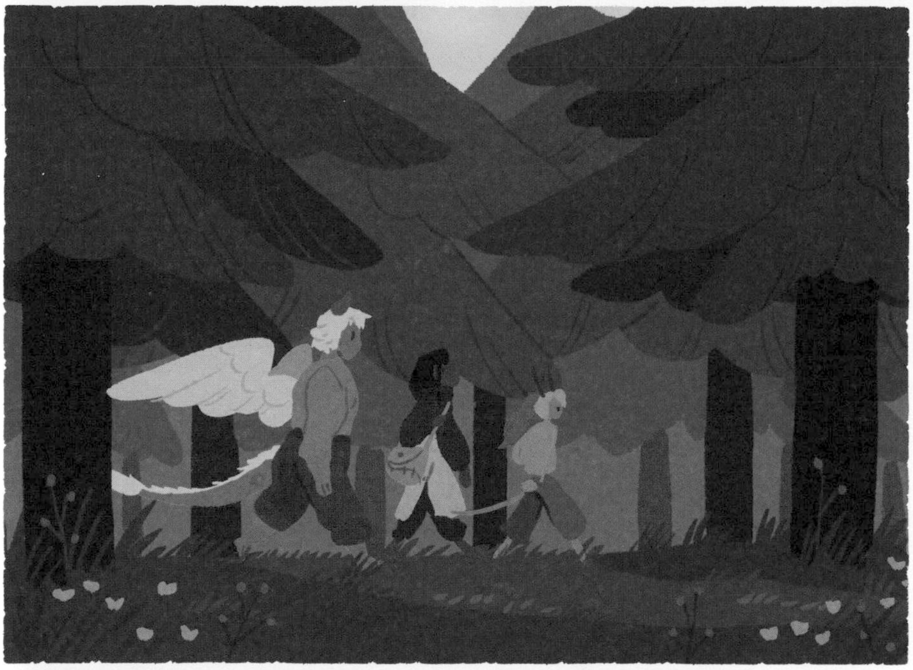

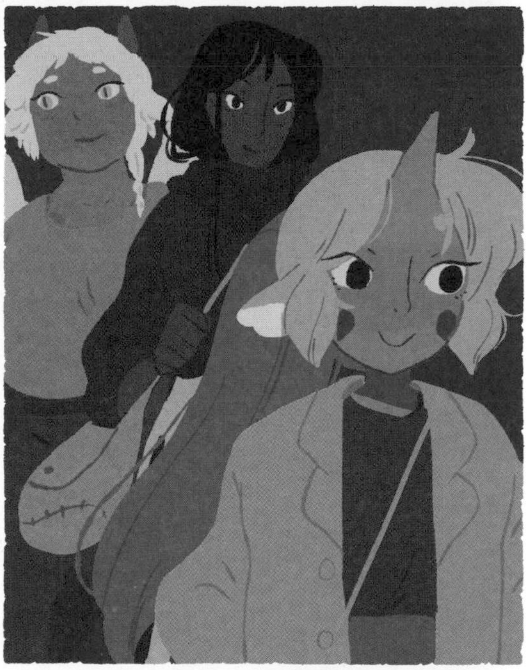

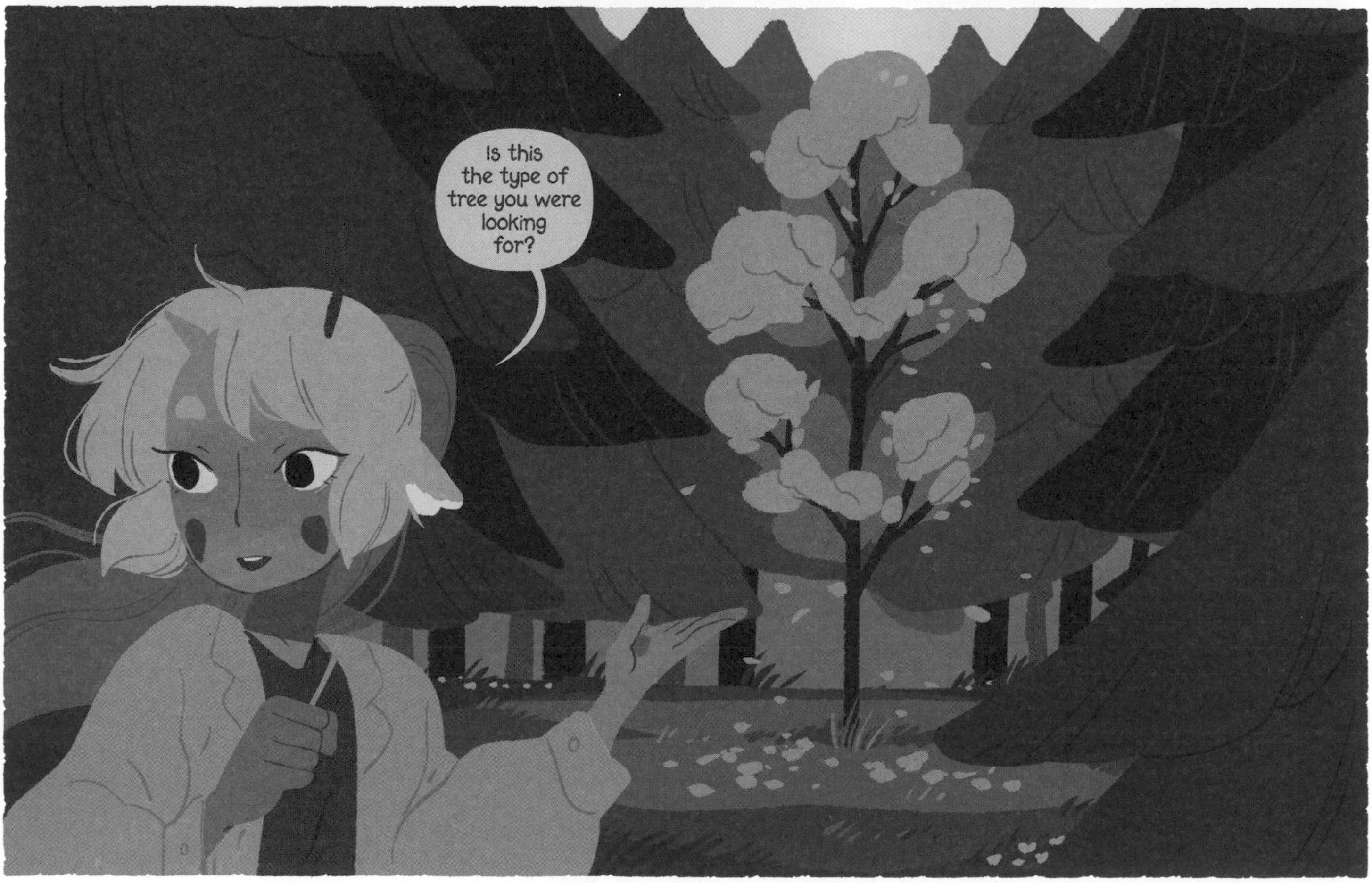
Is this the type of tree you were looking for?

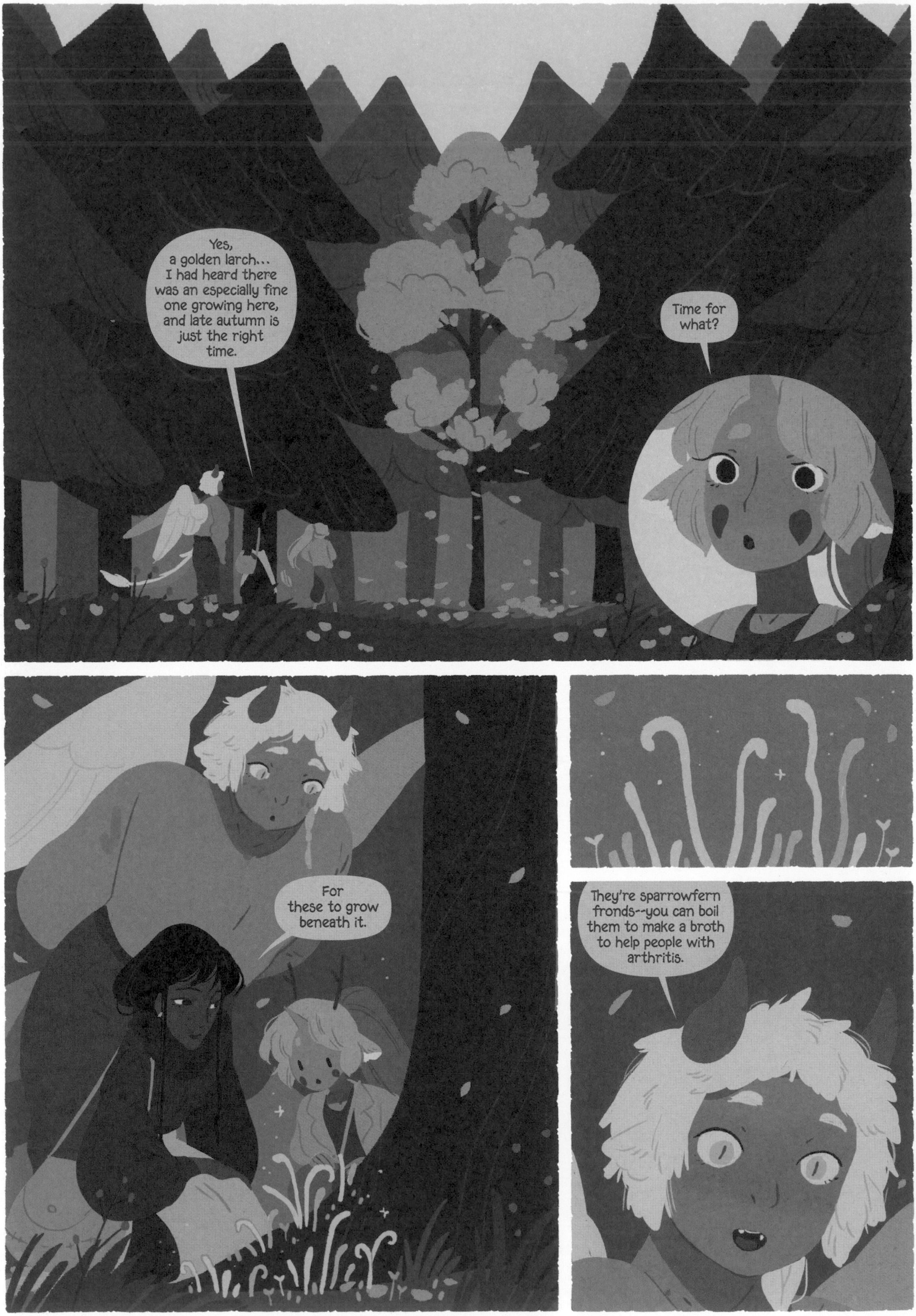
Yes, a golden larch... I had heard there was an especially fine one growing here, and late autumn is just the right time.
Time for what?
For these to grow beneath it.
They're sparrowfern fronds--you can boil them to make a broth to help people with arthritis.

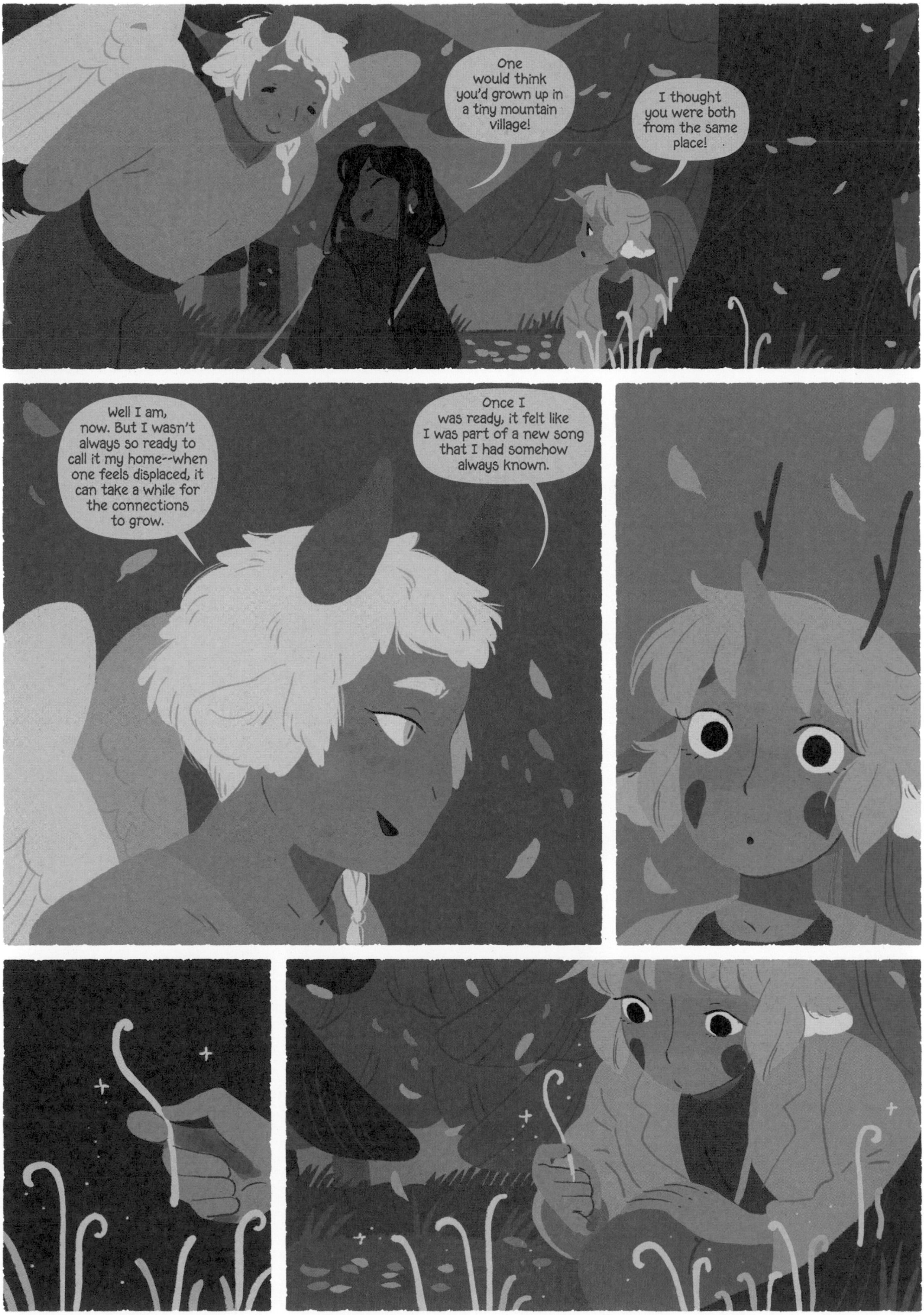
One would think you'd grown up in a tiny mountain village!
I thought you were both from the same place!
Well I am, now. But I wasn't always so ready to call it my home--when one feels displaced, it can take a while for the connections to grow.
Once I was ready, it felt like I was part of a new song that I had somehow always known.

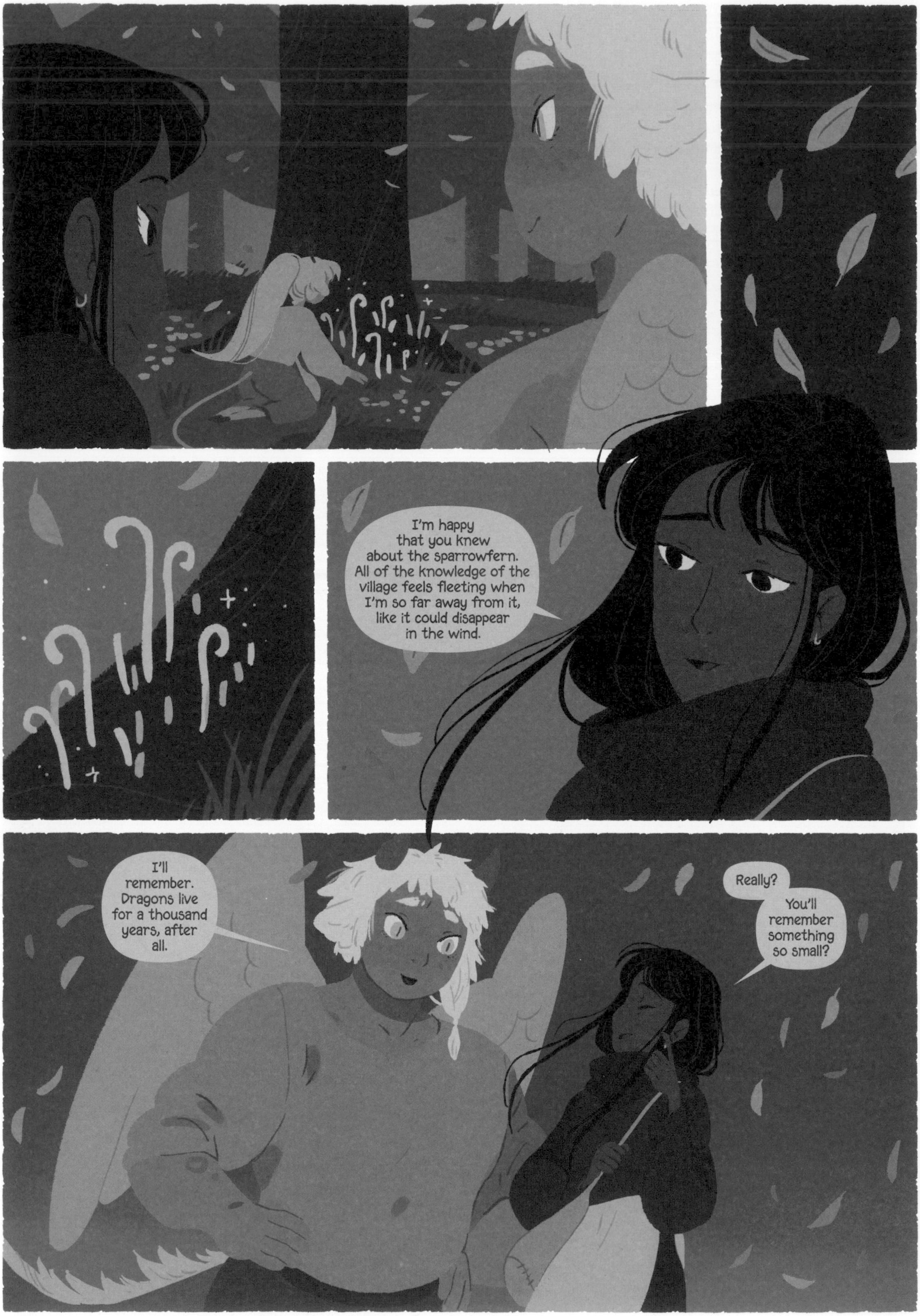
I'm happy that you knew about the sparrowfern. All of the knowledge of the village feels fleeting when I'm so far away from it, like it could disappear in the wind.
I'll remember. Dragons live for a thousand years, after all.
Really?
You'll remember something so small?

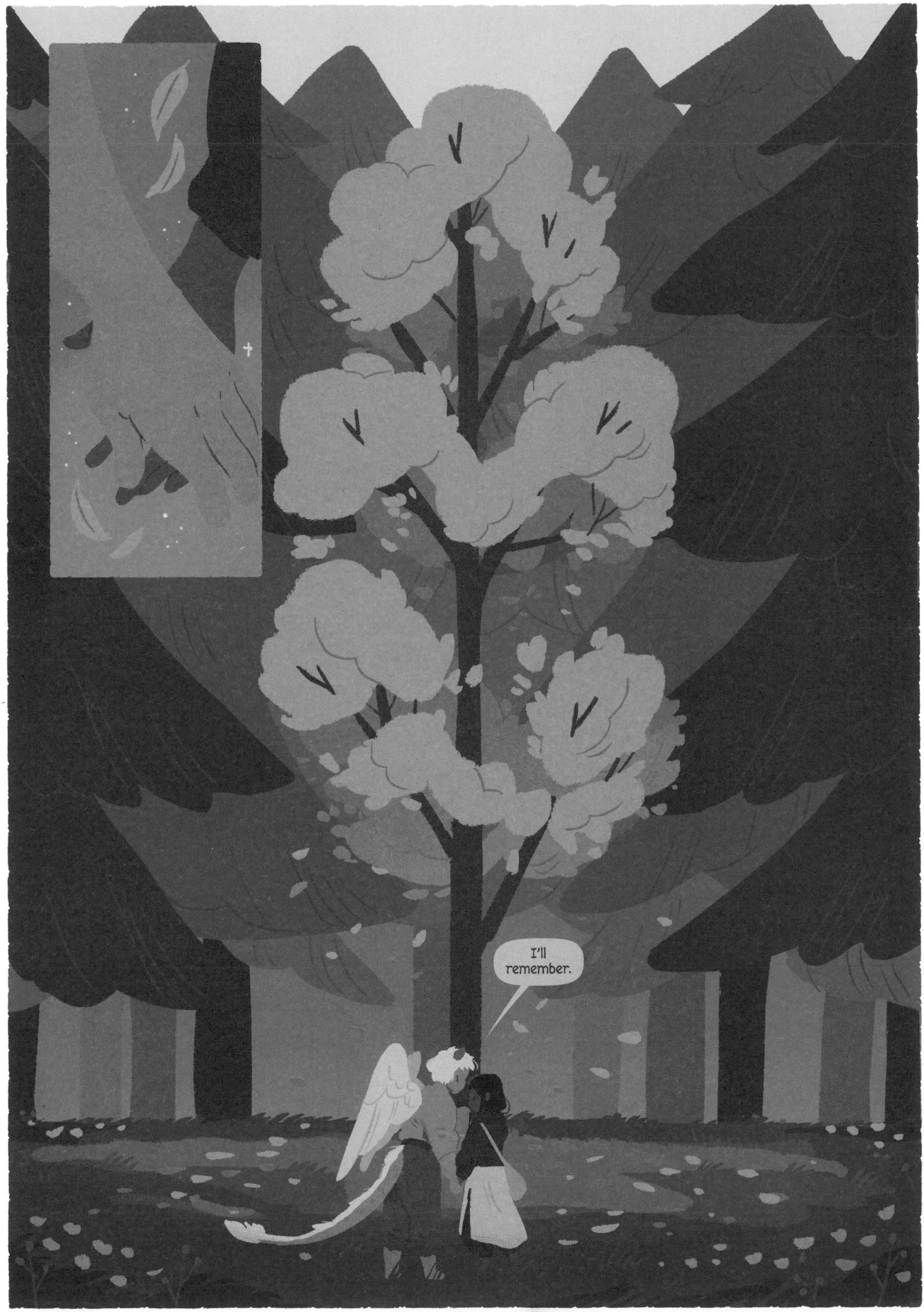
I'll remember.

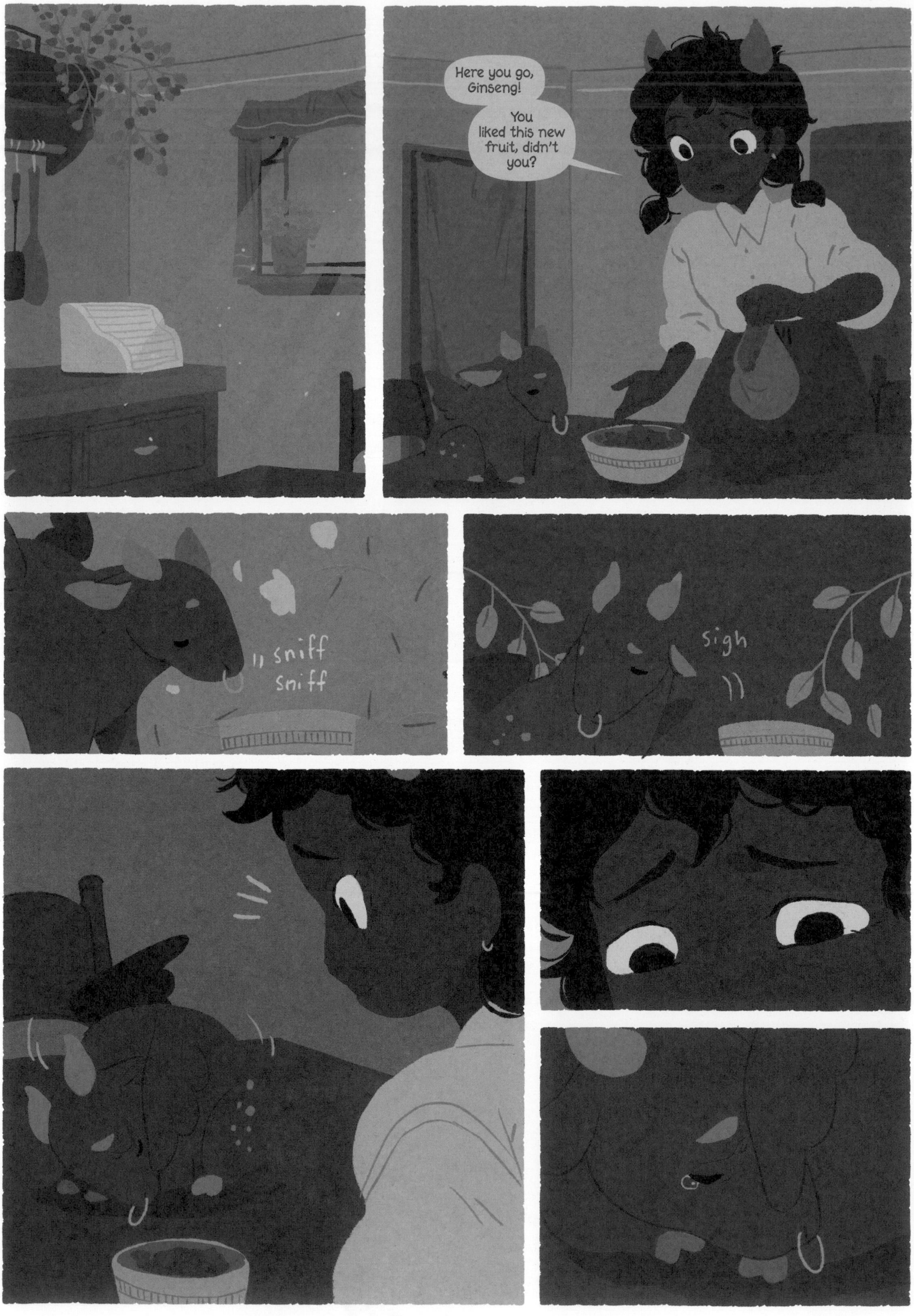

Here you go, Ginseng!
You liked this new fruit, didn't you?
sniff sniff
sigh

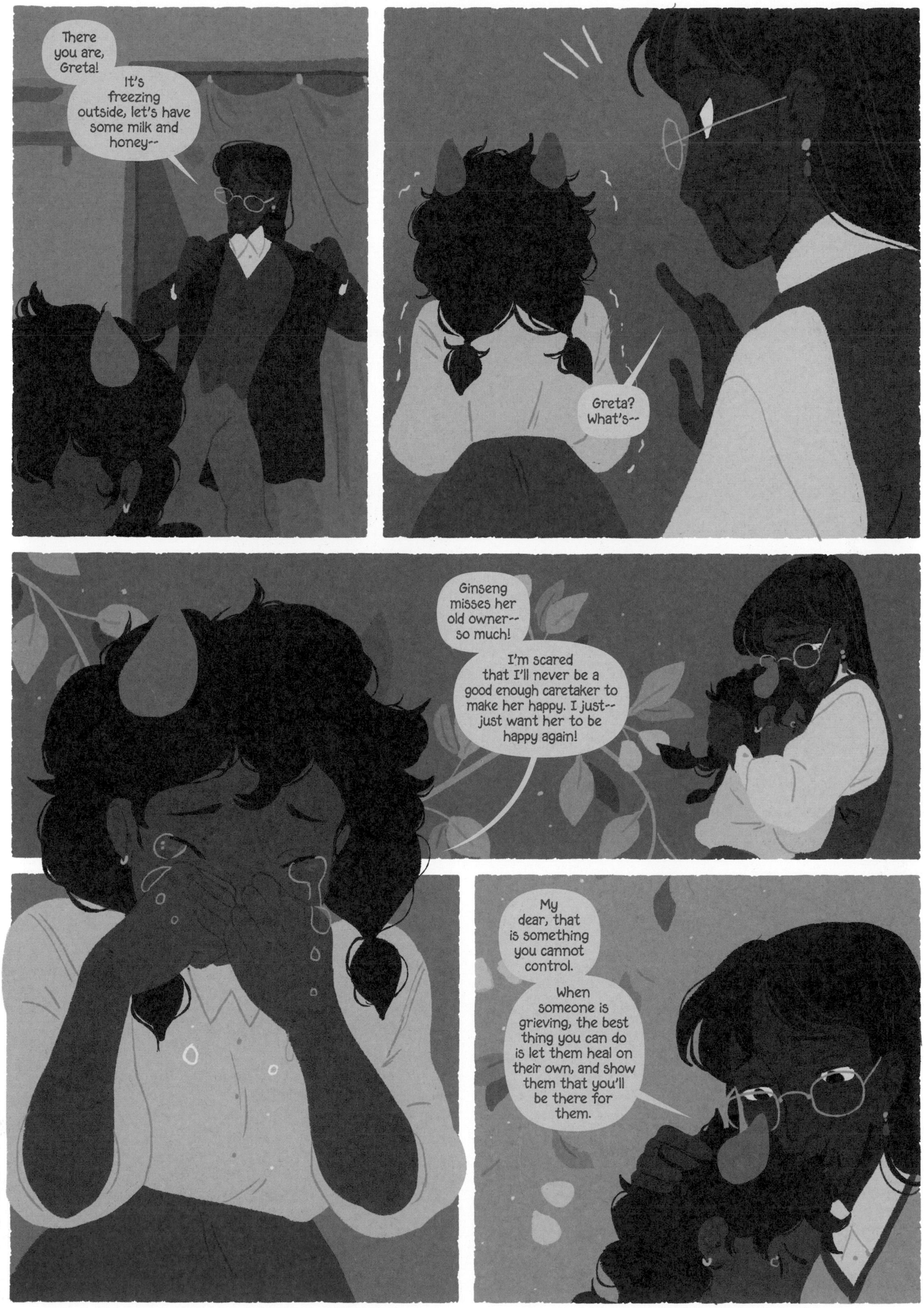
There you are, Greta!
It's freezing outside, let's have some milk and honey--
Greta? What's--
Ginseng misses her old owner-- so much!
I'm scared that I'll never be a good enough caretaker to make her happy. I just-- just want her to be happy again!
My dear, that is something you cannot control.
When someone is grieving, the best thing you can do is let them heal on their own, and show them that you'll be there for them.

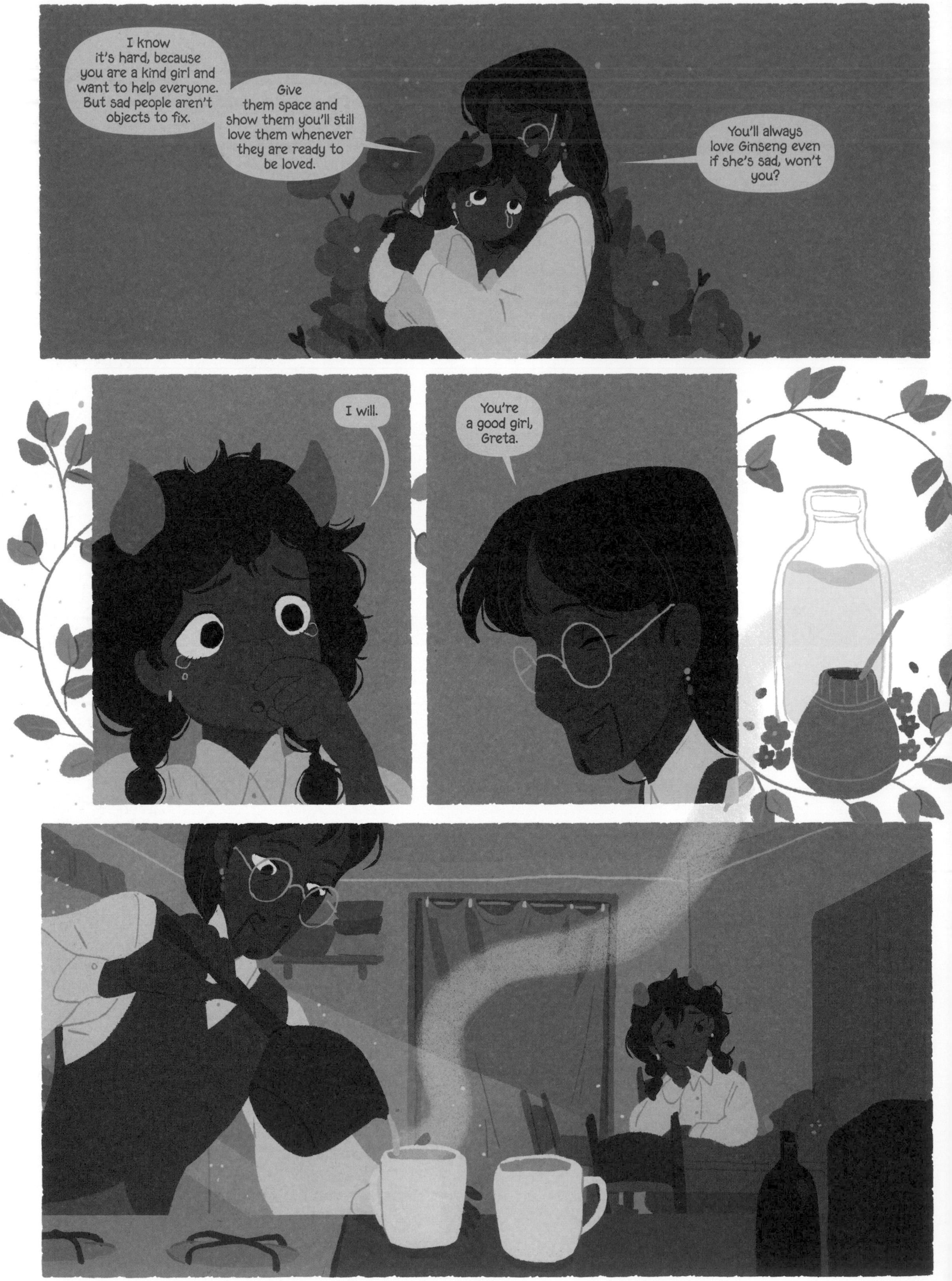
I know it's hard, because you are a kind girl and want to help everyone. But sad people aren't objects to fix.
Give them space and show them you'll still love them whenever they are ready to be loved.
You'll always love Ginseng even if she's sad, won't you?
I will.
You're a good girl, Greta.

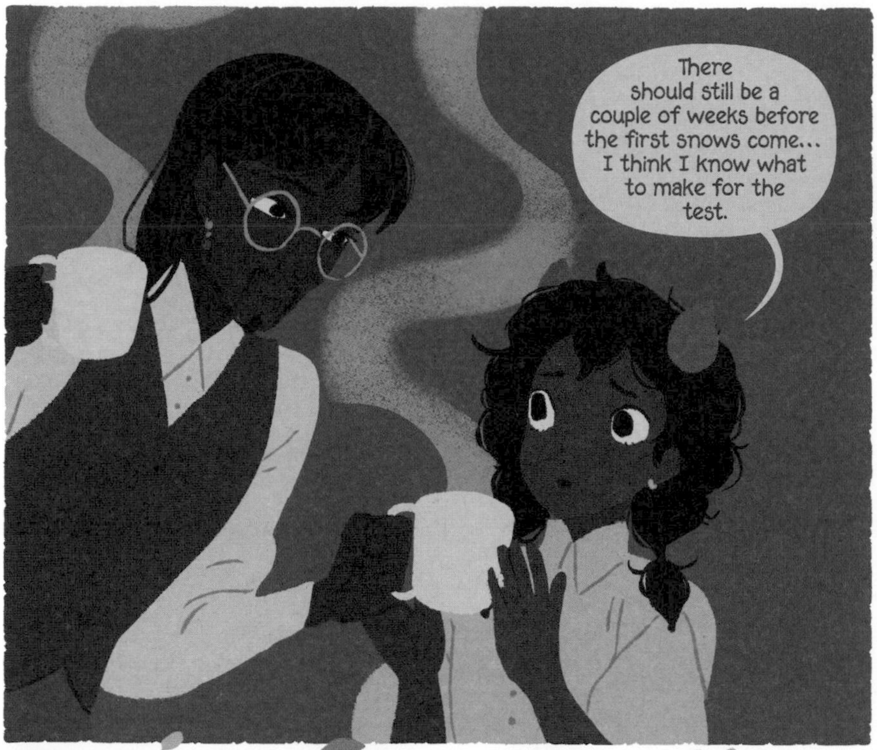
There should still be a couple of weeks before the first snows come... I think I know what to make for the test.
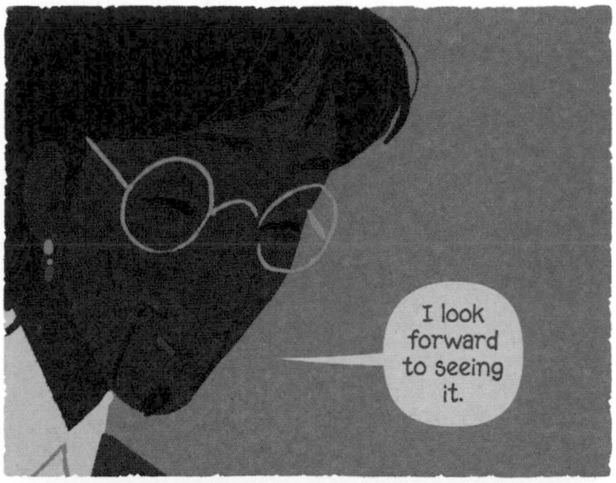
I look forward to seeing it.
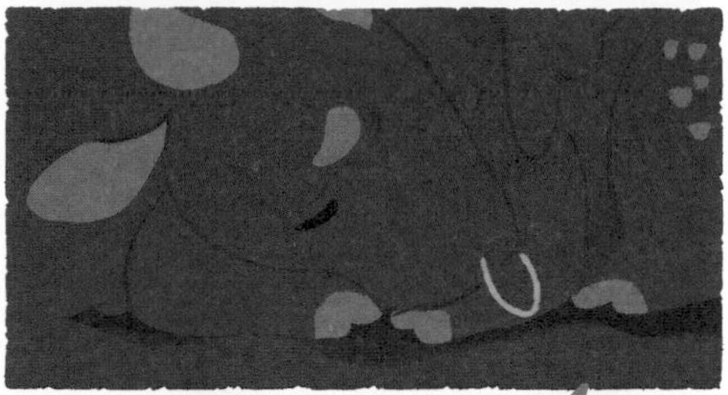
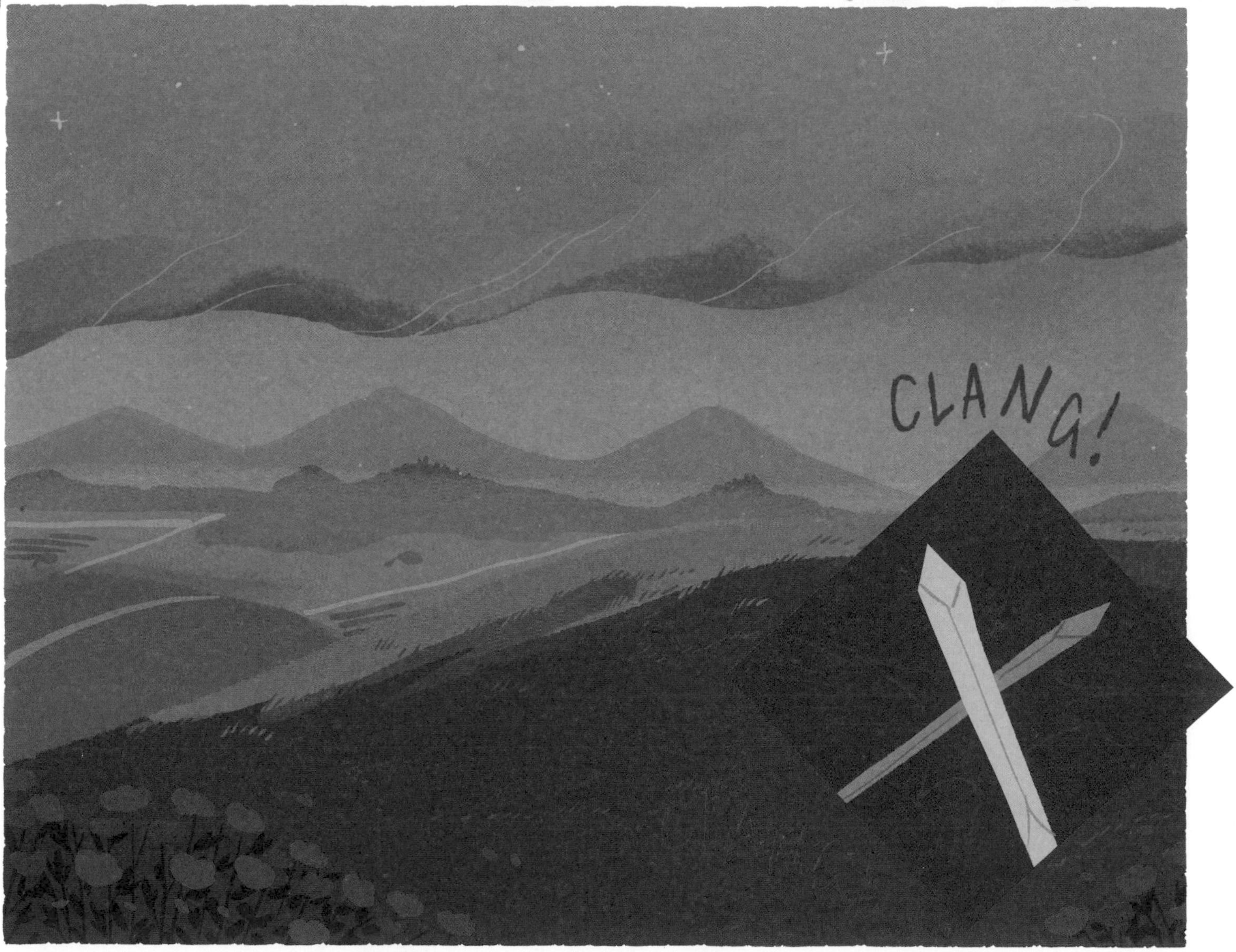
CLANG!

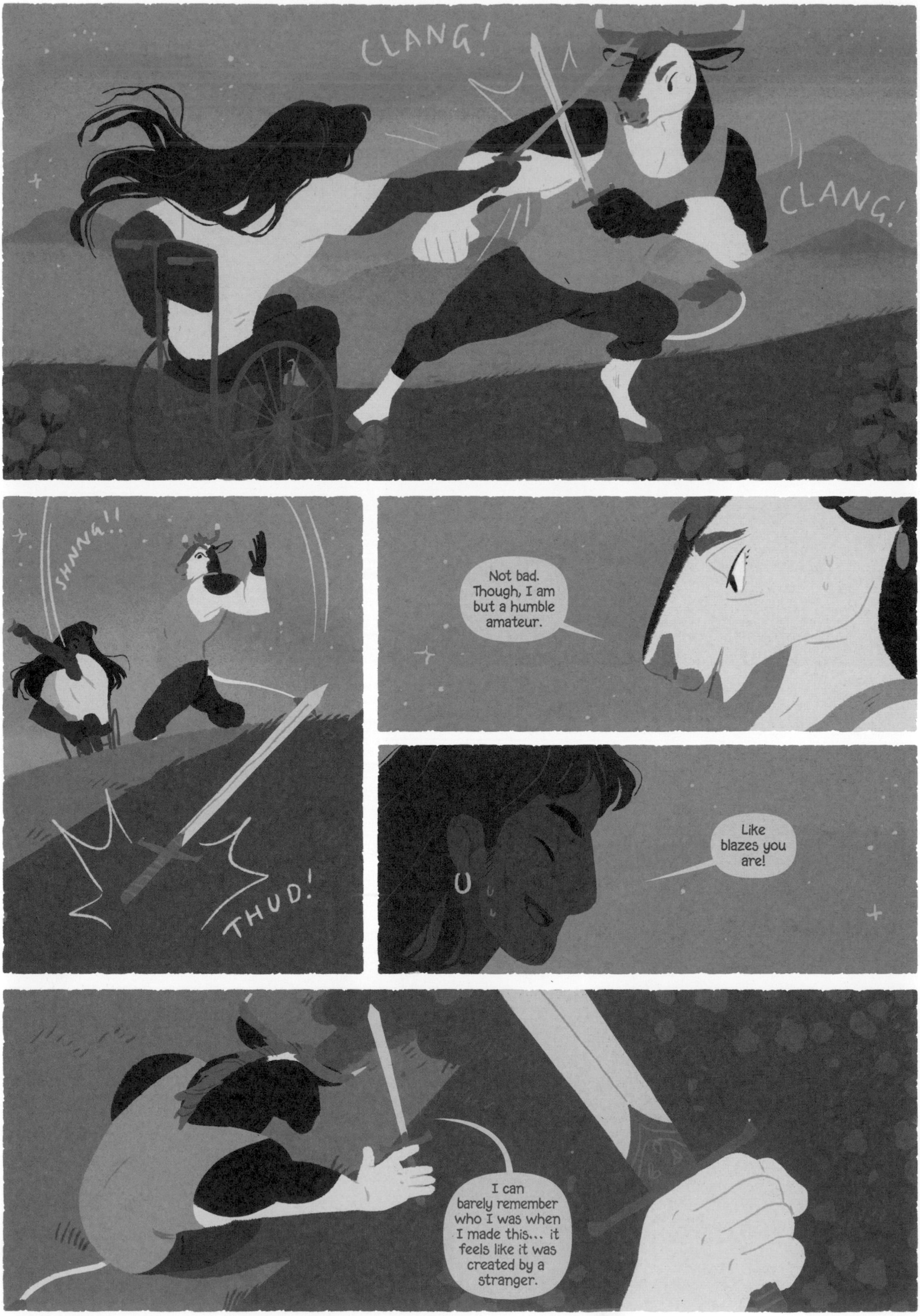
CLANG!
CLANG!
SHNNG!!
THUD!
Not bad. Though, I am but a humble amateur.
Like blazes you are!
I can barely remember who I was when I made this... it feels like it was created by a stranger.

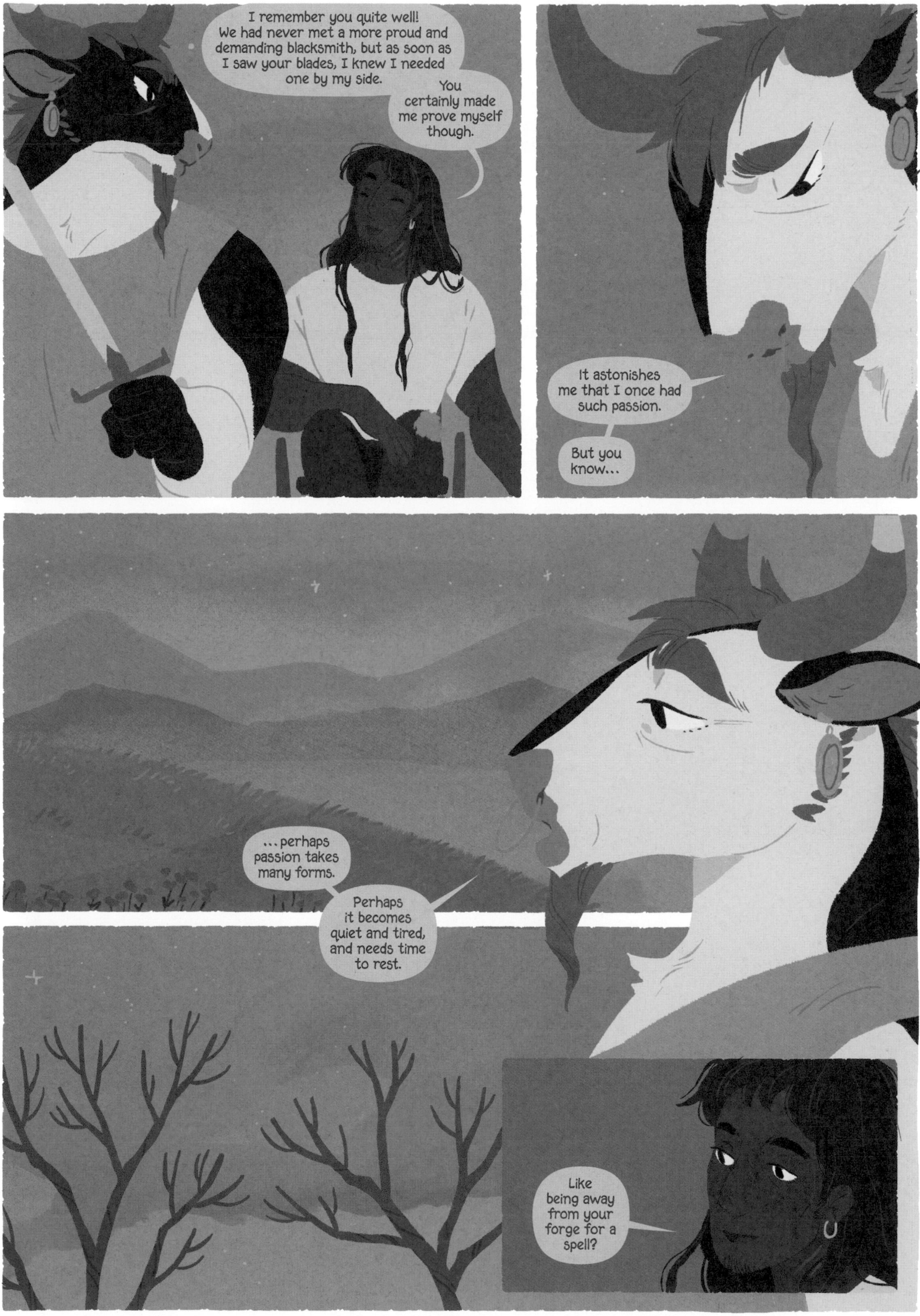
I remember you quite well! We had never met a more proud and demanding blacksmith, but as soon as I saw your blades, I knew I needed one by my side.
You certainly made me prove myself though.
It astonishes me that I once had such passion.
But you know...
...perhaps passion takes many forms.
Perhaps it becomes quiet and tired, and needs time to rest.
Like being away from your forge for a spell?

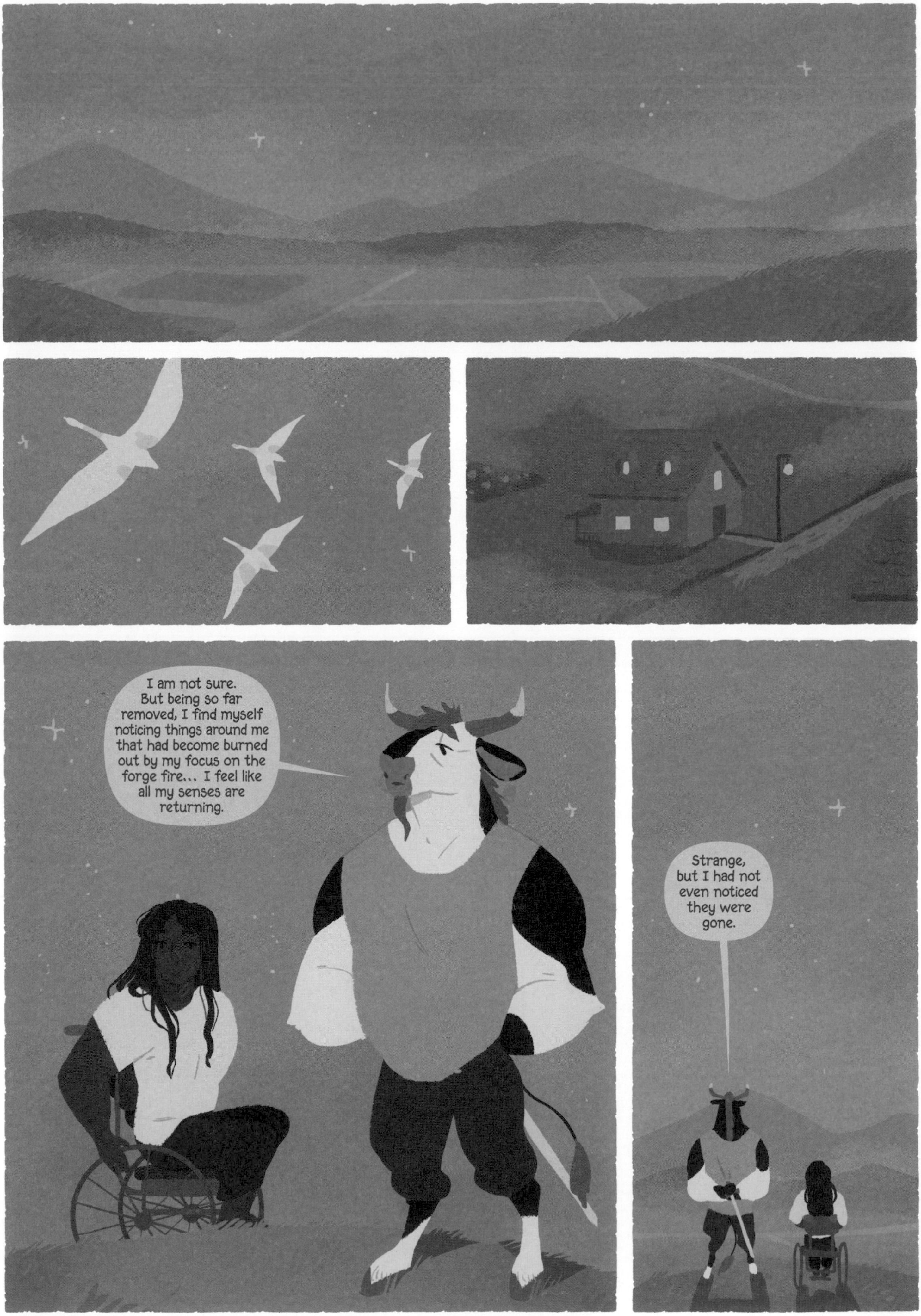
I am not sure. But being so far removed, I find myself noticing things around me that had become burned out by my focus on the forge fire... I feel like all my senses are returning.
Strange, but I had not even noticed they were gone.

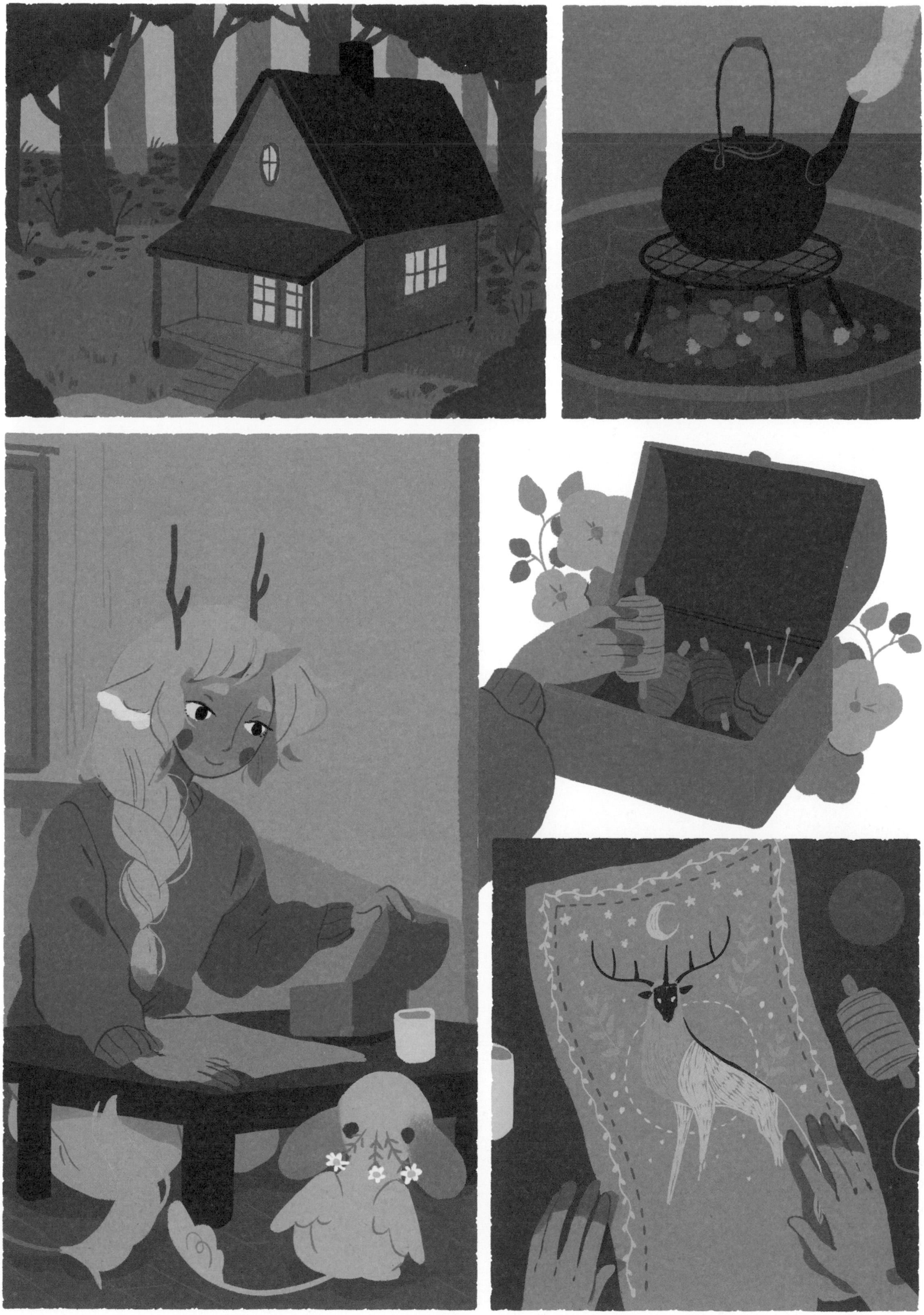

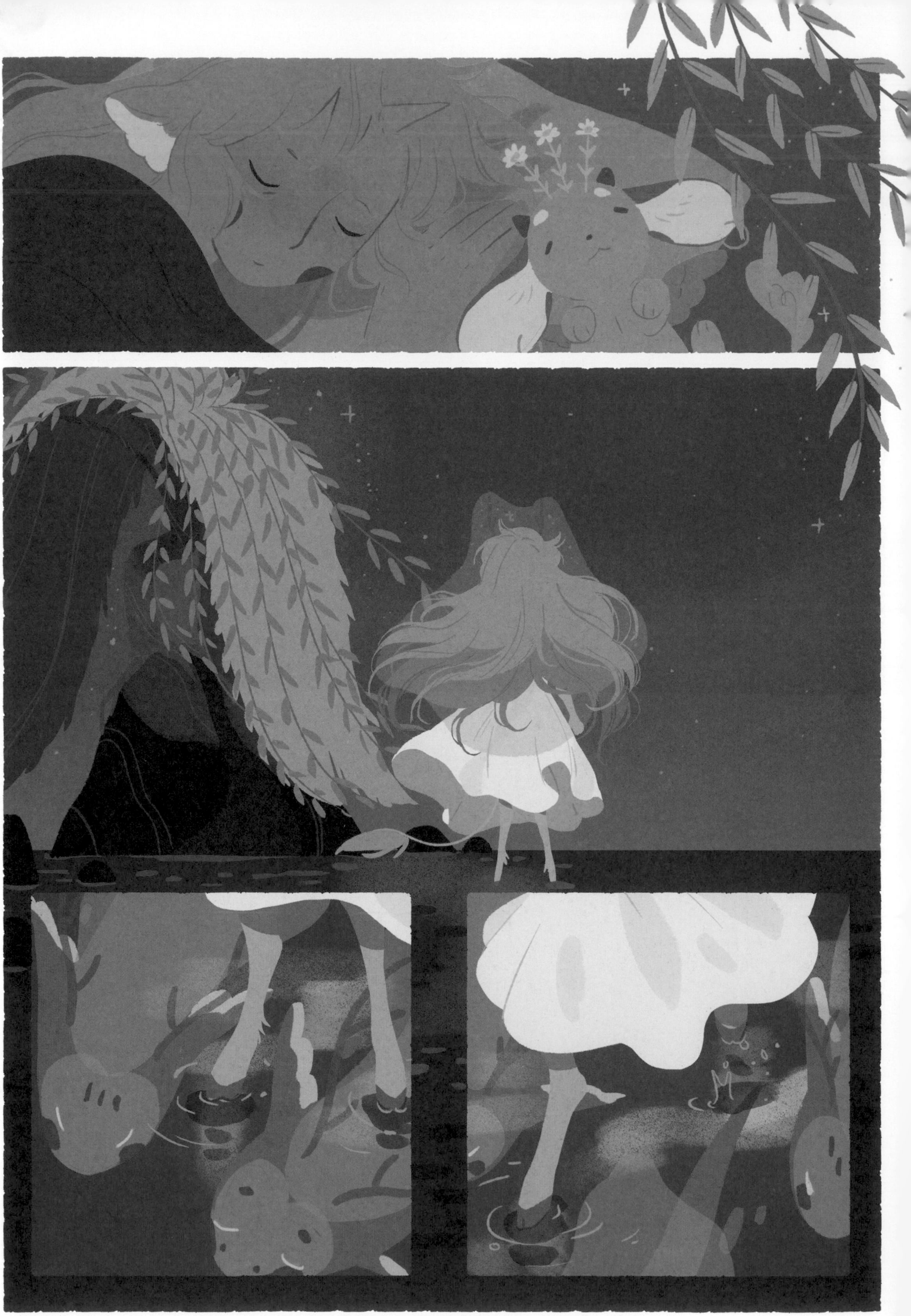

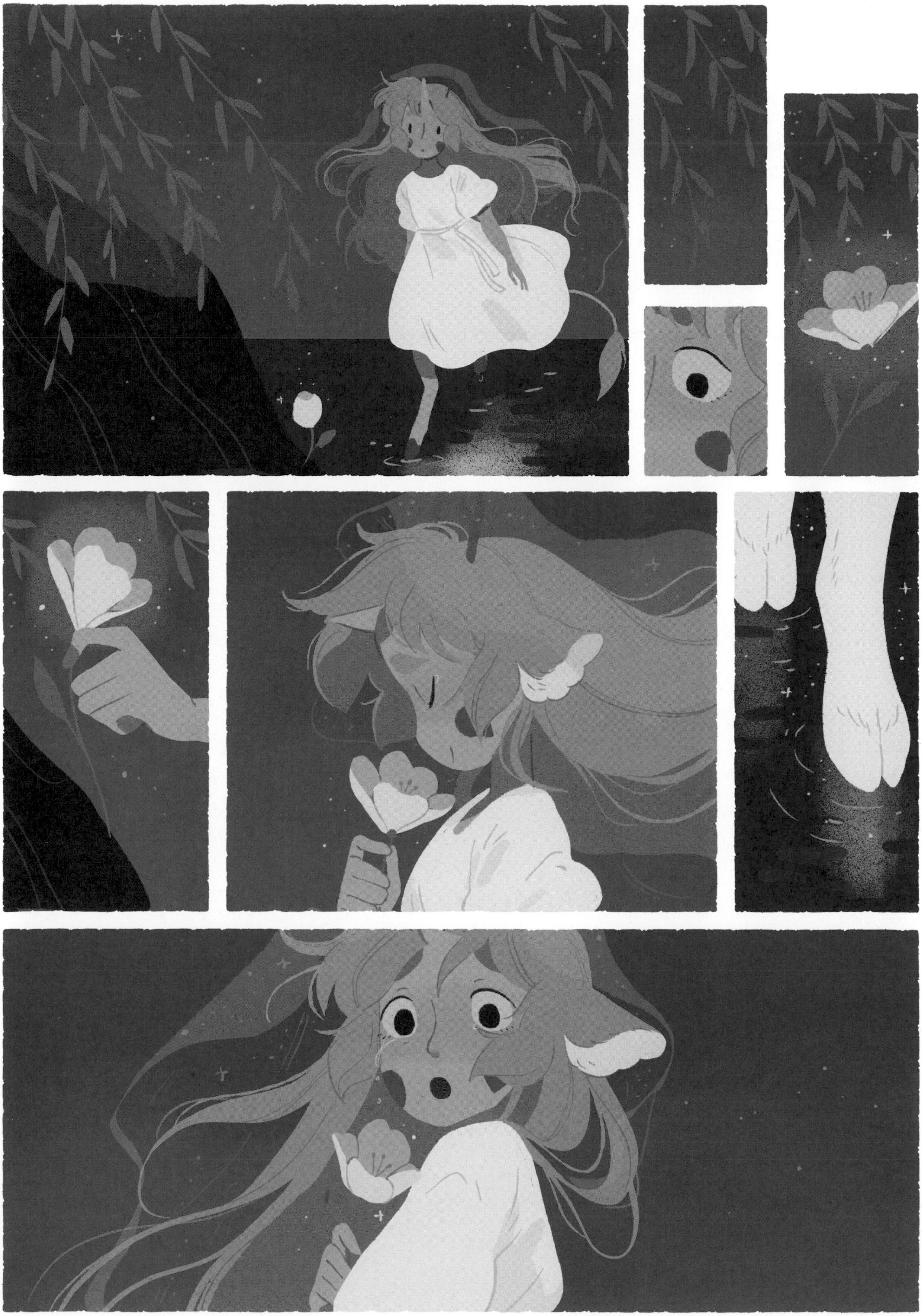

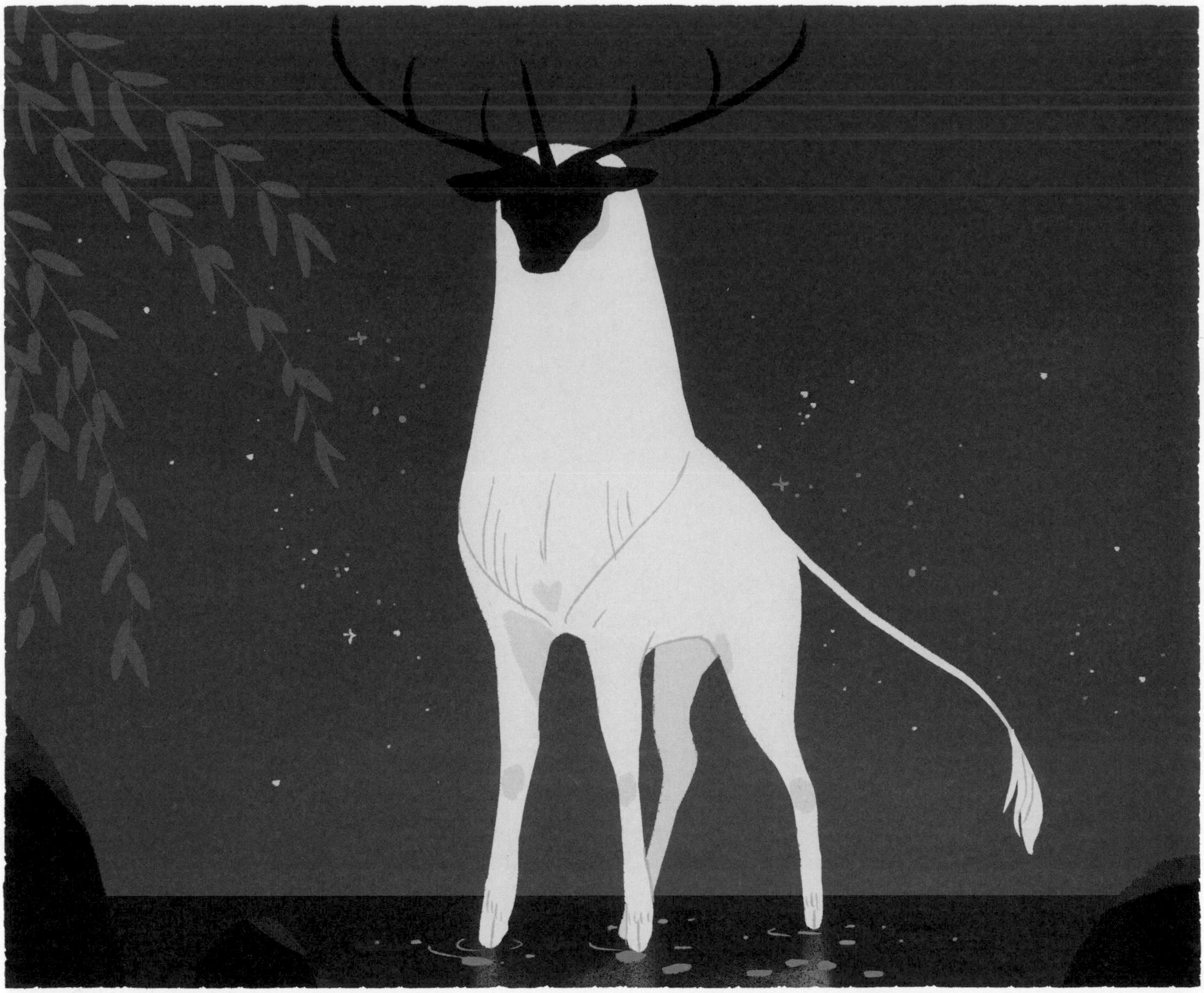

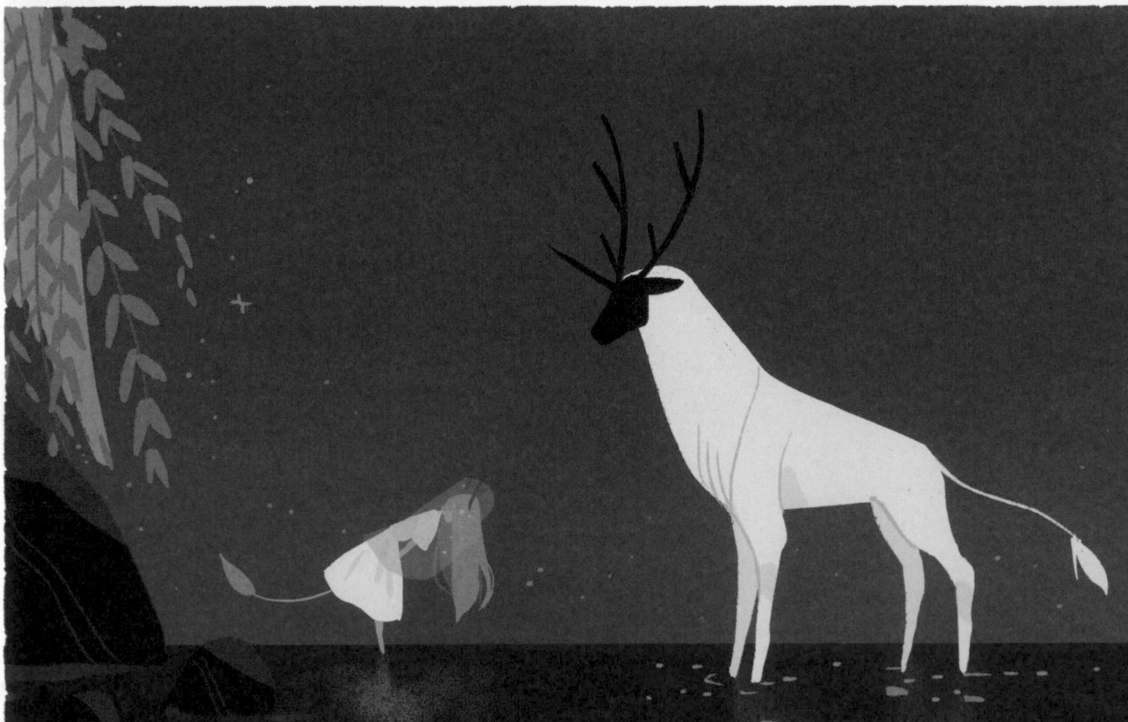

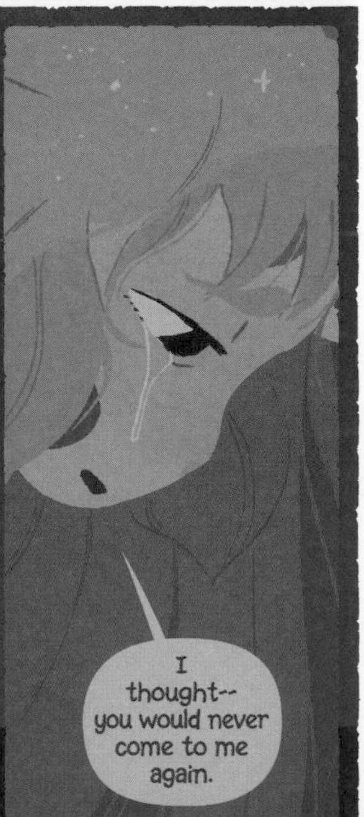
I thought-- you would never come to me again.

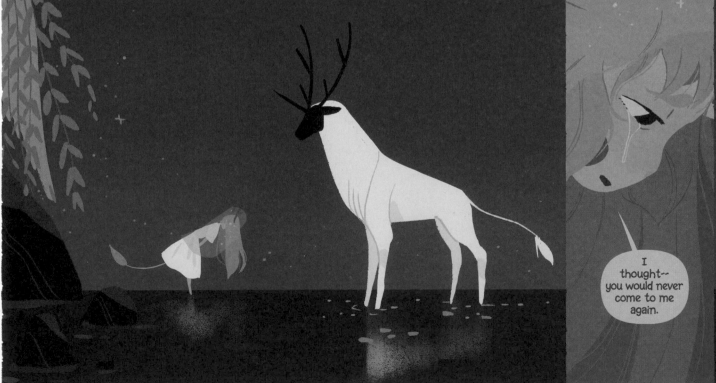

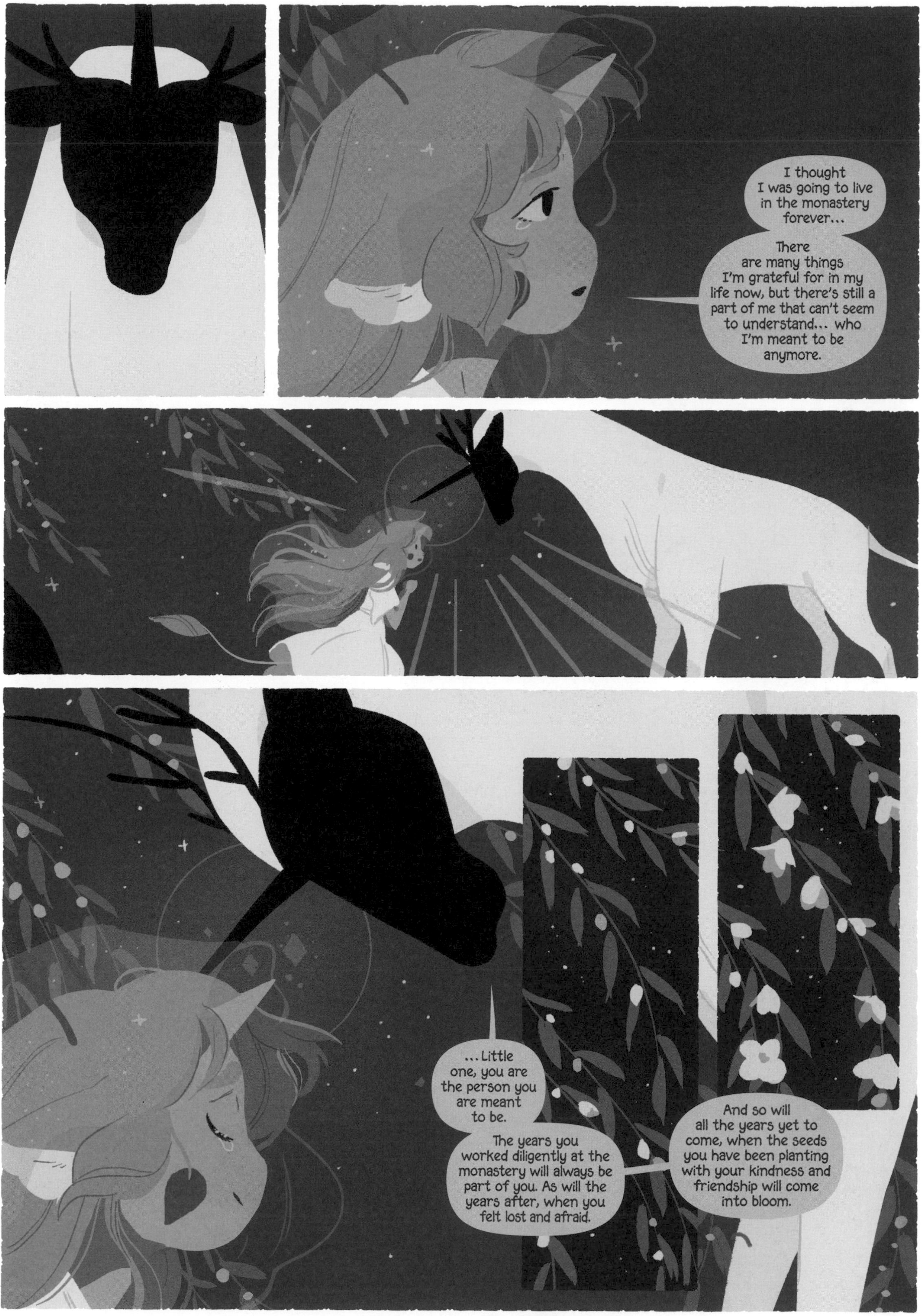
I thought I was going to live in the monastery forever...
There are many things I'm grateful for in my life now, but there's still a part of me that can't seem to understand... who I'm meant to be anymore.
...Little one, you are the person you are meant to be.
The years you worked diligently at the monastery will always be part of you. As will the years after, when you felt lost and afraid.
And so will all the years yet to come, when the seeds you have been planting with your kindness and friendship will come into bloom.

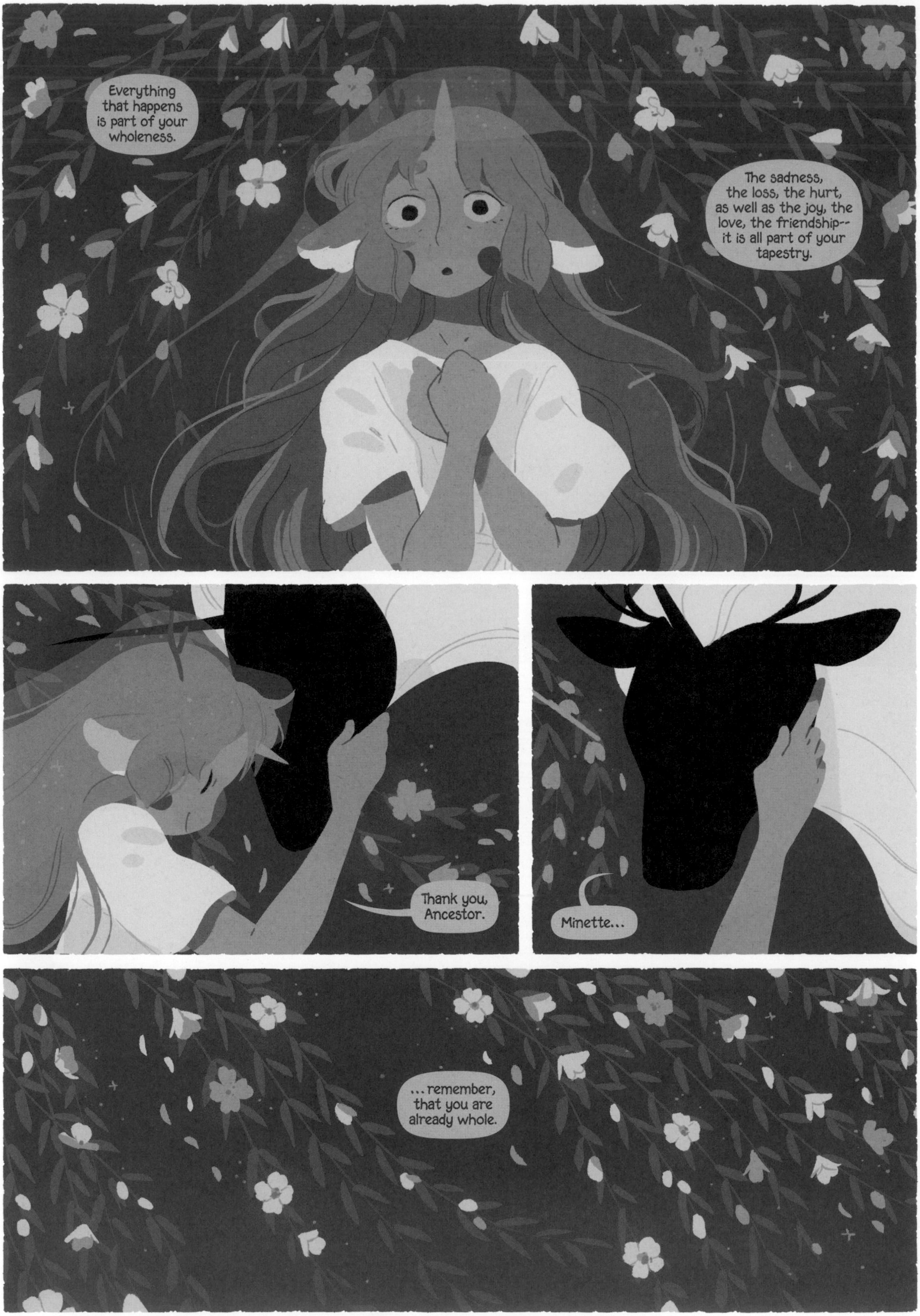
Everything that happens is part of your wholeness.
The sadness, the loss, the hurt, as well as the joy, the love, the friendship-- it is all part of your tapestry.
Thank you, Ancestor.
Minette...
...remember, that you are already whole.

Chapter Six

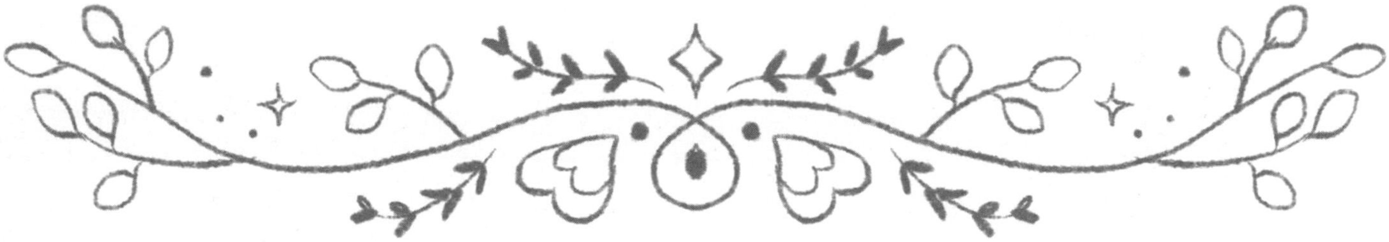

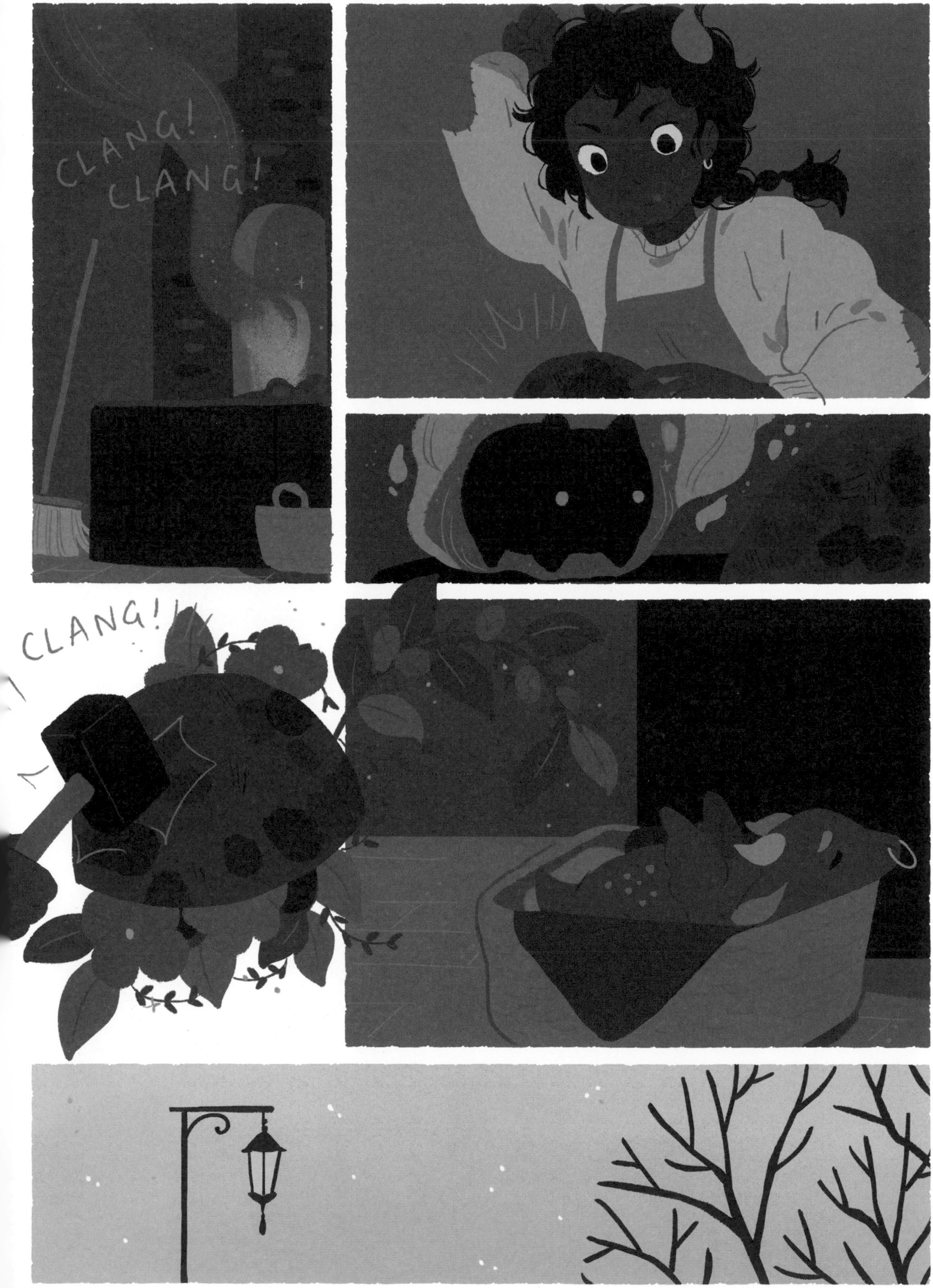
CLANG!
CLANG!
CLANG!

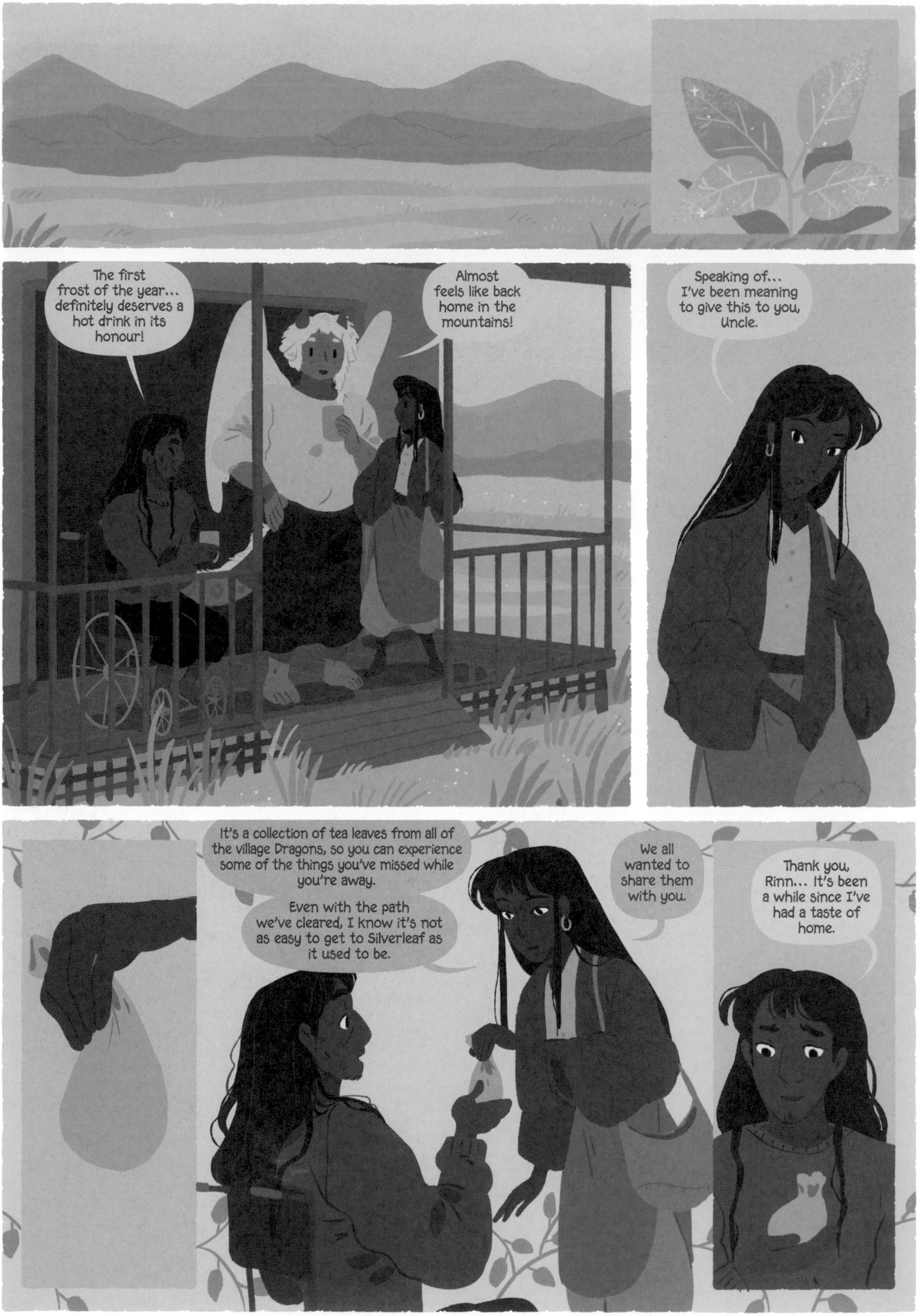
The first frost of the year... definitely deserves a hot drink in its honour!
Almost feels like back home in the mountains!
Speaking of... I've been meaning to give this to you, Uncle.
It's a collection of tea leaves from all of the village Dragons, so you can experience some of the things you've missed while you're away.
Even with the path we've cleared, I know it's not as easy to get to Silverleaf as it used to be.
We all wanted to share them with you.
Thank you, Rinn... It's been a while since I've had a taste of home.

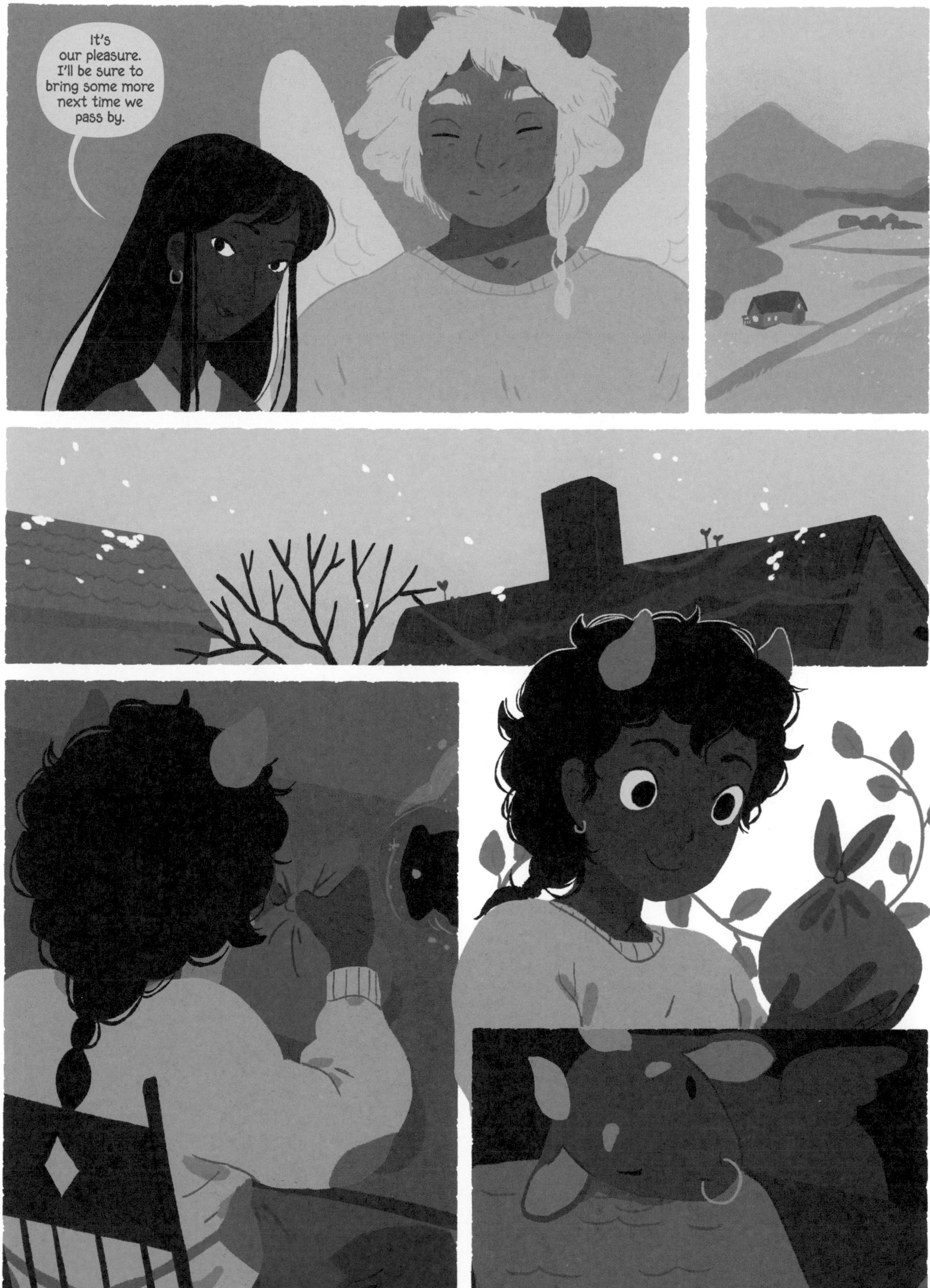
It's our pleasure. I'll be sure to bring some more next time we pass by.

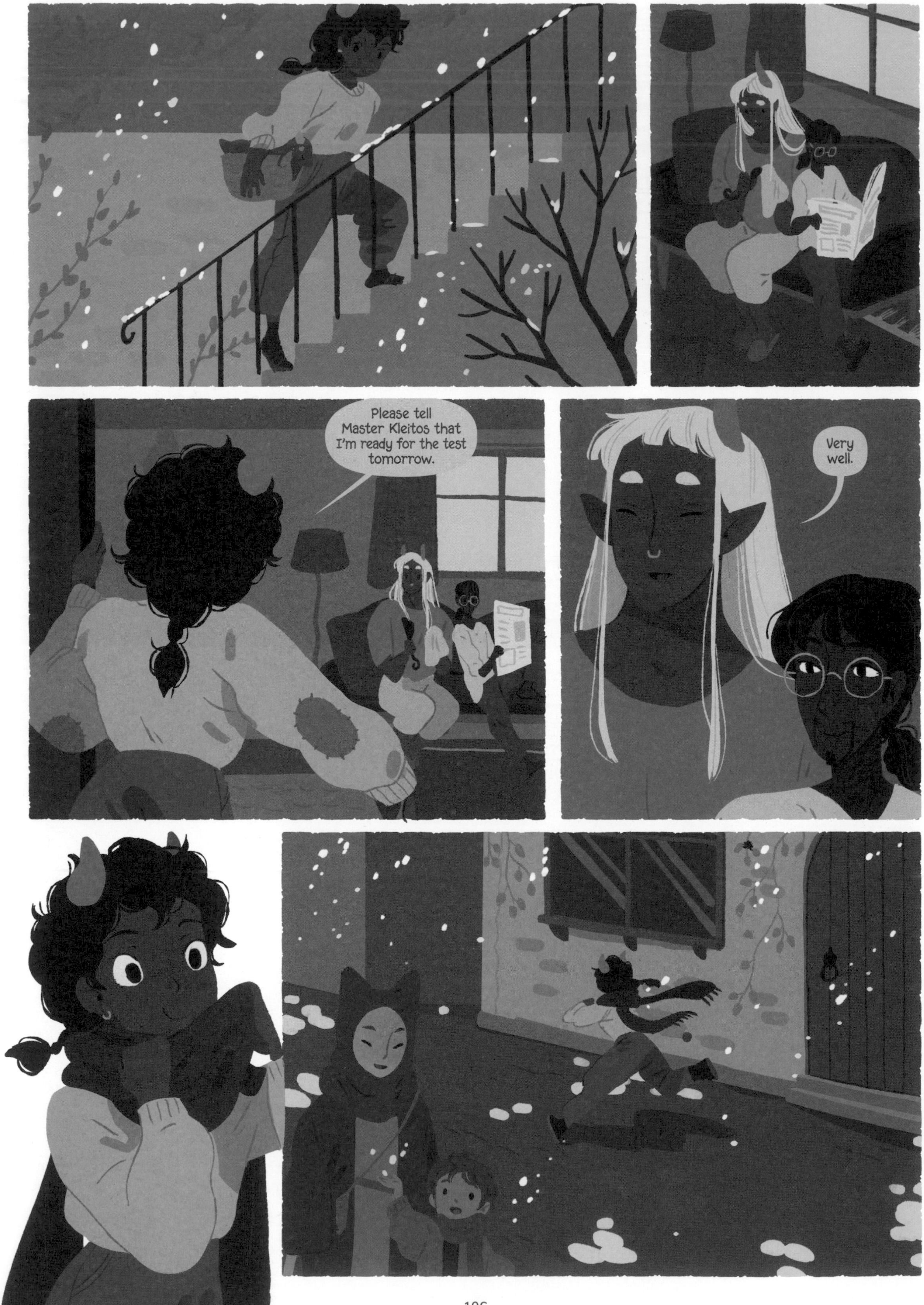
Please tell Master Kleitos that I'm ready for the test tomorrow.
Very well.

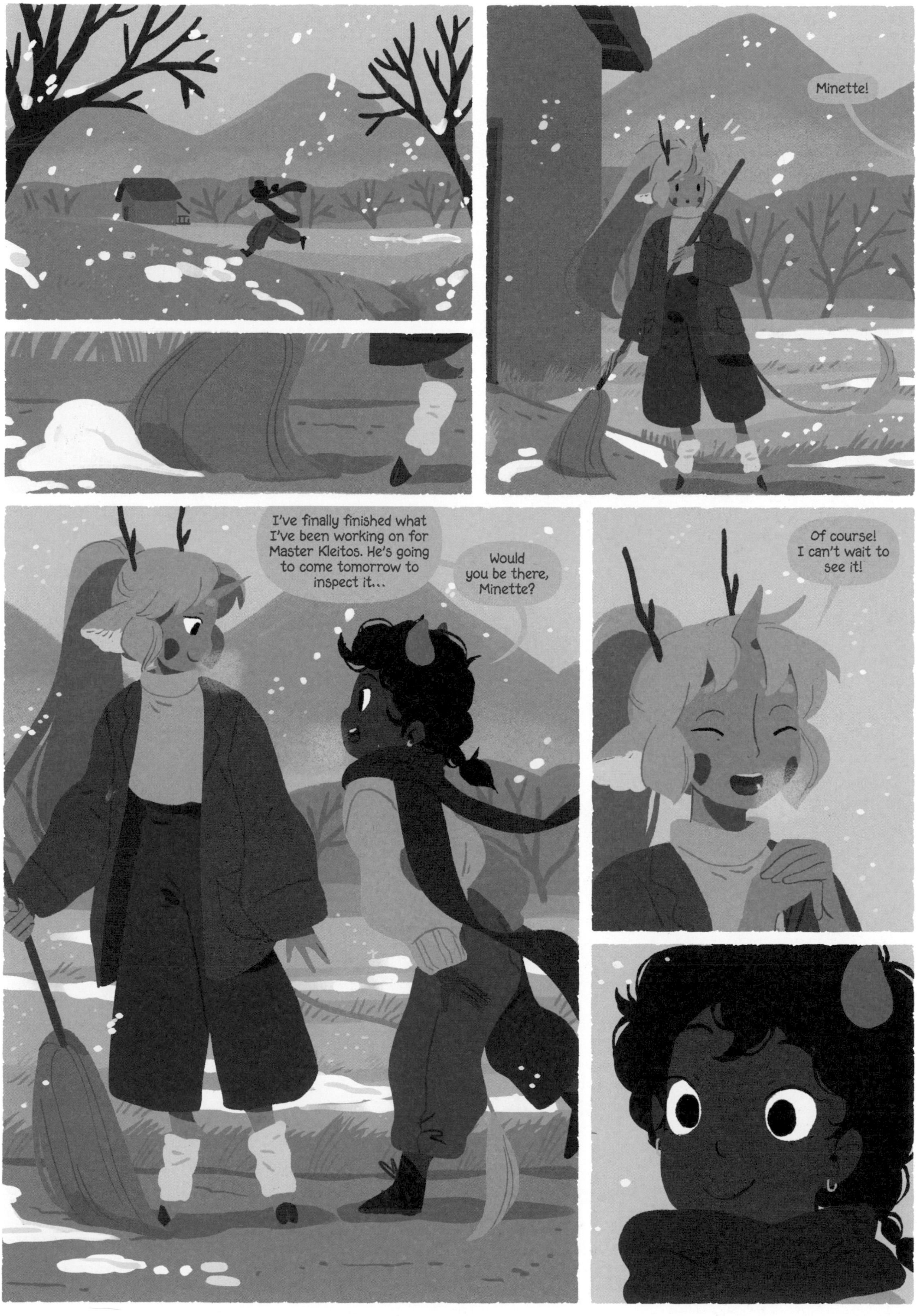
Minette!
I've finally finished what I've been working on for Master Kleitos. He's going to come tomorrow to inspect it...
Would you be there, Minette?
Of course! I can't wait to see it!

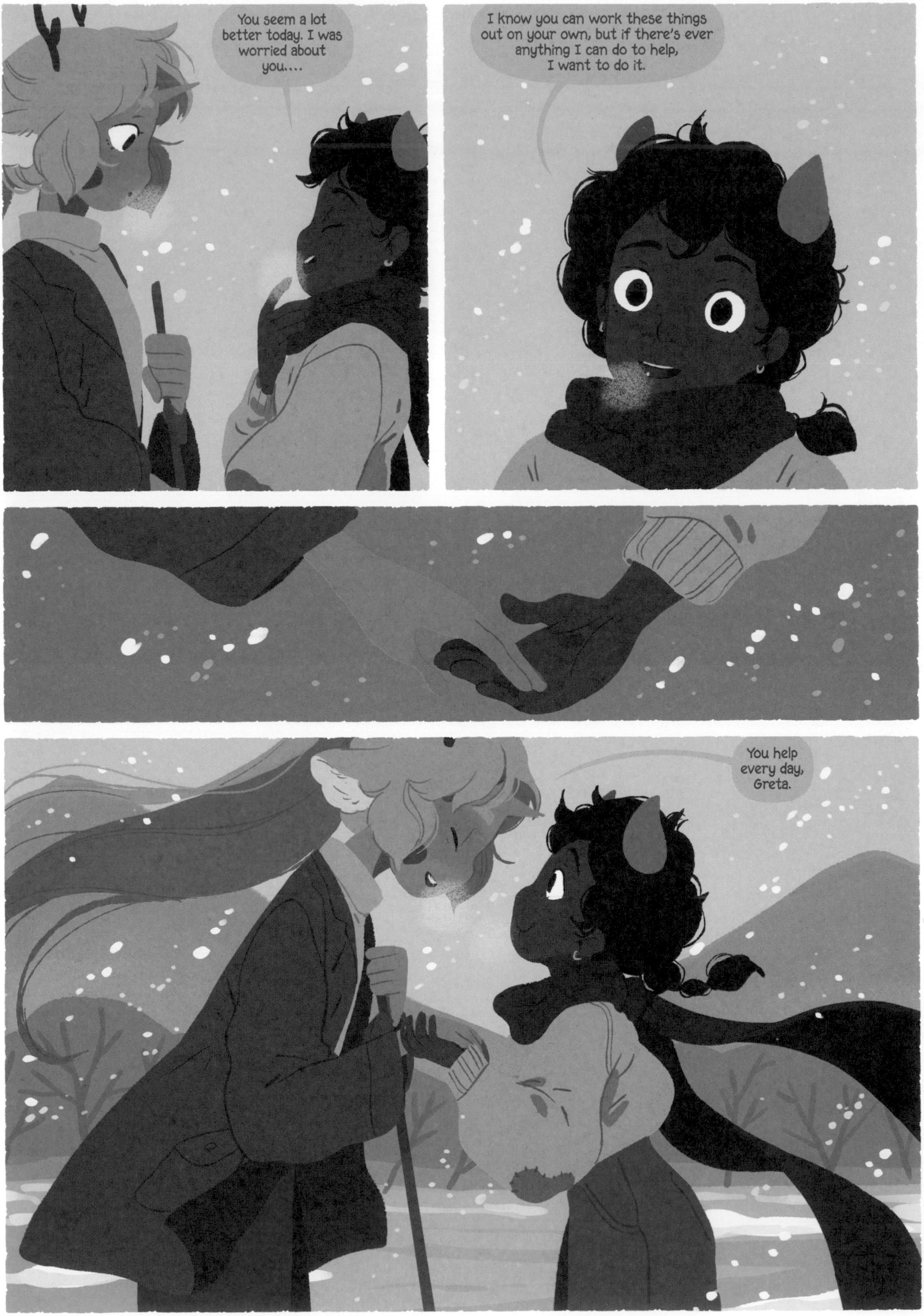
You seem a lot better today. I was worried about you....
I know you can work these things out on your own, but if there's ever anything I can do to help, I want to do it.
You help every day, Greta.

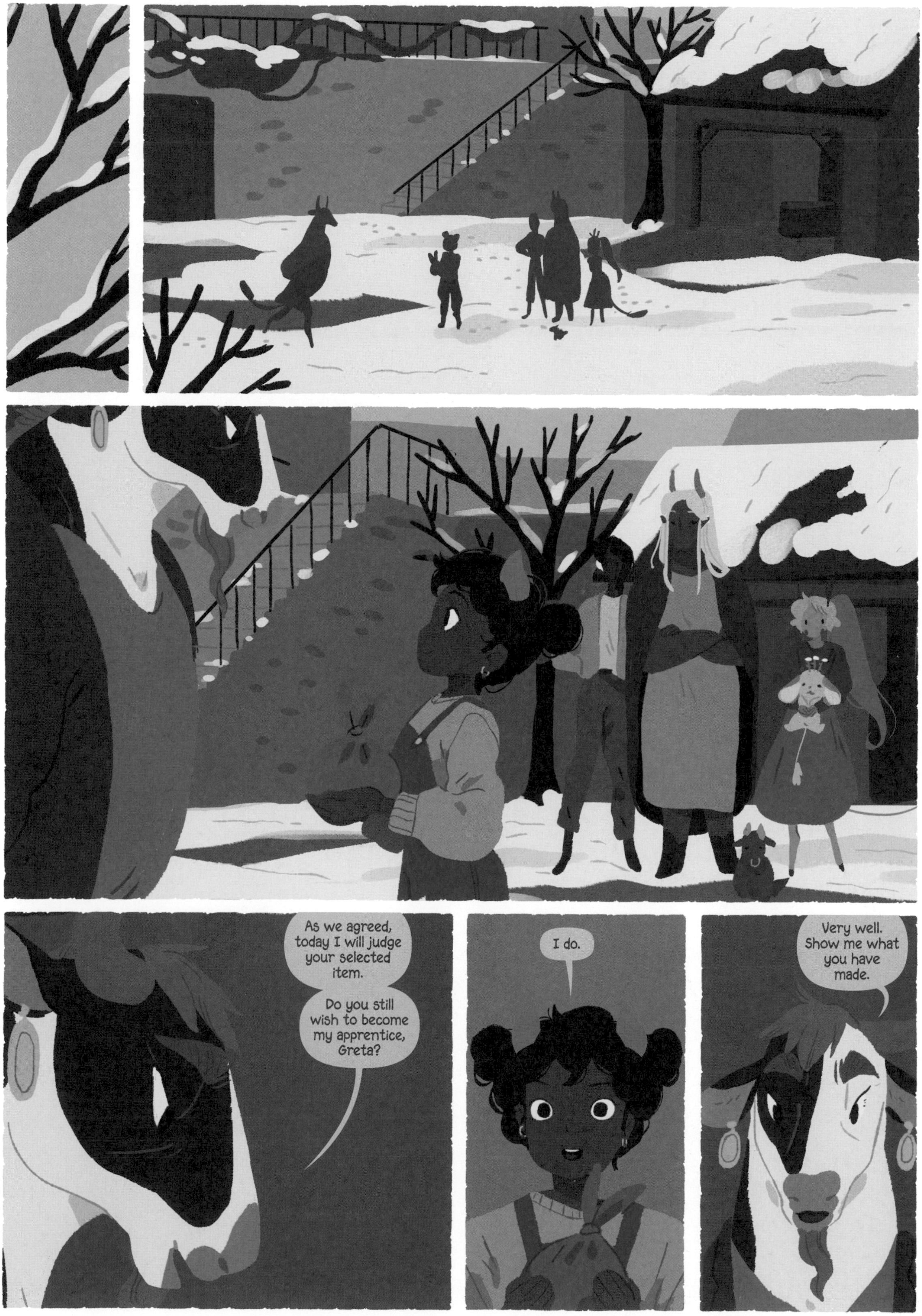
As we agreed, today I will judge your selected item.
Do you still wish to become my apprentice, Greta?
I do.
Very well. Show me what you have made.

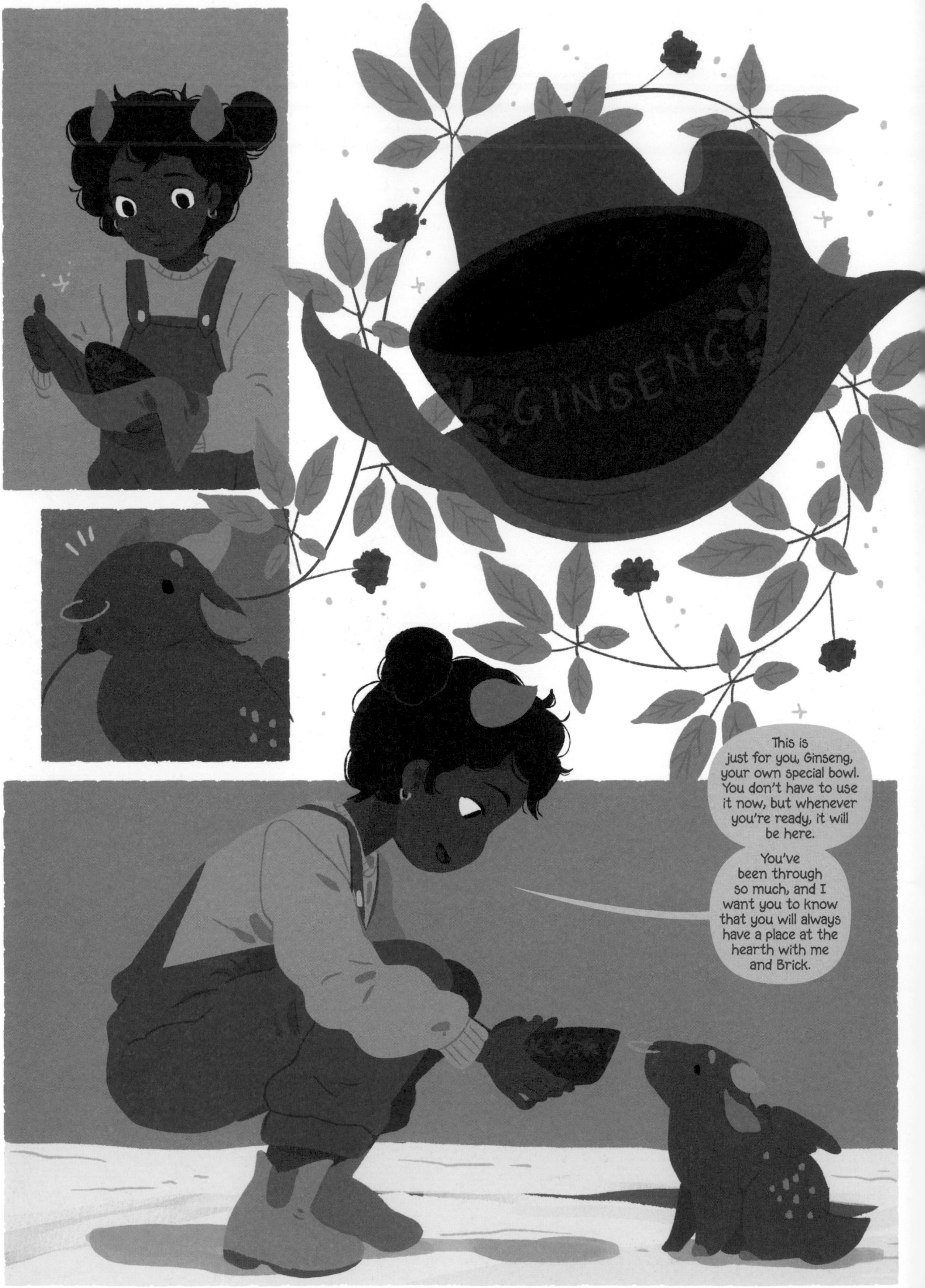
GINSENG
This is just for you, Ginseng, your own special bowl. You don't have to use it now, but whenever you're ready, it will be here.
You've been through so much, and I want you to know that you will always have a place at the hearth with me and Brick.

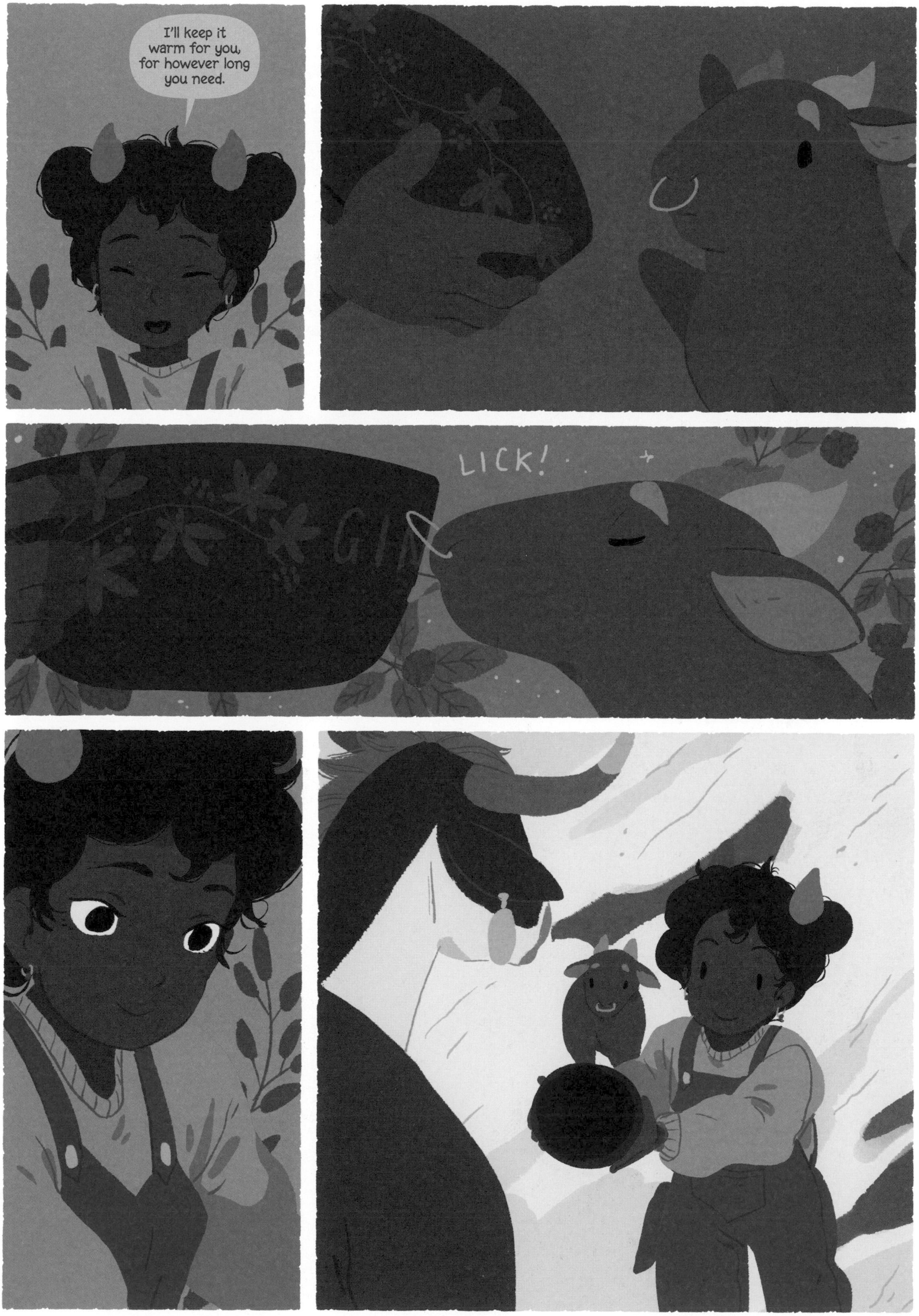
I'll keep it warm for you, for however long you need.
LICK!

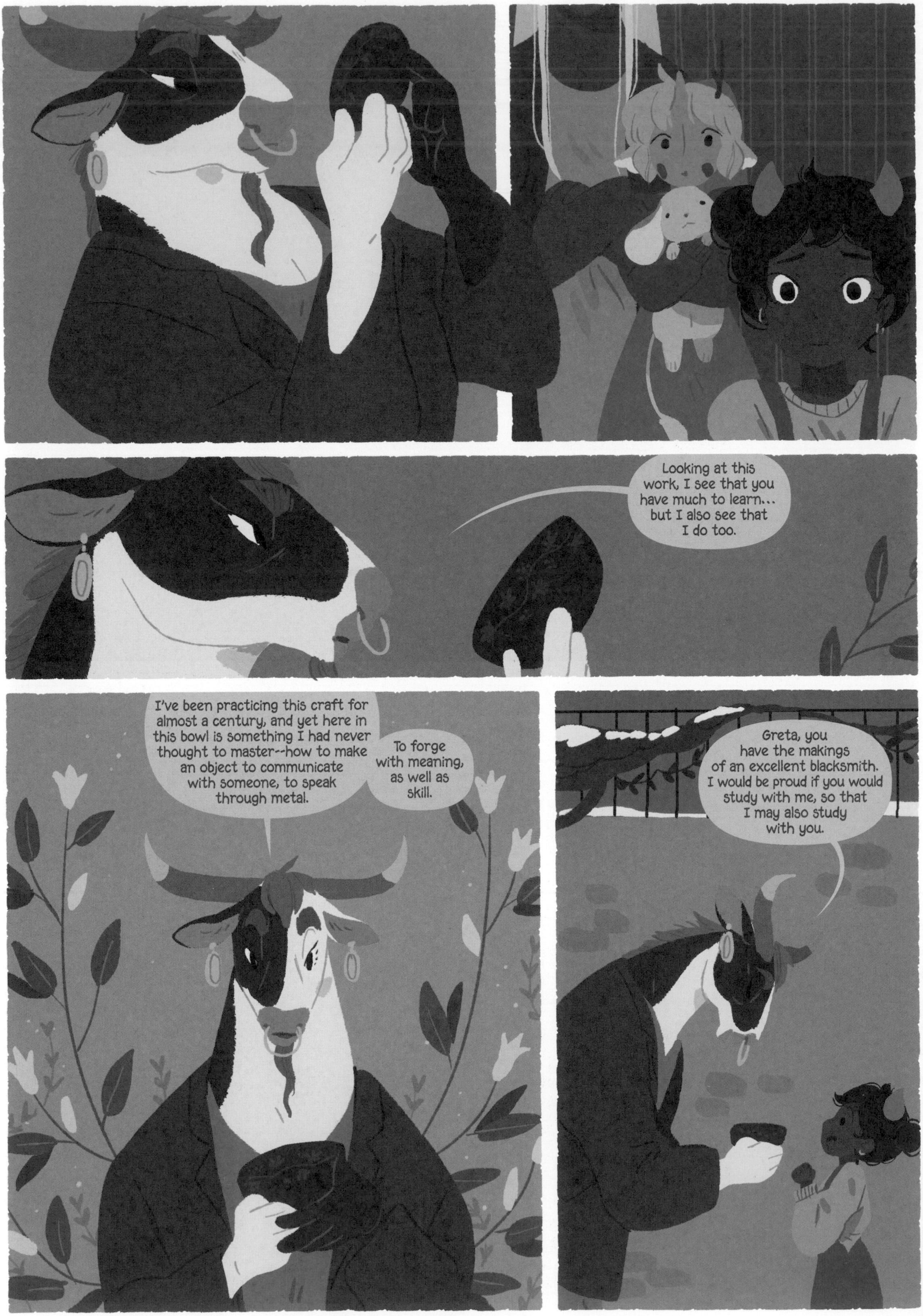
Looking at this work, I see that you have much to learn... but I also see that I do too.
I've been practicing this craft for almost a century, and yet here in this bowl is something I had never thought to master--how to make an object to communicate with someone, to speak through metal.
To forge with meaning, as well as skill.
Greta, you have the makings of an excellent blacksmith. I would be proud if you would study with me, so that I may also study with you.

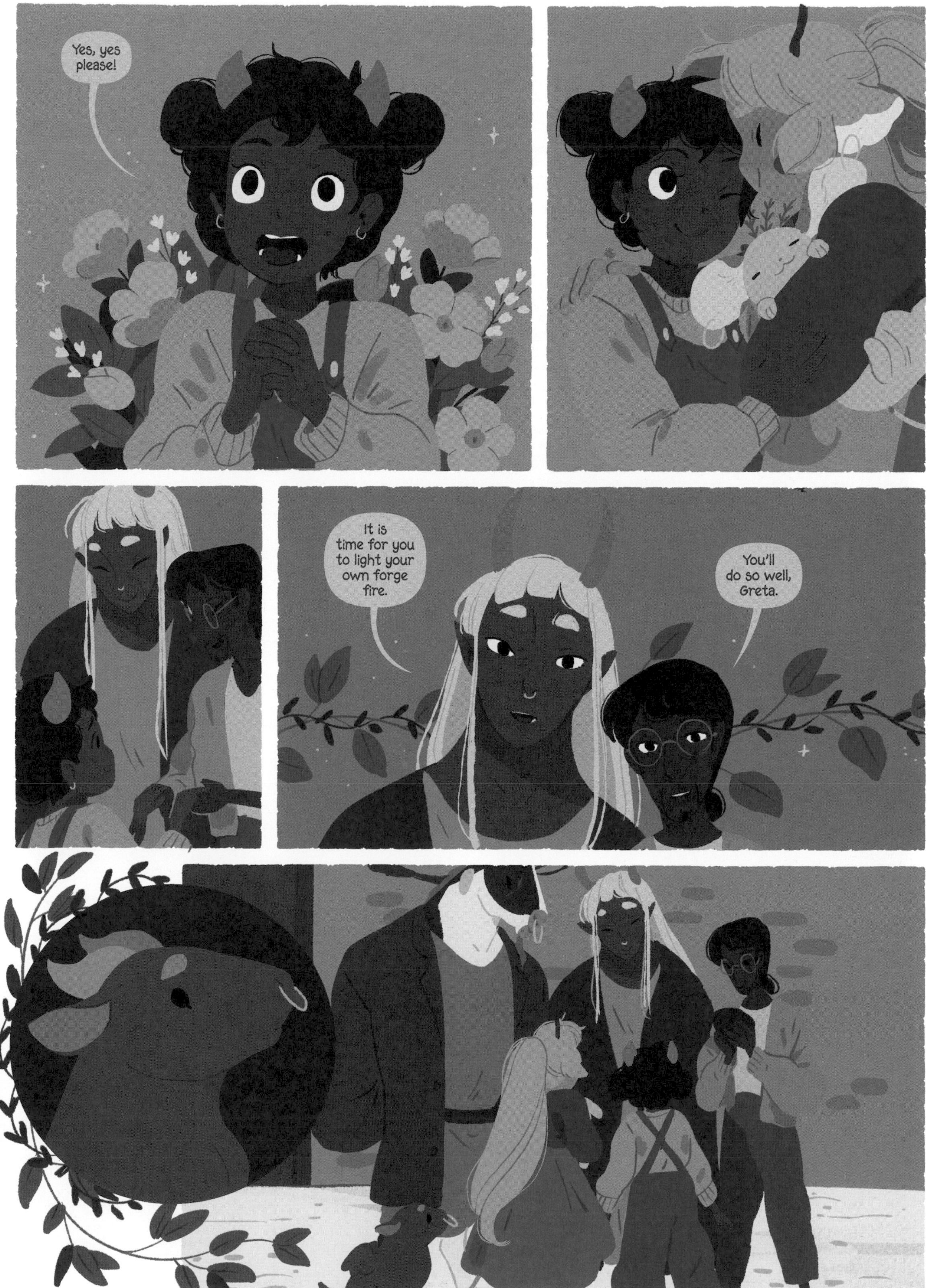
Yes, yes please!
It is time for you to light your own forge fire.
You'll do so well, Greta.

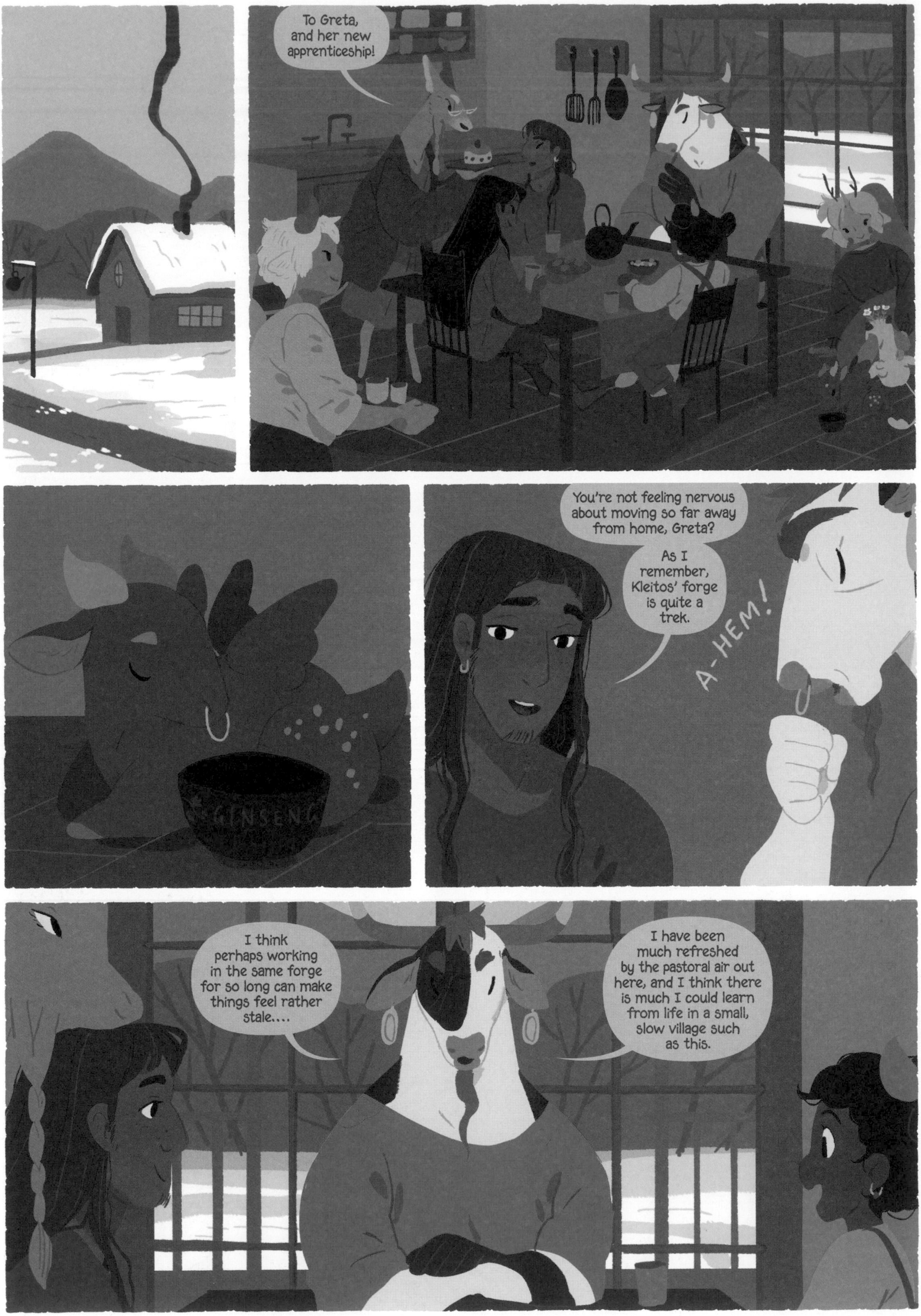
To Greta, and her new apprenticeship!
GINSENG
You're not feeling nervous about moving so far away from home, Greta?
As I remember, Kleitos' forge is quite a trek.
A-HEM!
I think perhaps working in the same forge for so long can make things feel rather stale....
I have been much refreshed by the pastoral air out here, and I think there is much I could learn from life in a small, slow village such as this.

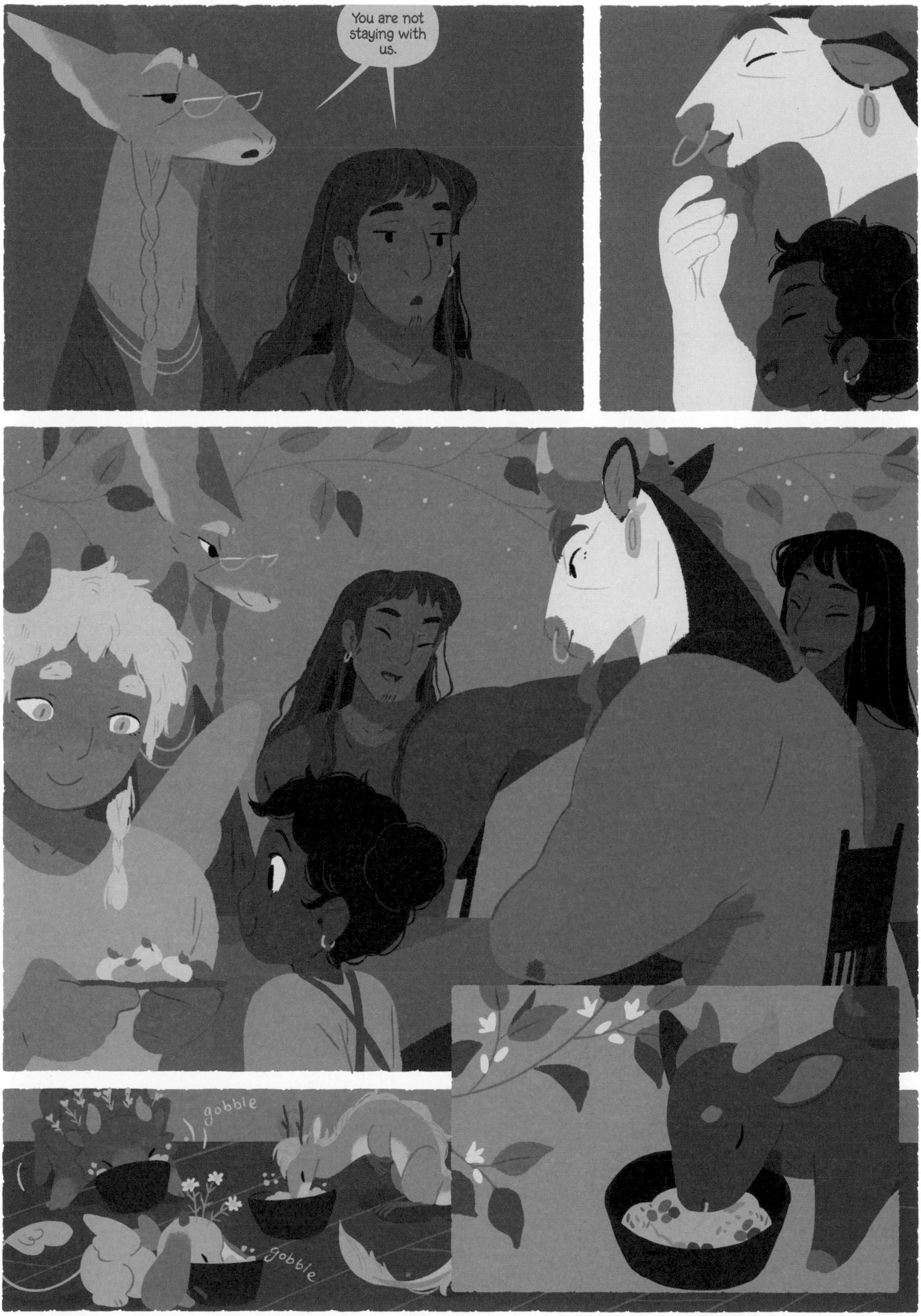
You are not staying with us.
gobble
gobble

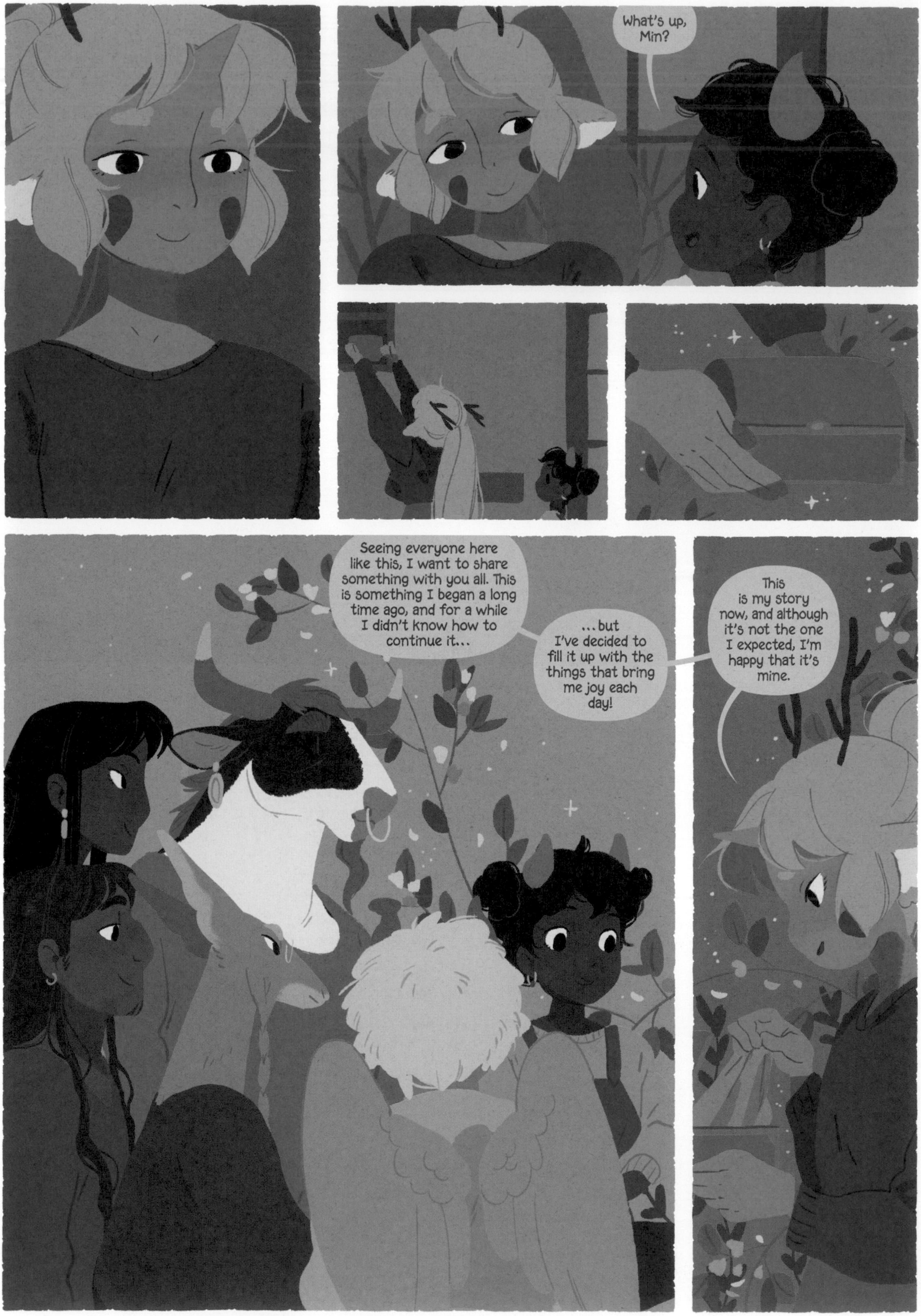
What's up, Min?
Seeing everyone here like this, I want to share something with you all. This is something I began a long time ago, and for a while I didn't know how to continue it...
...but I've decided to fill it up with the things that bring me joy each day!
This is my story now, and although it's not the one I expected, I'm happy that it's mine.

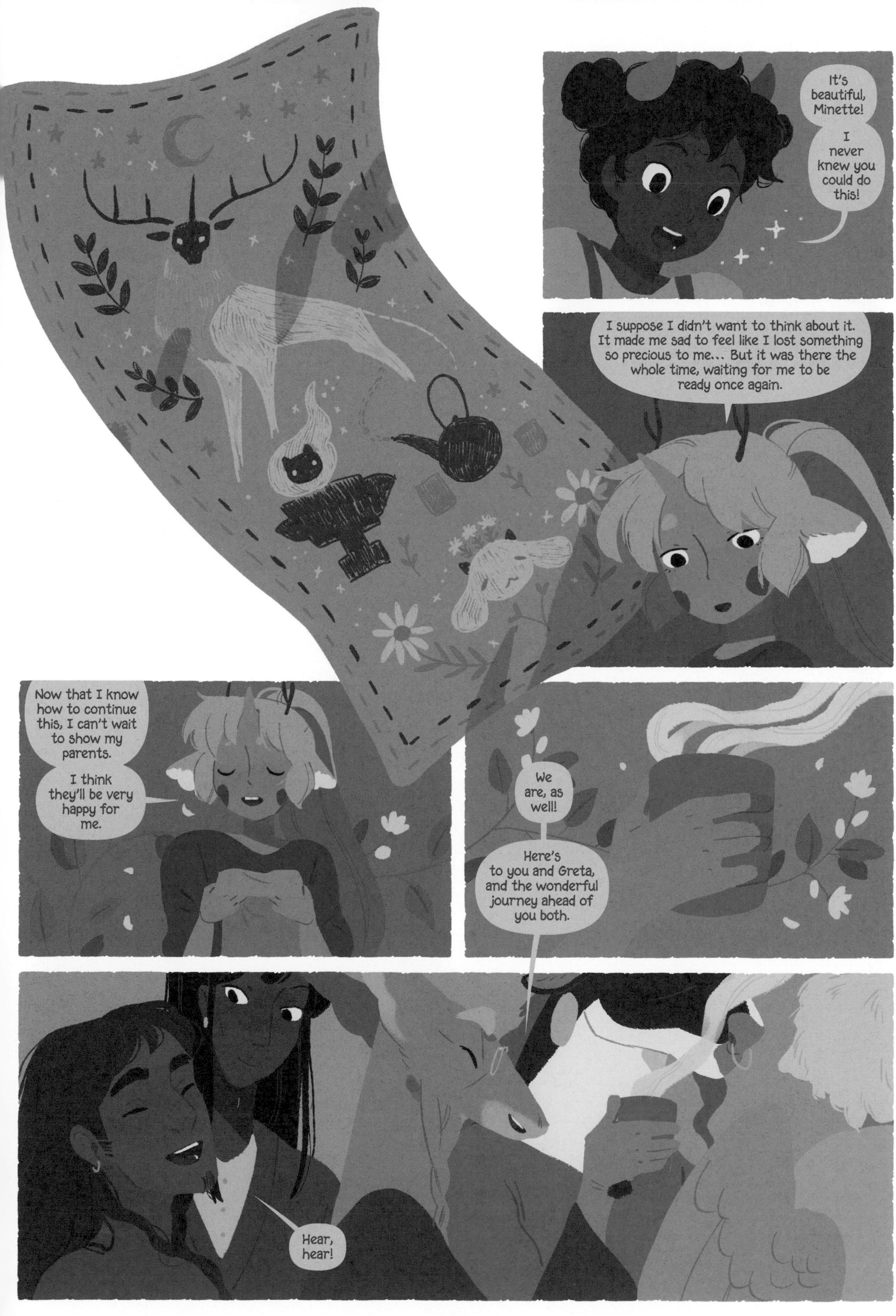

It's beautiful, Minette!
I never knew you could do this!
I suppose I didn't want to think about it. It made me sad to feel like I lost something so precious to me... But it was there the whole time, waiting for me to be ready once again.
Now that I know how to continue this, I can't wait to show my parents.
I think they'll be very happy for me.
We are, as well!
Here's to you and Greta, and the wonderful journey ahead of you both.
Hear, hear!

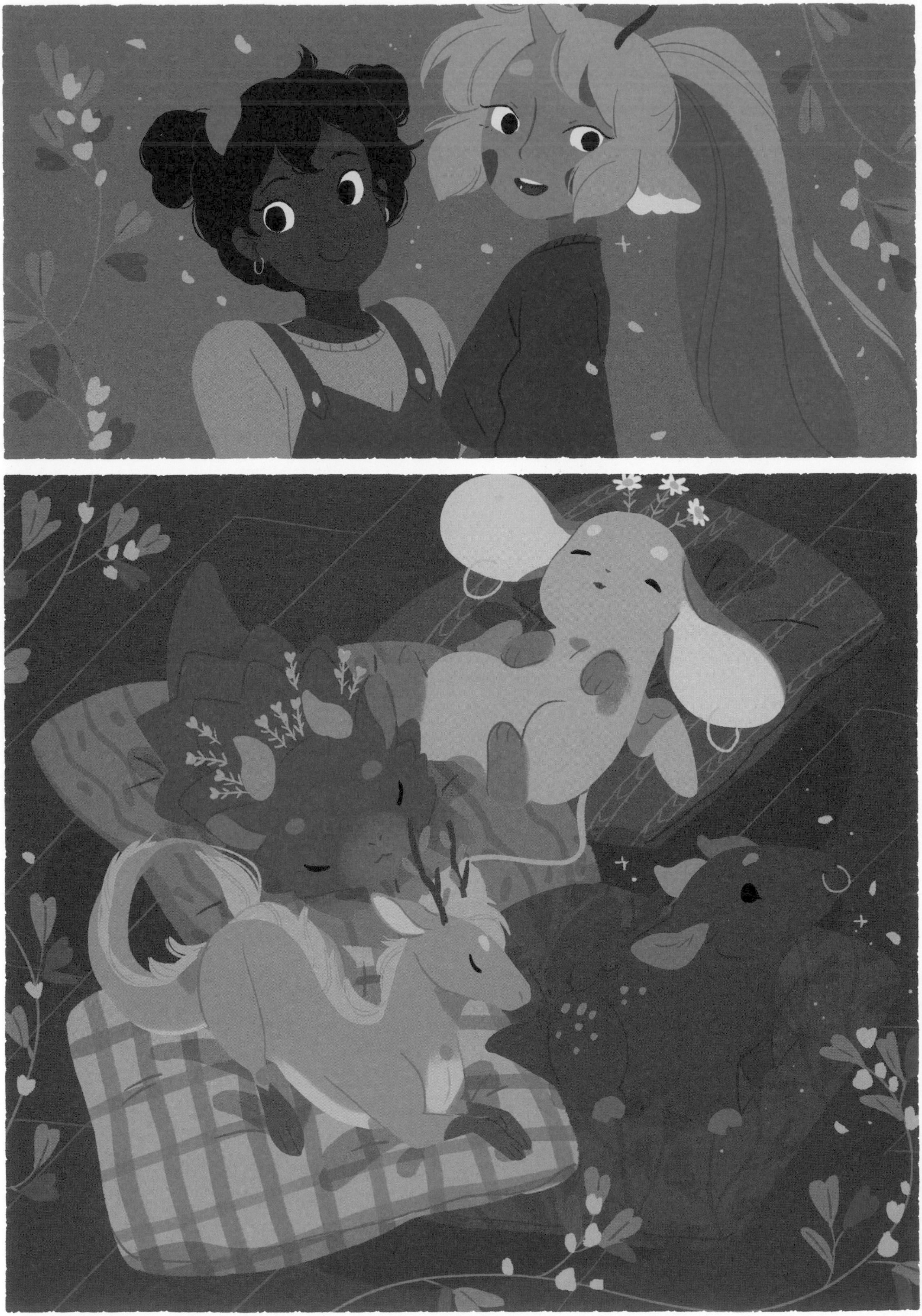

The End

Epilogue

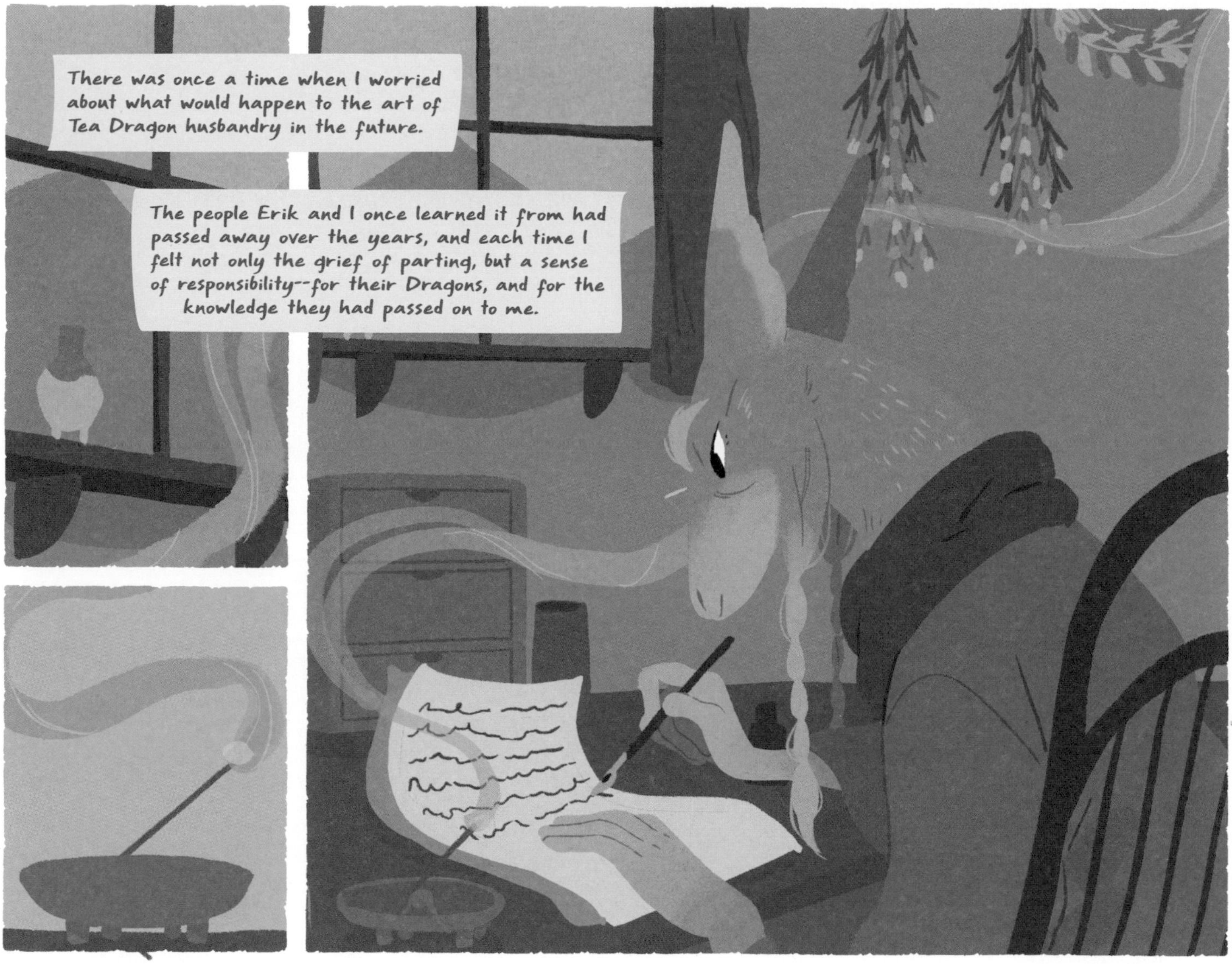
There was once a time when I worried about what would happen to the art of Tea Dragon husbandry in the future.
The people Erik and I once learned it from had passed away over the years, and each time I felt not only the grief of parting, but a sense of responsibility--for their Dragons, and for the knowledge they had passed on to me.

As the years went on, I found it increasingly difficult to find anyone to share it with in turn, and my worry grew.

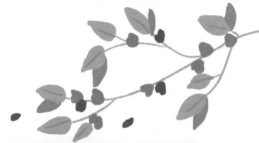

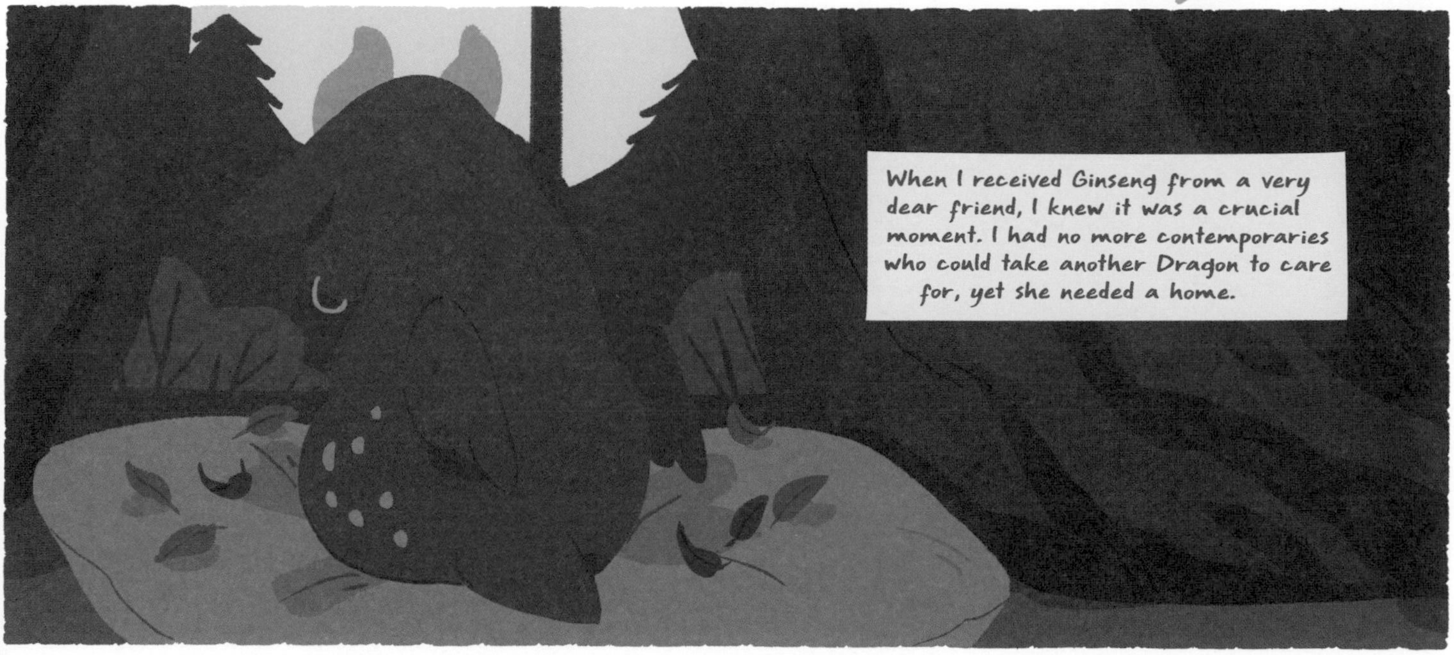
When I received Ginseng from a very dear friend, I knew it was a crucial moment. I had no more contemporaries who could take another Dragon to care for, yet she needed a home.

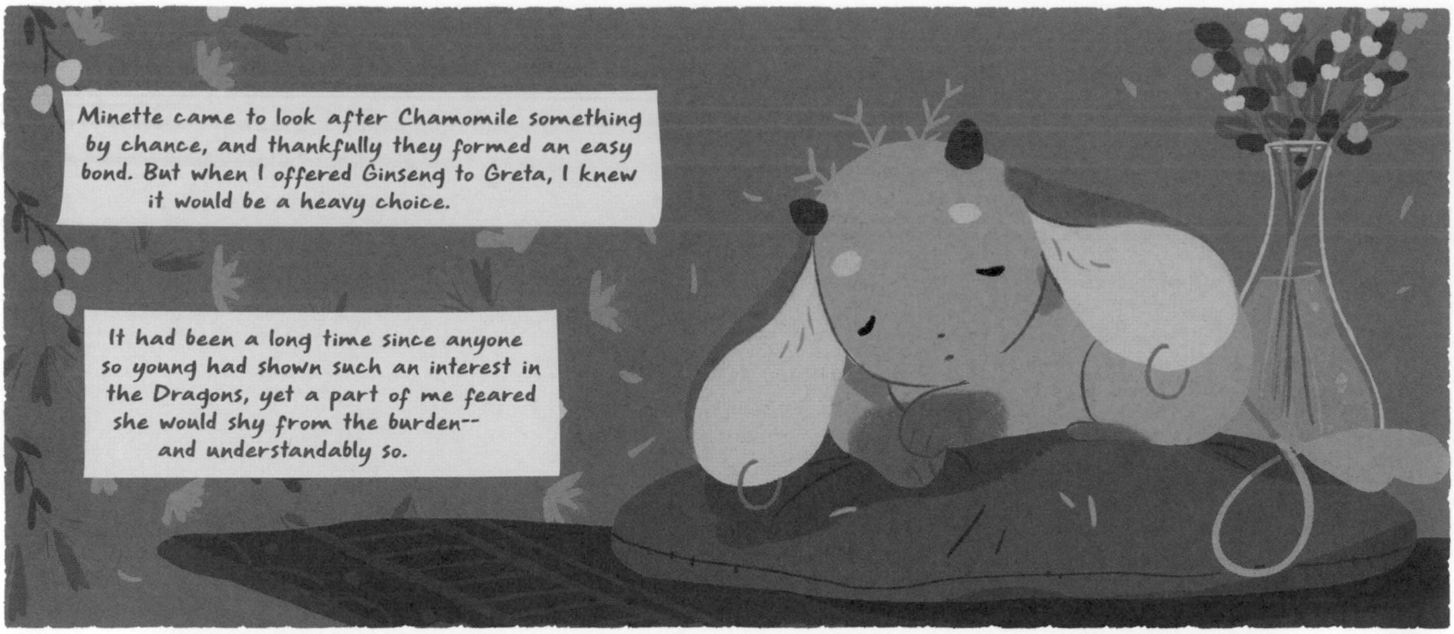
Minette came to look after Chamomile something by chance, and thankfully they formed an easy bond. But when I offered Ginseng to Greta, I knew it would be a heavy choice.
It had been a long time since anyone so young had shown such an interest in the Dragons, yet a part of me feared she would shy from the burden-- and understandably so.
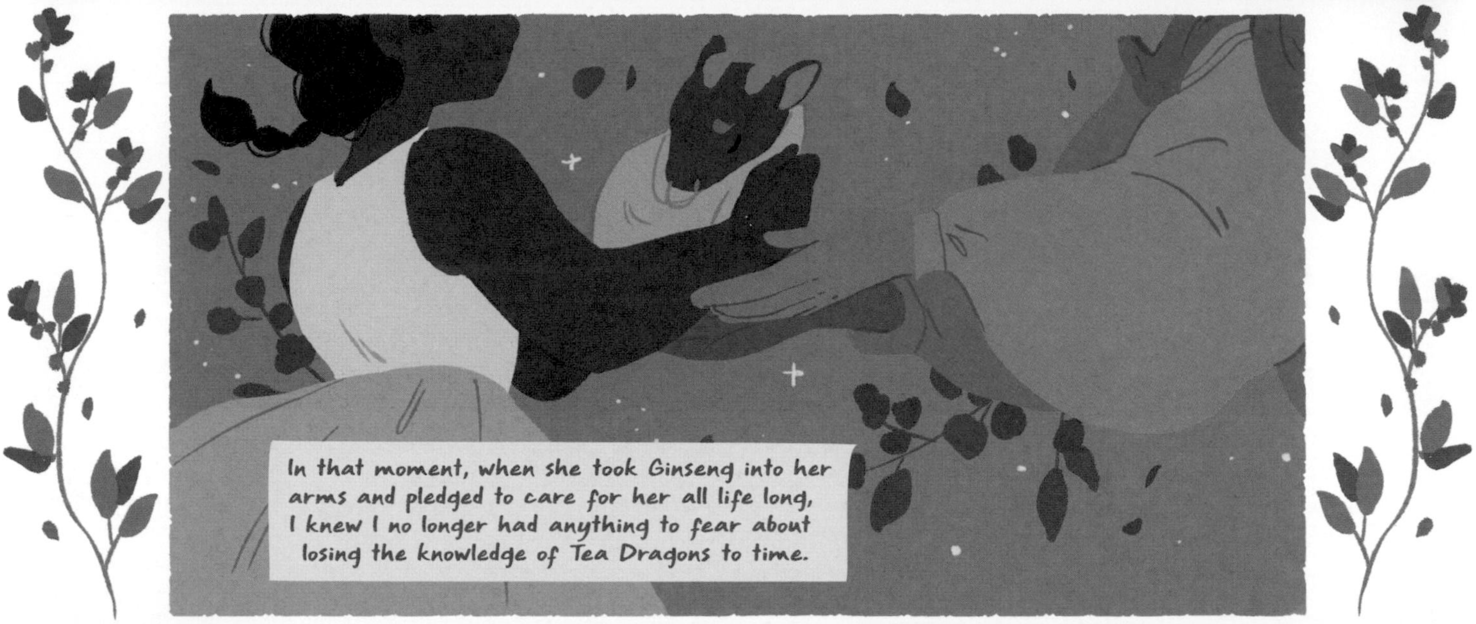
In that moment, when she took Ginseng into her arms and pledged to care for her all life long, I knew I no longer had anything to fear about losing the knowledge of Tea Dragons to time.
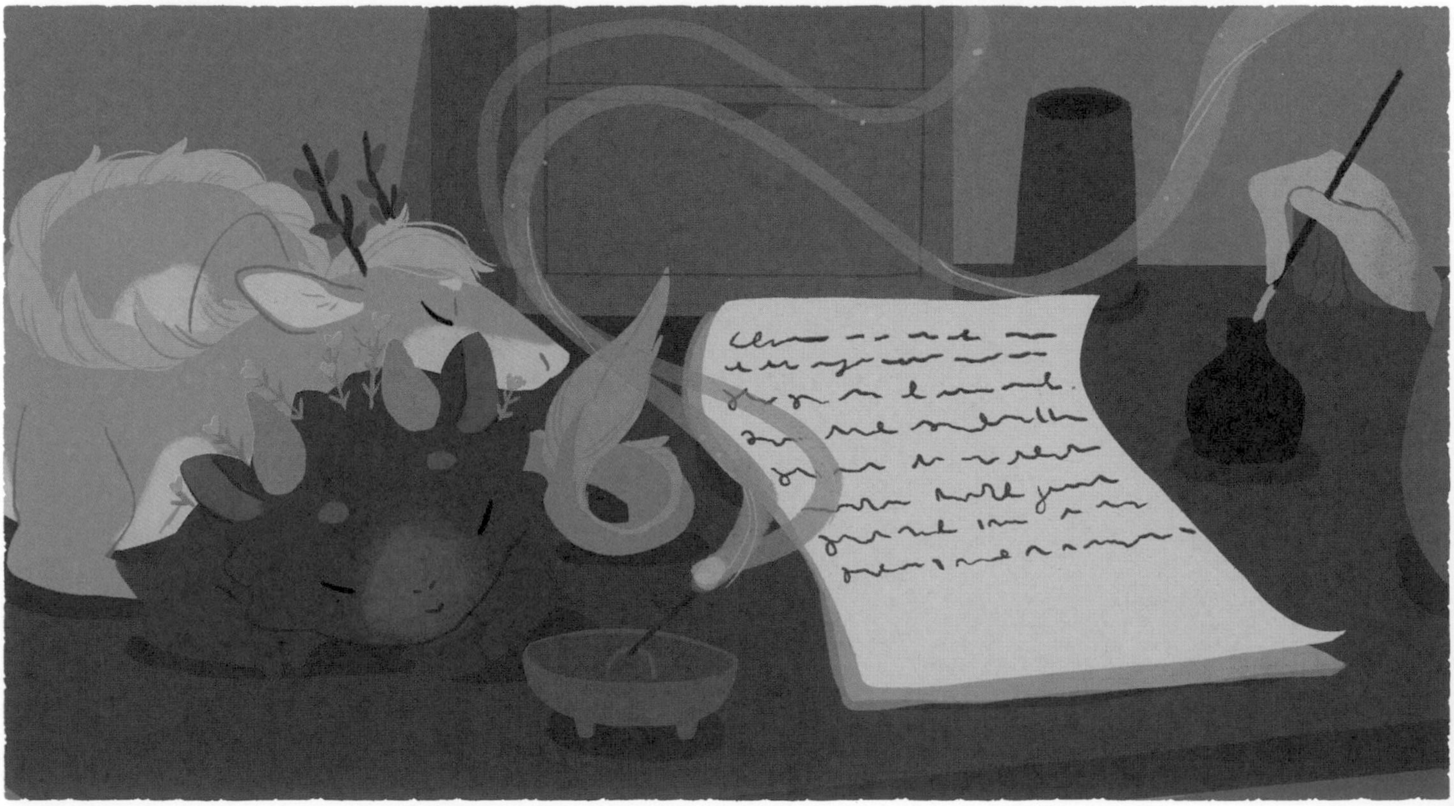

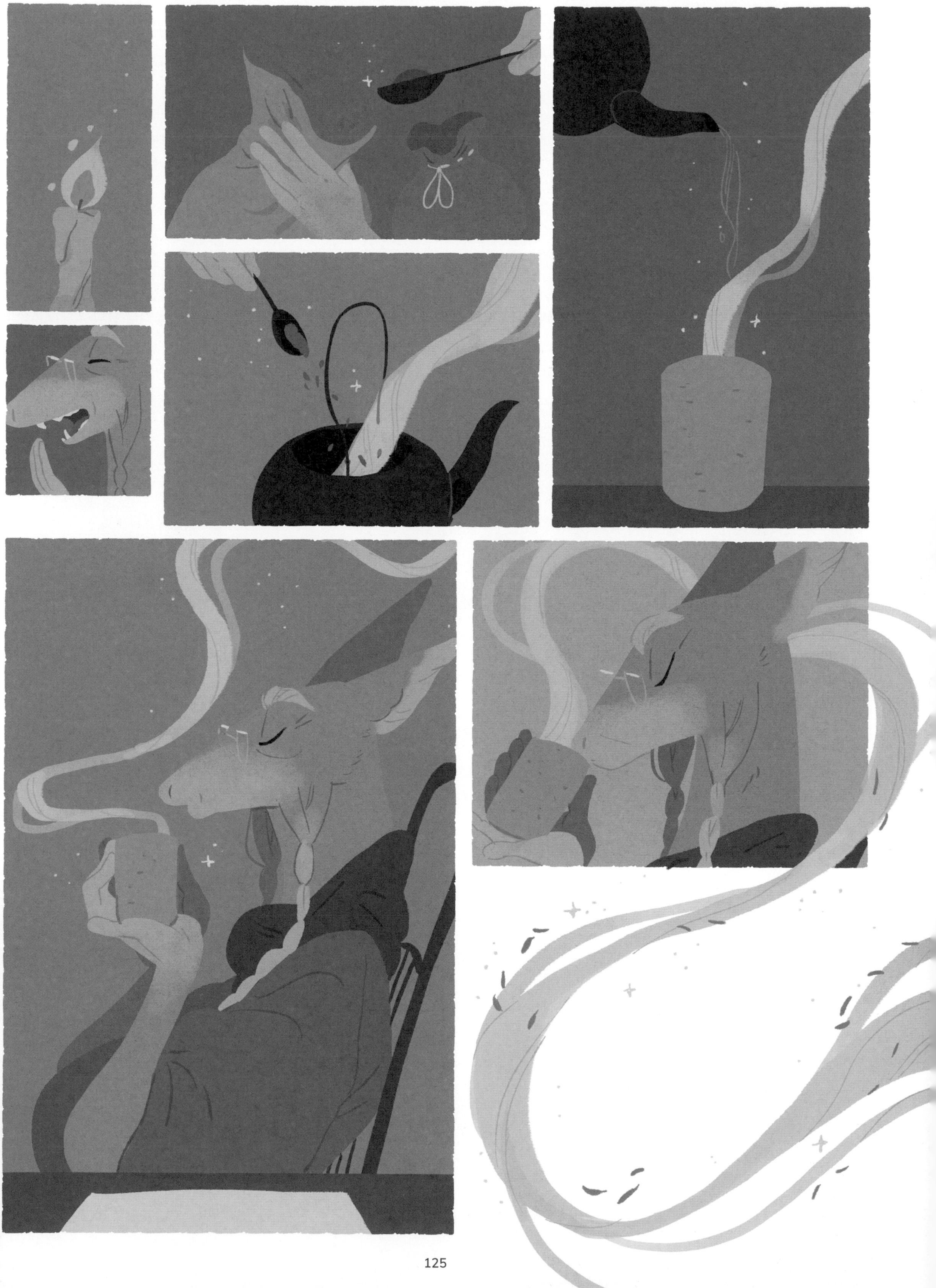

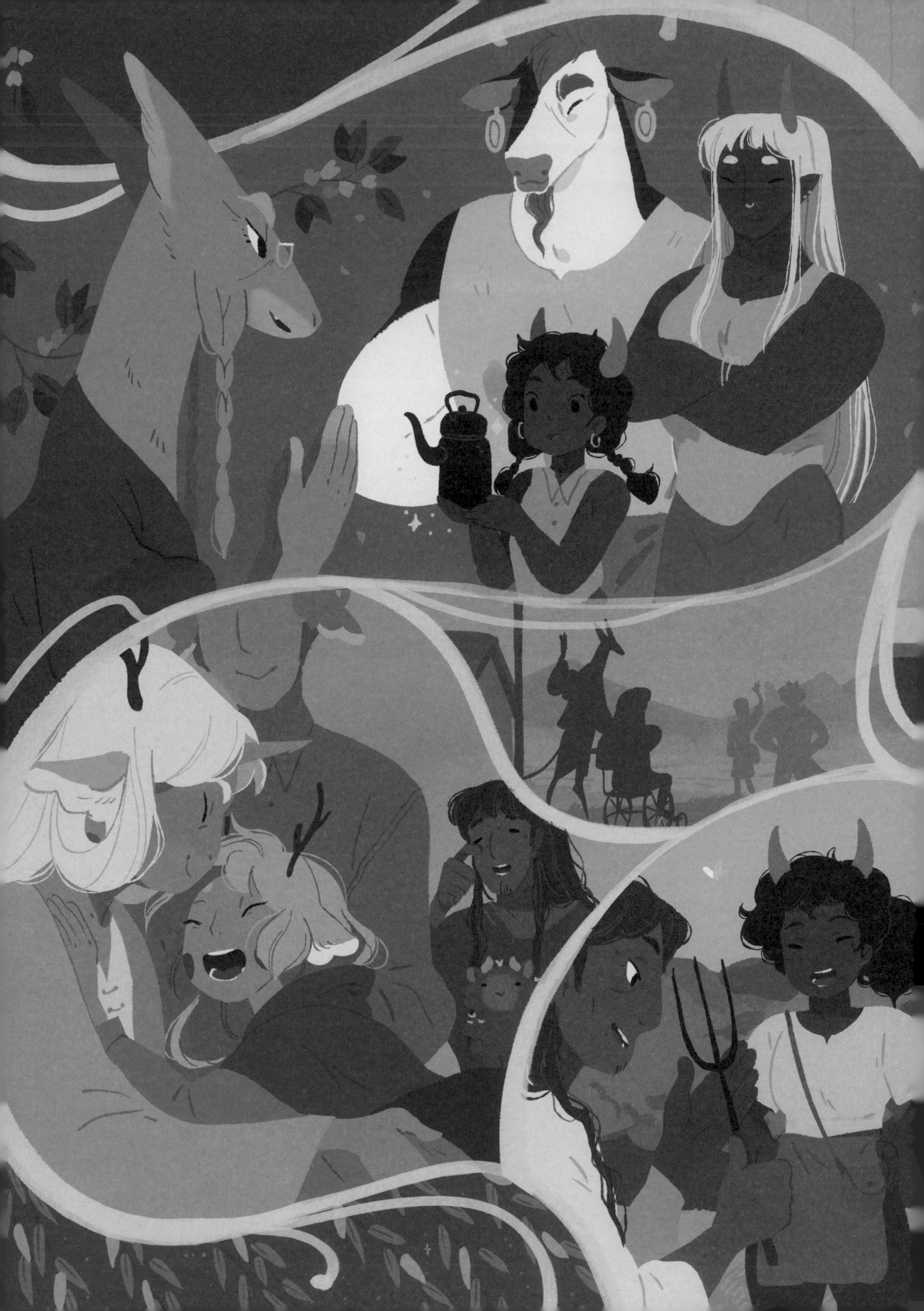

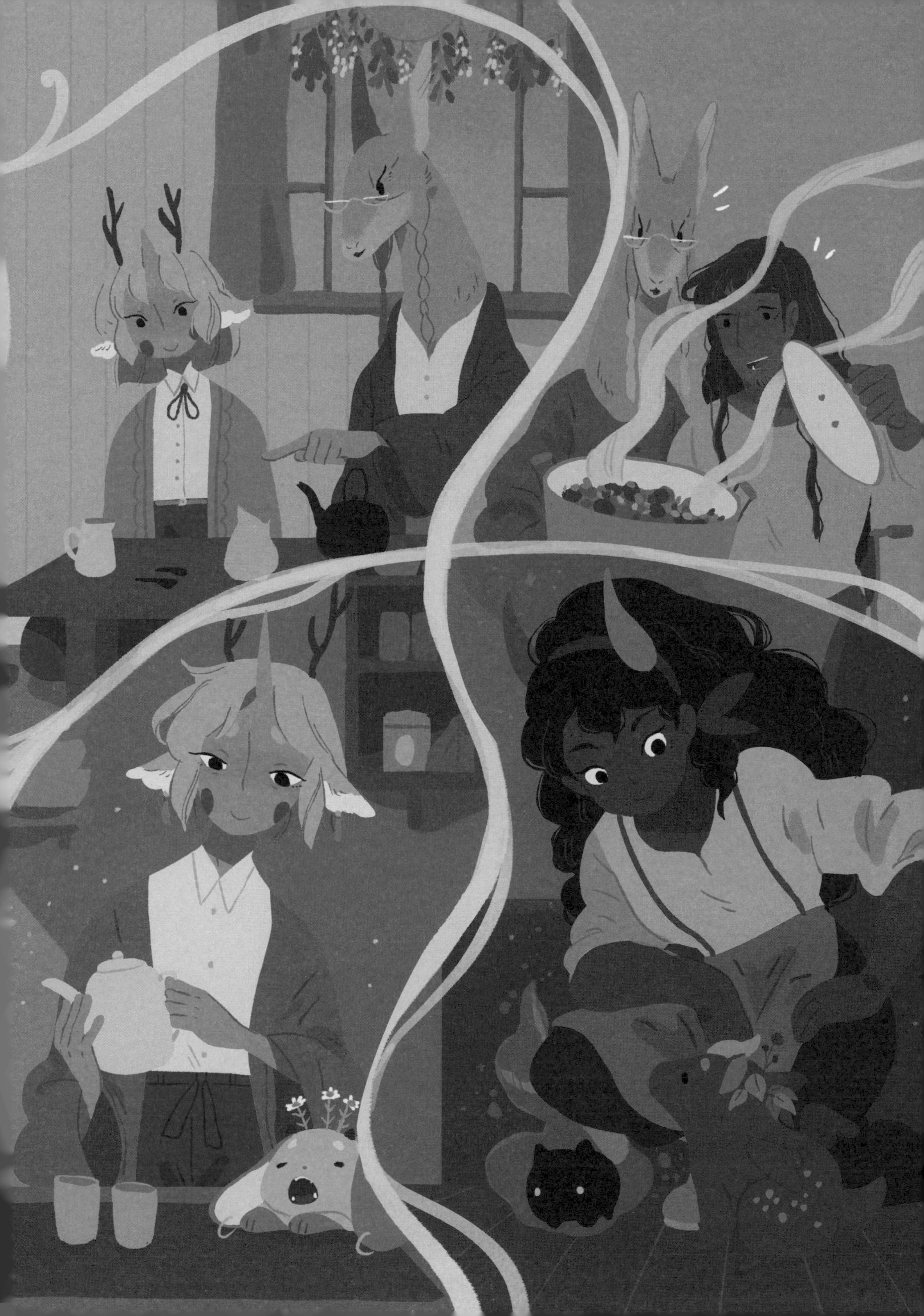

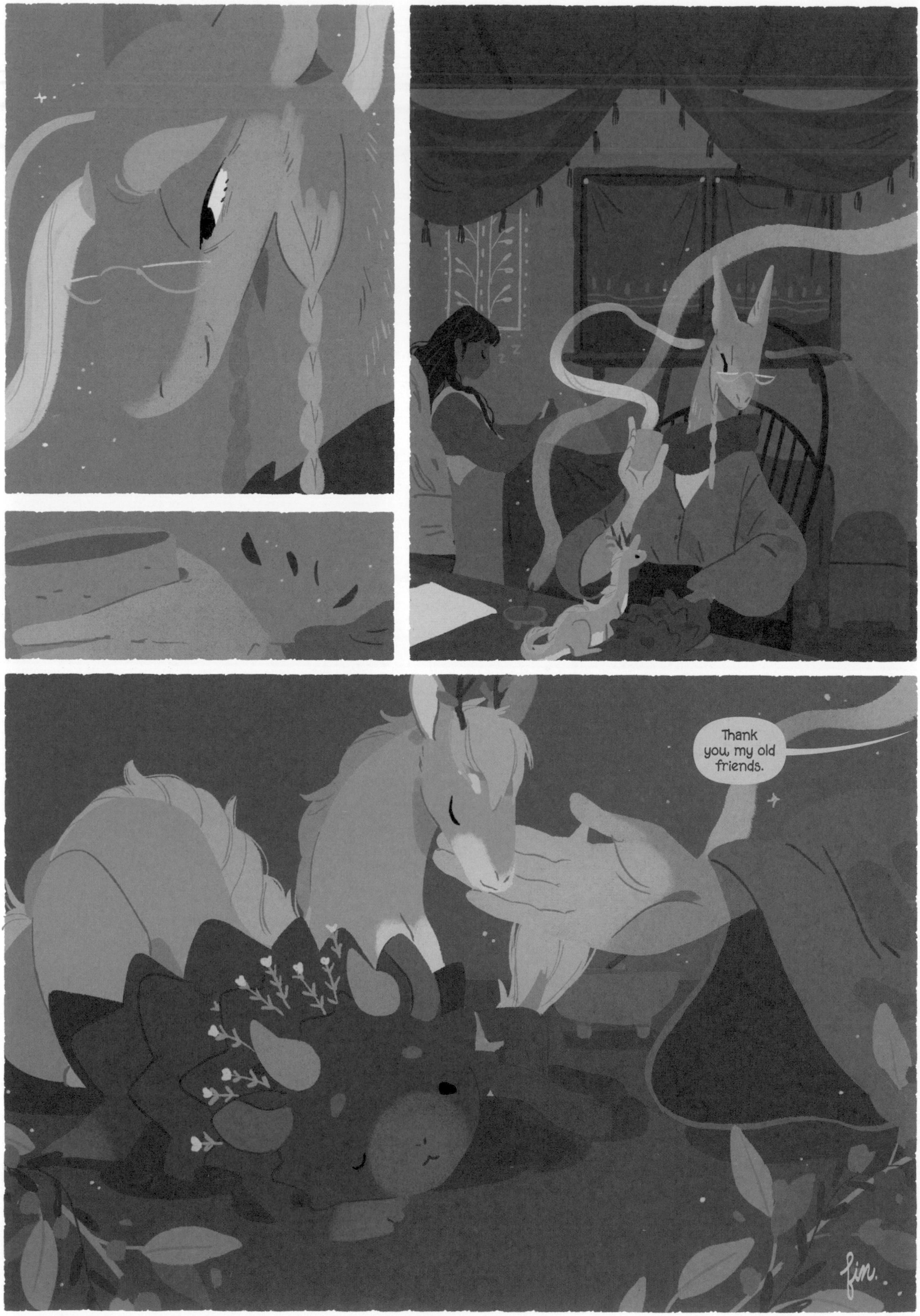
Thank you, my old friends.
fin.

EXTRACTS FROM

The Illustrated History of Tea Dragons

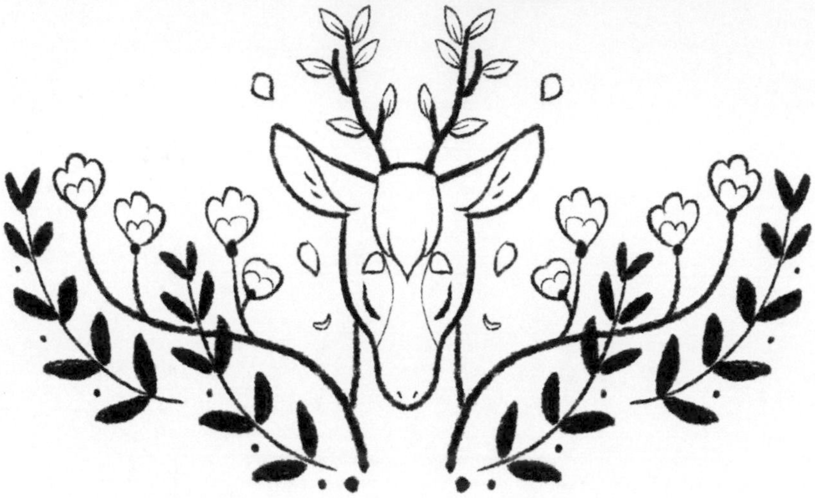

THE FIRST TEA DRAGON

For a long time, the origins of Tea Dragons were something of a mystery, with only oral traditions and folklore to guide us. However, in recent decades, an incredible discovery was made—an ancient Sylke journal written by the very person who encountered what became the first Tea Dragon. Despite being written in an almost extinct language, Sylke anthropologists have managed to translate and summarise the notes that reveal to us the origin of our beloved Tea Dragons.

The ancient book begins by describing a small species of wild dragon that grew little herbs on its horns, about the size of a bantam hen. One day, thousands upon thousands of years ago, a young Sylke biologist was observing these dragons. She and her fellow scientists had climbed for days through dense mountain forest to reach the small patch of grassland where the herb-growing dragons tended their young. While one of the nests was unguarded, she hastily worked away at sketching a clutch of eggs.

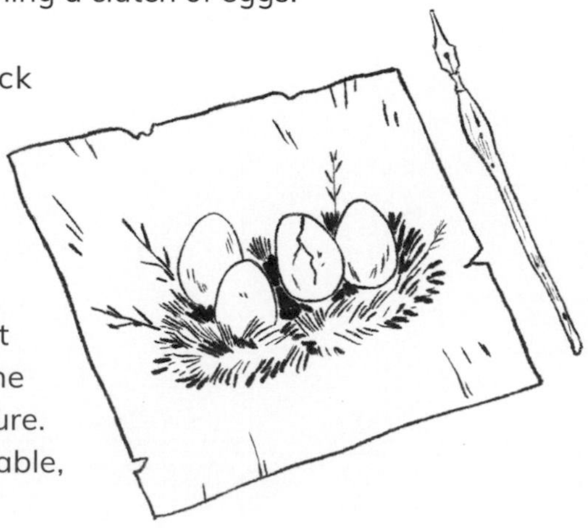

She was so absorbed in her work, she didn't notice a crack beginning to appear in one of the eggs. Suddenly she heard a cry as the baby dragon hatched right before her eyes! To her shock and dismay, the little one bonded to her as its guardian and refused to be left with the rest of the clutch. The biologist felt very conflicted, as the team had never intended to disturb the dragons from their native habitat. But they could see no other option, as it showed no sign of understanding that it was, in fact, a dragon. She reluctantly took it with her, vowing to do her best to nurture the creature. From then on it followed her everywhere, and they became inseparable, though the little dragon needed lots of care and looking after.

The Sylke and her dragon continued exploring the world and making notes about the new species and habitats that she came across. Wherever she went, she would bring some tea leaves from her home village—tea is very important to Sylkes, as they value good hospitality above all else. In their many journeys together, she and the dragon shared a lot of tea, and made a lot of memories. She had by now learned that this species of little dragon lived for several hundreds of years, and knowing that she would have this creature by her side throughout her life made her feel a strange tenderness and peace that she had never felt before.

One day, the Sylke noticed the leaves that naturally grew from her dragon's horns looked different than before. She gave them a sniff, and to her surprise, found that they had become tea leaves!

Brewing this tea produced an amazing aroma, and when she took a sip, the memories of all her experiences with the little dragon came flooding back to her, as if she were reliving them again. She had never experienced anything so incredible in all her life.

She made excited notes about this remarkable discovery. Many who read them thought of it as a folktale, but a few tea-lovers believed the truth in her words. They wrote to her explaining that they would be honoured to have a little tea-bearing dragon of their own. The Sylke sought out other folks throughout the world caring for small domesticated dragons. She explained to them the amazing transformation that had occurred in her dragon, and brewed them some of the tea so they could experience the sensation of the memories for themselves. Some weren't particularly moved, but others were enchanted by the magical bond and wanted to feel that too. They learned about the culture of tea from the Sylke, sharing it with their dragons and those around them in their lives.

These became the very first Tea Dragons, the ancestors from which all other Tea Dragons are descended. The group of people who shared their knowledge, friendship, and passion for tea to produce them became the very first Tea Dragon Society.

The original species of herb-growing dragon that the Sylke accidentally befriended is now very rare in the wild, and babies are protected so that they cannot be taken from their home. It was quickly decided that it would be better to breed from existing Tea Dragons rather than trying to hatch new ones. Not only would this protect the wild populations, but it allowed the Dragons to be carefully bred and to grow into their new cultures, climates, and homes.

TEA DRAGON BIOLOGY

Each species of Tea Dragon is very different. Certain physical and emotional traits are best suited for growing certain types of tea, and these characteristics have strengthened over time through careful breeding, as well as influence from environmental factors. Tea Dragons that produce flowers or fruit on their horns need to be a lot sturdier and stockier than those that produce only leaves. The largest Tea Dragon is Hibiscus, as it needs to be able to hold up its huge flowers. The smallest is Peppermint, and the tiniest specimen ever recorded could sit in an adult human's palm and grew just a few leaves at a time.

One reason caregivers go to such lengths to look after their Tea Dragon (besides being hope-lessly besotted) is that happy, healthy Tea Dragons produce much more vibrant and delicious tea. Tea Dragons store sad memories in their leaves along with the joyful ones, but as a natural part of a rich and varied life, these form the slight bitter notes that many tea drinkers appreciate as part of a good brew. Thankfully, very few Tea Dragons are mistreated or neglected, but an unhealthy Dragon will produce fewer tea leaves, and the memories will be patchy and blurry.

Each species is very visually distinct from one another, while variations within the species are a bit more subtle. Chamomile Dragons, for instance, are almost always yellow, but it may vary from a light buttery colour to a warm gold. You can also tell them apart by the different number of leaves or flowers, horn shape or size, different coat patterns, or the jewelry the Dragon has chosen to wear. It is important to note that all accessories (particularly piercings) are selected by the Dragons themselves, not the owner. Though they tolerate ribbons and ceremonial jewelry for special occasions, most will not be persuaded to wear miniature clothing.

Sometimes mutations in Tea Dragons occur, due to the huge magical power stored in the dragon lineage. This can result in extreme growth in the horns and leaves, odd colours or coat patterns, wings where the species would not normally have them, and sometimes even infusing the tea with minor magical powers.

Tea Dragons live for roughly three hundred years, regardless of species. Once they're fully grown (which takes between thirty and fifty years), they look pretty much the same throughout the first two hundred years of their life. Over the last fifty or so years, they will start to produce fewer and fewer tea leaves, will sleep much more than usual, and may slowly lose their appetite. The memories stored in the leaves will become focused on the Dragon's favourite moments of their lives, with all the owners they may have had in the past. Gradually, they become less energetic, and when they finally shed all their leaves and do not grow any more, the owner knows it is soon time that they will go.

TEA DRAGON VARIETIES

Astute tea drinkers will notice that many Tea Dragons produce a brew that is not strictly a tea; teas must be derived from a particular type of leaf, rather than herbs or fruits which are called tisane. Most Tea Dragon caretakers will cheerfully admit that they condense the terms together for the sake of practicality—the importance is more in the bond between caretaker and Dragon, enjoying the brew, and of course experiencing the memories contained within.

Over the thousands of years since the very first Tea Dragon came into existence, Tea Dragons have changed a lot. Carried by dedicated tea lovers back to their homes throughout the world, they have adapted to suit new cultures and new environments. Some have become more energetic, more regal, grown more fur or become more velvety in texture, duller or brighter in colour, more sociable or more shy. In every region they produce tea and memories, though how these are collected and brewed also varies a great deal from place to place.

Tea Dragons commonly evolved towards whichever local tea leaves, fruits, or berries are most frequently drunk. It only takes two or three generations for a Tea Dragon line to shift completely towards producing a certain type of leaf, if it is consumed frequently enough by its predecessors. They are very adaptable creatures in this sense, which is probably also why they have completely lost their survival instincts within a relatively short span of time living in domesticated comfort.

While it is true that no wild Tea Dragons exist, there are a few small isolated populations that could almost be described as such. There are known to be places—mostly ruined villages or infrequently used shrines—where a small population of Tea Dragons is able to get by without a primary owner. They aren't very adept at finding food, and rely on kindness from travellers, tourists, or a local priest or monk, but are overall cautious and wary of people. They have a stronger social bond with each other, and revert to many of the behaviours of wild dragons.

There are a few extinct varieties of Tea Dragon—types of ancient tea that no longer exist outside of the Dragons, who became so few in number that it was not possible to continue a healthy breeding line. And so they were mixed in with other more common kinds and eventually vanished. Others were kept by folks who simply had no interest in breeding them, and so they naturally died out.

A few carefully preserved tea leaves have been kept from some extinct Tea Dragon varieties, and are brewed on very special occasions. It is considered an honour to whoever raised the Dragons, and to the Dragons themselves, to continue to share their memories over time. After all, the aim of every Tea Dragon caretaker is to have lived a good and generous life with their Dragon. Having tea leaves to pass on is a sign of a life well lived.

LIVING WITH TEA DRAGONS

Tea Dragons get along with other pets better than one might expect, but they generally dislike boisterous animals. They can sometimes get a bit jealous of the attention given by their owner, but in the end they satisfy themselves by feeling smug that they know that they will live much longer than the other animals. All Tea Dragons love and respect chickens, who they see as a different, much more confident species of dragon.

Most Tea Dragons prefer a set routine, and will approach the same tasks with fresh interest and curiosity each day, no matter how many times they are repeated. Change can be difficult to cope with for Tea Dragons, causing them stress and anxiety. The best way to help them through change is to keep as many things the same as possible, such as food, mealtimes, grooming, and blankets. Though it can take quite a while, they always seem to adapt in the end.

Tea Dragons love being out and about with their owners throughout the day, and cannot be left at home alone for long periods of time or they will become depressed, or start making a nuisance of themselves. Most Tea Dragons are small enough to be easily portable on daily errands and tasks and have good stamina for snooping, but owners are advised to bring a "supply kit" of dried fruits and vegetables, warm blankets, and even a basket or bag in which the Dragon can sleep if it becomes tired from taking in all the different sights and sounds.

Even if they're drowsy, they can still be aware of their surroundings and pick up all sorts of memories throughout the day. Upon later drinking the tea collected from their Dragon, many owners will discover that their Tea Dragon noticed some small moment that they themselves missed that the Dragon thought was special and interesting enough to store as a memory. As a result, the owners often find themselves more attuned to noticing these little moments for themselves.

It can be tricky to figure out exactly what a particular Tea Dragon likes to eat, but luckily they are all herbivores (with the exception of enjoying a nice boiled chicken's egg), so it's usually a combination of fruit, seeds, nuts, grains, and cooked vegetables. They're quite picky about presentation, and can be put out if they think their owner's meal looks more delicious than theirs. They usually do best with small, frequent feedings throughout the day, as they will usually try to finish their plate out of a sense of pride. If they eat too much, they will be unable to move for several hours.

THE TEA DRAGON SOCIETY

The Tea Dragon Society was formed almost at the same time as the first Tea Dragons, in order to promote their wellbeing, as well as to exchange knowledge and ideas. Many cultures throughout the world have different rituals and practices regarding tea, and it was quickly realised how beneficial it is to learn about a range of different ways store, brew, and share tea in order to find the method that best suits a particular type of Dragon.

Each culture also grew to have their own stories and myths around Tea Dragons, and many Tea Dragon guardians make journeys to different countries to learn a different perspective on these beloved creatures. Along the way, they would stay with other Society members—the group was also a chance for people to come together with a common passion, and many friendships were formed that lasted a whole lifetime. Throughout the world in different countries, meetings are held every five years—a mixture of chit-chat and catching up, theory and demonstration, and of course, enjoying the tea.

Once, these societies were vibrant and active, but over time the numbers attending the meetings have dwindled. Fewer people have the time to make a long, meandering pilgrimage. In some regions, only one or two members of the society remain. What will the fate of Tea Dragons be if there is no community of guardians, sharing skills and teaching one another? This is why many of the older generation of Tea Dragon caregivers are excited for youngsters to learn the secrets, and to understand why the joys of raising Tea Dragons are worth the hardships.

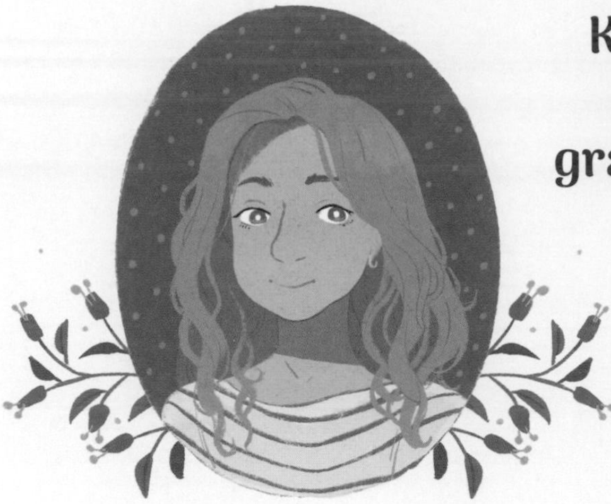

Kay O'Neill is an Eisner & Harvey Award-winning illustrator and graphic novelist from New Zealand.

They are the author of *Princess Princess Ever After, Aquicorn Cove, Dewdrop, The Tea Dragon Society, The Tea Dragon Festival,* and *The Tea Dragon Tapestry,* all from Oni Press. They mostly make gentle fantasy stories for younger readers and are very interested in tea, creatures, things that grow, and the magic of everyday life.

ALSO FROM KAY O'NEILL

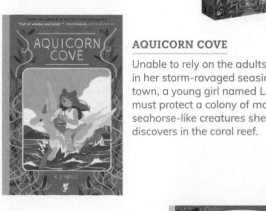

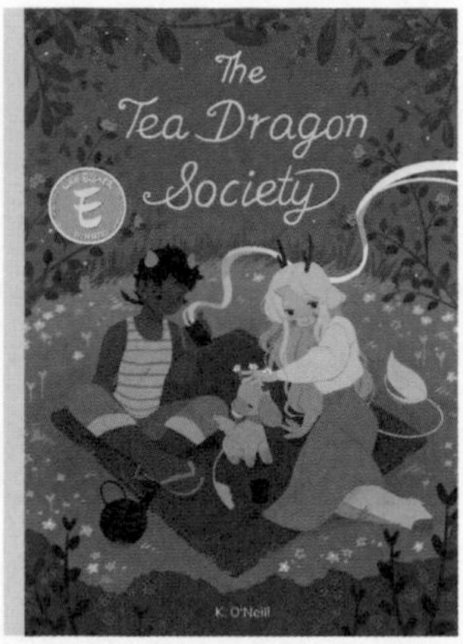
The Tea Dragon Society
K. O'Neill

THE TEA DRAGON SOCIETY

The Eisner Award-winning gentle fantasy that follows the story of Greta, a blacksmith apprentice, and the people she meets as she becomes entwined in the enchanting world of Tea Dragons.

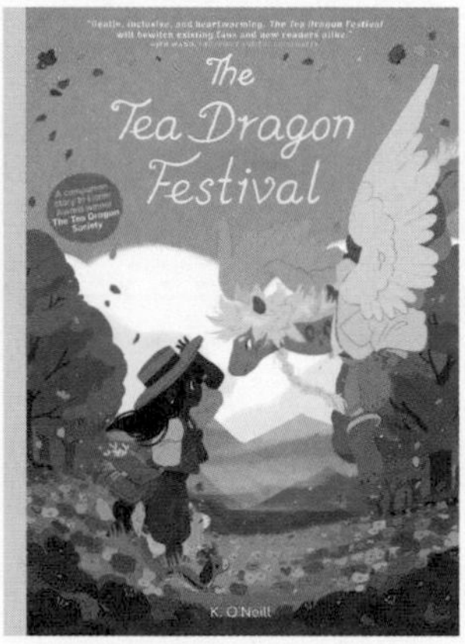
The Tea Dragon Festival
K. O'Neill

THE TEA DRAGON FESTIVAL

Rinn has grown up with the Tea Dragons that inhabit their village, but stumbling across a real dragon turns out to be a different matter entirely! A charming story about finding your purpose and the community that helps you along the way.

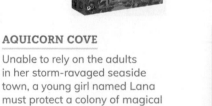

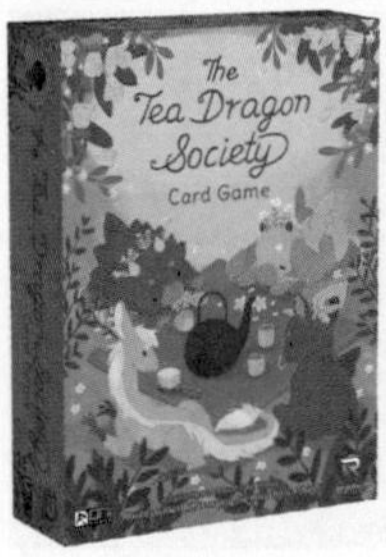
The Tea Dragon Society
Card Game

THE TEA DRAGON SOCIETY CARD GAME

Create a bond between yourself and your Tea Dragon in this easy-to-learn card game based on the graphic novel!

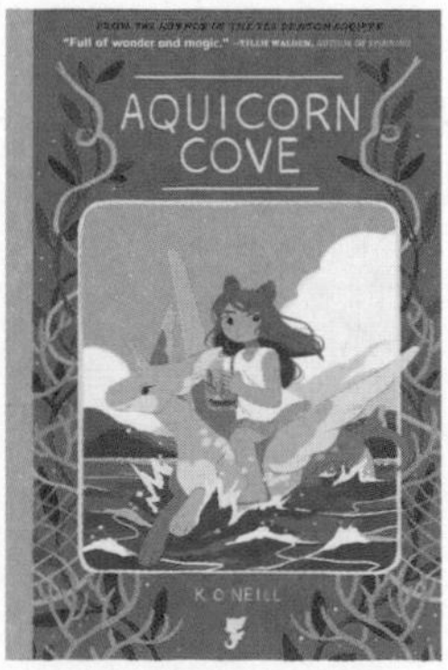
AQUICORN COVE
K. O'NEILL

AQUICORN COVE

Unable to rely on the adults in her storm-ravaged seaside town, a young girl named Lana must protect a colony of magical seahorse-like creatures she discovers in the coral reef.

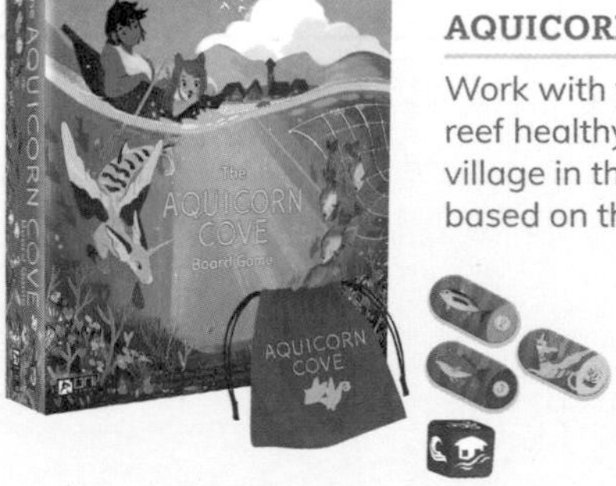
AQUICORN COVE

AQUICORN COVE BOARD GAME

Work with your friends to keep the reef healthy while taking care of your village in this cooperative board game based on the graphic novel!

DEWDROP

An early reader story about an adorable axolotl who cheers on his underwater friends as they each bring their talents to the pond's sports fair!

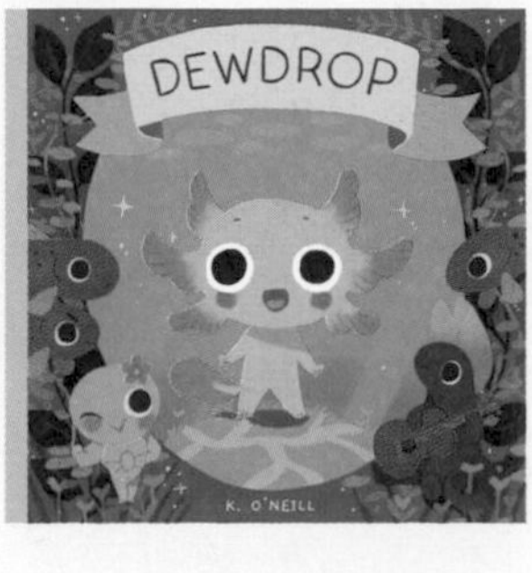
DEWDROP
K. O'NEILL

PRINCESS PRINCESS EVER AFTER

Join Sadie and Amira, two very different princesses with very different strengths, on their journey to figure out what "happily ever after" really means—and how they can find it with each other.

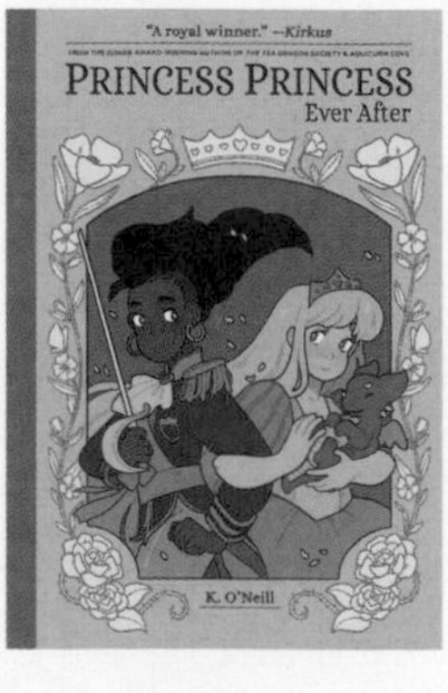
"A royal winner." —Kirkus
PRINCESS PRINCESS
Ever After
K. O'Neill

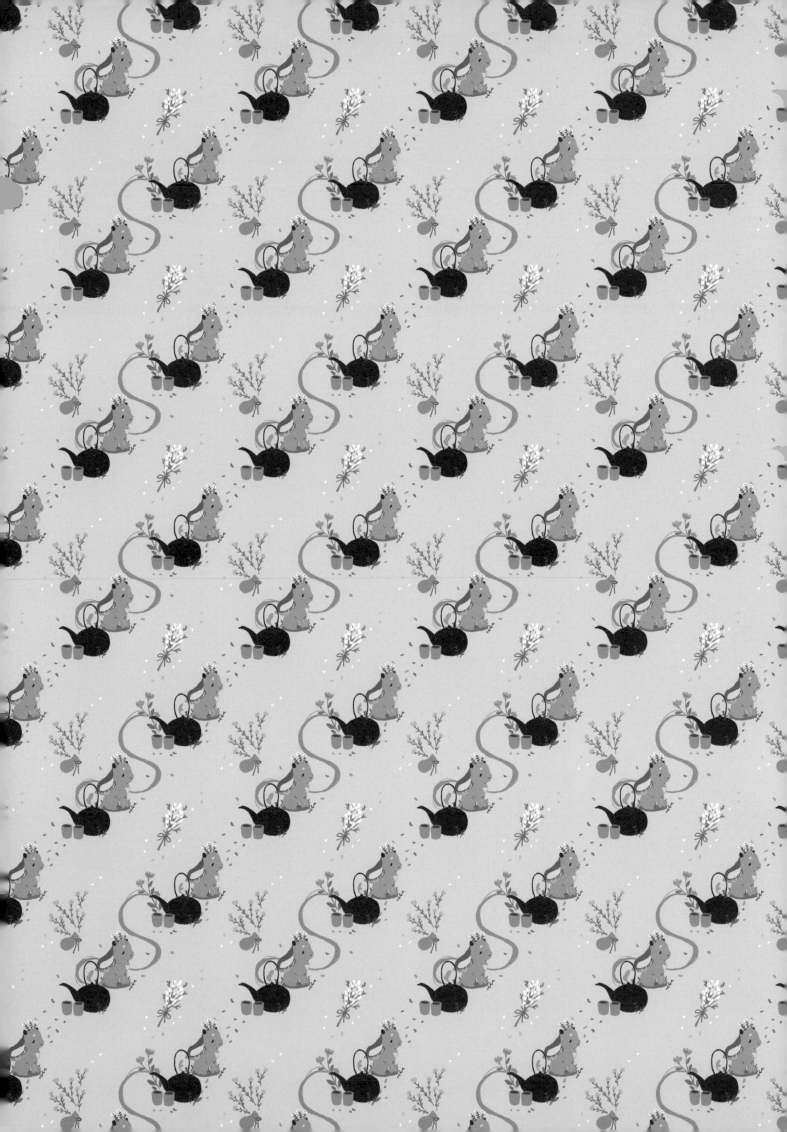

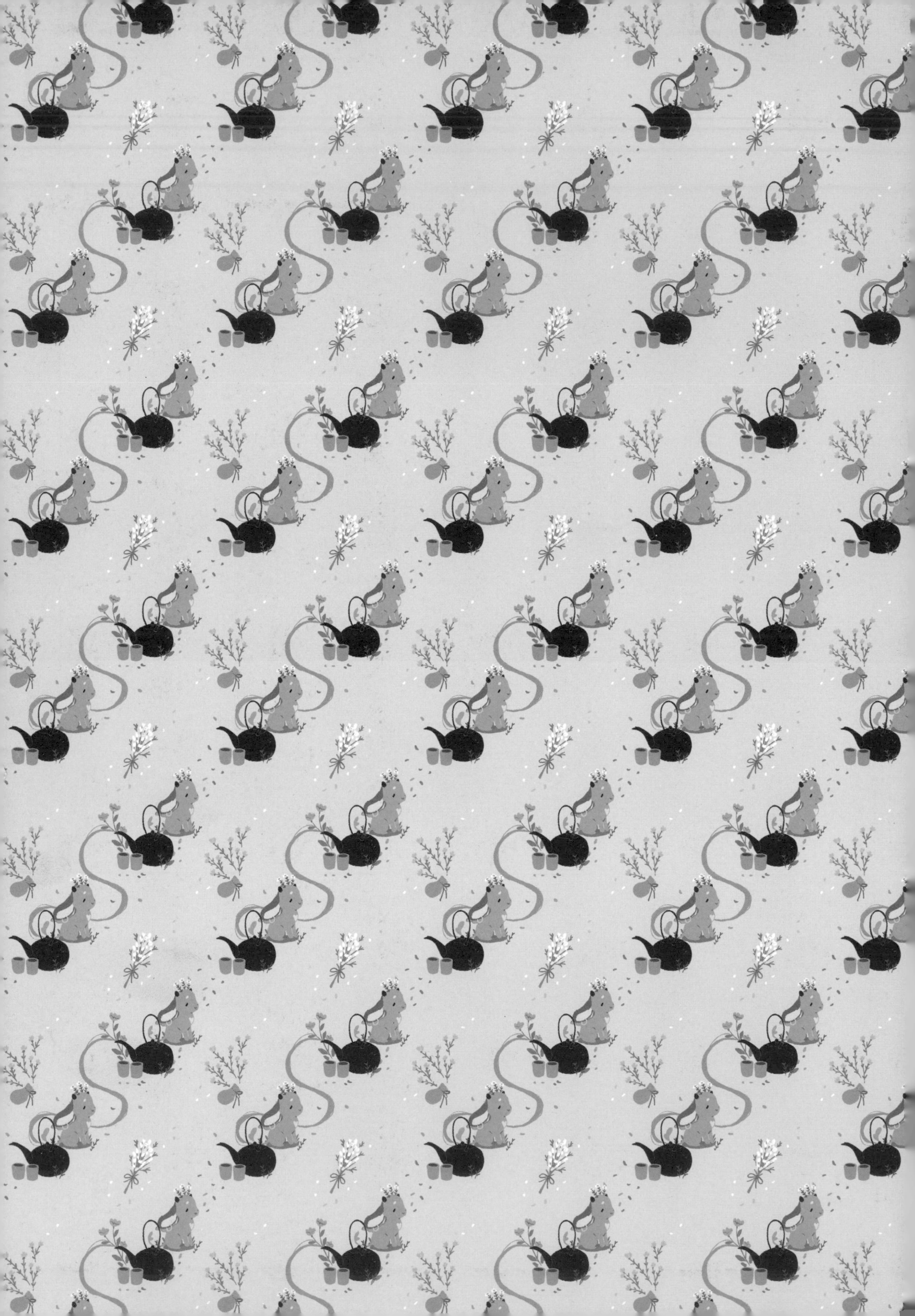